MALLORY BURGESS

WILD LAND, WILD LOVE

AVON
PUBLISHERS OF BARD, CAMELOT, DISCUS AND FLARE BOOKS

For Pamela Hingston Roderick,
who showed me Scotland,

and with very special thanks
to Warren Pratt.

WILD LAND, WILD LOVE is an original publication of Avon Books.
This work has never before appeared in book form. This work is a novel.
Any similarity to actual persons or events is purely coincidental.

AVON BOOKS
A division of
The Hearst Corporation
1790 Broadway
New York, New York 10019

Copyright © 1986 by Sandy Hingston
Published by arrangement with the author
Library of Congress Catalog Card Number: 86-90906
ISBN: 0-380-75167-4

First Avon Printing: November 1986

AVON TRADEMARK REG. U.S. PAT. OFF. AND IN OTHER COUNTRIES, MARCA
REGISTRADA, HECHO EN U.S.A.

Printed in the U.S.A.

K-R 10 9 8 7 6 5 4 3 2 1

Prologue

Dumbarton, Scotland, 1426

Genna set her taper to the last of the torches, watching anxiously as the warmed tallow sputtered into flame. Then she stood back, hands on hips, and surveyed the cavernous banquet hall of Dumbarton Castle. The newly polished armaments along the walls caught the light from the bracketed torches and danced it back and forth as though exchanging partners; gay banners and pennons rippled gently in the April breeze that streamed through the casements; and above the huge hearth even the rampant red lion of the Scottish kings seemed seized with the festive spirit, his cocky tail and blazing mane appearing more sprightly than ever. *"Nemo me impune lacessit,"* read the Stewart motto beneath his paws: "None attacks me with impunity."

Nodding her sleek dark head with satisfaction, Genna turned to her godfather. "Well, Papa John, what do you say?"

Red John Stewart came and kissed her forehead. "I say, dearie, that you've truly outdone yourself this time."

"Then you're pleased?" She smiled up at the tall, gaunt man and tugged his whiskers with gentle affection.

"Pleased? Sure as the sun comes up in the morning. Though I still say 'tis too much fuss and pother to make over an old cadger like me."

"It's not every day a man has his fiftieth birthday," Genna reminded him calmly, pulling at the edge of a splendid gold and blue tapestry to straighten it. "Best sit yourself back and enjoy it, and quit your grumbling."

"Enjoy myself while I can, don't you mean, lass?" Red John hunched up his shoulders and set his wide mouth in a doddering grin as he staggered toward her with an old man's shuffling footsteps. "Aye, I'm not long for this world now," he cackled, voice high and quavering. "When ye think of me, darlin', after I'm dead and buried, prithee, be kind."

1

Genna giggled. "Oh, Papa John, stop it. You know perfectly well you intend to outlive us all."

Red John straightened up to his full height and drew closer, his weathered face aglow with mischief. "Now that I'm all of fifty, do you think I can still beat you out to the kitchens?"

Genna's dark eyes returned his challenge as she gathered her skirts in one hand. "On your mark, set, go!"

They tore off across the flagstone floors to the hallway, scattering the freshly strewn rushes, Genna's long black braid whipping the air behind her. Red John glanced back over his shoulder as he rounded the turn to the kitchens. "You're losing, darlin'!"

"'Tis these horrid skirts," she panted, trying to kick out from beneath a tangle of dark green serge. "I'd like to see you run in acres of this damned stuff!"

Old Taggert appeared in the hallway before them, sturdy arms crossed over her broad chest, disapproval plain in her glance. "I'll be washing your pretty little mouth out, Genevieve Fleming, if I hear that word again. How am I ever to make a lady of you? And look at you, you old fool!" She glared up at Red John. "Acting more like five than fifty, that's certain. And not even dressed yet, with your guests due here any moment. Get up those stairs now, both of you, and into your fancy things."

Red John gave Genna a broad wink. "King James may have made me governor, but Taggert still rules the roost!" He pulled at the housekeeper's skirts like a spoiled youngster. "Please, mum, can I lick the spoon from the frumenty?"

"You'll get a licking from the back of my fist, Gov'nor or none, if you don't head up those stairs right now!"

Her master shrugged, sighed, and held out a hand to Genna. "Very well, then, Taggert. But I was winning, wasn't I, darlin'?"

"Honest to God," Taggert said darkly, "I don't know sometimes which of you's more the child."

"He," said Genna.

"She," said Red John. They dissolved into giggles together.

"Up those stairs or else!" Taggert threatened, brandishing a spoon.

Not cowed in the least, Genna and her godfather headed up the long stone flight.

"Look!" Genna exclaimed, clutching his arm as they passed

along the upper gallery and by a window. "She's right; they're already arriving!" They peered through the opening to the rock-strewn bailies and over the curtain walls to the banks of the Clyde. Far in the distance a band of a few dozen riders was wending its way along the river road to the castle, helms and halberds gleaming in the rays of the afternoon sun.

"Drat," said Red John, and spat noisily through the window. "They're more than two hours early!" He gazed down at Genna, blue eyes hopeful. "I don't suppose there's still time to call this whole matter off."

"What, and disappoint all those eager soldiers?" She laughed, tucking his arm more firmly through hers. "And who'll be the one to tell them there's no free ale to be had here after all?"

"Taggert," he said promptly. "She can fight 'em off with her spoons."

"Nay, Governor Stewart. The whole county is coming to pay its respects to you on this grand occasion."

"'Twould suit me better if they'd just pay their rents," he grumbled, and let himself be pulled up the stairs.

Genna smiled to herself, knowing that despite his protests Red John was keenly awaiting the evening ahead. He adored being the center of attention, showing off his handsome silver plate, his fine musicians, the delicacies Taggert prepared for his table—to say nothing of his goddaughter! She paused at the door to her apartments. "If you can bear to put off dressing for a bit longer, I've something to show you, Papa."

"Sure and I can!" he said brightly. "What is it?"

She put a hand on the latch. "Close your eyes."

He complied, grinning. "A surprise then, eh? You know how I love surprises." Genna grasped his elbow and led him inside. "Can I look now?"

"Not quite." She turned him to face the door, then went to the big oak loom that stood in the corner. Red John tapped his foot with eager anticipation.

"Now?"

Genna held up the tunic. "Aye, now."

Red John turned slowly, hands still over his eyes to lengthen the moment. Then he moved one finger upward, and another, until he could see the gift.

For a few seconds he stood speechless. Then he stepped forward slowly, reaching out gingerly to touch the finely wrought linen, tracing the subtle patterns she'd worked into the weave. "Oh, Genna, darlin'. What have you done here?"

"See, there are your lions," said Genna, pointing to the dark red creatures, "and here are the checks from the Stewart shield, and the purple thistle. Here's your governor's badge, and these are bulls, for your birth sign. These hearts here at the bottom—well, they just stand for me."

"*Just* for you?" Red John peered in wonder at the tiny intricate emblems. "Why, Genna, I've never in my life seen anything so lovely. It must have taken you ages to make this!" He leaned closer, lifting the tunic to catch the waning light. "What are these here, these little gray things?"

Genna's jet black eyes glinted. "Crossed spoons."

Red John threw back his head and laughed, gathering her into his arms, his big hand running over her hair. "Genna Fleming, I love it. And I love you, my dearie."

"Happy birthday," she whispered, standing on tiptoe to kiss his leathery cheek. "I love you, too."

They stood that way for a moment, then he stepped away from her embrace, brushing his eyes impatiently with the back of his hand, clearing his throat. "I'm going to put it on right now and wear it tonight. Taggert's spoons here next to my lions, eh? What a clever little minx you are."

"I just hope it fits you! Speaking of which—" She turned her back and indicated the fastener at the small of her waist. "Pray you, undo this button for me. The way Taggert shrinks all my clothes, 'tis a wonder I'm growing at all."

Red John fumbled at the button with his thick fingers, looking down at his goddaughter's silky black head and slim shoulders, then spun her around to face him. "Genna. Come and sit down by the window. I've something to give you, too."

"What is it, Papa John? 'Tis not my birthday."

He let out a heartfelt sigh. "Nay, dearie. But on your next anniversary, do you know how old you'll be?"

"Of course, silly. Seventeen. Why?"

He set her down on a stool by the window and sat beside her, shinbones creaking. "You're growing up, Genna. Growing up very quickly, indeed. In no time at all I'll be losing you to some fine man, with bells on his shoes and a plume in his cap."

"Not I," said Genna, and snorted. "You can have all that

courting and kissing nonsense, thank you. I don't care a fig for such stuff."

Red John smiled slowly, wisely. "Not just now, perhaps, child— There I go again! You're not a child any longer, Genna. And someday soon, very soon, some young man will come a-wooing, and you'll be gone."

Genna opened her pretty red mouth to protest, and he laid a finger gently against her lips. "Trust me. It happens to all of us, sooner or later."

She settled herself more comfortably on the three-legged stool. "Did it happen to you, Papa John?"

His blue eyes were suddenly distant. "Aye," he said wistfully, "that it did."

"Tell me about it," she begged.

But he shook his head. "Nay, another time, darlin'. 'Tis your mother and father I want to speak of now."

Genna cocked her head to one side attentively; she was curious to hear what he had to say. Her memories of her parents were so shadowy that she felt no sadness when she thought of them, merely a twinge of regret. Papa John was the only father—the only real friend—she had ever known.

"Once upon a time," Red John began, and Genna smiled at the familiar opening. "Once upon a time, in a place not far from here, there lived a remarkably dashing young man named Malcolm Fleming. His best friend was an equally dashing prince of the House of Stewart—a left-hand prince, but a prince nonetheless." Genna blushed a bit at Red John's easy reference to his bastardy; he caught it, and grinned.

"'Tis better to be the illegitimate offspring of a king than the son of a crofter, now, isn't it? Not"—he raised a cautionary finger—"not that I would ever wish such a thing on another. 'Tis the woman that suffers from such goings-on, and don't you forget it. My poor mother..." He shrugged it away. "Don't forget that when your lovers come courting, Genna. Promise me."

"I promise," she said, with great certitude.

Red John looked at her askance for a moment, and let it pass. "At any rate, this prince, whose hair was still fiery red in those days"—he ran a hand over his bushy white head—"and Malcolm decided to see a wee bit of the world, and off they went. First to France, then to sunny Spain, and lastly to Rome, the Holy City. It was a sort of pilgrimage they were making, you might say. And, like all pilgrimages, it ended with love. Malcolm Fleming fell head over heels in love with the prettiest little black-eyed lass you might ever hope to see, there in Rome."

"But she didn't want to come to a strange harsh place like Scotland," Genna went on, filling in the pause in the story as she began to unbraid her thick hair. Red John smiled.

"Nay, that she didn't. But Malcolm wheedled and begged— Oh, he was a handsome fellow, your father! And the prince wheedled and begged as well, and at long last Bianca—for that was her name, Bianca—said she would marry the man. So he brought her back to Scotland, to his home at Strathaven, and after a bit they had a wee bairn, a girl who was just as black-eyed and pretty as her mother."

"Me," said Genna delightedly.

"Aye, you. And for what seemed a very long time, they were all very happy together." Genna screwed her eyes up tight, trying to picture the dashing young Malcolm and the mother she resembled, but could not remember. "I stood as godfather to you," Red John said softly, "promising to look after you should aught happen to my friend." His voice grew husky. "And then the plague took them, as it has so many, and I cried an ocean of tears, and took you home with me."

Genna nestled against his shoulder. "And you've been as good a father to me as anyone ever could be."

"Thank you, darlin'." He planted a kiss on the top of her head. "You've heard that much of the story before, I know, but there's something else I never told you. When your father was very sick, and feared he might be dying, he gave me a present to keep for you, until you grew big enough to—to be leaving."

"I'm not leaving," Genna said fiercely.

Red John paid her no heed, reaching into the purse that hung from his girdle. "It was something he wanted you to have when I might not be there anymore to tell you his story, or your mother's, either. That time is coming, Genna. So here it is—your last gift from your father." He pressed it into her palm.

Genna felt the cool, still weight of gold in her fist, and opened her hand. It was a brooch in the shape of a love knot, rich and old-fashioned in its opulence, bright with tracery and studded with Scottish pearls. She pressed it to her cheek, clutching it tightly, and into her mind's eye an image from many years past came slowly struggling to the surface. "I see them!" she cried suddenly. "I see them, Papa John!" That tall, slim, smiling man with the beard, that was Malcolm, and the tiny raven-haired woman beside him was Mama—Bianca di Ghirlandaio—her black eyes flashing gaily as she held out her arms. "Oh," said Genna with awe, staring at the milky pearls, "'tis a magical gift, for it makes me see them again, as clear as day."

"Keep it close to you always," Red John said gruffly, and got to his feet. "I'd best leave you now and put my new tunic on, or Taggert will murder us both."

"Wait, Papa John." Genna handed him back the brooch and slipped behind her dressing screen, yanking off the green serge dress. "Could you— I'd like you to pin it on for me when I wear it tonight, for the very first time."

"Very well." Red John smiled at the glossy black head that barely showed above the gaily painted screen. It was just like her to sense his sadness, the impending loss he was feeling. That Italian blood, he thought, that's what does it, makes her mood change like quicksilver to suit the emotion of whomever she's with. Bianca had had that talent as well. He could remember as if it were yesterday the first time he and Malcolm had seen Bianca—dancing at the great ball in the Caperdian, dark and tiny as a swallow, as unlike the tall, hardy Scotswomen as night was from day. Genna had her mother's exotic coloring, snow white skin that took a rose blush so easily, coal black hair and red lips, and Bianca's big, black, almond-shaped eyes as well. Right now, Red John suspected, Genna's rare, striking appearance was a source of embarrassment to her. He hoped that would change, someday.

In the meantime, woe to the lad or lass who dared tease her about it! Genna's temper was Malcolm's legacy, that was certain. Taggert might do what she would, but the child's spirit was a wild and willful thing. Red John grinned, staring absently out the window, admiring the Clyde's blue waters, aflame with the mellowing rays of the spring sun, and the low hills draped in shadows of hazel and gray.

His grin turned to a frown as he heard a muttered curse from behind the screen. Perhaps, after all, he might have done better at seeing the girl was taught womanly arts—dancing, curtsying, flirting with pretty speeches. She had a disquieting habit of saying exactly what was on her mind, and not always in the most proper language. It was a trait that Red John admired in a woman, but he wondered whether it would appeal to the fops and dandies who seemed to make up the court retinue these days. Not like when he and Malcolm were young and long-haired, God knew.

Well, there would be plenty of time for that now she was getting older. He could seek out one of the neighboring ladies —the Widow Tavish, perhaps, or Estelle Pearson—and ask for her advice in the matter. He nodded his head, his decision made. This time he wouldn't be dissuaded by Genna's arguments. She was a gem, all right, but she lacked a bit of polish to make her shine even more brightly.

He looked again at the tunic she'd made him and nearly laughed aloud as he remembered how hard she had worked to learn that one feminine art, on the loom her mother had left to her. What a trial it had been for the girl to sit still for more than a minute at a time! But she'd set her mind to it, wading her way through the tangles of warp and weft, plaincloth and twill, not speaking a word of her efforts to anyone until, beaming, she'd presented him with the first fruits of her work —a neckerchief; not quite square or tight, but a neckerchief nonetheless. That had been seven years past, and as she practiced and learned, Genna's skills had come to rival those of any weaver in the town.

He held the garment to the window, admiring the subtle play of the patterns, the soft glowing colors of the wools she had dyed herself, with weld and madder and lichens she gathered from the woods, and the precious woad he sent for from France. Bianca would have been so proud...dear, gentle, beautiful Bianca. Red John's smile faded as he thought, as he did so often these days, of Bianca and her Malcolm, and all the other loved ones who had gone on ahead and left him to face the changes, some sweet, most bitter, that time could not help but bring.

Genna paused in the midst of lacing up her soft silk drawers. "What was that, Papa John?"

He pulled himself from his reverie. "What was what, darlin'?"

"That sound—did you hear it? Like something shattering a casement—"

It came again, the sharp crack of iron on glass, followed by a babble of low men's voices. "Do you smell smoke, Genna?"

Red John asked idly, his long nose probing the air. "P'raps Taggert's gone and burned the clootie dumplings again."

Genna hushed him with a wave of her hand and skittered from behind the screen to the open doorway, still clad in her drawers and corset, feeling the planked floor chilly beneath her bare feet. Peering over the balcony railings, she saw the banquet hall two stories below packed with soldiers, their hinged mail and long swords clanging as they pulled the bright torches down from the brackets, and set the drapery and hangings aflame.

She pushed the door shut silently and leaned against it, the pounding of her heart like drums.

"What is it, darlin'?" Red John tried to move past her to the hallway, but she thrust him back sharply, finger to her lips.

"Soldiers," she whispered. "Stewarts, by their banners."

"Our guests, then," said Red John, bewildered.

"Papa," said Genna, "they're torching the hall."

"Well, I'll soon put an end to this!" He paused, hand on the latch, as footsteps thundered up the stairs.

Taggert's voice cut through the growing commotion in a piercing wail. "They're comin' for ye, milord, they're comin'! Oh, sweet Mother of Christ—" The rest of her words were lost in a bone-chilling scream.

"Get out here, Red John, ye scurfy bastard!" The hoarse shout was echoed by jeers and whooping. "We've a message for good King James!"

Red John turned back to Genna, and she saw the sudden glimmer of fear in his eyes. "Jamie Stewart's men—it must be! He's revenging himself against the king for the imprisoning of his brother. Hide yourself, child, hide yourself!"

"No," she whispered, leading him behind the dressing screen. "You must hide, Papa. Down here—" She pushed him to the floor, hurriedly tumbling tunics and robes and gowns down from the shelves and piling them over his white head. "'Tis you they're after; I'll be safe enough. Now, stay down, and stay quiet! Whatever happens, don't you come out!"

She'd no sooner covered him with the garments than the door burst open, and a tall, beefy man with scraggly red hair and whiskers gazed coldly around the room. Genna stepped out from behind the screen, clasping her hands together to hide their shaking.

"Who in the hell are you?" he demanded, narrowing his

bloodshot gray eyes. Genna could smell the ale on him from across the room.

She took a deep breath. "Wouldn't it be more fitting for you to explain what you're doing in my chambers?"

He lumbered closer, and she drew back nervously toward the loom in the corner, seeing the cold malevolence in his gaze. "I'm looking for Red John Stewart, lassie. And if ye know where I might find him, there'll be something in it for you. Here." He pulled open his purse and flung a handful of marks to the floor. "Fine silver, lassie. Enough for you to buy yourself something to wear." His eyes raked over her thin drawers, the corset that was laced tightly between her gently swelling breasts.

Genna could hear the marauders' heavy footsteps all around her: on the staircases, in the galleries, crashing on the rafters overhead. Fighting back her terror, she eyed the silver cunningly, as though tempted. "What is it you'd be wanting with him?" she parleyed, and bit at her lip as her voice broke.

The man stood staring boldly, thumbs hooked in his gussets. "We've a message to send to his nephew, the king," he said at last, idly plucking a dagger from his boot, running a coarse finger over its gleaming edge.

"What message? From whom?" Genna felt her fear dissipate as anger boiled up in her heart. Were the intruders nothing but drunken brutes, eager to bribe and frighten helpless children and servants?

"From the Duke of Albany's son, Jamie," he said, sneering, coming closer still.

"And the message?" Genna demanded, black eyes flashing. "Do you think the king fears a parcel of lowborn drunken fools?"

His peculiar pale gaze glinted. "Suppose we forget Red John, then," he snarled, still whetting his dagger. "I can give my message to you."

Genna scrambled back behind the sturdy loom as he advanced. "I'm not afraid of you," she hissed, praying desperately that Papa John would trust her, would stay safe beneath the bundles of clothing. She forced her voice to be firm and calm. "Get out of my rooms this instant!"

He grinned and lunged for her across the loom. Genna sank her teeth deep into the back of his hairy hand with grim determination. The man sprang back with a violent curse and began to unbuckle his breastplate. Genna made a mad dash for the door, heard his hoarse voice at her shoulder, felt his hands grip her waist. "Not so quick, lass," he murmured into her ear. "There's that matter of the message."

He pawed at her corset, the laces snapping beneath his thick fingers like straws, his breath hot and close. Genna kicked back at his legs, his groin, but he laughed at her efforts and flung her around against the wall. The edges of his cuirass cut coldly at her breast as she writhed in his grasp.

He fumbled beneath his tasset, one huge hand pinning her by the hair, and Genna closed her eyes tight against the sight of his twisted, rapacious face. The dagger tickled against her throat as he grappled at his hose.

"Leave the girlie be, you scum."

"No, Papa John!" screamed Genna, the cold dagger slicing her skin. The man whirled around, torn between the satisfaction of cornering his quarry and fury at having his assault cut short.

Genna pressed a hand to her throat, gagging as it came away covered with blood. Then she threw herself at the intruder's mail-clad back, wrapping her fists in his red hair and pulling with all her might. "Leave him alone!" she cried, battering helplessly against him. "Run, Papa John!"

He threw her off easily, shoving her to the floor and advancing on Red John Stewart. The old man balled up his fists against the dagger, feet set firmly, fire in his eye. "Come and get me, ye murderous thievin' traitor! Fight a man if ye will, and not a wee child."

The man with the dagger slashed out, leaving a jagged streak of blood across Red John's knuckles, then slashed again. Genna, her head spinning from the blow he'd struck her, crawled weakly forward and pawed at his hose with clawed nails. He swung his foot back sharply, catching her shoulder, leaving her gasping for breath.

"Here's the message for your nephew," the man hissed, tossing Red John to the floor like a sack of barley. He set the point of his dagger behind the governor's ear and drew it slowly, relentlessly toward the other, straight across Red John's throat.

"Oh, sweet Christ—" Genna watched in horror as blood

spurted from the wound and spattered the chamber, as Red John's eyes, blue as the River Clyde, rolled wildly for a moment and then glazed over. She dragged herself across the floor, reaching for his hands, pressing them to her face. "Oh, Papa John—"

The murderer laughed viciously and grasped a thick hank of her hair, tugging her away. "Leave death to the dying, lass," he hissed, lust shadowing his pale eyes. "We've business to conclude together." He pawed at her breasts with rough fingers, twisting her head up to face him, lowering his mouth to hers.

Stunned, shaken, Genna felt her knees weak as water beneath her. She gave an anguished cry as his hand tore away her drawers, as he knelt above her, leering, and pinned the dagger to her throat.

Footsteps paused in the hallway. The door flew open, and Genna shuddered as she heard the red-haired man laugh. "I'll be done with her in a moment," he called out over his shoulder. "You can wait your turn—"

Two huge hands grabbed him by the neck, wrenching him away with such force that the dagger skittered out of his grasp and across the floor. The murderer let out a low angry snarl of pain and rage as the newcomer flung him bodily toward the doorway with a mighty crash. There was a moment of quiet, marked only by the two men's harsh, short breaths; Genna scrambled toward Red John's body, searching for the dagger, a stick, her scissors—anything with which to defend herself. Her godfather's stiffening fingers fell open, and she saw the pearls and pale gold of the brooch still clenched in his fist.

When the door slammed shut, Genna turned to find the red-haired man was gone. But another of the intruders was advancing on her, looming over her. "Keep your distance," she spat, her back arched like a cat's.

The man glanced at the doorway, then back to her. "Poor child, poor wee thing, what's he done to you?" He took another step forward as Genna recoiled, staring up into his grim angry face. He reached out a long arm toward her; Genna saw the room go spinning around her like a crazed tilting top as his fingertips grazed her hair. His eyes are even bluer than Papa John's, she thought briefly, distractedly, before fear and horror overwhelmed her, and she sank in a heap to the floor.

* * *

Alexander Mac Donald pulled the girl's still, small body away from the bloodied mass that had been Red John, then looked with urgency toward the door. If he gave chase now, before that red-haired son of a bitch escaped...But as he glanced down at the ghost-pale girl in his arms, he thought for some reason of an old Roman coin he'd unearthed once at Aros. The high, proud lines of her cheekbones, her dark brows, the faintly hooked nose and sculpted lips he saw reminded him of the image some long-dead engraver had pressed into that ancient gold.

She was cold as marble to his touch; hastily Alex ransacked the room for a bit of clean clothing. He found a linen shirt behind the screen in the corner and slipped it over her head, lifting up the masses of thick black hair that billowed over the floor, smoothing the cloth down past her tiny waist and round hips. As he touched the smooth white flesh of her thigh he felt a flash of fire in his loins, so strong that for an instant it took his breath away. "Christ, I'm no better than he," he muttered angrily, and, furious with himself, he began to pinch her pale cheeks and chafe her wrists, fighting back the heat in his blood.

Smoke from the smoldering hangings and beams began to swirl up from beneath the door, filling the room with billows of harsh black fumes. Alex grimaced and redoubled his efforts to revive her, but still the girl lay limp as death. Finally he leaned back on his haunches, considering the corpse beside her. Naught to be done for him, that was certain. He cursed as he heard the voices of Jamie Stewart's men through the window, drifting up from the bailey. News of the murder had spread fast, he thought bitterly, listening as they mounted their horses with shouts and clanging weapons. Hoofbeats galloped off down the river road.

He stared down at the tiny black-haired girl, turned for the door, and then turned back. He had his own reasons for catching Red John Stewart's murderer, but they would have to wait. He sensed in some part of his soul that it was more vital now to save this unknown girl. Bemoaning his intuition, Alex caught Genna up in his arms and pulled the chamber door wide.

Great gusts of thick black smoke poured in, making his eyes

burn. There was no sound in the castle now but the steady roar of the fires. With a last apologetic glance at the murdered man, Alex pulled the girl's head tight to his chest and drew his cloak over both their faces.

He groped along the gallery balustrade until he felt the turn for the stairway. The banquet hall below had become a raging inferno, its rich carved panels and elegant tapestries sending red and gold flames shooting toward the ceilings. Alex fought through the heat and smoke, gagging for breath as he tried to remember which way he'd come in. To the left, he decided, ducking to avoid a fiery rafter that crashed past his head in a hail of bright sparks. He stumbled through another dark hallway, and caught a whiff of burnt pudding—the kitchens. Then he burst through an open doorway and into the bailey at last.

Whipping the cloak from his mouth, he gasped in the cool twilight air, letting it fill his lungs with welcome sweetness. A cluster of servants had gathered by the water gate, the men forming a haphazard bucket line, the women wailing out lamentations in high, desperate voices. Alex felt the girl move in his grasp, her small arms reaching up to circle his neck, and again he felt a kindling in his blood. "Papa?" he heard her murmur as she settled against him. "Papa, don't leave me."

"Hey, you!" One of the men by the water gate sprang forward, dropping his bucket, and rushed across the courtyard. At the sight of his crazed, angry expression, Alex tugged the cloak back over his face and ran in the opposite direction. There was no telling what had gone on here, where she would be safe.

He reached the drawbridge gate and whistled, a single high, clear note that brought Bantigh charging toward him out of the gathering shadows, hooves pounding on the paving stones. "That's my fine lady," Alex crooned to the horse, bracing the girl as he swung up into the saddle. "Go, lady!" And the huge white mare gathered her strength and vaulted the gate in a bound. Alex urged her over the drawbridge, beneath the dark holes of the barbican that stared down like empty eye sockets, then across the rocks and into the sheltering woods.

"To the river," he whispered, and gave Bantigh her head, letting her pick her own way through the tall, shadowy trees to the banks of the Clyde. By the time they reached the river, Alex's parched, raw throat was aching for a draught of cool water. He leapt from the horse and set the girl down on the mossy bank, wrapping her tightly in the cloak. Then he drank ravenously from his cupped hands, leaning over the calm, still waters.

His thirst finally sated, he scooped up another handful and splashed it gingerly across her small, pale face, patting her cheek with his palm, first gently, then with more fervor. "Damn it," he muttered, Bantigh nuzzling curiously over his shoulder. "What's the matter with you? Wake up, for God's sake!"

Genna's pale eyelids fluttered. "Papa?" she whispered fretfully. "Papa, is that you?"

"Nay, I'm not your papa. Wake up, now." He spilled another handful of water across her white brow.

She pulled herself up on one elbow, brushing back hair from her eyes. "Oh, Papa, I had the most monstrous dream—" She broke off with a cry of fright, staring at the stranger who knelt over her.

Alex slipped his arm beneath her shoulder. "Are you all right, then?" He pushed Bantigh back; the horse was nibbling contentedly at the girl's black hair.

Genna's wide eyes, dark and still as the Clyde's night waters, considered him curiously. He had long golden hair that the wind had swept back from his face to show a high forehead. His mouth was wide and full, his skin baked bronze by the sun, and he had deep-set, heavy-lidded eyes that stared straight back at her, with a flicker of fire in their depths. Beneath his steady scrutiny she felt suddenly shy; Genna tugged down the shirt she wore to cover her knees, pricking her finger on the clasp of the brooch that had caught in the cloth.

"Are you all right, then, lass?"

Her gaze strayed to a point beyond his wide shoulders, where bright flames had begun to dance against the indigo sky. Alex saw the blaze reflected in her eyes as she gave a small hiccup of a sob, her hand at her mouth. "Oh, sweet blessed Jesus, tell me it was a dream!"

"I'm sorry, lass." Alex reached out his hand to stroke her pale cheek, to comfort her, and was startled when she scrambled from his reach.

"You—you came with them! You killed him, you beasts, you devils."

"No, lass, no. It was I who saved you, pulled you out of the fire."

"Don't touch me, you murderer!" she cried, facing him on hands and knees like a wild thing.

Alex shrugged impatiently, tossing back his mane of gold hair. "Don't be a fool, girl, I'm no murderer."

Her dark eyes flashed at him. "What do you call it, then? A man defenseless, unarmed— You cut him down like a dog. Oh, you're brave fighters, aren't you, you men of Albany? Taking on me and Papa John, both at once!" She choked back an anguished cry of despair.

Alex's hand hovered over her tangled black hair, seeking to soothe her, quiet her. "I'm no man of Albany's, girl. I'm my own man, and no soul else's."

"You're not a man, you're an animal!"

Alex took a long, slow breath. "By God, I'll make excuses for what you've been through, but watch your tongue!"

"Go on and make me, murderer," Genna spat.

Alex's spine stiffened. "I give you my word, I had nothing to do with your papa's death."

"Your word," she said, sneering. Her fingers tightened on the brooch, fumbled to undo the clasp. As he leaned toward her she slashed out furiously, aiming the sharp pin at his eyes. Alex caught her arm just in time; even so, the point pulled a jagged line down his temple.

"Why, you little—" He twisted the brooch from her grasp, nearly crushing her wrist. Tears of pain and frustration sprang up in her eyes. Alex pulled out a kerchief, wet it in the river, and dabbed at the scratch she'd made. Then he considered her bleak, bloodstained, ash-blackened face, and held out the cloth. "Wash off your cheeks; you look a sight."

"Go to hell," Genna snarled, slapping him away. "You kill Papa John, and now you want me to wash my face?"

"For the last time, I had nothing to do with his killing! On my honor!"

"Honor?" She laughed, a harsh, tight sound. "What would a weasel like you know of honor?"

"More than a spoiled half-wit child!"

She clawed at his face. "Murderer! Traitor!"

"Gutter rat."

Genna's red mouth was tight with rage. "Ox's ass. Bastard."

"Whore."

That stopped her dead. Alex stared down at her, grinning slightly.

"Now, do you feel better?"

"You called me— Oh!" She was sputtering in her fury. "I'm not what you called me!"

"And I'm neither a murderer nor a traitor—nor a bastard, at that. You should learn not to bandy strong words if you can't take them tossed back at you. Here." He presented her again with his kerchief. "Wipe off your face."

Genna did as she was told distractedly, running the wet linen over her chin and nose and down her neck. "You missed a spot," said Alex, taking back the cloth and dabbing at her throat. Blood welled up beneath his fingers. "You're hurt, aren't you? Here, let me see."

She slapped his hand away. "I don't want your help. Leave me alone."

Alex sighed. "Tell me where I should take you, then. Back to the castle? Where is the rest of your family, your clan?" She just stared at him, chin held high. "Well, I can't leave you here in the forest, girl! Be sensible!"

"Sensible?" Again Genna felt the hot sting of tears, and blinked angrily. "You burn down Dumbarton, kill Papa John in cold blood, and now you want me to be sensible?"

Alex looked away, flushing slightly. "I'm sorry. That was a fool thing to say." Apology had never come easy to him. He chewed on his lip. "I'll gladly pay for the damage to the castle."

Genna's black eyes narrowed with fury as she remembered the murderer, and the silver he'd thrown at her feet. "You bastard," she said slowly, distinctly. Alex turned back, startled by the loathing in her voice. "You think you can buy anything, don't you? Even a man's life."

"That's not what I meant."

Genna drew herself to her feet and faced him, hands on hips. "Get the hell off this land," she cried, and spat at his face. "Go back to your thrice-damned Albany friends. But so help me God, I'll see that you hang for this." She shook her small fist at him. "Nay, hanging's too good for you. I'll chop you up in small pieces, and feed you to dogs."

Alex stared for a moment, taken aback by the tiny creature's bloodthirstiness. Then he too clambered to his feet.

"Have it your way, you stupid ungrateful wench," he shouted, tossing the brooch at her. "I should have left you to burn in the castle!"

"You'll wish you had someday!" Genna screamed, glaring at him as he stood towering over her. "And I wish you had, too!"

Alex stared down into her huge, dark eyes, saw her breasts heaving raggedly beneath the thin linen shirt, and took a long, deep breath. Her rage had only heightened her strange, dusky beauty, and again he felt fire stir in his groin as desire seized him. He shook his head angrily, willing the sensation away, but its strength was close to overwhelming. God, was he mad? How could he even think such thoughts, with all that she had been through?

Genna's dark gaze glinted; she had seen the flicker of fire in those sleepy blue eyes, saw the muscles tighten across his broad chest, his clenched hands, and knew their meaning. Abruptly she smiled; Alex caught his breath as she stepped toward him, her white arms outstretched. "Forgive me," she murmured softly, her black eyes pleading. "Have mercy on a poor, helpless girl who is in your debt, and overcome with grief. Let me give you a kiss for your trouble, won't you? So strong, and so handsome. . . ."

That was more like it, thought Alex, grinning as he went to meet her, to gather her into his arms. God, what a beautiful creature! "Milady," he murmured, entranced by those wide dark eyes, her white throat, her pale naked legs, her tiny feet.

As he moved toward her, smiling, Genna smiled back sweetly, then brought up her small white foot and kicked him right in the groin with all her might.

Alex felt the breath go out of him in a loud whoosh as he doubled over, gasping, sinking to his knees. Genna crashed away through the underbrush, laughing, as he swallowed a billow of nausea and watched her vanish, a wisp of white wraith, into the night. "That ought to teach you, bastard!" he heard her call to him, her voice once more harsh with hate. "That will teach you to try and rape me!"

"Damn you, come back here!" he shouted. "I wasn't going to rape you, girl!"

The forest was still and quiet as death. Bantigh whinnied, the sound carrying like a clarion call through the gathering darkness. Alex groaned and stood up, his groin aching furiously. "Who'd want to rape you, anyway?" he bellowed after her. "You ugly, scrawny little beast!"

He hobbled over to Bantigh in disgust, moaning again as he swung himself up into the saddle. Obviously the child was quite capable of looking after herself. Overcome with grief, indeed. Alex glanced into the forest and thought he saw her flit across the strand, a tiny white spirit with long black hair. He grimaced, clutching his gut.

So much for trusting intuition, he thought, and laughed at his own naïveté. There were more important matters at hand —such as catching the murderer. He dug his knees into Bantigh's sides, and galloped away.

"I tell you, sire, I saw her! A young man carried her from the kitchens!"

"What young man? One of the household?"

The stablehand shook his head tentatively, pulling at his chin. "He did not come with the others, sire. A tall youth, with wheat-colored hair."

King James sighed, flexing his powerful hands. The stablehand was lying to cover his own negligence in the matter, of that he was certain. Most likely the girl was dead, raped and murdered, or being held by the Albanys for ransom. He cursed mildly and considered his choices. It had been a hard ride from Stirling in response to the reports of the sacking at Dumbarton, and his men needed ale, and food. But if the stablehand was telling the truth, if the girl was alive . . .

He gazed up once more at the smoldering husk of the castle, thinking of his uncle, Red John. He too might have turned against James during the long years of the Albany regency— after all, the first regent, Robert, had been his half brother. But despite the fact that he had never been acknowledged as a legitimate heir, Red John had remained a true and faithful servant to James, though it had brought him little in return, except his horrible death. James owed him something for that.

He took off his helmet and ran a hand back through his long auburn hair. "Very well. Mac Teague!" The captain of the cavalry stepped forward. "Take twoscore men and scour the lawns and woods. Who knows? We might be lucky." Mac Teague nodded and rallied his men.

James sat down heavily on a bridling stone, signaling for wine to be brought. If he *was* lucky, he reflected bitterly, it

would be for the first time in his brief reign. Eighteen years
he'd suffered as a captive of the English kings, while his uncle
Robert, the first Duke of Albany, ruled Scotland as regent.
And did little enough to work for my release, he thought
grimly.

James knew of the rumors that said it was Robert who ar-
ranged for the ship carrying the twelve-year-old king to safety
in France to be seized by Henry IV of England in the North
Sea. Thus had those long years of captivity begun. After Robert's death had come his son Murdoch as regent, and more of
the same. When James had finally managed to win his release
from the English and return to Scotland, only two years before, he'd found the Albany family still cozily ensconced in
power. James had immediately had Murdoch's eldest son,
Walter, arrested for treason, in an attempt to consolidate his
authority, to prove to the headstrong S~ottish nobles that this
Stewart was determined to rule his realm whatever the cost.
And the upshot was this: Murdoch's youngest son, Jamie, running wild throughout the west, burning the king's fortresses,
cutting down an old man and a helpless girl.

The situation had grown too volatile for half-measures to
serve. James remembered with an ironic grimace the words
he'd spoken so firmly at his coronation: "If God grant me but
the life of a dog, I will make the key keep the castle, and the
bracken-bush the cow." That task was proving harder than
he'd anticipated. Scotland had been in Albany hands too long;
the country's coffers were empty, private wars were rampant,
and the Isles were one recurring headache. Still, James was
determined to bring his sprawling, wayward dominion under
one man's rule—his rule. He sipped eagerly at the wine a
servant brought him. The Albanys would have to be dealt
with, rigorously, as an example. Red John's brutal murder was
the final straw.

In the meantime, James drained his cup and got up to go
through the castle, to determine what the costs of reappointing
it might be.

It was nearly two hours later when he heard the blast of a
horn from the wood. Hooves came thundering over the drawbridge, and a shout went up from his troops. James hurried
down from the charred gallery he'd been inspecting and into
the castle yards.

Mac Teague drew up on his steed, a limp bundle slung over his saddle skirt. "We found her, sire."

James's cool eyes met those of his captain. "Alive?"

"Aye." Mac Teague dismounted gingerly and reached back for the bundle. "Down by the river, curled up like a snail. She has a couple of wounds on her neck and shoulders; nothing deadly." The young captain tapped at his forehead. "But she's still a mite muddled, if you catch my meaning."

"Well done, Mac Teague. Bring a litter, someone," James called sharply, clapping his hands. Two foot soldiers scrambled in their packs as James took the girl in his arms and tugged the heavy dark blue cloak back from her head. He brushed away a stray lock of pitch-black hair, smiling down at her tiny heart-shaped face, the long curled lashes and rosebud mouth. "Wine," he ordered, and took the cup that appeared in his hand, pressing it to the girl's lips. Genna stirred slightly as the hot sweet liquid coursed down her throat. Her dark eyes opened, and she stared up at the king.

"Who are you?" she murmured dreamily, as he laid her down on the litter. A ripple of laughter ran through the troops.

James smiled. "Drink a bit more of this, lass, can you?" She swallowed another mouthful. "They call me James Stewart."

"James Stewart," she echoed, pale eyelids closing. Then they flew open. "'Twas your men that killed Papa John!"

"Nay, lass, not mine." He smoothed a hand across her brow. "What makes you say 'twas so?"

Genna shifted on the litter, frightened and confused. "Papa John told me—it was Albany's men, his son Jamie." She looked up at him again. "If you're not that James Stewart, then you must be . . . Are you the king?" Her gaze was wide.

He exchanged amused glances with Mac Teague. "Aye, lass. Tell me, did you see the men who killed Red John?"

"Aye, they came to the celebration early . . . bearing Stewart banners and shields." She clenched her eyes shut. "We heard them in the hall there, and then they came up the stairs."

"And then?" asked Mac Teague, leaning forward eagerly. Genna shrank back in horror as the images swarmed up in her mind: the murderer, grinning, bitter ale on his breath; his unbuckled cuirass cutting against her; the glint of the sun on the dagger as he held it to Red John's ear. "Papa," she cried vaguely, "oh, Papa John . . ."

James signaled for blankets to be brought and waved the captain away. "Later, Mac Teague," he said briefly. "Rest now, lass. There will be plenty of time for talk later on."

"But what is to become of me?" Genna cried, the blue cloak clutched tight in her hands. "What will I do, without Papa John?"

"Hush, child. I will take you back with me to Stirling."

"And Papa John?"

"We will bury him at Stirling," he promised, "in a royal grave."

Genna lay back wearily on the litter, somewhat appeased, then started up again. "My loom! I cannot possibly go to Stirling without my loom! Where is it? Was it burned?"

James hid his smile. A loom was hardly the sole thing any female of his acquaintance would have asked after under the circumstances. He patted the girl's thin hand. "We've plenty of looms at the castle. You needn't worry."

"But not like this one! You see . . . it belonged to my mother. And Papa John kept it for me for all those years." A single huge tear trembled for an instant on her eyelid, then slid down her cheek.

James cleared his throat. "Ah, yes, well, I'm afraid it's gone now."

"No, it isn't, Your Majesty!" one of the soldiers piped up. "At least, I think not. There's a big loom in the bedchamber right by the stairs."

James scowled at the soldier, looked at the distraught girl, and shook his head. "I'm sorry, young lady, but we can't very well march with a loom."

Genna pulled herself up on her elbows, struggling out of the litter. "Then you can march without me, as well!" She held her chin high, and her black eyes were flashing even as her knees began to give way.

James sighed and reached out to steady her; Mac Teague bit his cheek, ready to wager who would win. The king might be a great and fearless leader, but he was no match for a woman's stubbornness—or even a girl's.

The king turned to the soldier who'd spoken. "Go and get the bloody loom, then," he barked, "and you can lug it thirty miles for your help!" He glared at Genna. "And you, get right back on that litter. Now!" Genna crawled in gratefully, with a hint of a triumphant smile. James moved off a few paces and beckoned to Mac Teague. "Keep her under close guard until we get to the castle. She can testify at the next Parliament. She's the only real witness we have."

And even as his heart felt pity for what the child had endured, his politic brain was thinking: she is smart, and spirited, and lovely. How fortunate.

She should prove the best witness against Jamie by far.

Part I

**Stirling Castle
May 1427**

1

"Sit!" Katy said sternly, and reluctantly Genna perched on the chair before the polished tin mirror. "And you too, sirrah!" The maid glared down at the little black terrier that was nipping at her heels.

Genna patted her lap, and the dog bounded into the air and landed with a thump, settling down eagerly in the folds of her new silk gown, scratching at his tail.

"Ach, now, you'll have fleas and fur all over you, girl," Katy grumbled, pulling a tortoise-shell comb through a tangle of thick black hair with great vigor. Genna winced, clutching her ears.

"Katy, damn you, that hurts!"

"Well, too bad for you. If you'd been ready an hour ago like you were supposed to, I wouldn't be rushing." She peered down her nose at her mistress. "Aren't you all excited to be going before all those grand lords, girl? Why, the whole castle's abuzz with talk of the trial."

Genna sighed, running her hands through Nero's silky fur. "No, Katy. I am *not* excited."

"Just think, you'll tell 'em what happened, and then those brutes what done in your papa will get what's coming to them at last." The wiry maid's eyes gleamed as they met Genna's in the mirror. "Whoosh!" She made a quick chopping motion with the brush. "'Twill be, 'Off with their heads!'"

Genna shuddered and huddled in her chair. She'd spent the past year at court trying to forget that awful night at Dumbarton, hoping against hope that the king would forget his orders that she testify. After all, so much time had passed, and no one had been able to find Jamie Stewart or his band of marauders. They'd escaped to Ireland that night, and were in exile there. But now King James had somehow decided to try his uncle Robert and the other two sons, Walter and Alaster, for the

27

crime, holding them responsible for Jamie's dirty work. And at any minute the bailiff would appear to summon Genna to the Great Hall—the thought made her squirm on the seat.

Katy rapped her knuckles with the brush. "Hold still, I said. You don't want to look like a ragamuffin in front of all those great men, do you?"

"What does it matter how I *look?*" Genna wailed, leaning her elbows on the dressing table, and her chin in her hands.

"Why, girl!" Katy clucked her tongue and winked slyly above Genna's head. "Out of all those rich, important lords there's sure to be one who'll take pity on a poor little helpless orphan, 'specially one so pretty, and take her home for his wife."

"Don't be a damned idiot, Katy!" Genna stuck out her tongue at the maid's reflection. "Who'd want to marry one of those gnarled old codgers?"

"Hoo, such language!" Katy yanked viciously at a tangle. "They're not all old and gnarled, either, when it comes to that. But you wouldn't know, since you spend all your time up here working at that loom, 'stead of dancing and making merry with the other young ladies."

Genna sighed as Katy ran on; the theme was a familiar one. Dancing and merrymaking, she thought wryly. And with whom would she do such things? With the queen's ladies, who treated her with the scant civility they'd grant to a troublesome younger sister? Or with those beastly courtiers, perhaps, the ones who teased her incessantly, calling her Gypsy, or Romany. "Hey, little gypsy!" they hooted when they saw her. "Hey, gypsy, come tell my fortune!" The bloody fops, all pointy shoes and curled-up hair and frippery—was it any wonder she preferred to stay in her room?

She scratched Nero's floppy ears absentmindedly. The pup had been a gift from Queen Joan, one of the strays she kept taking in over her husband's objections. Kittens, puppies, birds found broken-winged in the gardens—even a bear cub that had wandered through the gates last month had been welcomed into her menagerie. Joan Beaufort had an innate sympathy for all lost things, which explained, Genna thought ruefully, why the queen had been so kind to her over this past year.

King James himself had been a lost thing when Joan first met him, for that matter. Genna thought of the chivalrous story and sighed again. He'd been imprisoned in the Tower of London, waiting to be ransomed, and had looked down and seen the beautiful young daughter of the Earl of Somerset walking in a hedge maze below. All Europe knew how he'd wooed her with songs from his window, and how Joan defied the objections of her powerful Lancastrian family to give ear—and then her heart—to the captive king.

Some thought it strange that James, after all those years of imprisonment in England, should have chosen an Englishwoman for his wife. But Genna well understood why he'd lost his heart to Joan. The queen was tall and blithe and gold-haired and merry, and she loved her husband with a fierceness unheard of in an age when royal marriages were without exception made for reasons of state.

What would have become of her had Joan not taken her under her wing, Genna could not imagine. She had no family now, no lands or dowry, nothing but the gold and pearl brooch she wore at her throat. That and her loom were all she had in the world to call her own. Even the yellow silk gown she had on now had been a gift from the queen, especially chosen for this appearance before the Parliament.

Katy had finished with her charge's hair, plaiting the rich black tresses into three long coils and looping them together at the nape of Genna's neck. Now she wet her forefinger in a beaker of walnut oil and rubbed at the girl's thick dark eyebrows to coax them into order. "Katy, what in God's name are you doing?" Genna demanded, wriggling out of her grasp.

"Her Majesty said I was to make you out a lady, girl," the maid said grimly, "and so I shall. Get back here while I put this here rouge on your cheeks."

"The hell I will," Genna snapped, backing into a corner. "Queen or no, I'm not going out looking like an alehouse bawd!"

A gay bright laugh burst from the doorway. Genna looked up, saw the queen standing there, and blushed bright red. "Your Majesty," she stuttered, dropping in a curtsy, "I beg your mercy, I did not hear you come in."

"Never mind, then, dearie, never mind." Joan came and pulled her to her feet, then examined her thoroughly from head to toe. Genna stood quaking as the queen's critical gray eyes scrutinized her, but at last Joan nodded and smiled. "You look perfectly lovely. Katy, she's quite right about the rouge. Young and innocent, that's what we want the lords to think."

"Young 'n' headstrong's more like it," Katy muttered.

"All right, Katy, you may go."

Still mumbling to herself, Katy gathered up combs and pins and potions in her valise and curtsied, then left them alone.

Joan reached out and pried Genna's clenched fists from the folds of the yellow gown, noting that the girl's knuckles were blanched white. "For heaven's sake," she scolded gently, "look how you're mussing that silk. And do stop gnawing on your lip; you'll put a hole in it." Genna laughed, somewhat shakily, as the queen smoothed out her skirts. "Frightened, aren't you?" Genna nodded. "Well, don't be. They're not going to eat you alive. You already know most of the peers, anyway— the earls of Douglas and Mar and Menteith and Sutherland and so on. And the king's uncle, Atholl—you remember him, Genna, don't you? The red-faced old fellow with the great bush of whiskers? He'll ask you the questions. Just tell them the truth, dearie. That's all His Majesty asks."

"Yes, Your Majesty," Genna whispered, her hands once more twisting the cheery silk of her gown.

Joan smiled kindly, tucking a stray wisp of ebony hair behind Genna's ear. "I truly am sorry to put you through this, Genna, but you must believe there is no other way. The Duke of Albany and his sons have been His Majesty's foes for a long, long time now, since before you were born. This is James's chance to . . . well, to pay off an old debt, let's say. And in order to do so, he needs you. You do understand."

"I—I think so." Genna jumped as she heard a loud knock at the door. Joan stepped back, made one last survey of Genna's appearance, and nodded with satisfaction.

"Who's there?" she called.

The bailiff, huge and unsmiling, pushed open the door and bowed. "Lady Genevieve Fleming is ordered to stand before the lords of the kingdom in the Great Hall."

Joan nudged Genna forward. "Go on, then, dearie! And remember, just tell them the truth."

With a growing sense of dread Genna followed the bailiff's tall, straight figure through the echoing corridor. His heavy-soled boots made sharp clicking sounds all the way down the long flagstone stairs, and the carved wooden staff he carried thumped with every step. Genna could hear her heart thumping in her chest, every bit as loud.

The bailiff stood aside at the vaulted entrance to the parliamentary chamber. Genna stood uncertainly in the archway, gazing into the high-ceilinged hall. The side walls were lined with rows of high-backed benches on ascending platforms, each row separated by heavy balustrades. At the far end of the room, seated on a huge carved chair, a table before him, was the Earl of Atholl. When he saw the girl in the doorway he rapped at the table with a mallet. "Order, please!" he called. The dozens of lords who were milling about, elegantly bedecked in their robes of ermine and velvet, slowly took their seats on the benches. Atholl beckoned Genna forward. She swallowed as she heard the iron doors behind her close with a mighty clang.

Staring at her slippers, Genna walked slowly through the vast, echoing chamber until she stood at the table, trying to ignore the hum of comment that followed her. "All right, let's get this done with," Atholl grumbled. "Genevieve Fleming?" She bobbed her head. "Speak up, girl!" Atholl barked from behind his bush of whiskers. "How do you expect the scribe to hear you? Your name is Genevieve Fleming?"

"Yes, milord," Genna whispered, her throat gone dry.

"And Red John Stewart was what to you?"

"My godfather, milord."

He leaned back in his chair, eyeing her expectantly. "Well, girl?"

"W-well what, milord?" Genna felt her color rise as the peers burst into laughter. Atholl frowned and smacked the mallet again.

"Well, tell us about the murder, for the love of God!"

"Yes, milord." Staring down at the slate tiles on the floor, Genna took a deep breath and haltingly began to recount the events of that long-ago afternoon, beginning with the lighting of the torches. There was an undercurrent of laughter in the big room as she told of the footrace, and Taggert, but it died away when she turned uncertainly and glanced up into the benches, tears bright in her jet black eyes. "We were jesting, you see," she explained, turning back to Atholl, "and we looked through the window and saw the riders coming. We thought they were guests. And Papa John said . . . he said, 'Is there still time to call this off, then?' I told him no, and we went upstairs." Her voice trailed off into a sob; she bit her lip, fighting back a sudden rush of tears.

"He was telling me a story in my chambers, and I heard the sound of glass breaking. And Papa John sniffed the air and said, 'Faith, the cook must be burning the dumplings again.' But I looked out the door and saw them down in the hall."

"Saw whom?" Atholl demanded.

"The—the men."

"How many were there?"

"I don't know. A score. A lot. And their insignias were Stewart. I told Papa John that, and he said, 'Well, they must be our guests.' But then I told him they were torching the hall. He wanted to go and fight them, but I hid him, down behind a screen. And then the door opened, and he—the man—he came in."

"What did he look like?"

"He was big, huge, with red hair, and his eyes were gray. He asked where Papa John was, and I said why did he want to know. He told me he had a message for the king—from Jamie Stewart." The lords shifted and whispered in their seats. Genna's thin hands were tying the cheery silk of her gown into tight knots. "He offered me money to tell where Papa John was hiding, but I wouldn't say."

Genna heard a sudden sharp intake of breath from somewhere high in the chamber. She continued to stare at her toes.

"And then?" asked Atholl brusquely.

Genna gnawed her lip. "He said—he said in that case he'd give the message to me. And he chased me, and tried to— He had a dagger, and his tasset was unbuckled, and he pushed me against the wall." Involuntarily her fingers reached for the scar on her throat, as if she felt the chill steel blade there once more.

Atholl was drumming on the table with his fingers. "All right, lass. What happened then?"

"Then I heard Papa John tell him to leave me alone, and he whirled around. I would have been all right, I could have borne it, borne anything, if only Papa John had stayed hidden!" The words were rough, ragged sobs. "But the man kicked me down, and put his dagger to Papa John's ear, like this . . . and then he just—he just—all the blood came rushing—" She shook her head, tears streaming down her face.

"I would not have thought, milord, there could be so much blood in a man."

Atholl cleared his throat. "I see. Can you tell me whether the murderer held the knife in his right or in his left hand?"

"For God's sake," a deep voice growled, "let her be. Hasn't she suffered enough without your endless questions?"

Genna blushed, rubbing her eyes on her sleeve. The last thing she wanted from any of these heartless men was their pity. "My dear boy," Atholl was saying over her head, his tone rich with condescension, "I know this is your first time sitting with us; you clearly don't understand our procedures—"

"To hell with your bloody procedures," the voice interrupted steadily. "And I'm not your dear boy."

A low murmur of outrage swept through the chamber. "Ill-mannered upstart," Genna heard one peer mutter angrily, and another called, "Cheeky boor!"

Atholl's normally ruddy face had turned brilliant scarlet. He pounded his mallet on the table. "Order!" he cried, peering across the room. "Now, my dear b— I mean, Your Lordship. Surely you realize we have a duty to ascertain what went on—"

"By badgering a helpless girl?" Genna could sense the rage that lay, barely restrained, beneath the surface of that low voice. "She told you the villain killed him. What more do you need?"

"Of course, Mac Donald, you'd know all about villains, wouldn't you?" one peer chimed in slyly.

Atholl rapped on the table. "All right, Henry."

"Learned from the best, didn't you?" the slick voice went on. "From your dear late father."

"Milord Argyll," Atholl shouted, "that's quite enough!"

Out of the corner of her eye Genna could see the lord being chastised; he was leaning forward in his seat, a cocky grin on his narrow dark face. "Well, 'tis true, isn't it?" he appealed to the lords around him. "Spawn of a traitor, I can make out the stench of him from here." And he straightened his wide velvet collar with slow disdain.

"You bloody bastard," that deep voice spat. The peers were laughing openly now, goading Argyll on with whispered encouragement.

"Order!" Atholl called sharply. "Order, everyone! Will the Lord of the Isles please get back in his seat?"

"Send him back to his bloody Isles till he learns some manners!" somebody cried out, and a chorus of jeering hoots answered: "Nay, that won't work!" "How could he learn manners there?"

"By God, I'll take on every damned one of you!"

Genna heard a thunderous roar as a huge figure broke through the balustrade and crashed into the row of benches where Argyll sat. The elegantly clad lords scrambled out of his way, knocking benches and one another over in their haste.

Argyll had taken refuge in the top row, crouching behind the benches. "If you ask me," he called above the uproar, "'tis Mac Donald and his heathen clan chiefs that should be on trial, the bloody barbarians!" The man clambering after him made a lunge for his throat.

"Guards! Guards!" Old Atholl was pounding his mallet furiously. A half-dozen burly men-at-arms gingerly came forward to grapple with the giant, clinging to his back. He growled and flexed his arms, throwing them off, and they fell among the scattered benches with a mighty thud. The sound shocked the room into silence. Genna turned and watched as the huge man leapt down to the floor, fists ready, every muscle in his long, strong body tensed.

She stared in disbelief at that flushed, angry face, the crown of dark gold hair, skin baked bronze by the sun.

"Order!" old Atholl bellowed, flinging his mallet through the air. "Alexander Mac Donald, your behavior is a blight on the honor of this assembly! This session of Parliament is dismissed! Unless— You, girl!" Genna looked back at him reluctantly. "Have you anything else to say?"

She turned and stared into those hooded blue eyes; they considered her coolly. Alexander Mac Donald met her gaze, unflinching, waiting for her to condemn him.

Atholl pounded his fist on the table. "Dammit, I asked you a question, child! Have you anything to add to your testimony here?"

shook her head slowly, still staring into those fath-
eyes. "No, milord. There is . . . nothing more to

2

The black-hooded headsman raised his long double-bladed axe, and a hush fell over the crowd that lined the gates to the Heading Hill. The bright spring sun glistened on the waters of the River Forth far below, and the keen edges of the axe seemed to glisten as well. Murdoch Stewart, Duke of Albany, stepped haughtily forward, calmly rolled down his collar to bare his sturdy neck, and leaned over the cold gray stone.

Alex turned away as the axe fell with a dull, sickening thud. Only the hearty cheers from the throngs who'd gathered to watch the execution told him it was finished. There was no joy in these beheadings for him, God knew. He slipped a finger beneath his own collar and rubbed his neck, thoughtfully.

From his vantage point above the crowds he could see the sleek dark head of Genevieve Fleming, bowed low as though in prayer, and he wondered once again what emotions were hiding behind those solemn black eyes. He'd known her at once when she'd entered the Great Hall that morning, tiny, trembling like a bird, her small hands tangled in the folds of her gown. He thought of her bitter tears, the bleak pain in her voice as she'd whispered, "I would not have thought, milord, there could be so much blood in a man." Christ, it was worth the calumnies he'd endured from Argyll that morning, if he'd managed to spare her any further grief.

"Alley! Alexander!" A yank at his doubtlet pulled Alex back to the present. It was Davey Mac Leod, his old leather cap perched jauntily atop his blazing red hair. "I've been lookin' for ye everywhere, Alley! Tell me what went on at the trial."

Alex started up the wynd toward the castle gates, grimacing at his friend's blithe smile. "You can see the result there on the Heading Hill, can't you? What more do you need to know?"

"Well, for instance, that wee girl who came out with old Atholl, the one with the black hair—what a beauty, eh, Alley? Do you know her?" He was skipping to keep up with Alex's long strides. "What's her name, do you remember?"

"No. What of it?"

Davey gave him a sidelong glance, saw the taut creases in his forehead, and shrugged. "Just wondered, Alley, 'tis all. What plans are you makin' for this evenin'?"

Alex ran a hand through his long gold hair. "I'm heading back to Mull, just as fast as I can."

"Back to—What, man, are you crazy? There's the banquet the king is holdin' tomorrow, with gorgeous women, and fine food, and all the ale you can drink—and two more beheadin's, as well!"

"Ghoul," Alex muttered.

Davey went right on, unheeding. "Did you see how cool and steady that Albany was on the block there, rollin' down his collar as calm as can be? I wonder, Alley, would I die so well. Do you think that you would?"

"I've no desire to find out," Alex said wryly. "So I'm heading back to Mull."

Davey paused, taken aback, then ran to catch up, pulling off his cap, making a sweeping bow. "Ah, come on, Alley, let's not go back to the Isles just yet. Let's stay on a wee bit longer. You forget, this is my last summer as a free man!"

"What would Meggie say if she heard such talk?" Alex demanded, grinning despite his preoccupation.

Davey's broad face creased in a smile of pure joy. "Faith, you know how well I love yer sister, Alley. The day on which we're wed will be the happiest of all my life. But still"—his green brown eyes sparkled as he tossed his cap in the air—"you would not begrudge a condemned man a final indulgence!"

Distracted by the conversation, Alex hadn't noticed that they'd come within a few paces of the queen and her ladies, and the usual bevy of eager, fawning courtiers. He saw Henry Argyll's tall, thin figure among them, and hastily pulled at Davey's jerkin to lead him away.

"What are ye doin', man?" the redhead hissed indignantly. "There's that little black-eyed beauty I was askin' about—"

"No, Davey!" Alex growled, but it was too late. Queen Joan turned and saw him, her eyes lighting up.

"Well, ladies, see who has finally come to join us!"

Alex halted reluctantly; it would be folly to offend the queen. But Davey stepped forward eagerly, sweeping off his cap. "Davey Mac Leod, Yer Majesty, at yer service. Do you suppose I might request an introduction to this ravishin' beauty by yer side?"

"Oh, you men of the Isles!" The queen wagged a beringed finger, then extended her hand. Davey planted a hearty kiss on it, then turned to Genna. "Genevieve Fleming," Joan said, laughing at Davey's debonair bow, "this is Davey Mac Leod."

"Well, well, well." At the sound of Argyll's smooth, slow drawl Alex felt his jaw tighten. "If it isn't the Lord of the Isles."

"Your Majesty." Alex bowed stiffly to the queen.

She smiled graciously, a hint of coquetry in her manner as she looked up at the handsome lord. "Alexander, we've not seen much of you since your arrival at court. Considering the roguish tales I heard of you from your mother, I expected to have to keep my ladies under lock and key all throughout your stay!"

Alex felt his face redden as the women giggled. He looked at Genevieve Fleming; she was standing shyly by the queen, her eyes downcast. He felt his breath catch at the sight of her beauty, remembered vividly for so long. She raised the heavy fringe of her lashes, and met his gaze.

"It would be more to the point to lock up the stables," said Argyll with an angry sneer.

Alex's huge fists clenched instinctively; he saw a flash of something like pity in Genevieve Fleming's dark eyes as the men with Argyll snickered.

"What's that about the stables, Henry?" Queen Joan asked, fearing she'd missed a clever joke.

"I only thought that after the exhibition His Lordship put on for the Parliament this morning," Argyll went on suavely, "he might find the company there to his taste. You do keep your asses there, don't you, Your Majesty?"

The queen considered Alexander Mac Donald curiously; a vein on his forehead was pulsing out in bold relief.

Davey Mac Leod knew what that look meant. He slipped his arm through Alex's, tugging him away. "If you'll pardon

us, Yer Majesty," he cried gaily, "perhaps we will have a look
at the stables. Asses at least are good for something, which is
more'n I can say for silk popinjays."

A burst of laughter rang out from the ladies. Davey tightened his grip and pulled Alex through the gates and up the
staircase to their rooms.

"Now, would you mind tellin' a soul what that was about?"
he demanded.

Alex paced over to the window and stood staring down into
the yards. "I don't know what you mean."

Davey yanked him around and glared up at him, freckled
face wrinkled bullishly. "Don't you be givin' me a fistful of
feathers, Alley Mac Donald. Haven't we been best of friends
for twenty years now, since we were babes in arms? That's
long enough for me to tell when you're angry—and you are
angry! What went on at that session of Parliament?"

"Nothing," Alex muttered, not meeting his eyes.

"Nothin'? Oh, nothin's why that slimy bastard out there
was jeering at you? Nothin's why all of a sudden you're leaving the court?"

"Nothing important, Davey, I swear it. I—I lost my
temper a bit at the trial. That's all."

"Lost yer temper a bit meanin' you spoke out of turn or
somethin', Alley? Or lost yer temper meanin' you threw some
chairs?"

Alex grinned reluctantly. "I didn't throw any chairs, but
there were a few flying about."

"Oh, lordy"—Davey shook his head in dismay—"I knew it
was too good to last, the women and the food and the ale and
all. Alley, why can't you just learn to think before you act?
And they say 'tis redheads that have the tempers."

Alex flopped down in a chair by the hearth. "You'd have
done the same thing, Davey, if you could have heard old Atholl bullying that poor girl. And then when I tried to step in,
Argyll started in on my father, calling him a traitor, and—"

"Whoa, slow down, then!" Davey held up a hand. "Bul-
lyin' what girl?"

"The girl who was at Dumbarton, the black-haired girl.
Genevieve Fleming."

"What was he doin' to her?"

"Oh, asking her what hand the murderer held the knife in

and such. Christ, Davey, if only he could have seen how terrified she was that night—" He broke off abruptly.

Davey came toward him slowly. "What night, Alley?"

Alex swallowed and said nothing.

"Seen her what night?" Davey said again stubbornly. "You
told me you didn't know her."

"I don't know her. Not—not really."

"My God." Davey stared down at his lord's flushed face.
"My God. Don't tell me you were there—"

"It's not what you're thinking, Davey! All right, I was
there. But I didn't ride with Jamie Stewart's men." He sighed.
"Do you swear to say nothing of this to anyone? Ever?"

Davey tapped his chest, wide-eyed. "On my honor as a
Mac Leod. You were at Dumbarton?"

Alex nodded. "But I didn't lie to you, Davey. I don't know
her. I didn't even know her name."

Davey pulled up a stool and sat across from him. "I think
you'd best begin at the beginnin', old friend."

Alex leaned forward. "Do you remember last Eastertide,
when my father sent me off to find Ranalt Mac Ruarie?"

"Yer uncle Ranalt." Davey's mouth twisted. "I might have
known *he'd* be tangled up in this somewhere. Sure, I remember. Meggie told me yer father was all in a rage, said she'd
never seen Donald so angry, but he wouldn't say why."

"He wouldn't tell me, either, just told me to find Ranalt
Mac Ruarie and bring him back to Mull, whatever it took. I
tracked Ranalt to Greenock; he'd joined up with a pack of
Jamie Stewart's men who were hiding out there. I was that
close"—he held his fingers apart—"but when I reached
Greenock, I heard they'd all ridden off to Dumbarton for some
celebration. So I set off after them. I wasn't more than half an
hour behind. And then when I got to Dumbarton, there
wasn't any celebration—just fire and smoke and confusion. I
heard a scream, so I ran into the castle and up the stairs. I
found that girl lying on the floor, next to Red John Stewart's
corpse. And guess who was standing over her, his knife still
dripping with blood?"

Davey's eyes narrowed. "Ranalt Mac Ruarie. That murderous cur," he growled, his teeth clenched. "The Mac Leods
should have slit his own throat years ago, after he killed my
aunt."

"You know, I never believed he'd done that, Davey, not

until I saw him bending over that girl, his little eyes glittering, pawing at her breasts."

"And did you kill him?"

"I never had a chance. I pulled him off the girl, and he ran away, like the coward he is."

"Well, why didn't you follow him?"

"What, and leave the poor girl there to burn?"

"All right, all right. Go on with your story," Davey said grimly.

He listened as Alex told how he'd taken the girl from the burning castle and down to the banks of the Clyde, not interrupting until Alex said he'd offered to pay for the castle. "Christ, that was bloody stupid of you, Alley."

"You don't know the half of it. At the trial she said Ranalt tried to bribe her to say where Red John was hiding."

Davey whistled between his teeth. "If she thought you were one of Jamie's men, then why weren't you keeping the Duke of Albany company on the block today?"

"Because she didn't tell the lords I was there!"

"Well, why didn't you tell them, Alley? After all, you did nothing wrong."

Alex stood abruptly, his brows knit together. "Who do you think would believe I just happened to show up at Dumbarton that day?"

"The king would believe you!"

"Not a chance," Alex said shortly. "Have you forgotten about the Harlaw?"

"The Harlaw. Christ, man, that was sixteen years past! No one remembers the Harlaw."

"Argyll remembers. He threw it in my teeth at the trial today. Called me the spawn of a traitor."

"Ach, Alley, 'twas the Albanys Donald was fighting against at the Harlaw. The king wouldn't hold that against you."

"No? King James is determined to make a show of his power, Davey. His uncle Murdoch was nowhere near Dumbarton that day, and is dead as can be."

"So you're tellin' me you were afraid to testify? Bullfeathers, Alley. You may be a lot of things, but you're no coward. And you'd go to the block just to prove you weren't, you're so bloody stubborn. Why didn't you testify?"

"Oh, Davey, can't you see?" Alex paced across the room and turned, his blue eyes dark with frustration. "If I'd testified, I would have been under oath. When they asked me who the murderer was, I'd be honor bound to tell them."

"So what?" Davey cried. "Don't tell me you're tryin' to protect Ranalt Mac Ruarie!"

"No, no! But what would *she* think, if she found out it was my uncle who caused her such woe?"

It was on the tip of Davey's tongue to ask, Well, who gives a damn what she thinks? But another look at Alex's stark, proud face silenced him. As I live and breathe, he thought, and nearly chuckled. Alexander Mac Donald has fallen in love.

"So what finally happened, there in the forest with the girl?" he asked curiously, gently.

A bright spot of color showed high in each of Alex's cheekbones. "She—uh—she attacked me."

"That wee little thing attacked you?" Davey repeated, incredulous.

"She kicked me." Alex grimaced, remembering. "Right here. Her aim was extraordinary."

Now Davey did laugh. "The little hellcat. Guess she's not so helpless as she looks. What did you do?"

"I lost my temper, of course. I left her, there in the forest. I set off after Ranalt. I was going to kill him myself for what he'd done to her. And then I reached Knockmoy, and found a ship there, from the Isles, with a message. Donald was dead."

"And you were Lord of the Isles."

"I had no choice but to return."

Alex moved to the window once more, staring out over the spring green fields, the river that shimmered with the dying rays of the sun, and wondered himself at the way the girl had lingered in his mind. He'd thought of her at the oddest times . . . In his bath, when he washed the jagged scar her brooch had left at his temple. On that grim day when he'd been acknowledged as his father's successor to the lordship, standing atop the ancient cairn at Islay, the silver belt of office heavy in his hand. At night, when he saw her flicker through the dark forest of his dreams, a tiny black-haired spirit.

"So that's where you disappeared to all last winter," Davey said thoughtfully. "You were in Ireland, looking for Ranalt." Alex nodded. "You should have told me, Alley, I'd have gone with you."

"I didn't tell anyone. I thought it would be a simple task to find him." He shrugged, his eyes dark and moody. "It wasn't."

And then I got word the king had summoned me to Parliament."

"Do you know what I don't understand, Alley? Why did you name Ranalt's son Euan your tanist, if you knew Ranalt to be a murderer?"

Alex's voice was soft but bitter. "Don't I know well enough, Davey, what it is for a son to suffer for the sins of his father? I've got no quarrels with Euan. Christ, I haven't even seen him in twenty years. And besides, Mary begged me to." A sharp knock sounded at the door. Alex stalked over and threw it open. "Well, speak of the devil. Hello, Mother."

Mary Leslie, Countess of Ross, swept grandly into the room and held out her smooth white cheek for a kiss. Alex obliged. "Hello, Alexander." She ignored Davey, as she usually did. He eyed her warily. Alex and his sister Meggie both took after their mother in looks—though not in temperament, thank God. As a girl Mary had been counted one of the greatest beauties in Scotland, but now, at age forty-four, her gold hair still shone a bit too brassily, her red cheeks and lips were suspiciously bright. Other women passed gracefully, gently into the particular soft beauty that age brought. Mary, Davey thought, chuckling to himself. Mary was determined to fight it, tooth and nail.

"Good heavens, Alexander." Mary batted her lashes at her son. "What a peculiar expression you're wearing. Am I interrupting?"

"You're certainly looking well, Mother. That's a handsome gown."

"Don't trifle with me, Alexander, you've seen it a million times. If you were stricter about the rents and tributes, I'd not be forced to go about wearing last year's fashions." Her pale eyes glittered. "What were you talking about before I came in?"

"Alley was telling me about a lady," said Davey, swallowing a laugh.

Mary pulled at the magnificent necklace of pearls that ringed her throat. "A lady? What lady?"

Davey had opened his mouth again, but Alex forestalled him with a warning glare. "I can tell what you're thinking, Mother. It's nothing like that."

"Now, darling." Mary reached up to straighten his collar.

"Don't you know that you can trust me utterly? What lady is this that's caught your eye?"

"The one who testified at the Albany trial today," said Davey cheerfully, avoiding Alex's stare.

"That funny little gypsy girl?" She paused, her hand still on her throat. "What on earth do you see in her, Alexander?"

"I don't—I'm not—"

The Countess of Ross turned on her heel. "Very well, then, if you prefer not to confide in me." She went to the mantel above the huge fireplace and picked up a cobalt jar, idly examining the potter's mark. "These are fine apartments you and Davey have been given, I must say. Far more spacious than my own."

Alex sighed. "We'd be more than happy to change with you, Mother."

"There's no need, my dear." She gave her son a wide, innocent glance. "That's the girl who was at Dumbarton, isn't it? The one who saw the old man murdered."

"And nearly was raped herself," Davey put in. "It was a lucky thing for her that—"

"Was there something you wanted, Mother?" Alex broke in hurriedly. This time not even Davey could ignore the thunder in his eyes. "Isn't it time for you to go to supper?"

"Well"—her smile was gay—"some friends are getting up a little game of cards this evening, and have asked me to join them. Quite important friends, I might add. The sort who could do a young laird a world of good if word were dropped at the right time, in the right place."

"I'm sure," said Alex. "How much?"

Mary set the jar back on the mantel. "Four hundred marks?"

"Four hundred." Alex laughed in disbelief. "Mother, that's two months' income from the estates!"

She swished toward the door in a whirl of pale blue satin. "Very well, then, Alexander. If you prefer to squander your money on your lady friends, while you create a spectacle of yourself in public at every opportunity. Oh, I heard all about your little to-do in the Great Hall this morning, believe you me. All I'm trying to do is advance your prospects, but do I get any help from you?" She dabbed at her eyes with a lacy kerchief. "Thank God your poor dear father isn't here to see the way our only son treats his mother."

"Father left you ten thousand marks of your own," Alexander pointed out gently. "It's not my fault if you ran through all that in less than a year."

"I suppose I can always sell off my jewels," the countess said with a sniffle. "After all, *somebody* has to uphold the family's good name."

"Indeed." Alex reached for his purse. "Would a hundred marks help?"

"Oh, you dear sweet boy!" Mary cried, throwing her arms around him, planting a kiss on his cheek. "You couldn't possibly make it two hundred?"

"One hundred," he told her firmly. Mary made a pretty moue, holding out her hand, and Alex poured out the silver. "That's all, now," he cautioned. "I'm not about to bleed my lands dry so you can lose at cards."

"Don't worry, darling." She patted his stern face. "I'm sure to win back four times as much. Well, I'm off to try my luck! And good luck to you with this girl. What did you say her name was?"

"Fleming," Davey supplied helpfully. "Genevieve Fleming."

"Fleming." Mary tasted it on her tongue. "Not a very distinguished name, is it. Pity. Farewell!" With a wave of her hand, she was gone.

Davey closed the door behind her and looked at Alex. They both burst into laughter. "Not a very distinguished name," Davey mimicked adroitly. "Lend me a million marks, you dear *sweet* boy." He went to the table in the corner and poured himself a tankard of wine. "I don't know how you put up with her, Alex, I swear I don't."

"Oh"—Alex's tone was apologetic—"she's just a silly, unhappy woman. She's been so lonely since Father died."

"That's not the way I hear it," said Davey, and bit his lip.

Alex looked at him sharply. "What do you mean by that?"

"Nothing." Davey's eyes were wide with innocence. "She must have plenty of friends to keep her company, though, the way she loses money at cards."

"I'm not such a fool, Davey," Alex said quietly, "that I don't see Mary has faults." He sat and stretched his long legs toward the coals in the hearth. "If it gives her pleasure to flirt a bit, and to gamble, who am I to say her nay? She's known little enough joy in her life. Ranalt hurt her once too, you know."

"There's two sides to that story," Davey said stubbornly. "Speaking of which, does she know why Donald sent you off to find Ranalt?"

"Nay. She said she's more in the dark about it than I am."

"You didn't tell her, then, what you saw at Dumbarton?"

"Of course not, Davey. You know she can't keep a secret for more than two minutes." He sighed, staring into the glowing embers. "I'd best get packing. Who knows when Genevieve Fleming may take it into her pretty little head to tell the king I was at Dumbarton?"

"Maybe she doesn't intend to tell him, Alley. Maybe she's as much in love with you as you are with her."

"And who says I'm in love with her?" Alex demanded irritably.

Davey shrugged. "My mistake." He walked over slowly to refill his wine cup. "Ach, 'tis just as well, considerin' the way Henry Argyll was oglin' her there on the wynd this afternoon."

"Argyll!" Alex leapt to his feet. "Why, if that filthy scoundrel so much as *thinks* of laying a hand on her—" He stopped, brought up short by Davey's burst of laughter.

"You big bloody ox." The redhead pushed his lord toward the doorway. "Go on and find her. You at least owe her thanks for having saved your life."

3

Genna flung herself down on her bed, face buried in Nero's fur, trying to block out the memory of the beheading that she'd just witnessed. It had been a specific request from King James that she attend the executions. "And I know why too, Nero," she told the dog, ruffling his ears. "I'm not so young as everyone thinks I am. Why should the king chase after a ruffian like Jamie Stewart, and catch the real murderers? They're not so dangerous as the Duke of Albany. He's got land, and an army, and all those friends he made while he was regent for the king. Papa John's nothing but an excuse."

"Girl? You talking to someone?" It was Katy, poking her head through the door.

"Just Nero," said Genna, blushing.

"Hmph. Well, get off that bed, girl, and get yourself downstairs for supper."

"Oh, Katy." Genna flounced over onto her back. "Everybody will be talking about the trial and the beheadings; I just can't face it." She looked over pleadingly. "Could you please bring me up a tray?"

Katy came and laid a reddened hand on her forehead. "You haven't gone and caught a fever what with all that excitement, have you?"

"All what excitement?"

"Why, that ruckus at the trial this morning! Tell me, is it true that the Lord of the Isles tried to horsewhip one of the peers?"

Genna sighed. "Will you bring me up a tray, Katy?"

"All right, girl, but then I want to hear *all* about it!" The maid bustled back through the door.

Alexander Mac Donald. Lord of the Isles. For the first time Genna had a name to put beside the rugged, handsome face, the amazing blue eyes she'd conjured up in her mind so often

47

over the past year. The hero who'd saved her from the murderer at Dumbarton was her own precious secret, one she'd
held close to her heart for all that time. When the courtiers or
the queen's ladies made her wretched with their teasing, she
held her tongue, but inwardly she cried out, Say what you
will! Once the handsomest man in the whole world carried me
off in his arms on a fine white horse, and saved my life.

Only it hadn't been *quite* that way. When she'd looked up
there in the Great Hall and seen those cool blue eyes staring
down at her, the beautiful bubble of dreams she'd spent so
long constructing had suddenly burst. True, he had been
handsome. And true, the horse was white. And he *had* saved
her life . . .

He'd also treated her like a spoiled brat—and called her an
ugly, scrawny little thing.

He hadn't even remembered her at all. Well, why should
he have? she thought angrily. He was a rich, important lord.
Look at the fuss Queen Joan had made over him, teasing him
about his ways with the ladies. Why should he pay any attention to an ugly, scrawny child?

She hadn't given him away, though. How could she? Seeing him again had made her speechless, breathless, giddy as if
from wine. She'd forgotten the way he towered over her, the
splendid breadth of his shoulders, how his dark gold hair fell
down over his eyes . . . those amazing eyes.

Katy reappeared with a tray of roast mutton and bread and
a beaker of cider, set the supper on a stool by the hearth, and
eyed her mistress expectantly. "Well, girl, let's hear it. Is it
true that Henry Argyll floored Mac Donald with a single
punch?"

"Who told you that, Katy?"

"Third cook downstairs got it from the bailie's wife, who
got it from Argyll's valet." She peered at Genna more closely.
"You sure you ain't got a fever, girl? You surely do look pale."

"I'm tired, Katy, 'tis all. Stop fussing over me, for God's
sake."

"Hmph! Guess I can tell when I'm not wanted. All right,
I'll go. But don't you be staying up all night at your weaving. I
warn you, you'll ruin those pretty eyes!"

"Yes, Katy," Genna said dutifully, and grinned. "I promise
not to work past midnight." Katy sniffed, and marched out the
door.

Genna nibbled at the meat and bread, then fed her supper bit by bit to Nero, who sat up on his hind legs begging. She sighed, presenting him with a choice bit of skin. The queen's pet puppy, that's all she was. More than likely she'd be shuffled off to some convent now she'd told her story to the Parliament. Or worse yet, married to one of those beastly courtiers. *If* any of them wanted a pathetic little thing like her. After all, the prevailing fashion was to be tall and buxom and blond, like Queen Joan.

She set the plate on the rush-strewn floor for Nero to lick and wandered to her loom, then sat and threaded the shuttle with a long twist of golden silk. The baldachino fabric she was making sparkled with delicate scrollwork and devices, and it took all her concentration to keep the multihued warp yarns in order. Usually weaving calmed her nerves, but on this night the threads kept knotting, the warp strings broke, and the squeak of the heddles rising and falling made her grit her teeth. After an hour's work she had only an inch of finished cloth to draw up on the roller. She threw down the shuttle in disgust and went to her window.

The lights of the town were flickering gaily far below, small welcoming beacons to call the merchants and laborers home . . . home. Genna thought of Dumbarton.

Nero stared up at her with mournful dark eyes. She reached down to pat his head with a little laugh. "Heavens, do I really look that dreary? Papa John always said self-pity was worse than useless. Let's go out for a walk, then, shall we?" His stubby tail wagging furiously, the terrier bounded to the door. Genna opened the sturdy oak chest at the foot of her bed and pulled out a mantle she'd woven of soft rosy wool.

Beneath the mantle lay the midnight blue cloak that Alexander Mac Donald had left on the banks of the Clyde. I should return that to him, thought Genna, then shrugged. Why bother? He was a lord, wasn't he? He could buy a dozen cloaks just as fine. He'd offered to pay for Dumbarton. He could buy anything he pleased.

She drew the mantle over her shoulders and went out, Nero jumping excitedly at her heels. From the banquet hall below she could hear gay music and laughter; she turned away, to the left, toward the outer stair.

What kind of woman would attract a man like Alexander Mac Donald, Genna wondered, her heels clicking on the flagstone steps. Someone tall, like him, and golden-haired. A clever woman, who could make him laugh at her jests. A woman in furs and satin and jewels, older, voluptuous, experienced, who knew all about life, and love.

Well, I hope they'll be happy together, she told herself viciously, and kicked open the garden gate. "Dammit." She bent down to rub her sore toes. Nero darted through and dove into a hedge of briar roses, hot on the trail of an imaginary rabbit. Genna kicked out at the gate again.

The twilit air in the gardens was sweet with the scent of hawthorn blossoms, the trees so heavy with flower that they draped down over the path. Genna stood on tiptoe to twist off a cluster of the snowy blooms, pulled loose the plaits Katy had woven of her hair, and reached up to twine the twig between two long strands.

"I want to talk to you."

The hand that clasped her elbow, the deep voice at her ear made Genna jump with fright. She whirled around, wide-eyed, a torrent of black hair whipping the air. "Let go of me, damn you!"

Alex stared down at her, unsmiling. "I said, I want to talk to you."

She glared up at those sleepy blue eyes. "Take your hand off me, or I'll sic my dog on you!"

His wide mouth curled in slow amusement. He let out a whistle, and Nero came tumbling from under the briar roses and fell at his feet on the path, tail thumping as he groveled and squirmed. Alex raised one dark gold eyebrow. "Vicious, isn't he? I can see he takes after his mistress."

Genna shook off his hand, irked by his air of calm assurance. "What do you want?" she demanded.

Despite her pique she could not help but notice the splendid figure he made in his tanned leather jerkin, pale linen shirt, and leggings of dove gray twill. The clothes were perfectly plain, unembellished, but their very simplicity pointed up his immense height, the muscles that lay tightly wound beneath the layers of cloth.

He took note of her perusal and grinned again. "Does something about my outfit displease you?"

"Why should I give a damn what you wear?" Genna snapped, feeling a hot red blush steal up her throat. "For all I know you could be stark naked."

"An intriguing thought," said Alex, moving a step closer. "Why did you lie for me at the trial today?"

His face was in shadow, but the moonlight played over his hair as it rippled in the night breeze. Genna searched the darkness for his eyes. "I didn't lie. I just didn't tell all the truth."

"A fine point," Alex conceded. "But you still haven't told me why."

"Oh, what does it matter?" she said with a hint of bitterness, turning away. "The whole trial was naught but a sham. The king doesn't care a whit who killed Papa John. He's only using that as an excuse to punish the Albanys."

"And you don't think it's right, what the king is doing?"

"'Tis not my place to say if the king's right or wrong. Why can't everyone leave me alone?"

His hand on her shoulder was gentle, turning her again to face him. "I need to know why you lied."

"Because I owed you a debt." Genna wrenched out of his grasp. "I like to pay my debts.'

"That's all it was, Mistress Fleming? Tit for tat?"

"That's all it was," she said coolly. "Now, will you excuse me? Nero, come along."

He towered over her, blocking the path, and Genna could discern the scent he gave off, heady and rich like fresh-turned loam.

"One minute." Alex stared down at her. Christ, she was even more lovely than in his dreams, those flashing black eyes, her moon white skin, the thick waves of ebony hair. She'd crossed her arms over her breasts, as though shielding herself, and she reminded him of a tiny dark fighting cock that found itself hopelessly mismatched. He reached out a hand, his long fingers brushing her cheek, and she shied from him, just as he'd known she would. As a bird shies away from the net.

Genna shivered as his fingertips swept her throat. "Well? What is it?"

"You still owe me something. A kiss."

"Oh, for heaven's sake." She tried to sweep past him on the path, but he slipped an arm around her waist, drawing her back to him. He bent down to touch his mouth to hers, saw her night black eyes grow enormously wide.

"One might think you had never been kissed before, Mistress Fleming," Alex said with a laugh. He saw the sudden shy affirmation of his careless words in the depths of her eyes. "You haven't, have you?" he said, more gently.

A hint of bright rose red stood out on her cheeks as she tossed her head indignantly. "Of course I have! I've been kissed by hundreds, thousands of men! Sometimes I'm kissed by a dozen men in a single night."

He cupped her chin in his big hand. "Then surely 'tis no great matter to be kissed by one more."

As if in a dream Genna felt his arm tighten on her waist; his heavy-lidded eyes were wide awake now, and aglow with some strange dark fire. She could feel the quick pounding of his heart as he pulled her against his chest, saw that wide, sure mouth descending on hers. "No," she whispered, "please—"

His mouth covered hers, stifling her protest, swallowing her words. Genna gasped as his tongue probed between her teeth, hungrily probing, tasting her sweetness, searing her with his heat. She shivered as she heard his breath, quick and wildly uneven, as she felt the enormous strength of his arms pressing the whole great length of his body tight to hers.

She was being swept away, drawn relentlessly down into a whirling chasm that had opened at her feet, swallowed body and soul by his ravening mouth, his burning hands. The sensation was shattering, terrifying. With the last shred of sanity left her, Genna writhed out of his grasp and slapped his face as hard as she could.

"I consider all my debts to you paid," she said coldly, the harsh words belying the furor in her heart. "I trust you will do the same. Nero, come!" She turned and stalked haughtily through the gate, but the moment it clanged shut behind her she lost her nerve and tore off across the yard like lightning, the little dog yapping at her heels. Alex watched as her tiny figure vanished into the shadows of the wall, rubbing his jaw where she'd struck him, the taste of her sweet red lips still hot on his tongue.

"Not so easily as all that, Mistress Fleming," he murmured thoughtfully, and winced, feeling a bruise beneath his fingers. "No, you'll not be rid of me so easily as that."

Mary Leslie leaned back on her velvet-covered bed, artfully arranging clouds of pale silk skirts over her naked legs. Peering into her hand mirror, she applied a touch more powdered clay to her brow, then slipped a drop of belladonna into each eye to widen the pupils. Time, she thought, frowning at the webs of fine lines the powder covered. *The harshest of all my enemies.* She blew out one, then two, then three of the candles that flickered at her bedside, and checked in the mirror once more.

A single sharp staccato rap sounded at the window that led off the courtyard. Hastily Mary composed her features, smoothing back her fading gold hair, moistening her lips. "It's unlatched," she called, her voice throaty and low.

Ranalt Mac Ruarie pushed open the casement and swung himself over the sill to the floor. Mary smiled beguilingly from beneath soot-darkened lashes.

"Darling. I thought you'd never get here."

"Mary." He flung himself on the bed beside her, pawing at the lacy nightdress, tearing it away.

"Ranalt," she scolded, "your manners! Aren't you going to take off that sword?"

He knelt over her, unbuckling his belt impatiently, his gray eyes gleaming with lust. "Is the door locked?" he growled, flinging his swordbelt to the floor.

She nodded, and a slow smile twisted his mouth. "Good." He yanked down his hose and grunted, plunging eagerly between her wide-spread thighs.

"Ranalt," she said softly, a brief time later, twisting her fingers in a lock of his fiery hair.

"What is it, Mary?" he asked, shaking off her hand. "Leave me be now; I'm tired. I tell you, it's hell living this way, always on the run, looking over my shoulder."

"I'm sure it is. Do you love me, Ranalt?"

He peered over, suddenly on guard. "Of course I do. For Christ's sake, are you going to go through all that again?" He pulled himself up on one elbow. "Have you got any wine in here?"

Her fingers tightened on his hair. "I only ask, darling, because of something I heard today. About that business at Dumbarton."

He sat up, rummaging in the cupboard beside the bed. "Why do you always have this place so damnably dark, Mary? And what in hell are you talking about?"

"When you told me about your little escapade with Jamie Stewart, you neglected to mention the girl."

"What girl?" He found a wine flask and drank from it eagerly. Mary traced a line up his hairy back with sharp nails, and he turned to her, grimacing. "What the devil's gotten into you tonight?"

"The girl," she said evenly, "that you tried to rape."

His pale eyes were watchful. "I don't know what you're talking about."

"That's good, Ranalt. That's really a very good thing. Because I'm not the sort of woman who likes to be trifled with."

He bent down quickly to kiss her. "I would never trifle with you, Mary." He swigged again at the wine flask. "Who told you about this girl?"

"A friend of Alexander's. He says the girl is here, at court."

"I saw no girl at Dumbarton," Ranalt said shortly.

She smiled. "I'm glad. I would hate to have to tell the king all I know about what took place or, for that matter, all I know about my poor late husband's death."

Ranalt swallowed wine. "You wouldn't dare try it."

She lay back against the soft pillows, lashes lowered. "Wouldn't I?"

He considered her silently for a moment. "You know, Mary," he murmured, "someday you are going to push me just a bit too far."

She sat up again, running a long finger down his scraggly bearded throat. "What's the matter, darling? Can't you take a jest?"

He seized the finger and twisted. "That one lies too close to home."

Their eyes locked, each wary, testing. Then Mary laughed, and tweaked his chin. "Give me some wine."

He poured out a cup and handed it to her. "What happened at the trial?"

"It all went just as I promised. Murdoch Stewart was beheaded this afternoon, and his two sons will die tomorrow."

"And what was said about me?"

"Nothing."

He gazed at her, incredulous. "Alexander said nothing?"

"Not a word." She sipped at the wine. "Didn't I tell you he'd hold his tongue? So long as that rash idiot Jamie stays safely in Ireland, there's naught to connect you to the murder. Except, perhaps, a girl."

"I told you, I saw no girl. I don't understand it, Mary. Why should Alexander stay silent to protect me?"

She shrugged. "Blood is thicker than water. He has always been very fond of you."

"That bastard? He hates my guts." Ranalt frowned, pulling at his beard. "He's up to something, Mary. It's time we took care of him."

"Not yet," she said sharply. "It is still too soon. There is still talk in the Isles of Donald's death. Rumors."

"Has he heard them?"

"I doubt it. He'd not believe them if he had. But other people . . . other people might, if aught were to happen to him."

Ranalt pushed himself off the bed and stared moodily through the casement. "Euan is driving me mad," he said at last.

Mary's hard expression softened. "How is dear Euan?"

"The same as ever. Nay, worse. Christ's sake, Mary, how much longer till we make the next move?"

"How long have I waited for my revenge?" she demanded bitterly. "Fifteen endless years. And none of this would have been necessary had you kept your hands off that mewling bitch of a Mac Leod."

"How was I to know the old man would change his tanist because of one youthful indiscretion? You might have married me instead of Donald anyway."

She laid a hand on his arm. "You are too impatient, my darling, and you always were. All our waiting will have been worthwhile once Euan is laird." She picked up a silver-backed brush from the table beside her and began to pull it through her hair. "So long as Alexander is without issue, there's no reason to worry. The lairdship will pass to Euan upon his death. And then—"

"Aye?" he asked, leaning close, his mouth at her ear. "What then?"

Her blue eyes narrowed, gazing over his shoulder. "And then we'll be right where we want to be. You must bear with Euan a little while longer." She smiled, turning, pulling his mouth against hers.

It was just before dawn that she woke him, pushing his heavy legs from atop her, tugging the blankets away. "Be off with you now, before the sun rises."

Ranalt groaned, his head heavy from wine, and sat to pull

on his trunk hose and tunic. "How much did you get from him this time?" he asked, buckling his shoes.

She pushed a strand of brassy hair over her bare shoulder. "Fifty marks." She took it from her purse and handed it to him.

Ranalt weighed the silver in his palm. "'Tis little enough. You'd not hold out on me, would you, Mary?"

"Don't be a fool, Ranalt. Of course not."

"When will I see you again?"

"When I send for you."

He stood by the bed, looking down at her. "You're a witch, Mary Leslie, do you know that? I honestly believe you could lie to me without a qualm. And yet you've sworn you love me, and always have."

She bared one white breast at him, smiling enticingly. "Kiss me farewell."

He fell on her hungrily, biting at her nipple, his fingers scrambling for her thighs. Mary waited until his breath grew ragged and quick, then pushed him away. "Give my love to Euan," she said softly.

"Witch," he murmured, panting.

She smiled. "Be careful, my darling."

He hesitated a moment longer, then turned with an oath and climbed through the window again.

Mary listened to the scrape of his boots against the stone wall, and heard him drop to the ground with a heavy thud. The first rays of the sun poured through the unshuttered casement. She pulled the blankets over her head and buried her face in the pillows, shaking with silent laughter.

4

Genna plucked a dead blossom from the bundle of purple larkspur she'd set in a jar by the hearth, stood back, frowned, sighed, moved the flowers up to the mantel, chewed her lip, sighed, and set them back down on the floor. Katy let out a low growl as her mistress reached for the jar again. "Ain't you got nothing better to do than muss about underfoot while I'm getting this room straightened? Go sit at your loom, why don't you, or out for a walk?"

"I can't work," Genna said crossly, "I've a terrible headache. Fetch me some malmsey, Katy, will you?"

"Not on your life." Katy shook a warning finger. "Drinking at the start of the day's a foul habit to begin so young."

"I'll fetch it myself, then," Genna told her defiantly. "And since when is it your place to question the orders I give?" But at the look of distress that flitted across Katy's brow, she was suddenly ashamed. "Oh, I am sorry. I just don't know what's wrong with me today."

"There, now, lamb, I know you didn't mean it." Katy took her hand and led her to a chair. "Just sit for a bit, and I'll rub your poor head." Reluctantly Genna settled down, chin resting in her hands, while Katy put a bit of salve sweetened with betony into her palm.

"Katy," Genna began, as the maid stroked her forehead with practiced fingers.

"Aye, lamb?"

"Nothing," Genna mumbled, watching in the mirror as that telltale blush crept over her cheeks. She closed her eyes and tried to lose herself in the soothing motions of the maid's strong hands. But before long her curiosity overcame her. "Katy?" she said again.

"Aye, girl? What is it?"

"Have you ever—" She glanced up at Katy's reflection, saw

57

the playful gleam in her eye. "Just what, pray tell, is so amusing?"

"Why, nothing at all, girl, 'cept that I think I know what's got you all cross and fidgety this morning."

"Oh, you do, do you? And what might that be?"

"I've seen it before, with other young ladies I tend to, indeed I have." The maid nodded knowingly. "Oh, 'tis a sad, sad thing. They start pining and aching and wasting away, all melancholy and feverishlike. I thought when I saw you last night you were showing the symptoms."

"You did?" Genna swallowed. "What is it, Katy? The ague?"

"Oh, no, girl. Far worse than that."

"Worse?" She blanched. "Not the plague."

"Worse even than that, God help us," Katy crossed herself.

"God help us," Genna murmured.

"Aye, if you ask me, girl, you show every sign of being . . . in love."

"Katy Mac Millan, that's the stupidest thing I've ever heard!" Genna cried, bouncing out of her chair. "Why don't you just mind your own business?" And she burst into tears.

"There, now, girl." Katy laughed. "You may yet get over it. 'Tis nothing to—"

The knock at the door was loud as a thunderbolt.

"Don't you *dare* answer that!" Genna shrieked, but Katy saw the way her hands flew up to smooth her hair. She stepped toward the door.

"Could be a summons from Her Majesty, girl."

"Katy . . . oh, damn you, Katy!" Nero, alarmed at his mistress's tone, began to howl. The maid pulled open the door as Genna, fuming, turned her back.

She heard a brief bit of low conversation, then Katy called, "Milady? A gentleman to see you."

"Tell him to go to hell," Genna managed to say from between clenched teeth.

"A Master Davey Mac Leod, milady."

"Oh." A long pause. "Who?"

Davey poked his red head over the maid's shoulder. "Davey Mac Leod, mum. Her Majesty was good enough to introduce us yesterday, on the wynd."

"She was?" Realizing that she sounded like a dim-witted parrot, Genna swallowed a small lump of something that might have been disappointment. "Of course. The man with the cap. Do come in. Katy, *you* may go."

"Nice meetin' you, mum," Davey told Katy with a wink. She vanished into the hall as he threw the door open wide. "Oh, and I took the liberty of bringin' along a friend, milady."

White-faced, Genna turned and saw in the doorway the towering figure of the Lord of the Isles.

Nero made a wild leap for Davey's knees, still howling. With a desperate attempt to collect her thoughts, Genna called, "Down, Nero! Down!"

"Nero, eh?" Davey wrestled the pup to the floor as it snarled and tugged at his hose. "Why Nero?"

"They—they say Nero fiddled while Rome burned. This Nero would have barked. He is good for absolutely nothing, but he makes a great deal of noise."

Davey laughed. "Reminds me of a lot of courtiers I know, wouldn't you say, Alley? Oh, forgive me. I seem to recall that the two of you have never been formally presented to one another. Allow me, please. Genevieve— May I call you Genevieve?"

Why was Alexander Mac Donald staring at her that way? Genna had the unsettling feeling she'd left her buttons undone, or had jam on her face. She smoothed down the pearl gray skirts of her fustian gown and forced a small laugh of her own. "Please, don't. No one ever called me that except Papa John's housekeeper, when she was angry. Everyone else just calls me Genna."

"Genna," he echoed, "I like that. Well, Genna, this is Alexander Mac Donald, also known in some circles as the Lord of the Isles."

"Mistress Fleming." Alex took her hand in his and pressed it to his lips, his eyes still on hers. Genna felt her cheeks burn as she remembered the touch of his mouth at her ear. He knelt and snapped his fingers at Nero, and the dog came running to him eagerly, wagging his stubby tail.

Davey looked down ruefully at his paw-marked hose. "Some people get along well with dogs, and some just don't, and that's God's truth. Me, I don't."

Katy reappeared in the doorway, a kettle in her hand. "Your malmsey, milady." Avoiding Genna's furious glare, she hung the kettle at the hearth. "Well, aren't you going to ask the gentlemen to sit down?"

"I'm afraid the gentlemen won't be staying, Katy," Genna said haughtily.

"Oh, we've no place to rush off to, have we, Alley?" Davey grinned and planted himself on a stool by the hearth. Satisfied, Katy curtsied and scooted out again.

Alex stood up slowly, his great height seeming to fill the room, his lazy-lidded eyes running over Genna's small white arms, the narrow curve of her waist, the single thick black braid draped over her shoulder. Desperate to escape that steady gaze, Genna went to the hearth and leaned over the polished kettle, scooping up a cupful of wine and handing it to Davey. She turned back to Alex. "Milord?" she said icily.

"Please. And my name is Alexander."

"Only no one calls him that except his mother," Davey said with a laugh.

She held out a cup and found that her hand was trembling. Damn him, what was he doing here? Hadn't she made it plain enough the night before that she didn't want to see him again? She forced her voice to steadiness. "And why is that so amusing?"

"You'd know if you'd met his mother," said Davey. "Perhaps you have. Mary Leslie? The Countess of Ross?"

Genna pondered the name. "A tall blond woman? Very elegantly dressed?"

Davey nodded. "Very elegantly everything. Alexander!" His voice rose in an echo of the countess's. "Surely you don't plan to go out hunting in those *rags!* What will your subjects think?"

"Davey"—Alex's tone was dry—"I doubt Mistress Fleming is interested in hearing about my mother."

"Oh, not at all," Genna said with sweet vindictiveness. "I find it fascinating that such a gentlewoman could have come from so untamed a place as the Isles."

"She didn't," Davey said promptly. "She hates the Isles. Always has. Why, even before Alley's father died she hardly ever stayed there. She prefers the life at court, or on her own estates at Dingwall."

"I can't say I blame her for that." Genna perched on a stool and tucked her feet under her skirt.

"The Isles aren't for everyone," Alex said easily, leaning against the mantelpiece. "My mother cares too much for frivolous things to like it there. But for those who can see past the hardships, there's a paradise to be found."

"'Course, it helps if you like cold winters," Davey put in, grinning. "Those nights in December can be awfully long."

Alex's gaze was steady on Genna. "Long nights have their advantages, too."

Genna blushed furiously and stared into the fire. Determined not to be intimidated, she groped for something to say. "Perhaps someday I'll see these Isles of yours, and judge for myself."

She could feel those dark blue eyes bore into her as Alex said softly, "Perhaps you will."

"You're more than welcome to come and visit Meggie and me anytime," said Davey. "Meggie is Alley's sister. I'm to marry her at Lammastide. We'll be livin' in Alley's castle on Mull while he's here at court tendin' to business."

"Dear me"—Genna arched a dark brow—"I do hope your business won't keep you here very long. You must miss paradise a great deal."

"The court has its attractions as well," Alex said evenly, his deep voice like a caress.

Davey drained his cup and stood, stretching his stocky legs. "Well, I promised the Earl of Crawford I'd play him at golf before dinner," he said briskly. "Thanks for the wine, Genna. I've got to go."

"What a pity," Genna said coolly. "I've a great deal of work to do myself." She motioned to the loom in the corner.

"Are you a weaver, Mistress Fleming?" asked Alex, striding across the room to examine the loom. "What are you weaving?"

"Cloth."

His lip curled in amusement. "So I see. I don't know a thing about weaving. Would you show me how 'tis done?"

"I fear a great lord like you will find it tedious," Genna said shortly.

"Nonsense. A great lord must know all manner of things. Davey, enjoy your game."

"Thanks, Alley, I will. Farewell, Genna." He slipped out the door, Nero barking at his heels.

Genna stood in a rustle of silvery skirts. "You'd best be going as well, milord. I really must be at my work."

"Are you afraid to be left alone with me?"

"Of course not," she snapped.

"Very well, then. I'll watch." He crossed his arms and leaned back against the wall.

Genna stood for a moment chewing her lip. Then she shrugged offhandedly and took her seat at the loom. "Suit yourself." She picked up the shuttle and closed her eyes for a moment, trying to calm the pounding of her heart. What was it about this man that flustered her so? His huge shadow floated over the breast beam as he moved to stand directly behind her. Gritting her teeth, Genna threaded the shuttle and began to work.

He watched silently for a few moments, admiring the deft movements of her hands, her dainty feet as she raised and lowered the heddles. Then, "What's this?" he asked, reaching over her shoulder to point, his fingers brushing her dress.

"The batten. You use it to tighten the weave."

"I see." And, a minute later, "What are those pulleys for?"

"They work the heddles."

"What are the heddles?"

Genna sighed. "Look. This is the warp wool." She pointed out the long threads stretched between the back and breast beams. "These are the woof threads here, that run from side to side. You move the heddles up and down with your feet, and with this hand you pass the shuttle. With the other you push back the batten. Is it all quite clear?"

"Oh, yes. Quite clear now." He gazed down at her sleek black head, the smooth white nape of her neck, and grinned. God, she was lovely. He leaned over, close to her ear. "What's this pattern you're making?" His hand traced the elegant scrollwork.

Genna suppressed a shiver as his warm breath played down her throat, as he ran his hand over the cloth with slow, sensual pleasure. "The—the queen's initials," she told him, surprised at the breathlessness with which the words came out. "I thought to give her the length when I'm finished. She has been . . . very kind to me."

Alex moved his hand from the cloth to her shoulder, and felt her tremble at his touch, firing his blood. "I cannot imagine anyone being unkind to you," he whispered, mouth brushing her ear.

Genna bolted out of her chair and faced him, hands on her hips. "Not even your fine friends the Albanys?" she threw at him, black eyes flashing. She saw his jaw tighten, and was glad.

"The Albanys are no friends of mine. I've told you that before. It was nothing but chance that I happened on Dumbarton that night."

"Then why are you so concerned that the king will discover you were there?"

"I'm not."

"You were yesterday! Concerned enough to put on that bloody show before the peers, and disrupt the trial so I wouldn't be able to tell them about you!"

She gasped as he grasped her shoulders; she turned her head, and he pulled her chin back to face him. "Let go! You're hurting me."

"Not until you hear me out." He reached for her bodice.

"What do you think you're doing?"

He calmly unfastened the gold and pearl brooch at her throat and tucked it into his girdle. "If this conversation is to continue, I want you unarmed." He lifted the shock of gold hair at his temple. "I don't need any more battle wounds from you."

Genna colored faintly, staring at the small jagged scar that showed white against his taut brown skin. "I would not have done that again." She held out her hand. "Give it back to me."

Alex pulled the brooch from his girdle and weighed it in his palm, considering the intricate brightwork, the milky white pearls. Then he looked down at Genna. "I'll give it back when you hear what I have to say."

Her black eyes narrowed to slits. "You arrogant bastard. I don't owe you anything."

Alex clucked his tongue. "My, my, little Mistress Guttermouth. Where did you learn such language?" He put the brooch away again. "I'll just hold on to this until you're ready to listen." He turned toward the door.

Genna clawed at his sleeve. "Give it back to me, damn you!" He grinned, holding it high above her head, and she jumped to reach it.

"Say please," he ordered, "or I'll toss it right out the window." Still dangling the love knot beyond her reach, he moved to the open casement.

Genna's heart leapt into her throat as she saw his long arm

poised over the sill. "Please," she whispered, "please give it back to me."

Alex turned, surprised by the edge of fear in her voice, the little-girl whisper. There were tears shining in her dark eyes. Without another word, he handed back the brooch.

She took it and pinned it to her gown, then wiped her eyes furtively on her sleeve. "Would you go now, please?"

"I pray you forgive me." There was a heavy tinge of sarcasm in Alex's tone, as he thought of his mother. "I did not think you the sort of woman who would set such store by a bauble."

"It's not a bauble," Genna said angrily. "It was a gift from my father."

"From Red John Stewart?"

"No. From my—my real father. He and my mother died when I was only a baby. I can hardly remember what they looked like. This helps me to remember." Her thin fingers curled around the gold.

"Then I am sorry," he said gently. "I know what it is to miss someone you love. My own father died but a year ago."

"I shouldn't think you'd want to remember him," she told him spitefully.

Those sleepy eyes turned suddenly watchful. "Why is that?"

"He was a traitor, wasn't he? That's what the man said at the trial."

For an instant she thought he would strike her, so fiercely intense was his anger. With an enormous effort of will Alex forced himself merely to say, "He was no traitor. He was an honest man who made one grave mistake, long years ago. He dedicated the rest of his life to atoning for it."

"What mistake?" asked Genna curiously.

Alex met her dark gaze readily. "He went to war against the king's regent. Against the Albanys."

"*Against* the Albanys? Then what were you doing with Jamie Stewart at Dumbarton?"

"I told you I wasn't with him! I happened there only by chance." He smiled grimly. "I'd thought my father's sin was forgotten. Now I see there are men like Argyll who will not let it die so easily."

"So if the king learned you were there that night—"

"There would be no shortage of scoundrels to hiss in his

ear, 'Like father, like son.'" He reached out and took her hand, pried the fingers open. "So you see, milady"—he raised her hand to his lips, his eyes deep and solemn—"my life is lying . . . right here."

A thrill tingled along Genna's arm as his mouth lingered on her palm, then moved upward to her wrist. But at the same time her heart was suddenly heavy. "And that is why you sought me out in the gardens, and came here today."

"And why I kissed you? Oh, no, Mistress Fleming. For the sake of a kiss from you, I'd gladly lose my head." He smiled down at her, his blue eyes smoldering. "I'd hoped I could convince you my life is worth saving."

"How?" she whispered. A soul could drown in those eyes . . .

His fingers twined through her hair, drawing her to him. "This way." His mouth closed over hers.

The kiss began as a sigh, gentle as a whisper, his lips barely pressing hers, his arm just circling her shoulders. Then Genna felt his hands catch in her hair, slowly unbraiding the long plait, spreading the heavy mass of it over her shoulders like a rich black mantle, burying his face in its waves.

"Genna," he murmured at her ear, his breath quick and shallow. "Oh, Genna—"

The hands that had been gentle as a summer wind tightened their hold, lifting her up and into his arms. His mouth plunged down over hers, his tongue parting her soft lips and searching greedily, hungrily for hers. His fingers traced her eyes, her face, her throat, then slipped lower, pulling at the buttons of her bodice, tearing them away. Genna felt a spark of white heat kindle in her soul as his mouth bruised hers with his passion, as his hand wrenched aside gray silk and white linen that covered her breast. She shivered as his fingers closed on her nipple, catching, teasing, rubbing with tender persistence until it grew taut and hard beneath his touch. She sighed, a tiny involuntary sigh. Oh, Christ, she knew she had to resist him, knew this was wrong.

The sigh was all the acquiescence that Alex needed. She was soft and light as a sparrow in his embrace, and the sweet, cool scent of her hair, like jacinth blossoms, the swell of her breast in his hand had his senses ablaze. He wanted nothing in all the world but to pull her onto the bed, taste every tantalizing secret that rustling gray gown held hidden. His loins ached with need for her, throbbed with longing. He claimed her mouth again with his, carried her across the room, and laid her down against the soft white pillows. Then he knelt above her, swallowed her breathless objection with a kiss, leaned down to press his mouth against the impossible beauty of her round white breast.

"Alley!" A brief knock, and the door flew open. "Old Crawford's got the gout, can you believe it? I thought I'd drop back and see if you wanted to play."

Genna screamed and scrambled to her feet, clutching the tattered bodice together with her hands. Davey stopped dead, staring at the two flushed, breathless figures before him, sensing the mad hot tension in the air.

"Oh, lordy," he said finally, backing away, holding out his foot to the terrier. "Just start here, Nero, my boy, and work your way up to my neck."

Much later that morning, Alex knocked at the door to his mother's chambers. Hannah, Mary's thin, nervous little maid from the Isle of Mull, yanked the door open, finger to her lips. Alex grinned at the woman. He pitied any servant who had to endure his mother's temperament. Hannah had managed to hold her post for a year now, far longer than any other servant ever had. Alex was grateful. Searching out new maids for the countess was a challenging task.

"Hello, Hannah. Is she in?"

The maid bobbed in a low curtsy. "Aye, Yer Lairdship, but still abed. I'll tell her you're here."

"I'll tell her myself." Alex winked. "'Tis too fine a day to be lying about like a slug." Hannah let out a tentative giggle, then followed Alex's tall, straight figure as he strode to the bedchamber door. Now, there's a one, she thought, sighing, taking in the rippling dark gold hair, the breadth of his shoulders. She thought of her own stolid, steady husband, at work in the king's stables. Still, handsome is as handsome does. And the Lord of the Isles had a frightful reputation as a rakehell with the ladies. Why, his own mother talked often enough of the bastards he'd bred back on Mull. Of course, to be fair, Hannah told herself judiciously, he'd never once laid a finger on her. Not that she'd have taken offense, mind you. She picked up her polishing rag and went to work on the marble lintel of the bedchamber door, ear cocked at the keyhole.

"Good morrow, Mother," said Alex, going to the bedside and planting a kiss on Mary's pale forehead. The countess was leaning back against a pile of plump pillows, examining her lengthy nails. Her red mouth turned petulant when she saw her visitor.

"Alexander, you know I hate to be disturbed in the morning. I must look hideous." She made a weak effort to arrange her impeccably coiffed hair.

"Nonsense, you look splendid," he told her, straddling a chair by the high white bed. "And besides, 'tis already nearly noon."

"Is it really? I spent such a restless night. This old place is so chill and drafty. I don't believe I slept a wink. Well, what is it you want?"

Alex grinned. "You really do look lovely, you know. Hardly old enough to be a laird's mother."

"You're just like your father, Alexander," she said briskly. "He never could get to the blessed point, either. 'Tis too early for me to trade pretty speeches with you. What do you want?"

Alex twirled the tassels of the white coverlet between his long fingers. "Well, since we are speaking of Father . . . Do you recall the ring he left to me, to be given to the girl I wed?"

Mary pursed her lips. "A ring? I'm not sure."

"Oh, Mother, you must remember it. A bloodred ruby set in yellow gold, with diamonds flanking the stone."

Her brow cleared. "Oh, *that* ring. I am glad he left it to you; I never did care for it. Rubies always make me think of blood." She shivered prettily. "Why do you ask?"

"If 'tis here at court, I'd like to have it."

Mary felt a sudden stab of foreboding. "Why, whatever for?"

He grinned again. "That's fairly obvious, isn't it? I've found the girl I'm going to wed."

Mary's mouth fell open. It was a moment before she could speak. Then she snapped, "Are you moonstruck, Alexander? You are far too young to wed."

"I'm the exact age Father was when he married you," Alex pointed out, smiling.

"That was different. Your father had proved himself a man by then, a warrior. Can you say as much?"

Alex flushed. "Times have changed, Mother. A man proves

himself these days by keeping the king's peace, not by breaking it."

"You've no pluck, Alexander, and I always told Donald as much. The Lord of the Isles is a title far older than James's. Why should you scrape and kneel to that Stewart upstart?"

He reached for her hand. "Mother, must we go through all that again? I've told you, because he is my king. And because if this country of ours is ever to keep from being swallowed up by the English or French or Spanish, we must all stand united. There's no shame in being a man of peace."

Mary snorted, then composed her features. "And who might this young lady be who makes you forget your manhood?"

"The—the girl Davey spoke of yesterday. Genevieve Fleming."

"Oh, for heaven's sake, that dark little thing? She's not even Scottish."

"She's half Scottish," Alex said patiently, "and half Italian. Her farther was Malcolm Fleming, who fought with Father in the border wars."

"She looks like a gypsy changeling." Mary peered at her son with narrowed eyes. "And so this little treasure hunter has set her cap to wedding you, is that it?"

Alex laughed. "Hardly. At the moment, she seems to hate me violently."

Mary looked up. "You've gone and gotten this girl into trouble, haven't you, Alexander? Well, there is no need to marry her because of that, God knows! Settle a bit of money on her, and send her away for a time. No one will be any the wiser. 'Tis done in the best of families."

"Oh, for God's sake, Mother, of course I haven't got her in trouble. She's an honorable girl. I *want* to marry her. If she'll have me, that is."

Mary's pale eyes glowed with a strange light. "An honorable girl, you say?"

"Aye." He gave a rueful laugh, rubbing his chin where she'd struck him the day before. "All too honorable, I'm afraid."

"I see, I see." Mary smiled gaily. "She must indeed be honorable, to refuse a man who has bedded every single lass in the Isles."

"Mother, why do you insist on telling those stories about

me? Some people take them seriously. I've got an outrageous reputation, thanks to you."

"Well, what about *my* reputation? How do you think I like having to put up with people's sneers about your temper? At least in the stories I tell your hot blood is channeled into slightly more acceptable behavior than fisticuffs in Parliament!"

Alex's jaw tightened. "I'm sorry to be such a trial for you, Mother."

"Well, I just don't see why, if you're going to be a rebel, you don't put it to good use," Mary said peevishly.

"You just don't give up, Mother, do you? Just because you managed to talk Father into going to war against the crown doesn't mean you can do the same with me. I don't want to hear any more on the subject—ever. Is that clear?"

"Oh, Alexander, you shouldn't take everything I say so seriously."

"Believe me, Mother, I don't. Where is that ring?"

"I haven't got it."

"Well, where is it?"

"Just because you're a lord now doesn't mean you can bully your mother, young man! Ask me nicely!" She turned away, fluffing up her pillows.

Alex sighed. "Please, Mother, will you tell me where the ring is?"

"That's better." She kissed his cheek. "It's at Dingwall. I'll send a man for it, if you like."

"Would you, please? And ask him to hurry." He stood up, flashing her a grin. "Did you enjoy your card game?"

"My what? Oh. Oh, yes, I did, thank you." Mary fluttered her lashes at her handsome son. "This idea of your marrying has made me all flustered. I was getting rather accustomed to having you all to myself."

"I'm sure you'll have no trouble finding some other worthy young man to dance attendance on you," Alex said dryly. "Try and be discreet, Mother, will you? And remember, no more of those stories." He kissed her farewell and headed out, whistling gaily, nearly stumbling over Hannah and her polishing cloth.

Mary waited until she heard the antechamber door close, then swept the entire contents of the top of her dressing table onto the stone floor with a mighty crash. "God damn it to hell," she hissed through her teeth.

Hannah came running. "What is it, mum? What's the matter?"

"Run and get your husband from the stables," her mistress snapped, "and bring him here to me."

"Aye, mum," the maid said, bobbing in a curtsy. "I'll go right now, then, shall I?"

"Go!" Mary screamed, sending a bottle of pomade thudding against the wall. The heady scent of orange blossoms wafted into the air. Hannah hurriedly made her escape, cursing at Alex beneath her breath for having put the mistress in one of her moods.

She led her husband in but a few moments later; he still wore his work-stained leather apron, and the odor of hay and manure mingled with the flowery pomade for a moment, then overwhelmed it. Mary held two dainty fingers to her nose.

"Phew! Stand back a few paces, you stupid mongrel! You, Hannah, sweep up this mess." She indicated the shattered bottles and jars. "And don't let me catch you being so clumsy again!" Hannah opened her mouth to protest, then thought better of it. Mary pulled out a paper and quill and began to scribble rapidly. "I want you to take this message to the same spot as last time. You know the place I mean?" The stableman nodded uncertainly. "I want it there by tomorrow morning at the latest."

"But, mum, 'tis a full day's ride—and I've just now got back to the stable from the last time! I'll lose my post for certain!"

Mary eyed him balefully. "And your wife will lose hers if you don't do as I say. Is that what you want?"

Hannah's husband shook his head. Difficult as the mistress could be, it was a great honor for Hannah to wait on her. "Very well, mum." He watched as Mary blotted the parchment with sand and rolled it up tightly, fastening it with her wax and seal.

"You'd best get started. Here's for your trouble." She threw him a piece of silver. "Go, off with you! Hannah!" She rushed in, whisk in hand. "Find whoever the maid is who attends a girl named Fleming, Genevieve Fleming. Bring her here to me at once." A thin smile twisted her mouth. "I'd like to know more about her."

"That would be Katy, mum. But, mum," Hannah said hesitantly, "what about the ring His Lairdship asked for? Isn't that the one you had me sell at Market Cross a wee bit back?"

Mary stared coldly at her servant. "Don't you know better by now than to eavesdrop on your betters, girl? I should have you whipped for your impertinence."

"Forgive me, mum," said Hannah, wide-eyed. "I meant nothing by it."

"Be off with you, then, before I regret my indulgence of you."

"Aye, mum." Hannah dropped the whisk where she stood and flew out the door before Mary could change her mind.

Her plans in motion, Mary settled back against the pillows and began once again to consider her long sharp nails.

5

"Genna, watch out!" The queen lunged for the reins the girl had let slip and yanked her mount back from the rocky drop down to the Forth. Genna gasped as she saw how close she'd come to tumbling into the swift-running stream. Queen Joan eyed her curiously. "There are far safer places for day-dreaming than while riding a horse on the river highway."

"Yes, Your Majesty," Genna murmured, feeling the color rise on her cheeks. "I'm much beholden to you."

Joan smiled slyly. "Then repay me, prithee, by telling me what is occupying your thoughts so completely this afternoon. Though you ride beside us, your mind is obviously trotting a long way off!"

There was a burst of laughter from the knot of women accompanying the queen on her daily outing. "Aye, do tell us," cried Ellie Douglas. "What is it makes you blush so prettily?"

"One thing's certain; it isn't a man," Bess Foxworth teased. "I never in my life saw a girl with so little interest in snaring a husband."

Genna reddened even more deeply, and the queen, taking pity on her, waggled her crop at Bess. "You might learn a lesson from Genna in that, Elizabeth, for 'tis not always the fastest flying hawk that takes the prize."

This time the laughter was at Bess's expense, and Genna shot a grateful smile at Joan even as she chided herself for her inattentiveness. It was simply that the warmth of the spring sun against her face had reminded her of something: the touch of Alexander Mac Donald's mouth against her own.

She shook her head angrily and whipped the little gray mare to a trot, as if by riding harder she could escape her thoughts. She'd ordered the Lord of the Isles from her apartments, voice shaking with fury, after Davey had burst in on

73

them. She'd snarled that she never, ever wanted to see either him or his lecherous, pandering crony again. She'd vowed to behead him herself if he so much as tried to speak to her.

And then, to her horror, all the long night through she had dreamed of nothing but herself in his arms.

I'll not be fooled by him again, she thought bitterly, reining in her mount. I'll keep my distance and keep my wits, and if he even looks at me, I'll tell the king all about Dumbarton. The prospect cheered her considerably. She smiled, looking out over the clear blue waters of the Forth that sparkled a brilliant sapphirine beneath the cloudless skies. Genna pictured a pair of clear blue eyes . . .

"Look there! Riders approaching," Joan called gaily, waving her crop.

Ellie Douglas strained her shortsighted gaze to see the figures in the distance. "Oh, my glory, it's that absolutely magnificent Alexander Mac Donald. Wouldn't you know it, I didn't wear my new hat after all. Damn it to hell!"

"Now, that would be a match for our Genna," Bess said thoughtfully. "He's as chary of women as she is of men!"

"I don't know about that, Bess." Ellie was straightening her bodice. "I've heard that in the Isles he keeps whole castles full of women all for himself."

"His own mother told me he's bred bastards all over the islands," another lady added eagerly, "and that supporting them all is draining his coffers dry."

"Not only his coffers, I'll wager," said Ellie, and giggled.

"Ellie Douglas!" Joan rebuked her, shocked.

"More likely," Bess said wryly, "'tis keeping that mother of his that will bankrupt him. Did you see the pearls she had on last night?"

"That's enough, all of you!" Joan eyed her women sternly. "You sound like a flock of silly jaybirds. Alexander!" she called. "Won't you join us?"

"Oh," whispered Ellie, "if he even just looks at me, I will faint dead away!"

At the queen's invitation, Alexander and Davey drew up beside the group, their huge war-horses dwarfing the women's dainty mounts. The Lord of the Isles bent over Joan's hand with a brilliant smile. "Your Majesty. When we saw you and these ladies from a long way off, we thought we rode toward a garden filled with lilies."

"And now that you've ridden closer?" Joan asked, smiling back at the tall, handsome lord.

His blue eyes were on Genna as he answered gravely, "Now I see it is roses instead."

The ladies tittered prettily. Genna stared out at the river, stone-faced, as Alex deftly guided Bantigh between the queen's horse and hers, his hand brushing against her thigh so lightly that she thought perhaps she'd imagined it. He touched her again, more firmly. She glared at him, and saw him raise one dark gold eyebrow with innocent calm.

"A mighty fine day, is it not, mum?" asked Davey, riding at the queen's right hand. "In the Isles, we'd call this a day to count cows."

"And why is that, sir?" asked Ellie Douglas, dimpling.

His hazel eyes twinkled. "Because, lass, more'n likely the cowherd's been makin' love in the hills with his sweetheart. If his master has any sense, he'd best stand at the barn door this evenin' to be sure all his cows come home."

His explanation was greeted with another chorus of giggles. "Faith, milord," Bess Foxworth said coyly, "let me ask you something that puzzles me. Is it true, as I've heard, that in the Isles all of the cattle have horns?"

"Oh, aye, that's true."

"Not the females, surely," Ellie protested.

"Oh, aye, mum, them especially. Thank God."

"Why do you say 'Thank God'?"

"You've never been to the Isles, have you, any of you?" The women shook their heads. "I thought as much. If you had, you'd know why we're grateful the females are marked so. That way we can distinguish the herds from the maids."

"Ooh, you awful thing!" squealed Ellie, rapping his knuckles with her crop.

"Nay, 'tis true," he insisted, warming to his topic as he played to the appreciative audience. "You here at court are all spoiled by yer own beauty. I swear, if our island lasses didn't shave their faces, not even the horns would help!"

Genna continued to stare fixedly into the distance, refusing to join in the laughter. She never noticed Alex tugging at her little mare's cantle, slowing her down, or the others as they gradually drew ahead on the road. She knew if she looked to the side she might see the way Alex's breeches clung to his long, strong thighs, or the thatch of curling gold hair that just showed at the open throat of his shirt. She started when he leaned down from his saddle to whisper in her ear, "Come and meet me this night in the gardens."

She jerked away, once again nearly falling into the river. "Like hell I will," she hissed at him, and looked anxiously to see if anyone had overheard. But the ladies were still giggling at Davey's tall tales of life in the Isles. Only Queen Joan peered back curiously, then turned again to Davey.

Genna raised her crop to spur the mare on, but Alex reached across her easily and twisted it from her hand. "Give me that back," she demanded, her voice low but vehement.

"Why should I?" he asked, a lazy smile playing at the corners of his wide mouth. "There's no need to punish your mare; she can't go any faster. I've roped her to Bantigh."

Genna glanced back at the hind bow and saw it was true. Her black eyes blazed. "You bloody knave! Untie me this instant!"

"Now, what have I told you about that language of yours?" His blue eyes were bright with amusement.

"Untie me or I'll scream!"

"Not yet, Genna." His voice was like a caress. "Not until you promise to see me once more—alone."

"Damn you, I'll untie myself!" She twisted around and fumbled at the tightly knotted rope. Alex took advantage of the movement to lean toward her and cover her mouth with his.

At his touch Genna felt herself slip from the saddle. One of his long arms caught her, pressing her breasts firmly against his side, sliding up her white linen bodice as his tongue probed eagerly against her clenched teeth.

"Genna! Are you all right, dear?"

It was the queen, wheeling her horse about and riding toward them. "I saw you slip again. Thank God Alexander was there to stop your fall!"

"Oh, it was nothing, really," Alex told her, ignoring Genna's outraged stare.

The queen eyed Genna inquisitively. "I've never seen you have a bit of trouble riding before, dearie. Perhaps that saddle needs adjusting."

Davey and the queen's ladies had halted up ahead, wondering at the excitement. Genna looked at their wide-eyed gazes and bit off the angry accusation before she made it. "Yes, Your Majesty," was all she could manage to say.

"I'll just fasten her mount to mine," Alex suggested cheerfully, busying himself with the knots he'd already tied. "That way I'll be right here should it happen again."

"An excellent idea," the queen said briskly. "And when we get back to the castle, Genna, I want you to see the stable master right away. It's most unlike you to be so unsteady."

Genna opened her mouth, looked again at the curious women, and clamped it shut. Alex grinned down at her with kindly condescension. "Perhaps milady is overtired. Did you have trouble sleeping last night?"

"On the contrary," she said, smiling sweetly, "I slept very well, once I routed a rat from my chambers."

"A rat?" The queen was horrified. "I'll have to tell the king about that right away! We can't have rats running about in my ladies' apartments. Ugh!"

"I shouldn't worry, Your Majesty," Genna declared. "It was a very small, stupid sort of rat. And I told it quite clearly that I'd kill it should I find it there again."

"You *told* a rat?" The queen shook her head, bewildered. "You are a most peculiar girl, Genna Fleming." Then she shrugged. "Well, it's getting rather late. Let's head back to the castle, shall we?"

Alex made an unfavorable display of turning Bantigh about with Genna's little mare still linked to her, asking several times with hearty solicitude if he were going too quickly for her. Not wanting to call any more attention to her predicament, Genna said nothing. But her night black eyes were darting such fire that Alex, bemused, remarked to their fellow riders as he loosened his collar that he thought the weather was growing even more warm.

Genna sat silently fuming, as they crossed the Old Bridge, passed through the gate of the town wall, and headed up the castle hill. Davey continued to regale his audience with jests and stories, while Alex rode high atop his prancing Bantigh, sometimes whistling, occasionally glancing down at Genna with that infuriatingly confident smile. She held her tongue until they reached the stables; there he leapt down from Bantigh and reached out his long arms to help Genna dismount.

"You bastard," she hissed between her teeth. "I don't need any more of your help."

"That's twice now I've saved your life, Genna Fleming," he told her, "and you've yet to thank me for either time." His big hands encircled her waist as he lifted her down from the mare, then held her close for a moment. He felt his blood rush as he looked down at her thick black hair, coiled in ropes at the nape of her neck, at her angry black eyes and a red mouth that was ripe for kissing.

But right now it was cursing him again. "Stay away from me, by God, or I'll tell the king you were at Dumbarton."

His deep blue eyes searched hers. "You don't mean that, Genna."

She pushed his hands away and turned on her heel. "Just see if I don't," she yelled back over her shoulder.

"Meet me tonight in the gardens," he called after her.

She turned back, unable to believe his arrogance, and found she was shaking, too angry to speak. The Lord of the Isles winked.

Genna stamped her small foot and ran on after the others. "Oh, couldn't you just *die*," gushed Ellie Douglas, "to be riding so close to him? You lucky little devil." She groaned enviously. "Why didn't *I* think of trying to fall off my horse?"

"I didn't—I wasn't— Oh, dammit all!" cried Genna, and burst into tears.

The queen put a comforting arm around her. "If you ask me, Genna Fleming, I think you've come down with a touch of the vapors. You should drink a cup of hellebore purge and climb right into your bed."

There is nothing wrong with me, Genna thought viciously, that clawing that self-assured bastard's eyes out wouldn't cure! But to the queen she said meekly, "Aye, Your Majesty. I believe that is just what I'll do."

"You see the problem," Mary said softly to Ranalt. The storm that had descended on Stirling rattled at the shutters, sweeping through the cracks and buffeting the candle flames.

"There's no problem," he said shortly, flexing his reddened fingers. "We'll just have to murder the girl."

She looked at him with faint disgust. "Haven't you any imagination, Ranalt, dearest?"

"Imagination?" He nuzzled at her white throat, the bedstraw rustling beneath them. "I rode for eight hours through this storm at your summons, and all you want to speak of is this fool girl. I have imagination, all right. I imagined you sent for me because you wanted me near."

"I do want you near," she said, smiling seductively but pushing his hands from her breasts. "I want you near me forever. And to achieve that we must do something about the girl."

"Ach, he'll forget all about her in a week or two. Doesn't he always?"

"He has in the past," Mary murmured thoughtfully. "But he never spoke of marriage before."

Ranalt fumbled at the lacings to her nightdress, gray eyes narrowed. "Mary, for God's sake, you're driving me mad with all this talk."

She sighed impatiently, expertly evading his grasp as she rose from the bed. "Just another moment, my love. I've learned a great deal about this girl in the past few days. She has a scar on the back of her knee. Her favorite scent is jacinth. She likes to wear it here." Her long fingers brushed the vee between her breasts. Ranalt cursed and pulled himself up on the pillows, reaching for the wine flask.

"Oh, Mary, who gives a bloody damn?"

"Wait." The countess smiled. "The girl also has a dog that she is very fond of."

"Wonderful. The girl has a dog."

"Listen." Mary leaned toward him, whispering in his ear. When she'd finished, Ranalt smiled his mirthless grin. "And you think that would anger him?"

"I think it would enrage him. He is so like his father." She stroked his arm, purring. "Donald never could stand to share what was his either, you know."

"Like Donald in more ways than one." Ranalt spat in a corner. "He's got his damned cousins swarming all over Ireland looking for me, Mary. Sooner or later he'll learn I'm not there. And God help us then, with me dragging Euan along everywhere. Why can't he just stay here with you?"

"Now, darling, he's not that much trouble, is he?"

"For a six-year-old, no. But Lord, Mary, he's twenty-four years old! Oh, I know, I know, he can't stay with you because you don't want Alexander to find out his tanist's an idiot!"

Mary's hand whipped against his cheek. "Euan is *not* an idiot!" She wiped a bit of spittle from the corner of her mouth. "He is obedient. And cautious."

"He's a bloody idiot," murmured Ranalt, rubbing his cheek.

"I didn't hear you, *darling*."

"I said, you're right. He's not an idiot." He stretched across the bed, gulping more wine. "You think Euan can be trusted with this job? I'd be more than happy to do it for you."

"I imagine you would," said Mary dryly. "But remember, Alexander is to be looking on. He'd recognize you, even if the girl did not." Her pale eyes gleamed. "When falls the full moon?"

Ranalt counted on his fingers. "Three days' time."

"Have Euan here early that night, before the moon rises. Tell him which window to use. Make certain he understands."

"Mary, it'll never work."

"Oh, yes it will. Don't my plans always work?"

He grimaced. "You've been damned lucky so far. Now, for God's sake, let's have done with this talking."

A huge clap of thunder crashed overhead, drowning out Mary's reply. "I couldn't hear you," Ranalt mumbled, yanking her down on the bed.

"Why didn't you bring Euan here tonight, so I could see him?"

He pulled her atop him, hands scrambling at her breasts. "Because I didn't care to have him looking on while I did this." He bared his teeth against her throat. "And this." Pushing her legs apart, settling her into place, he strained his meaty thighs against her. "Ah, Mary . . ."

She wrapped her fingers in his red hair and leaned over him, smiling, as the lightning flashed around them, the pace of her movements quickening, riding him into the storm.

6

The twenty-first of May was the third anniversary of the coronation of James and Joan, and following a mass of Thanksgiving in the morning the king sponsored a huge festival, welcoming the burgesses and townspeople of Stirling into the castle yards. The craft guilds put on a competitive pageant, and masons and farriers, armorers and joiners, bowers and fletchers vied for their sovereign's favor with exhibits set on huge ox-drawn platforms. The theme of the pageant was, appropriately, the great kings of the Bible. The title of King's Favorite was finally bestowed on the brewers' guild for its representation of Solomon's palace, complete with bronze basins and baths. There was some grumbling among the other tradesmen that the brewers had cheated by having the fountains of the baths flow with new ale, from which the throngs along the parade route could fill ewers and cups and even their hands. But all in all, it was a popular choice.

Genna, watching with the queen's ladies from the balconies of the castle, had hoped the dyers' guild would win instead. They'd made a statue of Joseph, the son of Israel, that stood nearly ten cubits high. The paste-and-paper effigy was draped in a multicolored coat on which the guild had expended all the secrets of its craft. The rainbow-hued garment rippled down over the edges of the cart to conceal the drivers, and Joseph's hands held gold silk reins that looped over the oxen's horns. From the height of the balcony it appeared as though the huge figure was taking a parcel of ungainly pets for an afternoon walk.

Genna was so delighted with the sight that she failed to notice Davey Mac Leod as he wedged in beside her. When she turned to exclaim to Ellie over the colors of the cloak, she saw instead Davey's broad grinning face.

81

"Hello," he said cheerfully, twirling his cap on a fingertip. "Enjoyin' the parade, then, are ye?"

Genna inclined her head, just barely, and turned away.

Davey took no notice of his chilly reception. "I was wonderin', Genna, if you'll be goin' to the banquet this evenin'."

Genna eyed him suspiciously, but as always his countenance was benignly gay. "I'm going," she said stiffly. "All the queen's ladies will be there."

"Good, good"—he nodded—"glad to hear it. Well, till this evenin', then, Genna." And he slipped away as quietly as he'd come, leaving Genna to wonder what he might have up his sleeve.

She wondered again as she sat in her rooms that night, with Katy fussing beneath her breath as she tried to coax her mistress's heavy black hair into curls with the help of an iron, water, and a bar of scented wax. After half an hour's effort, Katy finally threw up her hands in despair. "I'm sorry, girl, but it's not holding! I don't know any more tricks to try!"

"Hm?" Genna shook herself from her reverie and peered into the tin mirror. "Oh, Katy, it doesn't matter. I'll just plait it back as I always do. Why don't you go see after Ellie and Bess now? They must be waiting for you."

"But, lambkin." Katy looked down at her tiny black-eyed mistress. "I haven't even gotten you into your dress."

Genna laughed. "For heaven's sake, Katy, I've been dressing myself since I was three; I think I can manage. Go on to the others; they need your help now."

"Aye, and I'll wager they'll be ready to bite my head off when I get there. Such a fuss they make getting themselves all prettied up! Well, they've got to work harder at it than you." She packed the iron and wax into her leather valise, then glanced sidelong at her mistress. "Tell me, will that strapping young fellow that visited t'other day be at the banquet?"

"Which fellow?" asked Genna, though she knew very well who was meant.

"Ach, you must be daft." Katy grinned. "The one who looks like a god, all tall and gold-haired, with blue eyes to drive a girl mad."

"How you do go on, Katy Mac Millan," Genna said airly. "I don't know if he'll be there. Why do you ask?"

"I was talking to his mother just t'other day," Katy said over her shoulder, laying out Genna's gown and underskirts.

"What was she like?"

"Oh, very nice, mum. Very curious about my work, and how I like it here at court. A most elegant lady she is, I'll tell you. 'Tis plain to see she's well-bred."

"I'm glad you got on so famously." Genna pinned the thick braid she'd made into a coil at the nape of her neck. "Perhaps she'll want you to come and work for her."

"No, thank you, child! Her Hannah—that's her maid— tells me she's got a temper to rival the devil when she's in the mood. Nay, I'll stick with my young ladies, at least for now."

"Unless you get over to your other young ladies' apartments, you're going to find them in a temper."

"Well, if you're sure there's nothing more I can do..." Katy ran her hand over the full skirts of the gown Genna had made for the occasion. "'Tis such a lovely dress. That cloth you wove is light as air. Puts me in mind of the summer skies, it does—"

"Katy Mac Millan!" Ellie barged through the door. "If you don't come and do my hair this instant, I'll boil you in oil!"

"Yes, milady!" Katy grabbed her valise, winked at Genna, and hastily followed Ellie into the hall.

Genna pulled on her linen drawers and corset, then tied the voluminous starch-stiffened petticoats at her waist. She unfastened the bone buttons of the gown to slip it over her head, underskirts rustling as the soft light cloth settled down in graceful folds. She'd woven and dyed the linen herself, with woad and just a hint of verdigris. The gown was cut simply, close-fitting at the bodice, with braided twists of a paler blue at the shoulders and high waist. The sleeves were long and full, gathered into little turned-back cuffs at the wrist, and the neckline squared off just low enough to show a hint of swelling breasts. The style suits me, thought Genna, though Ellie or Bess would have added ruffles and bows. But I'd feel foolish wearing those big fancy dresses; I'm far too skinny and short. Besides, the gown's simplicity of design showed the fabric to best advantage—the clear sky blue linen that reminded Genna of the waters of the River Clyde.

Or of Alexander Mac Donald's eyes. Genna grimaced, fastening the tiny carved buttons. She'd managed to avoid him since that last encounter on horseback three days past. The memory of his impudent touch on her thigh, his huge hands on her waist, made her furious—and at the same time filled her with an unfamiliar longing that she dared not admit even to herself. He was only toying with you, Genna, she told herself angrily. Remember those castles full of women and bastard babies. And remember what Papa John told you: "'Tis the woman that suffers from such goings-on."

He was so maddeningly self-assured, so certain that she'd fall a victim to his charms. He'd been just the same way that night at Dumbarton, ordering her around and acting the know-it-all. Well, little wonder, the way Ellie and the other women fawned over him. "It's revolting, isn't it?" she demanded of a napping Nero, who sat up eagerly at the sound of his mistress's voice. "Even you made a fuss over him, you naughty dog!"

If she saw him tonight, she would be haughtily serene, not deigning even to smile. And if he asked her to dance, she'd look him right in those blue eyes and just say no.

Genna tucked a few wayward strands of hair behind her ears, practiced her most queenly expression for the mirror, and went off to find Ellie and Bess.

The banquet was one long procession of noisy confusion, with the clang of platters and cutlery clashing against the notes of the gitterns and shawms and lutes. The wine was poured with unusual generosity, and more than one overindulgent courtier had to be carried from the hall. When Genna searched the men's tables across the room she told herself she was looking for Davey Mac Leod. When she saw neither him nor his lord she told herself she was glad.

At last, as the rinds of the cheeses and the fruit peelings were being cleared away, a semblance of silence reigned in the hall. King James leaned back in his tall carved chair, clasping Joan's hand and belching with satisfaction. The musicians scrambled down from the gallery to beg for scraps in the kitchens before the dancing began.

From the arched entrance to the hall a peculiar wheezing buzz of sound burst forth, and built to a wailing drone. Bess, sitting beside Genna, clapped her hands over her ears. "What's that ungodly racket?" she demanded, rising up in her seat.

A thin wisp of melody wandered into the room like smoke, filling the air slowly, growing into a wild tangle of dense music that to Genna was piercingly, achingly lovely. Beneath it all the solemn, steady droning pulsed like the throb of a heart. She looked toward the entranceway and saw half a dozen men clad in bright yellow tunics that billowed out from silver sword-belts clenched at their waists. The tunics ended above the knee, and the men wore rough gray stockings and leather shoes with wooden heels. As they fanned out into a vee, Genna saw that the man at the head of the group was Alexander Mac Donald.

They stopped just short of the king's dais. In the entranceway three pipers, dressed in the same yellow tunics, clutched the unwieldly bladders of the pipes to their shoulders, cheeks puffing out as they filled the bags with air. Genna tried to force herself to watch them as they played, but her gaze kept straying back to Alex, standing straight and solemn before the king, looking impossibly tall in his heeled shoes. Just to his left stood Davey, for once in his life without a grin on his face, his beard newly trimmed. At some imperceptible signal the men unbuckled their swords in a single flashing motion and began to dance.

Genna had watched groups of men dance for the king before, many times, but never with much pleasure; the dainty set pieces performed by the courtiers were precious niceties intended to show off well-turned shins and fine clothes. This dance was something else altogether. As the music of the pipes grew faster and faster, the men of the Isles twirled their long swords overhead, whipped them along the floor, and jumped and leapt around and over them as they called out to one another. This dance celebrated sheer strength and agility, with the swords in constant motion, glowing in the torchlight like silvery stars, while the dancers crouched and vaulted and turned in the air, so close to slicing off their own heads and arms and legs and those of their neighbors that one watched openmouthed, filled half with terror and half with amazed delight.

"My God," Ellie Douglas whispered, "have you ever in your life seen such beautiful men?"

Genna didn't bother to answer. Even the tables of raucous courtiers looked on with rapt intensity as Alex and Davey and their countrymen leapfrogged over each other's backs, shouting and laughing, somersaulting forward across a gauntlet of blades and then back again. Once Davey seemed to stumble, and a loud gasp circled the hall, but it was all a part of the intricate performance; he landed on his back and pushed himself up to a handstand, his sword between his teeth, and the onlookers screamed their delight.

Genna found herself wishing the dance would never end. She could have watched Alexander Mac Donald forever, his mane of gold hair flying, saffron skirts spinning, the heels of his boots tapping out the driving rhythm of the wild music. And each time he whirled past Genna his blue eyes swept over her like the tide, reaching, tugging, drawing her into their fathomless depths . . .

Swords held high over their heads, the dancers formed a high-kicking circle and spun like dervishes in one final mad orbit of the room, while those watching clapped in time to the quickening pulse of the pipes. Faster and faster they whirled, until the circle became a blur of saffron and silver and gold, so dizzying to the sight that more than one lady turned away in a swoon. Then the strange wild music of the pipes broke off abruptly, and the dancers tumbled in a heap to the floor, collapsing amid a chorus of cheers and shouts for more. Laughing, shaking their heads, they regrouped, bowed in a tribute to James, who signaled his pleasure with a broad smile, and hurried out of the hall.

"My God," said Ellie again, "weren't they *something?*"

"I *hate* that awful piping; it makes my head ache," Bess said petulantly. "Genna, what are you staring at?"

"Nothing!" She tore her eyes from the entranceway. Before the last echoes of the pipes had died away, the minstrels took their seats in the balcony and began again to play. The stilted courteous tunes they plucked out seemed dull and lifeless to Genna after the wild, haunting sounds of the pipes. She smiled and refused several offers to dance, preferring to stay in her seat, lost in thought.

Davey slipped into the chair Bess had vacated. "Well, Genna," he said heartily, hazel eyes alight with mischief, "could you spare a sip of that wine for a man who's gettin' too old for such displays?"

She handed him her cup warily, on her guard. "Your performance seems to have pleased the king."

"D'ye think so?" He nodded in satisfaction. "Ah, but did it please you?"

"What difference does that make?"

"All the difference in the world, darlin'. You see, that was a courting dance that we do in the Isles."

"Really. How very interesting."

"Glad you think so." He leaned forward conspiratorially. "Alley wanted to be sure you'd see it; that's why I asked this morning whether you'd be here. He hardly ever dances in public anymore."

"I don't see why; I should think he'd adore flaunting his talents," Genna said tartly.

"Well, you've got him wrong there. He's a very shy, timid sort of man."

"I could tell that the other morning in my chambers, when he attacked me!"

"Attacked you?" Davey's brow creased, then cleared. "Oh, you mean kissed you."

"I mean attacked!" Genna snapped.

Davey grinned. "Aye, well, that all depends on yer point of view. You and he will have to fight it out amongst yerselves."

"He and I are not speaking." She turned her back.

"Hello, Genna."

For a moment, looking up at him, she nearly fell under the spell of those sleepy blue eyes, his alluring smile. His bronze skin was still flushed from the exertion of the dance, the golden mane of his hair curled with damp heat, and the air around him was filled with his scent, warm and musky like ambergris. Genna felt the start of a telltale blush as she caught herself remembering the warm impassioned force of his mouth against hers, his hands at her breasts. She feared that if she tried to move, she'd betray her thoughts; she felt light-headed, dizzy from the aura of power and maleness he exuded. If he had touched her just then, she was sure, she would have offered herself to him.

But a cluster of giggling women suddenly surrounded him, pulling him away, demanding that he dance with them. Golden women, bright-eyed, elegant. Genna heard a rumble of displeasure from the partners they had abandoned to make their claims on the Lord of the Isles. "Bloody strutting cock," she heard one courtier hiss, and another hooted at Alex, making vulgar motions with his hands.

Alex flashed a look of hot regret at Genna, trying to disentangle himself from the clutching women, but she had already left her seat and fled from the hall.

Strutting cock was right, she thought angrily, hurrying along the passageway. It was a pity he hadn't impaled himself on his sword. A courting dance, was it? Well, let those other ladies fall for his sugared words, his long legs and golden hair. When—*if*—she ever fell in love, it would be with someone gentle, and kind, and compassionate. Someone who cared about her feelings, who didn't try to force himself on her with tricks and games. Someone who would truly love her in return, not some rake looking only for another maidenhead to add to his collection.

"Genna!" Queen Joan was running after her down the corridor. "Are you all right, my dear? Have you taken ill again?"

"No, Your Majesty," Genna said faintly. "I'm merely a bit overheated. I thought it best I return to my rooms."

"Well, wait one moment. I've something terribly important to speak to you about."

Genna glanced beyond the queen's shoulder and saw Alexander Mac Donald approaching, grinning widely. "I really do feel faint, Your Majesty," she said somewhat frantically, as he stopped a few paces off and leaned nonchalantly against the wall.

"Well, this will only take an instant," Joan promised. "I never am one to beat about the bush."

"No, Your Majesty," Genna agreed politely, eyeing Alex with a sense of dread.

"And of course, it's not as though this is totally unexpected," Joan went on, her pale forehead furrowed. "In fact, I've seen it coming for quite some time."

"Yes, Your Majesty, I'm sure you have," said Genna, bewildered but desperate to get away.

The queen smiled down at her, considering the girl's smooth black hair, her skin pale as snowdrifts. "In fact, I'm surprised it hasn't happened sooner, considering what a beauty you've turned out to be."

"I beg your pardon," said Genna, "but *what* hasn't happened?"

Joan stared, mirroring her confusion. "But it has happened, dearie."

Genna swallowed her muddled impatience. Alexander Mac Donald had crossed his long legs and was whistling a soundless tune. "*What*," she asked again, clearly and distinctly, "has happened?"

"Oh! I'm sorry. The king has had an offer for your hand."

"My—my hand?" Genna echoed weakly. "You mean a proposal of marriage."

"Naturally. Oh, Genna, isn't it exciting?"

"That's not exactly the word I would choose," said Genna, reddening as Alex looked on from a distance, still grinning complacently.

"Oh, but darling, every girl wants to be married. Surely you don't expect to stay a maid for all your life."

"As a matter of fact, I'd rather that than be wed to him!" Genna declared hotly. "I wouldn't marry him if he were the last man on earth."

"Now, how can you say that, Genna? He is tall and rich, and very good-looking. I think he'd make a lovely husband. And just think, you'll be the envy of all the other girls."

Genna heard her heart pounding wildly and took a deep breath, willing herself to stay calm. "When did His Majesty receive this proposal?"

"Why, just the other afternoon, after we'd been riding. The day that you took ill."

Genna's cheeks were burning. The nerve of that man! She tells him she never wants to see him again, threatens to expose him to the king, and he goes and asks for her hand!

"Well, Genna, what do you say? I know it's awfully sudden, but I'm sure if you just got to know him better..." The queen prattled on as Genna stewed silently. That bloody bastard, she thought. Just because all the other girls at court swooned over him, he was sure she'd jump at the chance to wed him. Despite the fact that he was insolent, and overbearing, and deceitful—oh, God, what a hateful man!

"After all, dearie"—the queen took her hand and patted it gently—"it's not every day that a girl gets an offer from a peer of the realm. So, tell me. What do you say?"

Genna drew herself up as tall and straight as she could, fire in her black eyes. "You may say to His Majesty the King," she said, clearly and deliberately, "that he can tell Alexander Mac Donald to go straight to hell."

It was the queen's turn to look bewildered. "Alexander Mac Donald? What ever has he to do with this?"

Genna felt her stomach sinking inch by inch to the floor. "Didn't... isn't he the one who made the offer?"

Joan laughed merrily. "Oh, no, no, my dear. Haven't you been listening to a word I said? It was Argyll, Henry Argyll."

"Henry Argyll?" Genna repeated incredulously. "Who in God's name is Henry Argyll?"

"The gentleman," Joan said patiently, as if speaking to a child, "who has asked the king for your hand." Her blue eyes were suddenly surprisingly shrewd. "What is all this nonsense about Alexander Mac Donald?"

Genna felt her knees trembling, and fervently wished she could disappear into the air. "Why, nothing, Your Majesty. I misunderstood you."

"So I see," the queen said thoughtfully. "So I see." Then, sensing Genna's embarrassment, she kissed her cheek. "Well, think about it, Genna, won't you? Argyll is a rich, well-connected lord."

"I will," said Genna, still blushing furiously. How much of the conversation Alex had overheard she had no way of knowing. But he had certainly caught her loud denunciation of him. "I promise. Please, will you excuse me?"

"Very well, dear." The queen smiled reflectively as she watched the girl go.

Genna ran to her chambers as quickly as she could, terrified that at any moment she would hear Alex's footsteps behind her. She flung open the door and snapped shut the bolt, then leaned against it, more mortified than ever before in her life. And somehow, as she thought about what had happened, it too became Alexander Mac Donald's fault. If he hadn't been standing there so insolently, she would have been able to concentrate on what the queen was saying. Oh, damn that man! He always made everything all twisted.

"Nero!" she called, and waited expectantly for his eager bark. She wanted to curl up in bed with the pup and forget the horrible blunder she had made. Whatever must the queen think of her? she wondered. "Nero! Here, boy!" she called again.

But no patter of paws, no yapping bark came in response. Genna shrugged, took off her dress, and stood before the mirror, unbraiding her long black hair. "I don't blame you, Nero," she told her reflection wryly. "I wouldn't want to be seen with me either, after I made such a fool of myself!" She pulled a freshly laundered nightdress from the chest at the foot of her bed, stepped out of her underskirts and stockings, and unlaced her corset. Shivering in the chill spring air, she tugged the nightdress over her head and called out for Nero once more.

Then, sighing, she snuffed out the candles on the table and crawled into bed.

She'd been asleep for hours when she woke with a start to hear a soft rapping on her chamber door. "What now?" she wondered drowsily, throwing off the covers and padding out barefoot to answer. Why, it had to be past midnight; the castle was quiet as death. Through the unshuttered casement pale moonlight poured in, bathing everything in the antechamber with a silvery pall.

The tall young man who stood on the threshold, red-haired and smooth-cheeked, had an anxious frown on his face. "Yes? asked Genna, clutching her nightdress together at the throat.

"Genevieve Fleming?" His voice was whispery and sing-songy, as if he were reciting a lesson learned at school. Genna peered at him more closely. There was something eerily familiar about his tall lank body, his broad brow. He was not so young as she'd thought at first, she realized, though his tentative manner and beardless face were like a boy's.

"Aye. Who are you?"

"They told me in the kitchen to fetch you," he went on in that odd soft voice. "You have a dog, don't you, a little black dog?"

"Aye. Why? Has something happened?"

"One of the stablehands came across him in the queen's gardens. A fox had got him; he is hurt pretty bad."

"Oh, no!" Genna's hand flew to her mouth. "But how did he get out to the gardens?"

"Sure and I know not, but you'd best come see to it. His poor little leg is near chewed off."

"I'll come right away! Let me just put on some clothing."

He grabbed her wrist. "There's no time, mum, not if you want to save him."

"Well . . . all right." And she followed as he hurried through the deserted passageways to the staircase, and out through the bailey door.

"Poor Nero!" she cried in dismay, as he pulled her across the yards toward the garden, her bare feet slapping on the flagstones. "He must have slipped through the door when Katy left me. Oh, dear, I do hope he's all right. Who found him, did you say?"

"One of the stablehands," he said again, his voice partly muffled by his cloak. With each breath he took she heard a high thin whistle from his nose. "He's back this way, by the rose beds." His hand tightened on her wrist.

"I don't understand," said Genna, panting. "Why didn't they bring him inside to me? Why did they leave him lying out here in the cold?"

"Can't tell you that, mum. But there he is, down there by that stone."

Genna clambered through the rose hedge, not heeding the thorns and brambles that tore at her arms and sheer nightdress. In the glistening light of the moon she could see a tattered bundle of thick black fur. "Nero!" she called, but he lay still and silent; not even his stubby tail wagged. Genna knelt on the ground beside him, lifting him up in her arms. The stranger towered over her, his shadow as long as a tree.

"I thought you told me his leg was hurt." Genna probed anxiously at the pup's hindquarters, then patted his limp black head and drew back her hand, feeling a warm stickiness on her palm. She looked up.

The man's teeth glinted white in the moonlight as he leaned down, covering her face with a cloth. She heard that faint high whistle as she wriggled in his grasp, gasping, falling. "Did I say that?" he whispered at her ear, the words rhythmic, singsongy. "I was wrong. His throat's been cut."

"Dear me." Mary Leslie patted the purse that hung from her girdle. "I know I had that ring with me at supper, but I simply forgot to give it to you then. Now, what could I have done with it? It's not here on my dressing table, and not in my purse . . ."

Alex tapped his foot impatiently. "Honestly, Mother, how can you be so simpleminded? If you had it just hours ago, you must know where it is."

Mary bit her lip, brow creased with worry. "Well, it was such a surprise to me when it turned up here after all. I never even thought to look in my jewel case. And now that man I sent to Dingwall will think me simpleminded as well."

"Just tell me what you did earlier this evening."

"Please don't be cross with me, darling; you know I can't stand that. Let's see. After the banquet I played at cards, there in the banquet hall."

"Did you have it with you then?"

"Aye, I know I did. I pulled it out to show to that old hag,

Atholl's wife. She thought it was charming. I actually believe she might have been envious of me. Imagine that, the great Lady Atholl jealous of little old me."

"Mother, *please*."

"I'm trying, Alexander! Don't rattle me. Let's see, then I went out to the gardens."

"You went to the gardens?" asked Alex incredulously. "Mary Leslie, who thinks fresh air is poisonous? Whatever for?"

"Well, darling, I needed to be alone, to think. It's very unsettling to face the prospect of losing your only son in marriage, especially to a girl like this Glenda."

"Genna," Alex corrected her.

"Didn't I say Genna? Anyway, a girl like her, whom I know so little about. I had a great deal on my mind, so I thought a walk might help."

Alex groaned. "Don't tell me. You looked at it, there in the gardens."

Mary crinkled her nose. "You know, darling, I believe I may have, to see if it needed cleaning. Of course, it didn't. Even when I'm only storing my jewels, I'm always very careful to keep them well wrapped."

"Come along, Mother," said Alexander.

"Where—where are we going?"

He led her firmly to her chamber door by the elbow. "Out to the gardens. I want you to show me exactly where you were walking."

"I was sitting!" said Mary indignantly. "You can't think I'd be so careless as to pull out a costly ring like that while I was walking about!"

Alex laughed despite his exasperation. "You really are an amazing creature, Mother. Come along."

Mary glanced up sidelong at her son as he pulled her across the bailey to the gardens. "We're lucky the moon is so bright tonight, aren't we, darling? We should be able to see as plain as day."

"Aye," he said shortly, holding open the garden gate. "Now, try and remember where you were sitting."

Mary put a sudden hand on his arm, finger to her lips. "Hush!" she whispered. "Do you hear that?" The murmur of a boyish voice floated out from beyond the ghostly hawthorn trees. "Someone's making love in there! Oh, come on, darling, let's spy!"

"Mother, have you no decency?" he hissed.

"Don't be such an old lady, Alexander; they won't see us. Just one peek," she begged prettily.

He shook his head, disapproving but amused. "If you must." And reluctantly he followed her to the rose hedge and stood, fists clasped behind him, feigning nonchalance as she shielded her hands from the thorns with her skirts and pulled the branches back.

"Sweet holy God," Mary murmured, and turned hurriedly away.

"What is it, Mother?" asked Alex.

She tugged at his shirt. "Come away, now, quickly. Oh, my poor sweet darling. Oh, my poor little boy!" She buried her face in her hands.

"What are you talking about? Who's in there?" Alex crouched down, pulling aside the sweet blossomy branches.

"Don't look," Mary said, sobbing, "please don't look, my darling. Oh, I'm so very sorry."

Alex stared through the green leaves that shimmered in the moonlight and saw the stranger who sat with his back to them, giggling and singing softly. And then he saw the girl the man held in his arms. Her black hair was tumbled carelessly around her, and her moon white breasts showed against the filmy nightdress that was all she wore. Her eyes were closed, her head thrown back in ecstasy as the man twined her hair in his fingers and crooned out his song.

Alex stood abruptly and stalked off toward the castle.

"Alexander! My darling!" cried Mary, running after him, pulling at his sleeves. But he shook off her beseeching hands, and did not once look back.

Mary hesitated, watching his proud, angry strides as he crossed the bailey and vanished into the shadowy bulk of Stirling's walls. Then she turned and called through the hedges, "All right, Euan, dearest. That's enough."

Euan looked up, smiling. "She's prettier than any doll I ever saw. Don't you think she's pretty?"

"If you say so, darling." She came and patted his cheek with a gentle hand.

"How did I do? Did I do all right?" Euan demanded eagerly.

"You were perfect," she assured him. "You're a very, very smart boy. Now, wrap her in the blanket I gave you, and bring her inside. And give me that kerchief back. You know you mustn't play with alchemics; they're very dangerous."

"Very dangerous," Euan repeated, obediently wrapping Genna's senseless body in the coarse green wool. "Very dangerous. Just like the doggy."

"That's right, dear. It was a mean, vicious doggy, and that's why it had to be killed." Mary put her arm around his thick waist as he hoisted the girl to his shoulder, then led him over the moonlit lawns to the castle doors.

Euan shifted the bundle he carried. "Zounds, but I'm hungry. Is there anything to eat around here?"

"I have cakes and barley water waiting for you," said Mary, smiling up at his eager face.

"Currant cakes?" he asked hopefully.

Mary laughed. "Of course! Don't I always give my smart boy everything he likes?"

Euan ran his thick tongue over his lip. "And then what? After the cakes?"

"Then we'll play a game, darling. Any game that you like."

"The secret game." His eyes lit up. "Why, we can play it with the girl, can't we?"

Mary put her finger to her lips. "Now, darling, you know you must never play that game with anyone but me. And you must never, *ever* talk about it to your father. Promise?" Euan nodded uncertainly. "That's my good boy. Come on, then. Let's leave the girl in her chambers, and get you your cake."

Davey woke with a start as the door to the room swung open, slamming into the wall. He groped for the dagger beneath his pillow. "What is it? Who's there?"

Alex said nothing, simply yanked his saddle pouches down from a shelf and began to stuff them with tunics and hose and breeches. Davey hastened to light a taper and saw the hard set of his jaw, the veins standing out on his brow. "Are ye—are ye goin' somewheres, Alley?" he asked tentatively.

"Back to Mull. Are you coming?"

Davey shivered a little as he saw the cold fury in Alex's blue eyes. "I don't understand," he said softly. "What about Genna? I thought you wanted to marry her."

Alex took a step toward him. "I don't *ever*," he said slowly, distinctly, "want you to mention her again. That's an order to you."

"But, Alley," he protested, bewildered, "you're in love with her."

Alex's fist clipped him sharply, catching him by surprise. "Never," he repeated, his hands still tightly clenched. Davey saw his eyes glittering, cold as blue ice. He rubbed his lip, tasting blood, and shook his head to clear it. Alex jerked the pouches closed, pulling the buckles taut. "Are you coming with me, or aren't you?"

"Christ's sake, Alley." Davey gave a shaky laugh. "'Tis the dead of night out there. Wait until the mornin', why don't ye? Think it over. Whatever has happened, it will look far different in the light of the sun."

A sudden haunting flicker of pain coursed across Alex's proud face, then vanished. When he spoke again his voice was harsh. "I've seen all I need to see—by moonlight. 'Tis no use to try and dissuade me. You can come with me, or no."

Davey took but a moment to decide. Whatever had happened, he was still a man of the Isles, and his place was with his laird. He nodded.

"Aye, I'm comin' with ye, Alley. What else could you think I'd do?"

Part II

Inverness, March 1428

7

Joan smoothed a soothing hand over her husband's furrowed forehead. "What is it now, my darling? Rats in the barns of Scotland? Snakes in the Highland heather?"

James frowned down at the reports strewn over the desk in front of him. "'Tis no laughing matter, love. This is the third rebellion I've had to put down in as many months. It seems the moment I gain a respite from the English borderers' raids, the Isles flare up once more." He leaned his head on his hands. "At times, Joan, I swear I'm tempted to let the clans go ahead and destroy one another. Cameron hates Mac Pherson, Mac Pherson hates Mac Phee, Mac Phee hates Mac Lean, Mac Lean hates Mac Leod." He threw up his hands. "I can't even keep their rivalries straight anymore. And where in hell is Alexander Mac Donald, who's supposed to be their overlord?"

Joan crouched beside him, resting her blond head on his knee. "You knew it wouldn't be easy, James. You knew from the start that it would take time to make a unified nation out of these bands of unruly savages."

He grinned down at her. "Not savages, love, and *you* know that. They're just frightfully prideful men who frequently behave like spoiled boys." He sighed, his fingertips playing through her pale hair. "Sometimes that's just what I feel like: a father with a whole parcel of bull-headed sons. I should give them all a good hiding." He stroked her cheek. "Ach, I don't know why I trouble you with my problems."

"Because I'm your wife and your queen, my darling. And I cannot bear to see you worry so." She knelt silently for a moment, reflecting on what he'd said. Then, "James," she murmured.

He smiled at the familiar tone in her voice. "What mischief are you thinking of, minx?"

She stood, grasping his hands. "Why *not* give them all a hiding?"

James laughed. "'Tis most irregular punishment for the clan chiefs of the realm, my pet. And how would I get them to submit to the whip?"

"Oh, I don't mean actually beat them. But they need to be taught a lesson, from what you tell me. As you say, they're like spoiled boys."

"What would you suggest?"

"Why not invite each here to a personal audience? 'His Majesty James Stewart, King of All Scotland, earnestly desires to parley secretly with Iain, Clan Chief of the Cameron,' that sort of thing. Don't you think they would jump at the chance to whisper in your ear about their feuds?"

"Of course they would. But what do I do when they get here? Those men can't even stand to be in the same room with each other."

"Give each one a private room . . . in your prisons."

"They would never forgive me!" James was horrified.

"Oh, I'll wager they would. You needn't keep them there long—just long enough for them to know you mean business. Then pardon them all, and let them speak before the Parliament, have their disputes aired before a lawful tribunal." She gazed down at her husband. "They'll know it was in your power to behead them, James. If you ask me, they'll be so grateful for your leniency that they'll forget all about their petty quarreling."

The king stroked his auburn beard. "'Tis a rotten trick to play, that's certain."

"Aye," Joan said slyly, "but effective. Is it not written in the Proverbs, 'He that spareth the rod hateth his son, but he that loveth him chasteneth him betimes'?"

James smiled slowly. "'Tis also written there, 'Whoso findeth a wife findeth a good thing.'" He crumpled a sheet of parchment in his powerful hands. "I've naught to lose by trying, I suppose. Forty men died in this last dispute between Cameron and Duffy. And over what? Some perceived insult, some trifling affront to Iain's dignity." He shook his head, saddened by the senselessness. "Forty good men."

Joan perched on the edge of his chair, her arm around his brawny shoulders. "Chasten your children, darling. It's what any good father would do."

He wrapped his hand over hers. "But what if they do not believe that I chasten them out of love?"

"No one who knows you," she said softly, "could possibly believe aught else."

James shuffled the reports together as his wife rose to her feet. "Send in my secretary, will you, my dear? I may as well get started on the summonses." He grinned. "Let history record it was a woman who urged this deception."

Joan threw him a kiss. "Fortunately for me, it will do no such thing!" She hesitated. "Will you be writing to all the clan chiefs, then?" He nodded. "And the Lord of the Isles as well?"

"Of course. He's the only one who might be able to get those stubborn old fools to listen to reason. If he hadn't run off from Stirling last spring without so much as a by-your-leave from me, I wouldn't be in this mess now. That young man has definite possibilities." He glanced at her. "Why do you ask?"

"No reason. I'm—I'm simply fond of Alexander."

James winked. "So is one of your ladies, you told me once. Genevieve Fleming."

"That was nearly a year ago, James! What a memory you have."

"A father must know all about his children," James told her, grinning wickedly.

"And a mother," Joan said complacently, "must see her daughters happily wed."

Genna had wandered a long way from Inverness Castle, following the twisting pebble-strewn banks of the River Ness. Ostensibly she was searching for saffrons, the tiny purple flowers whose stamens made a brilliant yellow dye for her woolstuffs. In truth, she thought, looking across the barren rocky hills, still showing dismal shades of gray and brown and sorrel, she was searching for spring.

Genna wrapped her thick kersey cloak more tightly against the harsh March winds that peeled off the rushing river, flush with the first snow melt from far-distant peaks. Why King James had chosen this bleak, desolate place to spend the winter Genna could not guess. She thought longingly of Dumbarton, where even now jonquils and heartsease and primroses would be poking their heads up through the green lawns, uncurling leafy fronds and shaking off soil from their nodding heads. This place—she kicked viciously at a stone that lay in the path before her—in this dark place, it seemed spring might never come.

She plucked a branch of dried heather from a bush by the road, admiring the tenacity with which the dead flowers still clung to a frail, snow-washed shade of pink. They crumbled at her touch into pale, powdery nothingness, and Genna felt a swell of sadness sweep through her as she looked across the dun-colored meadow to the far-off white-crowned hills. The landscape matched her mood completely: numbed, spiritless, waiting for something, anything, to bring it to life again.

She smiled a bit at her fancifulness. It was not as though she were miserable, after all. She had her companions at court, she was sharing her chambers with Ellie Douglas, and though the girl's silliness drove her mad at times, she could be good company too on long winter nights.

And there were suitors, lots of them now, though none that she cared about. Genna's mouth curved downward as she pictured Henry Argyll's thin dark face. He continued to press his request for her hand; he'd pestered her relentlessly all winter, popping out of shadowy corners to catch her alone, trying to fondle and kiss her. Henry was sly and bold at once, and his fox brown eyes seemed cold and calculating as they followed her everywhere. Some days she was ready to scream at him to leave her alone.

She shrugged it away. Thank God the queen was patient, and hadn't made her submit to a husband as yet. Though Bess had been wed in August, and Arabelle at Lammastide . . .

At Lammastide Davey and his Meggie had been married as well, she supposed. She thought of his jolly, laughing face, the way he'd beamed when he spoke of his sweetheart. That was how she wanted a lover to look at her. Not with Henry Argyll's insolent, lascivious stares.

The way Alexander Mac Donald had looked at her at Stirling, just before he'd kissed her . . . as though she were the most beautiful, fascinating creature in all the world.

Genna threw down the heather in disgust. Pretty words, she reminded herself, that is all you got from him before he disappeared without so much as a good-bye on that awful morning.

She'd simply awakened that morning so certain it had all been a dream, a terrible dream about the strange man in the garden. She'd hunted all over the castle for Nero, and then, laughing at her own foolishness, had gone out to search the briar roses at the foot of the hill. And she had found the dog's limp, bloodied body lying there, a long deep slash across his throat.

When Genna told the queen what had happened, Joan had paraded every single servant in the castle by her, one by one, and even made them each speak a few words. But none had matched the pale, mooncalf face she remembered, or that odd high singsongy voice.

That same day, Alexander Mac Donald and Davey had been gone. Genna had been too embarrassed to ask the queen if she knew where. Nonetheless, she had a pretty good idea. Back to the Isles, back to his castles full of mistresses and babies, no doubt. If he ever happened to think of her, he probably laughed, remembering how she'd been foolish enough to believe he wished to wed her. Why should he wed at all, when he was a mighty laird and could have any woman he wanted just by winking his eye? Relentlessly Genna's mind formed a picture of Davey and Alex sitting together beside a fire, drinking, trading tales. "She what?" Davey would ask incredulously. "She thought I'd asked for her hand!" Alex would tell him, throwing back his golden head, laughing uproariously. "Can you imagine? That ugly, scrawny little thing," he said, his blue eyes dancing in the firelight.

Genna blushed at the mere thought, starting up a steep rocky slope beside the river, hauling her crimson skirts above her ankles. To cheer herself, she began to sing. It was an old song that Papa John had taught her, and its air of loss and sorrow seemed to suit the cold gray day:

> Oh, waly waly up the bank,
> And waly waly down the brae,
> And waly waly yon burnside
> Where my love and I were wont to gae.
>
> Oh, waly waly, but love is bonnie
> A little time when it is new,
> But when 'tis old it waxeth cold,
> And fades away like morning dew.
>
> Had I but wist, e'er I'd been kissed—

"Damn!" She paused at the top of the rise to catch her breath, then bent down to pull out the pebble that had slipped into her boot. The chill wind whipped back the hood from her cloak, strewing long strands of coal black hair over her face.

Alex had pulled up sharply on Bantigh's reins as he heard the first high, clear notes of the song come drifting over the hummock, not quite able to believe his ears. He had never heard Genna Fleming sing, but the voice muttering the oath that cut the song short was unmistakable. For a moment he considered wheeling the horse around and galloping off. Instead, he held his mount motionless, staring at the girl who knelt not a hundred yards away.

Ten months he'd spent trying to escape the haunting memory of what he'd seen in the queen's gardens at Stirling: her long black hair tumbling wildly over her bare shoulders, the achingly lovely pallor of her throat, her breasts.

And the splotch the man's dark hands had made against her fair skin, his murmured pleasure as he stroked the willing body beneath him.

Ten months. And not battle nor hard work nor fevered lovemaking had served to drive that memory from his mind. He swallowed, trying to contain the resentment and fury that welled up like bile in his throat.

Genna shook out her boot, slid it back on her foot, and fastened the buckle with a resounding snap. She raised both hands to reach back for her hood, and saw the lone rider atop the tall white horse, his gold hair agleam in a sudden slanting stream of weak winter sun.

"Why, Mistress Fleming." His voice was as calm and self-assured as ever. "Are you waiting for someone? Your lover, perhaps?"

Genna struggled to her feet, crimson skirts blowing madly in the gusting wind, the gray cloak billowing around her. In the tangle of wind and wool she looked, thought Alex, like a child, fragile and small. Or like a wild bird, about to take wing over the water, soaring away.

He swung himself down from the saddle and came nearer, long legs swallowing the distance in measured strides. Genna stood silently, hands clasped before her, entranced by the way the sunlight played over his shoulders, making a golden halo of his windswept hair, setting the rest of that tall, straight figure into sharp relief. He was as magnificently handsome as she'd remembered. Changed, though, she thought with surprise; his expression was grim and stern, his blue eyes dark, in shadow.

He leapt up the hill in a single bound and stood towering over her, those cold, dark eyes sweeping her from head to toe. Then he reached down and grabbed her right hand. "No ring yet," he observed, denying to himself how the sight of her moved him, filled him with quickening desire. "Why not, my dear Genna? Are all your lovers so ignominious that not one will pay for his pleasures with his name?"

Genna was rapidly recalling why she despised this man. What right had he to touch her, speak to her in that insulting tone? "All my lovers?" she repeated, pulling back her hand. "I haven't the least idea what you're talking about."

His chilly eyes narrowed, blue turning steely gray. She looked, still, as unsullied and fresh as she had that night in the forest, when she had been a nymph, a spirit beckoning him into the darkness. He hardened his heart against the charms of her small pale face, the entrancing billows of black hair. "Still playing the coy virgin, I see," he observed, mouth twisting. "Surely most of the courtiers have grown tired of that by now. But then, you are such a clever little harlot, aren't you, Genna? No doubt you've managed to cover your tracks quite well."

She smacked his face. "How dare you call me that name?"

He caught her wrist and wrung it, bringing tears of hot pain to her eyes. "I call you what you are," he said evenly, "a whoring she-cat. Who was your redheaded paramour that night? A stablehand? The gardener's boy? Or perhaps you yourself are not certain. Perhaps there have been so many that you cannot remember his name."

"Take your hands off me," Genna spat, as his fingers grew tighter on her arm.

"You don't say that to everyone, do you, Genna? You didn't say that to him."

She stared up at him with wide dark eyes, suddenly frightened by his cruel strength, the venom in his voice. "Have you gone mad?"

At that moment he would not have denied it; the sight of her again after so long a time, the exquisite beauty of her face, her eyes, and his knowledge of the strumpet's heart that beat beneath the bloodred gown were filling him with ungovernable rage. "If I have," he growled, teeth clenched, "'tis the thought of you has driven me to it." His gaze swept the deserted meadow, seeing no one, and his lip curled in satisfaction. "By God, I've a mind to take you right here," he said slowly, drawing off his riding gloves finger by finger, reaching to unbuckle his sword.

Genna's eyes grew even wider. "What—what are you doing?"

"What I should have done a long time ago." He let the sword belt drop to the ground, eager to erase the memories that haunted him, to exorcise the ghost white girl he saw each night in his sleep. "This was what you wanted all along, wasn't it? All your fine show of innocence. Did you really think you could fool me? I know your kind. All soft words and blushes, but only till you part your knees."

"No," Genna whispered, backing away down the hillside. "No, you're wrong!" But he laughed, coldly, tightly, and reached for her breast. She screamed then, the sound eddying off in a swirl of wind, and plunged recklessly away, running from him like a deer from the hunter, fleeing the fury in his cold eyes. The brambles and briars beside the path clutched at her heavy skirts, tore at her stockings, and when she glanced over her shoulder in terror she saw that he was following easily, toying with her as a cat might play with a bird. Her lungs were raw and bursting, her heart pounded frantically, and her throat ached and throbbed with each panting breath.

And then she was falling, snagged by a root, and scrambling on hands and knees to escape him, clawing at his face, his eyes, as he caught her and pinned her down.

"There," he said, with a grim smile of pleasure. His dark face loomed over her, his gold hair wild with wind, and beyond him was nothing but the cloud-ravaged sky. Genna clenched her eyes shut, a fleeting cry of fear tearing from her as he caught her tangled tresses in his hands and pulled her to him, his breathing rasping and harsh.

Then his mouth covered hers, pressing with such fierceness that she thought he would surely crush her. He cupped her face between his huge palms, his lips like a brand against her, searing her with his need and longing, his anger vanished, leaving only tortured regret.

"Oh, Genna," he whispered brokenly, staring down as his hands fell from her, as she opened her startled eyes. "Oh,

Christ, how I might have loved you." His voice caught, faltered, and he stood abruptly, turning his back to her, whistling for Bantigh in a single clear note.

The white steed came charging over the winter-browned sedge, her hooves like thunder. Alex grasped the bridle, leapt into the saddle, and rode off beneath a scrim of skittering wind-torn clouds. Genna saw him circle back to the hummock, swing down from one stirrup, and catch up his belt and sword. And then they were gone, in a flash of white tail and gold hair, moving together like a single creature, half man, half beast.

Genna lay utterly still, hearing her heart beat loud as Bantigh's hooves, feeling the earth tremble beneath her as she let out her breath in a wordless prayer of thanks. Then she stumbled to her feet, clutching the thorn-tattered cloak about her, numbed by the fury of the storm she'd witnessed, the immense sadness in his eyes. "How I might have loved you . . ." What had he meant by that, and by the slurs he'd flung at her? She'd been so certain he meant to make good his threats, to assault her. Instead, he had only kissed her, and murmured those words.

He really has gone mad, she thought dimly, through a mist of terror and tears. He might change his mind, turn and come back for her now that night was falling. He might be searching for a secluded place where he could take her, where no one would hear her cries. Oh, God, she had to get safely back to Inverness.

Genna ran back down the path by the river, fighting the rising winds, not heeding the growing gloom of dusk, certain that at any minute she'd hear once more the pounding of Alex's horse's hooves, see him rise up out of the gathering darkness like a demon from hell.

A sentinel saw her stumble uncertainly up to the gates of the castle, took in her wild eyes and bramble-torn skirts, and caught her in his arms just before she collapsed. He carried her by the back stairs to the queen's chambers, soothing her like a child as she raved about thunder and clouds.

Joan took one look at the girl's disheveled hair, the tattered cloak and gown, and dismissed her ladies. "Get wine," she told the soldier quickly, fearing the worst, "and say nothing of this to anyone." Perhaps, she thought distractedly, she could keep the news of this shame from spreading, could yet salvage

Genna's honor. "Genna," she whispered, holding the wine cup
to the girl's mouth, "can you hear me? Who did this to you?"

Her wind-parched lips moved; Joan leaned closer. "Alexander," she heard her whisper. "Tell the king—warn him.
Alexander."

"Alexander Mac Donald?"

Genna nodded weakly. "Tell the king . . . Alexander is
mad."

"Did he . . ." Joan hesitated, thinking of the king's young
cousin, fearful of the answer. "Did he rape you, child?"

"Nay," Genna whispered, her face ghostly pale in the twilight. "He didn't. That is how I know he is mad."

Immensely relieved, but completely confused, Joan
propped the girl's head up with pillows, made her swallow
more wine, then matter-of-factly said, "All right, Genna. Now
tell me what happened, from the beginning."

As the story poured out in bits and pieces, Joan had to
admit that it did sound as though the Lord of the Isles had lost
his mind. Genna was quaking wildly by the time she'd finished. The queen wrapped her warmly in a blanket and moved
her chair closer to the blazing fire.

"You say he called you a harlot?" she asked incredulously.

"Aye." Genna nodded, her cheeks burning. "And a . . . a
whoring she-cat."

Joan shook her head in bewilderment. "Tell me again what
he said about the redheaded man."

"He asked who it was—the stablehand, or the gardener's
boy. He called him my—my paramour. Your Majesty," Genna
sobbed, her face in her hands, "I haven't the least idea what he
was talking about! He must be mad."

"The stablehand or the gardener's boy," Joan mused, racking her brain. "The gardener's boy or the . . . Genna!"

"What is it?" asked Genna, seeing the sudden gleam in
Joan's eye.

"Will you be all right if I leave you alone for a moment? I
have to go down to the dungeons."

"The dungeons? Why on earth—"

"By the strangest coincidence, Alexander Mac Donald
is—ah—is imprisoned there."

"Oh, thank God!" cried Genna. "Then you and the king
are safe!"

"Oh, aye, *we're* safe enough," the queen said mysteriously. "Now, promise me you'll stay right here."

When Joan returned to her chambers a scant hour later, her gray eyes were twinkling.

"Well?" Genna demanded, jumping up from her chair, the blankets tumbling to the floor. "He is mad, isn't he?"

The queen pushed her back down, tucking the blankets firmly around her. "You must sit quietly, Genna. You've had a fearful shock."

"But did you see him, Your Majesty, and talk with him? If you did, you must surely have known right away."

"Alexander and I had a most illuminating chat," the queen said calmly, picking up her broidery hoop, moistening the edge of her thread.

"A chat? With that madman? Impossible!"

"Oh, you're quite right about that. He is mad." Joan held her needle to a lamp to thread it.

"I told you," said Genna triumphantly.

The queen eyed her over the needle. "He is mad, young lady, about you."

"About me?" Genna's mouth fell open.

Joan was plying her needle in quick darting stitches. "Do you remember, Genna Fleming, when we were at Stirling last spring, and you found poor Nero in the gardens?"

"Of course I do." Even now, after all the time that had passed, the memory brought tears to Genna's eyes. "I cannot imagine who would be so cruel as to do such a thing."

"Nor can I, my dear. But do you also recall the man who came to fetch you in your chambers?"

Genna shuddered. "Oh, I shall never forget him! That awful pale face of his in the moonlight, and his bright red hair."

"Exactly." The queen set down her sewing. "You were not quite alone in the garden that night, dearie. Alexander and his mother were there."

"He was there? He saw me? And he did nothing to stop that horrible man?"

"Alexander was under the impression," Joan said carefully, "that you would not have wanted him stopped. I gather he was influenced in that opinion by his giddy mother."

Genna shook her head. "But I don't understand. What did he think was going on?"

"Alexander believed . . . that you were making love."

Genna's black eyes were round as saucers. "He thought *what?*"

"Alexander thought you were making love to the man," Joan repeated. "He was furious because you had once, ah, shall we say, spurned his advances? And so, in a jealous huff, he hied himself back to the Isles."

Genna folded her hands in her lap, trying to digest this unlikely information. "Oh, I do not believe that man," she said finally. "Couldn't he see I was in danger? What kind of fool cannot tell the difference between lovemaking and a—a foul attack?"

"I believe," said Joan, resuming her sewing, "that Alexander is in the dungeon at this moment asking the same question of himself. You see, dear, he really is mad about you."

"Well, I think he is a perfect idiot!" Genna said viciously, pulling the blankets tighter, staring into the fire. "I might have been killed—or worse."

"Don't be too harsh with him, Genna," the queen said gently. "Even the mightiest lord is a fool when he is in love. I should know."

"King James would never have made such a mistake!"

"I'm not so certain," said Joan, with a little laugh. "I think love's darts strike hardest in men like James and Alexander. Lords are the most solitary creatures on earth, Genna, because they can never be certain whether people really care for them, or only care because they're lords." She hesitated, resting her chin on her hands. "When I first met James, I wasn't impressed by his title or his handsomeness. He was a prisoner in England, a stranger in a strange land, and he touched my heart because he was so very much alone. It sounds rather odd, I suppose, but I felt sorry for him. Do you understand me?"

Genna was silent, thinking of the pain in Alex's voice when he'd whispered, "I might have loved you . . ."

"I don't know if I understand or not," she said finally, then tossed her head. "But I know one thing, Your Majesty. I hope he sits and rots in that dungeon for a good long time."

"That's according to His Majesty's pleasure, of course," said Joan, hiding a smile as she bent over her sewing again. "But however many days he spends there, I'm sure that to Alex it will seem a very long time."

8

"You look absolutely breathtaking in that gown, Genna," said Ellie Douglas, standing beside her at the mirror. "God, I wish I had your skill at the loom!"

"All it takes is a bit of practice, Ellie. You could learn to weave in no time."

"Oh, you know me; I'm much too busy to spend hours and hours sitting here in a room by myself. Though, I must say, for a dress like that it might be worth it." She looked enviously at the drape of the deep green linen, the low-cut bodice nipped in at the waist by a braided gold cord, and the long sleeves lined in golden silk. Genna's heavy underskirts rustled as she knelt to fasten her green leather shoes. Ellie eyed her friend's tiny waist and bared white throat and sighed.

"I don't understand why you haven't married yet, Genna. That Henry Argyll has been chasing you for months now. Why don't you give in to him, for heaven's sake?"

"Because I don't trust him," Genna said firmly, struggling to tuck the front of her hair into a tiny gold cap. "Or like him, either, for that matter."

"You silly goose, you needn't like a man to marry him! He's rich, and handsome, and there's talk the king will appoint him vice governor here. What more could any girl ask?"

What more, indeed, thought Genna, staring into the mirror. The warm dark green of the gown made her skin glow like polished ivory, and her eyes looked huge and black as coal beneath the little gold headpiece. She'd woven strands of gold twine into the three thick braids looped at the nape of her neck, and they caught the candlelight and sparkled like fine jewels. With a sigh she went to her dressing table and picked up the gold and pearl brooch, fastening it into the hollow between her breasts.

"Do you want to borrow my emeralds?" Ellie offered. "They'd look fabulous with that green."

Genna shook her head, smiling. "It's kind of you to ask, Ellie, but you know it makes me nervous to borrow your jewels."

"If you were wed to Henry Argyll," Ellie said slyly, "you wouldn't need to borrow. You could have all the emeralds and rubies you wanted."

"If I were wed to Henry Argyll, I should need more than a few jewels to make me happy."

"Oh, happy be damned." Ellie linked her arm through Genna's. "I don't understand you one bit. Come on, we'll be late for supper."

As they started down the passageway to the banquet hall, Ellie leaned her head close. "I heard from my cousin Janet that the clan chiefs are to be brought out tonight after supper and flogged right before our eyes. Do you think it's true?"

"How would I know, Ellie? All sorts of rumors have been flying around since the king tricked them into coming here." But the idea was secretly thrilling. How she would love to see Alexander Mac Donald flogged!

"I think it's just horrid for King James to have locked them all up in the dungeons," Ellie said peevishly, twisting the rope of pearls at her throat. "It's hard enough for me to find a husband without his keeping half the bachelors at court under lock and key."

"Ellie, you're awful." Genna giggled, rounding a corner. "Don't you ever think of anything except— Oh!" She felt the breath go out of her as she collided full tilt with a bundle of rose-scented satin and feathers. "I beg your pardon!"

"You damned idiot!" snarled Mary Leslie, clutching her huge ostrich-plume headdress. Her blue eyes narrowed as she saw the girl who stood before her. "Honestly, it's getting so the king will give any little nobody a place at court. Come along, Henry." She extended an elegant gloved hand to the man beside her.

"Good even, Genna." Henry Argyll ignored the countess's beckoning hand to make a low sweeping bow, peering into the cleft between Genna's breasts. His bold coppery eyes made Genna want to turn and run.

Instead, she said simply, "Good even, sir. We are just on our way to supper."

"As are we," said Argyll, smiling his thin tight smile. "Perhaps you'll allow me to escort you."

"Henry!" Mary Leslie snapped, shaking out her fan. "Come *along!*"

Argyll flashed Genna a look of hot regret before he led the countess away. Her purring voice carried back down the corridor: "As I was saying, before that stupid little thing nearly bowled me over, Alexander has made me a grandmother *again* —can you believe it? Oh, still no *legitimate* children, the rascal, but if all those mistresses don't care if he weds them, well, really, now, why should he?"

Ellie stared curiously at the retreating figures, then slipped her arm through Genna's once more, shaking her head. "I can't understand why any woman would talk that way about her own son. It's almost as though she doesn't want any decent girls to go near him. Do you know her?"

"Not—not really. I only know who she is."

Ellie's gray eyes danced with laughter. "Well, she can say what she pleases about him, and it won't change one thing. I would marry Alexander Mac Donald faster than you can say fiddle di-dee!"

They slipped into their places at the queen's ladies' table just as a loud bright blare of clarions heralded the arrival of the king. He was resplendent in a blue velvet doublet and yellow hose, and the heavy gold chain of office he wore gleamed in the torchlight. His auburn-bearded face was solemn as he stepped up to the dais, Joan's arm on his, then turned and surveyed the gathering. At last, his back held rapier-straight, he lowered himself onto his throne.

The courtiers and ladies were seated, and the first of a steady stream of servants appeared, bearing heaping platters of codlings and salmon and eels, presenting them first to His Majesty for approval, then offering them all around. The huge hall filled with sound as the ladies began to gossip and cast sidelong glances at the courtiers across the room. Genna sipped thoughtfully at a cup of cider and picked at her plate of eel, feeling not at all hungry. The encounter with Mary Leslie had unnerved her. Why, she'd never even met the woman. Why should the countess have eyed her with such malevolence? And as for that insolent Henry Argyll—she stabbed the eel with a fork—she'd as soon marry Alexander Mac Donald as him!

It had been a week since their encounter by the river. Genna smiled wickedly to think of Alex locked in the keep with rats and spiders for company. He'd not be so arrogant and proud when—*if*—the king finally released him.

"What are you looking so pleased with yourself about?" whispered Ellie.

"Nothing!" Genna said quickly, and hid her smile behind her cider cup.

The meal, as most at court did, went on forever. After the fish came spitted birds—geese, teals, woodcocks—and then whole roasted lambs that were slung up on staves between the servants. Then there were pasties and custards, and cheeses, and almonds, and wrinkly wintered-over apples. As Genna bit into the soft, squashy fruit she wished more heartily than ever that spring would hurry and arrive.

At long last the pies and sweetmeats were brought in, and the hounds were let loose to scavenge beneath the tables for bones. King James raised his hand for silence, and a hush fell over the hall. One final burst of loud laughter rang out. Genna looked across the room and saw Mary Leslie seated next to Argyll at a table crowded with the more dissolute courtiers, her color high, the bodice of her fine satin gown awry. Genna wondered fleetingly why the woman should be so carefree, with her only son imprisoned practically beneath her feet.

James frowned in the countess's direction. "Ahem . . ."

"I beg your pardon, Your Majesty," Mary called gaily, "but these gentlemen are slaying me with their jests." She slapped out at Argyll's wandering hand. "Ooh! Stop it, all of you, and hearken to your king."

James inclined his head, bemused. "Thank you, Mary. Now, if I may continue, I've news that concerns the countess —and a good many others. You may be aware that we have distinguished guests in our cellars. The clan chiefs of the Isles have been, er, enjoying our hospitality for the past few weeks. They have begged permission to come before us this evening, and we have granted their request. Squire, show them in!"

It was a bedraggled bunch that straggled through the arch-way, their hands bound before them, clothes tattered and grimy from their time in the keep. Proud Cameron, Mac Pherson, Mac Lean, Farquarson, Montrose, Mac Neil, Crichton— forty in all—filed into the center of the great chamber, and though their bodies were unkempt, their heads were held high.

"Look there," whispered Ellie. "*He* doesn't look as though prison bothers him a whit!"

It was Alexander, taller than the others by more than half a head, a new growth of golden beard curling over his squared chin. Like the others he wore only a long white shirt and loose breeches; his knees and feet were bare. But his mane of tawny hair rippled down over his shoulders like liquid fire, and his blue eyes were cool and provocative as they swept the room. His gaze lighted on Genna and lingered; on his wide mouth was a trace of a smile.

She stared hurriedly down at her plate. Why, he looks more the king in a beggar's clothes than James does in all his finery, she thought in amazement. Even the beard became him; it made him look older, fierce and grave.

"Genna!" She heard a hiss from the crowded floor and looked up to see Davey Mac Leod, freckled face grinning, give her a hearty wink.

"Didn't we meet him at Stirling?" asked Ellie. "Is he married?"

"I think so," said Genna, waving to Davey. "Hush, now; I want to listen."

James smiled in satisfaction as he surveyed the gathering. "Well, gentlemen, you craved an audience; we have granted it to you. What have you to say?"

Angus Mac Pherson, the eldest of the chiefs, stepped forward. "If it please Your Majesty—" His voice was a husky croak, his wiry white beard aquiver at the humiliation he was forced to endure. "If it please Your Majesty," he began again.

"Well, Angus, get on with it!" hissed Iain Cameron, the next oldest in the group.

Mac Pherson glared at him. "P'raps you'd be thinkin' 'tis you should have been chosen for the task, eh, Iain? Well, fine then. I give it to ye!" And he turned and headed out of the chamber.

"Sure and I'll take it!" Cameron roared at his back. "At least I won't stammer and start so, and put the whole lot of us to shame!"

"Shame, is it?" growled Mac Pherson, returning. "And what would ye know of shame, pray tell? You bloody upstart, my fathers were growin' good corn from the ground while yours were still searchin' for a way to crack oysters!"

"By God, I'll crack your idiot head," said Cameron, advancing.

"Crack it just like an oyster for him, Iain!" Brian Mac Intosh chimed in, choosing sides. "Ask him if he even knows who his father was!"

"I know yer father for a rutting goat, Mac Intosh!" yelled Mac Pherson.

"Aye, and your sister's a goat-hag!"

"My sister, is it? What about Iain's mother, who he ties to her bed each night?"

"Why, you bleeding bastard!" cried Cameron, and lunged for him, bound hands and all, knocking his rival to the ground and scrambling for his throat. The hounds set up a monstrous racket, Mac Intosh jumped into the fray, and the rest of the clan chiefs aligned themselves with one faction or the other, hooting and brawling, while James stood on his dais, hands raised above the clamor, bellowing for silence from all. Genna didn't know whether to burst out laughing or not; looking for Davey, she saw him take a diving leap headfirst into the fracas, issuing a wild yell. She laughed.

"That's enough!" roared Alexander, using his long legs to thrust Cameron and Mac Pherson apart. "Have done with it! Are you no better than animals, then? The king of Scotland has called you before him, and you behave like squabbling chickens." The din died away to silence as he glared at the chiefs. "Angus." He hauled him to his feet by the collar. "Finish your speech to the king."

"Nay, I'll not," the old man said sullenly. "Let Iain do it, if he thinks he's so clever. My sister, indeed!"

"Iain, the task falls to you."

"Not I," Cameron grumbled, shaking his hoary head. "If 'tis too hard a thing for Angus, 'tis too hard for me."

"You do it, Alley," urged Mac Intosh, pushing him forward. "You tell him what we've come to say."

"Aye, you do it, then," the others echoed. Angus Mac Pherson glared up at the tall young man.

"Ye are, after all," he snapped, "Laird of the Isles."

Alex paused, considering the men around him. "Very

well," he said finally, and stepped out in front. "Your Majesty."

James scowled down from the dais. "Aye?"

Genna could see the smile that tugged at Alex's mouth. "The clan chiefs come before you in all humbleness," he began.

"You'd be humble too," spat Cameron, "if you'd been fed naught but dried sprat and water for three weeks!"

The others shouted him down. "Go on, Alley!" "Aye, you tell him!"

"In all humbleness," Alex continued, unruffled, "to offer you their pledges of fealty, and swear their loyalty to none but yourself. They beg you to graciously accept those pledges, and release them from the loving protection—"

"Protection!" roared Mac Pherson indignantly. Alex thumped him in the stomach with his bound hands.

"In which you have so generously held them," Alex finished, his voice rising above a growing undercurrent of disgruntlement.

James tapped his heavy fingertips on the table. "There would be conditions . . ."

"They accept them," Alex said promptly.

The king drew a list from his doublet. "The clan chiefs are to dwell in their own manors, in their own districts, and are to travel with no more than twoscore men."

There was a loud groan from Cameron; Alex silenced him with a glare.

"Each chief is to keep the order in his district," the king continued, "and is to provide the crown with one galley rower for every four merks of land. The playing of golf is forbidden in your districts, with every man aged twelve and older to practice at archery instead."

"He'll make us into a bunch of bleedin' Frenchmen," grumbled Brian Mac Intosh, who was inordinately fond of golf.

"Dueling and rebellion—" The king paused, considering the list, then gazed out sternly at the chiefs. "Dueling and rebellion are outlawed *from this moment*. *All* offenders will be beheaded, their lands and goods forfeited, with no exceptions. Is that clear?"

"It is, Your Majesty," Alex said with a nod. "They accept the conditions."

"Now, just one moment," said Mac Intosh. "About the golf, Your Majesty—"

"They accept all the conditions," Alex repeated firmly. "Hush, Bri," he added in a whisper. "You surely can't play if you're locked in the keep."

"Well, then"—James appeared somewhat mollified—"what security do you offer me to guarantee their pledges?"

Alex glanced around at the clan chiefs. "Each of them must make his own security for his pledge, Your Most Gracious Highness." Then his blue eyes locked on Genna, and she realized with a start that he was walking toward her. "As for myself"—he came around the table and stood behind her, his huge hands alighting on her shoulder—"I can only say that I intend to wed this lovely creature just as soon as I work myself free of these bonds." He looked up at James and Joan. "And I can assure you that once I have done so, I'll be far too busy filling my castle with bairns to join these old codgers in rebellion!"

Genna whipped around in her seat and stared up at him, unable to believe what he'd said. The clan chiefs were erupting in cheers and whoops of appreciation. "You tell 'im, Alley!" yelled Cameron, and even old Mac Pherson beamed happily at his laird.

"His grandmother's sister was my father's aunt," he proclaimed proudly to those around him. "Ach, what a silver tongue there is on the boy!"

Genna was speechless with rage. It was awful enough what he'd said about wedding her, but that other—the bairns— Oh, Lord!

Alex chuckled, leaned over, and kissed her full on the mouth. "You can see she's overcome with relief at my impending release," he called to the king, grinning.

"You bloody bastard," said Genna, between clenched teeth. But the scene he'd already created was more than spectacle enough; she didn't dare worsen it by sticking her fork in his heart.

The king's cold eyes softened as he looked down at his cousin, and a trace of a smile creased his face. "That is all the security you have to offer me, Alexander?"

Alex gestured to Genna, blue eyes twinkling. "Look at her, Your Majesty. What sovereign could ask a greater pledge?"

James threw back his head and laughed. "Very well, then, I accept it. Squire, release him. I set you free, Alexander Mac Donald Mac John Mac Angus Og, scion of Somerled, high king of Norway. On the condition, of course, that you do indeed marry the girl."

"I'm eternally grateful, Your Majesty," Alex said, grinning. With his freed hands he was holding a sputtering Genna firmly in her chair. "We are both . . . eternally grateful."

"In a pig's eye we are!" Genna hissed at him. The king had turned back to the clan chiefs.

"Who's next? You, Cameron, what have you to say?"

"Alas, milord." The old man grinned toothlessly. "I'd make the same offer myself, but my good wife would flay me alive!" A burst of laughter rang out from the assembly. "But I'll pledge you five hundred marks, and my solemn word of honor."

"Accepted," said James, nodding. "Mac Pherson?"

"Oh, I'll match his offer and better," Mac Pherson said stoutly. "Five hundred marks, and twenty armed men, with horses, to serve at Your Majesty's pleasure."

"Very well, and thanks to you. Mac Intosh!" And one by one the clan chiefs stepped forward to offer their securities.

"If you think for one moment," Genna began, twisting her head to see Alexander, "that I would ever, *ever* marry you—"

He silenced her with a kiss that left her breathless, his hand cupping her chin, gold beard tickling, mouth plunging down on hers with hot passion. The look in his sky blue eyes was one of pure desire.

Genna pinched his arms with all the strength she could muster, stood up, and headed for the door. "Overcome with relief," she heard him repeat to Ellie. "She's simply overcome."

"Why, that closemouthed thing," gushed Ellie, "she never gave a hint to me that the two of you were betrothed. Oh, I just think it's so exciting."

That was all Genna caught, for suddenly Mary Leslie stood before her, hard eyes glittering. "I suppose you think you've won," the woman hissed venomously. "Well, you haven't, lass, not by a long, long way!"

Certain she had misunderstood, Genna simply stared.

Mary's eyes went beyond her shoulder to Alex, who was hurrying after his bride.

"Oh, my darling," the countess cried, throwing her arms about his neck. "Your father would have been so proud of you! Oh, my dear boy!" And she smothered his face with kisses.

Genna threw one murderous glance at Alex, then fled through the archway to the maze of passages beyond.

9

The next morning, just that suddenly, spring arrived. The skies which had been gray and leaden turned a brilliant cloudless blue, and the rolling hills of the Northwest Highlands doffed their dull coats to put on new cloaks with the barest tinges of gold and amethyst and green. Genna woke, saw the bright sunlight that streamed through the casements, and ran to look out with a cry of delight. For a moment she forgot completely the wretched restless night she had just spent. "At last," she murmured, leaning from the window, letting the warmth play over her upturned face. "Nothing could possibly go wrong on a day like this!"

But then she remembered the dreadful scene in the banquet hall, and Alex's infuriating self-assured grin as he'd held her in her chair and kissed her. Kissed her, in front of all those people, and had the gall to tell the king he intended her to be his bride!

There was about as much chance of that, Genna thought, viciously tearing off her nightdress and clambering into a wool skirt the color of lapis, as of her marrying the king of France! And after he'd come *that* close to raping her just a week ago. Did he really think she'd forget so easily the fright he gave her that day? Or was he just accustomed to having women do whatever he told them? Well, maybe those mistresses he kept in the Isles rolled over every time he snapped his fingers, but she wasn't about to! She yanked her wide blue belt tight with a vengeance. She'd get back at him, never fear.

But for now, the hills were waiting, the thrushes were singing, and the sun was shining.

"Genna, where are you going?" Ellie struggled up from beneath a mountain of blankets, shaking blond hair from her eyes. "You were sound asleep when I came in last night. I haven't even had a chance to ask you about your betrothal!"

121

"Later, Ellie," Genna said quickly, glad she'd had the foresight the night before to feign sleep. "Right now I've got to, ah, I've got to go and get breakfast. I'm simply famished!"

"But, Genna," Ellie wailed, "I've got a million questions to ask you. When is the wedding? How did it feel when he kissed you? Where will you live when you're married? How rich is he, anyway? Can I be a bridesmaid? What will you wear?"

"Oh, Ellie, shut up!" Genna snapped, and escaped into the hall, leaving Ellie to decide sleepily that love was a very strange thing, indeed.

Genna had no sooner shut the bedchamber door than she saw Queen Joan bearing down on her, smiling happily. "Oh, Genna, dear, I'm absolutely thrilled for you! Now, I have it all planned out. How does this sound? We'll have the ceremony right here in the chapel. James is dying to give you away — Genna? Genna!"

Genna had let out a wail of anguish and vanished down the servants' stairs.

Katy Mac Millan was just on her way up with an armful of the first cherry blossoms, fresh and soft pink and fragrant. "Oh, these are for you, mum!" she told Genna, thrusting the huge bouquet at her. "His Lairdship himself cut them this morning. God almighty, he's handsome. Where should I put them for you?"

"I don't give a damn where you put them!" Genna shrieked, tossing the branches at the startled maid's feet. "Why can't everybody just leave me alone?" And she ran blindly down the stairs.

She could hear the rattling of crocks and cutlery from the kitchens below, punctuated by the master cook's sharp voice as he scolded his scullions. Behind her on the stairs she heard the queen call her name, and Katy babbling. She turned a corner, saw the open door across the huge oven-lined room, and made a dash for it.

"Hey, you there! Out of my kitchens!" the cook bellowed, running after her, brandishing a cleaver.

Vexed beyond endurance, Genna picked up a tray of hot scones and threw it at him. "I'm *going*, you big old fool!" she cried, and raced through the door.

The cook's furious curses followed her as she darted across the yards to the water gate, where she had the pleasure of arguing with the porter for what seemed like hours over whether or not he would raise the portcullis. He finally relented only when Genna, certain that at any moment a whole string of curious women would pour out of the kitchens, burst into tears. "Ah, well, then, lass," the porter mumbled. "I suppose I could make an exception. But you'll have to come back in through the main gate, you know. King's orders is that this one is used *only* for provisions."

She thanked him breathlessly and hurried under the iron gate, finding herself free at last, panting with exhaustion, but blissfully, utterly alone.

"Genna, wait!"

"Dammit to hell," she burst out, whirling around, "what do you want?"

Davey Mac Leod loped toward her, looking puzzled. "Why, nothin', darlin'. I just happened to be walking this way."

"Bosh. No one walks this way; that's why I came here." She eyed him suspiciously. "How did you get past that porter?"

"I gave him twopence," he admitted with a sheepish grin. "How did you?"

Despite her anger, Genna giggled at his expression. "I cried."

"Well, then," said Davey, falling into stride beside her, "you owe me fourpence altogether. I had to soothe the master cook as well."

About to laugh, she stopped abruptly. "You were following me!"

"Aye, that I was. And now that I've caught up, could we go a wee bit slower? You ran like a bloody greyhound across the yards; I'd a devil of a time keeping up."

"In case the point was lost on you," Genna said icily, "I came here because I wanted to be alone."

Davey grinned his wide, guileless grin. "Can't a man simply say good day to an old friend without her jumpin' all over him?"

"Very well, then," snapped Genna, "say it and be done!"

"Good day, Mistress Fleming."

"Good day, *Master* Mac Leod."

But Davey showed no sign of turning back to the castle. "Meggie says good day to you as well," he went on cheerfully, "or she would, if she were here, I'm certain. She's back on Mull, tending to her gardens. But I'm sure if she were here, she'd tell you good day herself. I've told her a lot about you, you see."

"How nice," said Genna, through clenched teeth. "Why don't you go back to Mull right now and tell her I said good day?"

Davey put a hand on her sleeve and faced her. "Are ye angry with me for somethin', Genna?" His green brown eyes were wide and innocent.

"No," said Genna, shaking off his hand.

"Well, that's a good thing." He peered at her closely. "You're not—you're not angry with Alley, I hope."

"Angry?" said Genna, black eyes flashing. "Angry doesn't even begin to describe my feelings for that—that lout! How dare he say those things in front of the whole court? I would sooner marry a dog than him."

"I'm sorry you feel that way, Genna. But I'm certain Alley could change your mind, if you'd give him time."

She stared openmouthed for a moment, then closed her jaw with an audible snap. "You can go and tell your friend Alley that just as soon as I have the chance, I'm going to report to His Majesty that the Lord of the Isles told him a blatant lie!"

"Oh, dear, I was hopin' you wouldn't do that, Genna. You see, then Alley would be clapped right back into prison."

"Good. He belongs there!"

"Nobody belongs there, darlin'. I spent nigh on two weeks enjoyin' the king's hospitality in his dungeon. 'Tis a terrible grim place."

"And I suppose that gives your lord the right to tell vicious falsehoods? Why didn't he just put up money or men for his security, like the others?"

"Probably because he hasn't got any money," said Davey ruefully, rubbing his beard.

"Then he can cool his heels in the dungeon until he does."

"But he could be there for years!"

"I hope he rots there! And what do you mean, he hasn't got any money? Isn't he the high and mighty Lord of the Isles?"

"Aye, but you see, Genna, the harvest last autumn was poor, and the one the year before even poorer, so Alley let the clan chiefs go twice without payin' their winter rents. That's one of his most splendid aspects, really, is Alley's generosity."

"He's damned generous with his imagination, that's for sure!"

"Now, Genna," Davey began, in a tone of utmost reasonableness, "it'll kill Alley if he has to stay in that prison any longer."

"Bullfeathers, Davey Mac Leod. I saw him last night. He doesn't look one bit the worse for wear." She was still so angry that she failed to notice the bemused gleam in Davey's eye.

"If he looks well," he said softly, "'tis because he's finally found out the truth about that man and you in the gardens at Stirling. Faith, I've seen Alley angry, but never like that before. Genna, don't you understand? The man loves you."

"Well, I hate him. And if he thinks I'm going to help him deceive the king, he's sorely mistaken."

Davey clucked his tongue and frowned. "I know they say women are ungrateful creatures, but somehow I thought you were different."

"Ungrateful? What am I supposed to be grateful for?"

"Why, for—" Davey had been about to mention Alex's pursuit of Ranalt, but then remembered she knew nothing about that. "Why, for his saving you at Dumbarton, pulling you out of the fire."

"I didn't ask for his help!"

"And that time at Stirling, when you nearly fell off your horse."

"That was his fault I nearly fell off!"

"And for carin' enough about you not to go on and rape you t'other day."

"For that I should *thank* him? He scared the life out of me!"

"Well, if he hadn't been a man of honor," Davey said stoutly, "it could have ended up much worse! You can't blame the man for bein' in love with you, darlin'. Why not sit back and enjoy it? 'Tis no use fighting Alley once he's got his mind set on something. I know that well enough."

"Well, he's going to have to unset it, that's all."

Davey shrugged. "Do as you please, but don't say I didn't warn you. I've never yet seen Alley go after somethin' and not get it in the end."

Genna's eyes gleamed. "Never?"

"Not once in twenty-four years."

Genna took a deep breath of warm sun-tinged air. A challenge had always appealed to her. And it might be amusing to teach the Lord of the Isles that he wasn't so irresistible as he seemed to think!

But what would be the best way to go about it? She pondered for a moment. Wouldn't it be a blow to his pretty pride if she promised to wed him now, and then called it off at the last possible moment? Leave him standing at the altar, that was it. With the entire court looking on . . .

"Davey?"

"Aye?" He turned from his contemplation of two rose-breasted linnets swooping low over the river, threshing the water reeds with their wings.

She stared demurely at the ground. "Would you be so kind as to tell His Lordship that I am delighted to accept his proposal of marriage?"

"Genna! Ach, darlin', do you mean it?"

"Of course I mean it, Davey. What girl wouldn't be thrilled to death to wed the Lord of the Isles?"

"Oh, Genna!" Davey clutched her hands, nearly dancing with delight. "Oh, darlin', I swear, you'll never regret it! I've got to go tell Alley!"

Genna watched as he tore back along the river to the castle. "Oh, no, I'll never regret it," she murmured to herself. "But you can wager that the Lord of the Isles will!"

10

For nearly a week, Genna's plan went remarkably well. She allowed Alex to squire her about to suppers and dancing, sat beside him in the chapel on Sunday, walked with him each day in the gardens. She endured the eager chattering questions of Ellie and the other ladies, oohed and ahed over dresses for the wedding, and even let Queen Joan choose the date, just a fortnight hence.

And Alex? He seemed properly appreciative of the favor she'd bestowed on him, but except to take her arm at times, and kiss her hand when they met, he made no attempt to impose his affections on her, or press for liberties. He was in all respects the complete gentleman. In fact, Genna reflected—sitting beside him in the gardens one morning, she with her hands chastely folded in her lap, he with his clasped behind his head as he leaned back to catch the sun—in fact, the Lord of the Isles was proving rather dull.

"A lovely morning, is it not?" Alex asked gravely, seeing her black eyes slant toward him.

"Lovely," she agreed primly. Alex grinned to himself. Her sudden acceptance of his public proposal had not fooled him. Genna Fleming had something up her sleeve, that was certain. He glanced at the girl beside him, eyeing the thick black hair that was bound up in crimson ribbands to match her gown, the beautiful clean sweep of her white throat. Her long lashes cast charming fringed shadows against her cheeks as she stared at the ground. Alex felt his blood begin to heat as he contemplated the swell of her breasts beneath the red gown. Now if he could only restrain himself until she tipped her hand! He looked away hastily, whistling a little tune.

Genna scuffed the toe of her shoe in the grass, her delight in the warm sun and budding flowers marred by a vague sense of dissatisfaction. It was difficult to remain irate with the man when all he did was sit there and whistle.

A tiny brown sparrow alighted on the end of the bench, attracted by Alex's whistle. Genna shooed it away with a flap of her fan. Alex looked at her questioningly. "Don't you like birds, milady?"

"Don't I what?"

"Like birds. You know." He flapped his arms, hands tucked into his sleeves. "Birds."

Genna could not help it; she giggled. "What kind of birds?"

"All kinds. Big birds, little birds, scrawny birds and fat birds." He leaned back on the bench, his sleepy eyes half-closed. "I'm very fond of birds. As my betrothed, that's something you should know." He sat up again. "Speaking of birds, here comes that vulture Argyll."

"Do you think him a vulture, milord?" Genna asked, watching the tall, thin nobleman pick his way toward them through the sweet-scented herb beds. "I find him rather charming."

Alex looked at her, and for a moment she saw a cold flash of anger in his eyes. But "I'll wager you do" was all he said, his voice steady and calm.

"Hello, Henry," said Genna, smiling. Her dark gaze took in his splendid green silk doublet and leather breeches. "Are you going riding? How fortunate you are. My betrothed"— she indicated Alex with a disdainful wave—"never cares to do anything but sit in these gardens and stare into space." She started as she felt Alex's fingers clasp her wrist, as though in warning. She ignored it, and gave a pretty little sigh. "I envy you, Henry. 'Tis a splendid day for a ride."

Argyll, encouraged by Genna's unaccustomed civility, whacked his boot with his crop. "If you'd care to accompany me, milady, I'd be only too happy to explore the surrounding woods with you." His teeth gleamed white in the sunlight. "Though with you beside me, I would be hard-pressed to notice anything else."

"Why, Henry," Genna said with a giggle, "how very gallant you are."

By now Alex's fingers were cutting into her skin quite cruelly. Genna glared at him, then smiled graciously as Argyll bowed low at the waist, staring boldly at her breasts. "I know a place, milady," he murmured, "that is nearby, and very private. We could become better acquainted there."

Alex got to his feet abruptly, his great height and broad shoulders making even the long-limbed Argyll seem slight. "Get the hell out of here, Argyll. Genna's not interested in becoming better acquainted with the likes of you."

"Let the lady be the judge of that herself," Argyll suggested, licking his thin lips. "It seems to me that she welcomes my presence. If you're as churlish with her as with me, I don't wonder."

Genna saw Alex's back stiffen at the insult, and took it one step further. "Forgive him, Henry, I beg you," she said sweetly. "His Lordship seems to pride himself on living up to the reputation of his homeland—that it breeds wild, uncivil men."

Alex stared down at Genna with unmistakable fury as Argyll smiled and drawled, "I have heard that the king expects to make a docile little housepet of him. I wish James luck."

There was yet another pert reply on the tip of Genna's tongue, but the rage in Alex's blue eyes convinced her she'd gone quite far enough. She extended a hand to Argyll. "You must excuse us, milord; we were in the midst of a most intriguing discussion of birds. I hope to take up your kind invitation some other time."

"As milady pleases." Argyll shrugged, pressing his mouth to her hand, his lips lingering. "I look forward to that time with great eagerness." He bowed briefly to Alex. "Your Lordship." The corners of his mouth twitched. "I trust your stay here in civilized society will be a long one. King James has obviously set himself a Sisyphean task."

With a tremendous effort Alex held his temper until the courtier was out of earshot. Then he turned to Genna, his proud face set like stone. She smiled. "Sisyphus, milord, was a king of Corinth."

"I know bloody damned well who Sisyphus was," he growled. "I'm not a savage; my father went to Oxford. I even know how to read Latin and Greek, which is more than Henry Argyll can say. Who in hell do you think you are, mocking me that way?"

"Good heavens," she said airily, getting to her feet and starting away. "It was only a silly jest; you needn't make such a fuss."

His hand yanked her back, pulling her so close that she could hear his heart beat. His blue eyes were cold as steel. "Make another such jest and you'll regret it. And don't play games with men like Argyll. It's like playing with fire."

Genna shook off his hand. "I don't take orders from you. It just so happens that I find Henry amusing. I like the pretty speeches he makes."

"You damned little fool, didn't you see him staring at you, undressing you with his eyes?"

"Are you suggesting I should be insulted because he finds me attractive?"

"I'm suggesting you comport yourself properly if you're going to marry me!"

"I'm not *going* to—" She stopped, chewing her lip.

"Not going to what, Genna?" His arm tightened on her waist, drawing her against his long legs, and his hand tugged her hair, tilting her head back to face him. "Not going to what?" She felt the rough, controlled force in his grip, stared up into his angry eyes. Now, she thought, now he will kiss me.

But instead she felt him grasp her hand. "Come along."

"Where—where are we going?" she gasped, as he dragged her through the garden.

"You expressed an interest in riding," Alex said grimly. "We are going riding."

"I cannot go riding alone with you!"

"And yet you would have gone with Argyll?"

"I told you, I was only jesting." Genna wondered suddenly, with a delicious little thrill, if he were jealous.

"At my expense." He stopped suddenly, looking down at her, and she saw bitterness and regret plainly stamped on his face. "Where I come from, it's not considered clever or estimable for a betrothed woman to flirt with men other than her intended."

Genna stared at her toes. "Argyll has asked to marry me, you know."

"You are betrothed to me, though, are you not?" he asked, his eyes dark, impassive.

"Y-yes."

Alex considered her downcast eyes. "We'll take Davey with us," he said abruptly. "For the sake of your honor."

"With us where?"

"Riding," he said, his mouth still tight and angry. "Go put on something that doesn't show your breasts every time you move."

By the time she'd exchanged her red gown for a wide skirt of earth-colored wool, a white linen shirt, and a close-fitting jacket of warm honey brown, Davey was knocking at the door to her chambers. "Lord, but Alley's in a foul temper," he said, as they headed out to the stables. "I wonder why."

"That man has absolutely no sense of humor, Davey! Henry Argyll and I were teasing him about something and the two of them very nearly came to blows right there in the garden."

"Teasing him about what, Genna?"

"Oh, just about the Isles being uncivilized. Goodness, you'd have thought from the way he carried on that we'd impugned his virility." She giggled.

"You find that's amusing?" She looked at him in surprise; it was the first time she'd ever seen Davey angry. "Let me tell you something, Genevieve Fleming. It was in the Isles that Christianity and readin' and writin' were kept alive for the whole of Europe while Henry Argyll's ancestors were still paintin' themselves blue and speakin' in grunts. Alley can trace his forefathers back through fifteen generations. There were churches and castles and towns and ports on Mull while London and Edinburgh were naught but cattle-crossings. So just because Alley may dress differently from yer precious lowland lairds, or because his speech isn't so fanciful, or his hair short and curly as theirs, doesn't mean the Isles are one whit less civilized than anyplace else. They're different, 'tis all. And if you ask me I'll be bloody well pleased to get back there, where a man's judged on what's in his heart and his mind and not how many pairs of shoes he owns!" He paused for breath, noticed her astonished expression. "Well, I'm sorry to yell at ye, darlin'. But I've had it to here with Argyll and his kind, jestin' at us because they're too stupid to know their own history. Alley's a fierce proud man, and he cannot bear to be laughed at. And if you laughed at him, well, all I can say is you should be ashamed."

Genna opened her mouth, blushed, and closed it again. Then she looked up at Davey timidly. "Did his father really go to Oxford?"

"Does it matter to ye, one way or the other?" She shook her

head, and he smiled. "Aye, lass, he did. And just between you and me, he thought the scholars there the least civilized pack of creatures he'd ever seen."

Genna had plenty to mull over while Davey gave her a hand up onto the roan-colored mare Alex had saddled for her. He was already waiting atop Bantigh, his face still stern and forbidding. She followed in silence as he spurred through the castle gates and out to the meadows, with Davey close behind.

Then she was forced to concentrate all her attention on keeping up with the grueling pace Alex set, as if challenging her to beg him to slow down. Genna gritted her teeth, remembering the last time they'd ridden together, when she'd nearly fallen from her horse. She'd prove to him now that it had only been his unwelcome attentions that caused her to falter. They cleared the low plains beside the river, following its meandering course upward into the hills, and then Bantigh vaulted over a hedge of brambles that marked the edge of the castle grounds, galloping at full speed. Genna, though inwardly praying, wrapped her hands firmly in her mare's mane and did the same. She saw a gleam of approval in Alex's sleepy blue eyes as he pulled up to watch her take the fence; then he and Bantigh were off again, moving as always like a single creature, breathtakingly graceful, with Alex's long gold hair streaming out on the wind, rippling in the sun.

As they followed a narrow trail higher into the hills, into thick dense forest, Bantigh's gait grew more leisurely; Alex seemed to have left some of his tense anger behind when he left Inverness. He even smiled back at Genna once, when she swore at an overhanging tree limb that caught on her jacket, and doubled back on the path to help her untangle herself. Davey was still some few hundred feet behind them, and Genna took advantage of their moment alone to say softly, "I'm sorry I said what I did to you there in the garden. You know, about the Isles."

There was a glint of amusement in his dark blue eyes as he pulled a stray leaf from her hair. "Ah, the difference it makes, having a father who went to Oxford."

"That has nothing to do with why I'm sorry!" she said indignantly.

He grinned. "Sometimes you have absolutely no sense of humor, you know."

"Here, girl," said Davey, pulling up behind them and

yanking on his horse's reins. "Stop nibblin' at the honeysuckle, and stick to the path." Just ahead the trees opened into a clearing; he pointed off to the south. "Take a look at those mountains, will you, Genna? Isn't that a grand sight?"

Alex gazed over the treetops to the cloud-ringed heights in the distance. "I think we'd better head back to Inverness, Davey. It looks like a storm might be brewing."

"Nonsense," Davey told him briskly, "those mountains are always covered with mists. Besides, we're nearly there now."

"Where are we going, anyway?" Genna demanded.

Davey smiled mysteriously. "You'll see."

Genna gathered up her reins. "I'm going to turn around right now if someone doesn't tell me where we're headed."

Alex laughed. "Here," he beckoned, urging Bantigh forward through the trees. "Come and look at this."

Genna caught her breath as she saw for the first time the sparkling blue waters of Loch Ness stretching endlessly out in the distance between the green treetops. "Oh, Alex." She turned to him, dark eyes shining, not noticing the way his face lit up at her use of his name. "'Tis like a perfect jewel, set in the forest's crown."

"Welcome to Loch Ness," said Davey, clucking as he guided his horse down the hillside to the water. "The deepest loch in all of Scotland, I've heard. And some folks say there's a monster that lives in its depths, a dragon with fins and a three-mile-long tail."

"Do you think we'll see it?" she asked eagerly, following him along the trail.

"We might, lass, we might. Who's to say?"

Alex scanned the skies once more, frowning. "Davey, I think we should go back to Inverness. There are clouds moving in from the south—"

"Oh, please?" Genna begged, turning in her saddle. "I want to see the monster!"

"There is no monster; 'tis naught but an old wives' tale," he grumbled, but he started Bantigh down the hillside, casting one last anxious glance at the far-distant clouds.

"Look! A castle!" Genna pointed to the tall gray towers rising up from a bluff overlooking the lake. "Who lives there?"

"No one," Davey told her. "'Tis Castle Urquhart, of the clan of the Seafield Grants. The kinsmen were all lost at the battle of Harlaw. 'Tis said to be haunted by their ghosts, so no one will stay there now. There's plague in the dungeons too, folks say."

"Ghosts and plague and a monster!" Genna said, laughing. "I would not have missed this for the world!"

"'Twas Alley's father that led the Grants at Harlaw," Davey went on, leading the way through the sun-dappled trees. "They call it the Red Harlaw now, for 'tis said when the fight was finished the ditches ran red with blood."

"We'll not speak of it, though, will we, Davey?" There was a note of warning in Alex's tone.

"And why not, then, I ask ye? 'Twas a brave fight, to be certain. Donald's men were gravely outnumbered," he told Genna, "but they fought right fiercely, and brought down close to three thousand of the enemy."

That was the battle Alex had told her about at Stirling, Genna realized, the one mistake his father had made, and the reason he'd not wanted James to learn he'd been at Dumbarton. Her curiosity pricked, she asked, "What was the battle about?"

"Land, what else? See, Alley's mother's brother's daughter, Euphemia, inherited the earldom of Ross from her father. But she threw it all over to become a nun, and gave the earldom, not to Mary Leslie, but to her uncle John, who was already Earl of Buchan. Mary was absolutely furious, of course, and she managed to convince Donald that the land was hers by right. So he marched on Buchan and his cousins, the Albanys."

"Davey, please," said Alex. "That's enough."

"Aw, come on, Alley. 'Twas a noble fight."

"It was a rout," Alex said with sudden fury. "It was butchery, the knights swarming down on them like waves, he told me, and row after row of his brave boys falling, hacked and hewn into pieces, not screaming, he said, for that would have been beneath their honor, but just falling to the ground in pieces, covering the ground."

Davey and Genna looked at him, astonished by his vehemence. "I'm sorry," he said, more quietly. "But if you knew how he lived to regret what he'd done."

"'Tis too fine a day for talk of battles and whatnot, anyway," Davey put in quickly, swinging down from his horse as they reached the mossy banks of the lake. He helped Genna dismount, setting her down gently. "Here, come and feel the water."

She gathered up her skirts and knelt, rolling back her jacket sleeve and dangling her hand below the smooth glassy surface. "Brr!" she cried, shivering, "'tis cold as ice! Come see, Alex."

He came and knelt beside her, plunging his arms in to the elbows, splashing water on his face. Then, with a sly look at Genna, he scooped up two huge handfuls and pelted them at Davey. "Hey!" the redhead shouted, brushing off his tunic. Genna backed away hurriedly as they began to kick huge sheets of the chilly lake water at one another, teetering cautiously on the brink, laughing. The beads of water caught the sunlight and fell like sparkling diamonds through the clear bright air. Genna looked on, giggling, the momentary unpleasantness over the Harlaw forgotten, as Davey and Alex chased each other about like two mischievous ten-year-olds.

She sat on the emerald green bank and leaned against the trunk of a pale birch tree, picking idly at its loose bark, watching a red spider busily constructing a web in its leaves. The hot sun and the long ride had made her drowsy; she closed her eyes, drawing up her knees, feeling the soft warm rays against her face.

Alex looked over and winked at Davey, and they circled around behind her, swift and silent. "Do you want to see the monster, Genna?" Alex whispered at her ear. Her eyes flew open.

"Davey, what are you doing?" His hands tightened on her ankles. "Alex, let go of me!"

He grasped her by the wrists and together they swung her high into the air. "I thought you wanted to see the monster," Alex told her, grinning innocently.

"Aye," Davey put in, "close up!"

"Put me down this instant," Genna demanded, twisting in their clutches, her black eyes wide. "I can't swim, I'll drown if you throw me in there! I'll catch the ague and die!"

Alex nodded to Davey, relenting, and they let her tumble to the ground. "Ouch!" she cried angrily, rubbing her wrists, "you've hurt me. Look here, you've given me a bruise."

Alex bent over to see the spot she showed him. Genna smiled up into his concerned blue eyes, gathered her strength, and pushed him backward into the lake.

"Why, you little devil." He sat up in the marshy shallows, shaking droplets of water from his gold hair. "Toss her in here with me, Davey; she deserves to drown."

Genna scrambled to her feet and danced out of reach along the water's edge. "Do you see the monster, Alex?" she teased, laughing at his sopping tunic and plastered-down hair. "Is it big and mean?"

Alex's eyes suddenly widened; the water around him began to ripple wildly, and he let out a high-pitched scream. "It's got me, Davey!" he shouted. "Genna, it's got me!" He slipped down in the water, vanishing inch by inch. "Farewell! Farewell!" And he sank beneath the surface in a flurry of bright bubbles.

Genna stared at Davey. "He's just foolin' us," he assured her, sounding none too certain.

She looked out over the smooth, unbroken lake. "Oh, Davey, I don't know. Hadn't you better make sure?"

Alex's head bobbed up once more. "The monster!" he screamed, hands flailing wildly, and disappeared again.

Davey yanked off his boots and made a low flat dive into the water, landing with a huge splat. He paddled about for a moment, took in an enormous swallow of air, and cut cleanly down into the darkness.

Genna found herself counting her loud heartbeats as the seconds passed and neither reappeared. "Seven—eight—nine—ten—" Surely no one could hold his breath for so long!

She pulled off her own boots and stuck a stockinged toe into the water, gasping at its chillness. But it was her fault that Alex and Davey were in there. She had to try and save them. She breathed deeply, held her nose, clamped her eyes shut, and jumped.

She was standing ankle-deep in the murky lake bottom, the water lapping gently at her knees. Alex and Davey, laughing helplessly, waded toward her through the mud. "What a brave little gypsy you are, Genna," said Alex, coming toward her with his dripping arms outstretched. She sputtered wordlessly for a moment, murder in her eye.

"Good thing you held your nose, eh, Genna?" called Davey, tossing a handful of marsh grass her way.

"Now, Davey, it was a very valiant jump," Alex declared, "though a bit short of the mark." He hoisted her up in his arms, sodden skirts and all, and carried her to shore.

"You just leave me be," Genna cried, wriggling in his strong grasp. He obligingly set her down. "That was a horrid trick to play! I thought you were dead."

"I would think you'd be happy to see me dead. Then you could go riding with Argyll." Alex pulled off his soaked tunic and shirt and wrung them out, grimacing. Genna caught her breath as the sun glinted on his chest, pointing up the thatch of gold hairs there, the rippling muscles beneath his taut skin. How beautiful he was . . .

Alex saw her staring, and grinned. "What's the matter, Genna? Have you never seen a man naked before?"

Wide-eyed, she shook her head.

"Best turn about, then," Davey called cheerfully, "or you're about to see two!" Blushing, she hurriedly turned her back as they stripped off the rest of their clothing and wrung from it what water they could.

Genna looked off into the dark green woods, picturing again Alex's rippling chest, the trunk hose plastered tight across his long haunches. In that moment, with the late sun slanting across him, he had seemed suddenly magical, mysterious. Genna felt a spark of white-hot fire stirring within her. She thought of her own small white body, picured it lying close to his, and she shivered.

"Are you cold?" asked Alex, pulling a blanket from his saddlebag and wrapping it around her. He'd been more touched than he would admit by her leap into the water. Neither he nor Davey had meant for their jest to go so far.

Genna shook her head, not trusting herself to speak as his big hands folded the blanket over her shoulders. He'd looked like a god standing there, golden and omnipotent, his blue eyes fathomless as the endless waters of the lake.

"You know, Alley," said Davey, "I think you were right. It's going to rain." Genna looked up and saw dark gray clouds scuttling across the sky, crowding out the warm bright sun.

"Damn. I knew we should have turned back." Alex chewed his lip worriedly. "We won't get two miles before that storm breaks."

"No, but we might make it there to the castle," said Davey, buttoning up his clothes. "We could even spend the night there if we have to."

"Are you out of your mind?" asked Genna. Alex looked down at her.

"Afraid of ghosts?"

"Of course not!"

His blue eyes challenged her. "What *are* you afraid of?" For a moment she had the disquieting sensation that he could read her thoughts. Her chin jutted out at him.

"Nothing."

"Well, then." He lifted her up to the saddle, leapt atop Bantigh, and took off after Davey over the grassy berm.

A fine white mist rolled up from the lawns of the abandoned towers as they approached, and the skies had grown so dark that Genna could scarcely see the road ahead. The horses' hooves echoed the thunder as they pounded over the ancient causeway and into the nether yards. Weeds clutched at the walls and grew over the paving stones; the blank black holes of the casements looked like gaping mouths as lightning began to flash. The first big raindrops splashed down into a marble fountain choked with bindweed and ivy that made a fantastic mane around a huge carved lion's head.

"Damn!" Davey pushed with his shoulder at the heavy wooden door to the nearest tower, but it would not budge. "What do you think ghosts need with such a strong hurdle?"

"'Tis to keep us mortals out," said Alex, laughing. "Maybe the outbuildings are unlocked."

"We could try to climb in through a casement," Davey suggested, then shook his head, staring up at the sheer stone walls. "Nay, I guess not. Well, let's tether the horses here under the causeway, and find a sheltered place."

Alex helped Genna down from the mare, then handed her the blankets he pulled off the horses. "Hush, fine lady," he whispered in Bantigh's ear. "Hush, 'tis only a little storm." The big white horse whinnied fiercely as another huge flash of lightning lit up the shadowy yards. Thunder pealed out in a deafening crash, and then the rains began in earnest, coming down in torrential sheets that caused a din as they hit the paving stones.

"Over here!" Davey shouted from across the yards, gesturing wildly. Alex and Genna ran, slipping and sliding, across the slick stones. Davey held open a low door ahead of them, and they ducked through.

Genna stood catching her breath, staring into the pitch darkness. "Where are we?" she whispered, shivering in her soaked clothes. Her voice echoed weirdly around them.

Davey stumbled, ahead in the darkness, and muttered a curse. "I don't know, but watch out. There's some sort of high step here, and an iron rail."

Genna jumped as something fell to the floor with a mighty crash. "Davey! Are you all right?"

"Ouch! What is this bloody thing?" Genna felt Alex clasp her elbow, forging ahead. Davey was still mumbling to himself. "It feels like—wait, it is! It's a bloody candlestick, a great huge thing. And there's a candle here. What luck! Alley, have you got your flint?"

"Aye, but it's soaking wet."

"Never mind; I'll try to strike a spark on the step." They heard the harsh scrape, then saw his grinning face as the tinder flared. "There."

The wick of the candle sputtered as it caught. Genna looked about timidly in the wavering glow. "Why, 'tis a chapel!"

"So it is," said Alex, taking in the tall wooden altar, the crucifix on the wall above, and the elaborately wrought Eucharist rail.

"They must have left it open for pilgrims coming by," said Davey, setting the candle back in its stand. "Well, we'll be the pilgrims for now, shall we? Come, Genna, spread out those blankets and sit down."

"Do you think we should? It doesn't seem right, somehow." She stared out at the blank pews, the cold marble floors of the chancel, then up at the figure of the suffering Christ.

"It's a place of sanctuary, isn't it?" Alex asked, sitting on the rail and pulling off his sopping boots.

Davey wrapped a blanket over his head and followed suit, then padded noiselessly down the nave in his stocking feet, peering at the tarnished silver markers along the pews. Genna hesitated, shrugged, and pulled off her boots as well.

Alex laughed as Davey turned at the far end and headed back toward the altar. "That's perfect, Davey, that outfit. You look like a cowled monk."

"I'm your ghostly father," Davey told him, grinning. "Tell me, my son, what have you to confess?"

Alex looked at Genna, who was busily trying to mop her soaked hair dry with a blanket. It shone black as coal in the candlelight, rippling down over her shoulders in great loose waves. "What would you say, holy father, if I confessed that I find this daughter tempting me to sin?"

"Ah, I would have to absolve you," said Davey, "for she is an angel, and desire for an angel is no sin."

Genna tried to ignore their jesting, pulling off her honey brown jacket, rolling down her stockings. As she tugged the damp wool over her feet she felt Alex's eyes on her. Hurriedly she yanked the blanket up over her damp linen shirt, lifting out her hair and beginning to braid it.

"Leave your hair down, Genna," Alex said suddenly, his voice low and winning. "Let me look at you thus a little while longer. Please."

She felt a tremor run through her as she met his narrowed blue eyes. She blushed, but left off the braiding. "Your confessor's doctrine is faulty," she said softly. "Desire for an angel is sin, for did not God destroy Sodom because its men lusted after his angels?"

"That was unnatural desire," Alex pointed out, then added, "What I feel for you is woefully orthodox."

Davey cleared his throat. "What you must do then, my son, is marry her."

"I would wed her this instant," Alex said huskily, looking solemnly into her huge black eyes. "But she's told a good friend of mine that she'd sooner marry a dog."

Genna's color rose higher in her cheeks. "That's not necessarily true, milord." She twined a long strand of hair in her fingers.

"It's not?" asked Alex quickly.

"Oh, no, milord. First I would have to see the dog."

Davey laughed, and pulled the blanket tighter over his head. "Faith, I could marry the two of you now," he said, "for a feather and a coxcomb. Here, now, how does the service begin? Take her hand, Alley."

"Shouldn't we kneel, ghostly father?" he asked.

"Aye, kneel, sit, stand; it makes no difference to me. I belong to a most disorderly order." Genna giggled, then stopped abruptly as she felt Alex's long fingers curl over her hand.

"Let us pray," Davey intoned, looking down his nose at them.

"In Latin, ghostly father," Alex commanded. "Or don't you remember our schooling well enough?"

Davey wagged a finger. "Enough of your impudence, boy, or I'll make a monk out of you with my dagger! Where was I?"

"You hadn't begun yet," said Genna, smiling at his antics. It was remarkable how differently Alex behaved once you got him away from court. Davey was always amusing, of course, but she'd rarely seen Alex this way before, carefree, relaxed, no longer defensive or edgy. Why, I'll wager he's like this all the time in the Isles, she thought with surprise.

"*Kyrie eleison*," said Davey.

"*Christe eleison*," Alex responded, nudging Genna.

"*Kyrie eleison.*"

"*Gloria in excelsis deo, et in terra pax hominibus bonae voluntatis. Laudamus te, benedicimus te, glorificamus te.*" The blanket slipped over Davey's face, and he straightened it with a mock scowl. "*Gratias agimus tibi propter magnam gloriam tuam.*"

"Very, very nice, Davey," said Alex. "Father Gervase would be most proud of you."

Davey threw him a withering look. "Silence from the congregation! *Domine Deus, rex coelestis, pater omnipotens, domine filii unigenite, Jesu Christe altissime, domine Deus, agnus Dei, filius patris.*" He rapped his dagger on the candlestick, and it rang out like a bell. "*Qui tollis peccata mundi, miserere nobis, suscipe deprecationem nostram.*"

"Amen," Alex said.

Genna closed her eyes and heard the smooth slow cadence of the timeworn words as they echoed through the tiny chapel, caught the sweet cerate scent of the candle, listened as the rains clattered down on the eaves overhead. Alex's hand tightened on hers; she looked up and saw, over Davey's shrouded head, the shadowy wooden crucifix above the altar, the elongated lines of the Christ's nail-pierced hands and legs.

"*Et incarnatus est de spiritu sancto ex Maria virgine, et homo factus est,*" Davey went on quietly. "*Crucifixux etiam pro nobis sub Pontio Pilato . . .*"

A sudden gust of cold wind burst open the door, fluttering the candle; then, hinges moaning, the portal swung shut once more. Genna shivered, and Alex wrapped his arm around her. She glanced up and saw his hair still dark and curling from the rainstorm, remembered the laughter in his eyes as he rose up, grinning, from the loch, and the way the sun had gleamed on his smooth brown skin.

"Do you, Alexander, take this woman, Genevieve, to be your wife?"

"I do," said Alex, his eyes dark as night.

"And you, Genevieve, do you take this man for your husband? Do you promise to love and obey him?"

Genna pulled away from Alex, half frightened, half fasci-

nated. He had turned to face her; now he took her hand and
pressed it against his tunic. Beneath the damp wool she felt his
heartbeat, steady as drums, or bells.

"It's only a game," she protested.

He searched her small pale face. "Then why not say it?"

She wrinkled her nose at him. "All right, then. I do."

Davey's hand fluttered on her dark hair. "Let us pray. Our
Father, which art in heaven, hallowed be thy name. Thy kingdom come, thy will be done . . ."

"On earth," Alex echoed softly, "as it is in heaven."

A final bolt of lightning crackled through the skies, flashing
odd ethereal white light through the empty casements, illuminating the two supplicants at the altar, and Davey's blunt figure, wrapped in the saddle blankets.

"Forever and ever. Amen."

Davey stood silently for a moment, his ear cocked to the
rafters. "Rain's stopped," he announced at last. "I'll go see
after the horses." He moved to the door, the blanket falling
from his shoulders, and stared out at the black sky, just barely
sprinkled with stars. "Matter of fact, it looks as though 'twill
be a fine night now. I might just sleep out here, I'm thinkin',
underneath the shining moon."

He glanced back to the altar, and saw the Lord of the Isles
reach out to touch Genna's ghost-pale face. "Aye, that's just
what I'll be doin', then," he murmured. "Good night to you,
milord, milady." And God have mercy on us all, he added
silently, closing the door.

"Wife." Alex smiled, kneeling beside her, running his hand
through the thick black tresses that tumbled over her shoulders
and to the floor.

"Don't be silly, Alex." Genna heard her voice come out
thin, breathless. "Davey's no priest; he cannot marry us. It
was only playacting."

He pulled her hand over his heart once more. "Is this playacting?" he asked, as she felt his life's blood pounding. He
moved her hand lower. "Or this?"

Genna stood abruptly, awed by the power she'd sensed beneath her touch. He knelt before her, his blue eyes fired by
candlelight. "I meant what I said there, Genna. I love you. I
have since the first time I saw you, naked, white as a bird,
there at Dumbarton." He pulled her toward him, groaning,
the strength of his desire causing a physical aching in him.

"Do you and Davey play these sorts of games often?" she demanded, steeling herself aginst the tremor that ran through her at his words. "Is this the usual method of seducing a girl in the Isles?"

He laughed. "Of course not! What are you talking about?"

"I've heard the stories about the women you keep in your castles, your bastard babies!"

"Who told you such lies?"

"Everyone says it," she cried angrily. "The queen, all the women at court."

"They're wrong."

"And your own mother," she finished triumphantly.

"Oh, Christ." He got to his feet and paced down the aisle. "I haven't got any women hidden at my castles. And I have no children."

"If that's true, I'm sure 'tis not for want of trying!"

"What does it matter to you?" He turned back to her, his blue eyes blazing. "You never intended to wed me, did you, Genna? What about the game you're playing—how do you plan to have it end? Are you going to throw me over for Henry Argyll? Leave me standing at the altar?" He saw the blush on her cheeks. "So that's it. You'd enjoy that, I wager. Well, let me tell you something, Genevieve Fleming. Every night for two years I have dreamt about you. I have seen your face, your eyes, your wild hair." He reached out as if to touch her, then drew his hand back. "If love is, as they say, desperation and longing, then I am in love with you. God help me. You told me once I would wish someday I had left you there in that castle to burn. By Christ, I do."

She looked at his strained, angry face, saw the pain in his eyes, and knew she should rejoice. This was the way she'd longed to see him, stripped of his confidence, his arrogant pride. But somehow, now that she'd accomplished it, she felt awful, vicious, small.

"Why did you say what you did to the king, there at the banquet?" she whispered.

He let out a harsh little laugh. "Because I longed like the devil for it to be true. You know, Genna, before I met you I never knew what it was to be alone. And now I know you'll never love me." He turned, picked up Davey's discarded blanket, and headed for the door. "I'll leave you now."

The words that Queen Joan had once spoken flashed

through Genna's mind: "Lords are the most solitary creatures on earth . . . He touched my heart . . . because he was so very much alone."

"I'm sorry," she said contritely.

He laughed again, without humor. "Oh, no, Genna. It is I who am sorry."

She stepped forward timidly, putting a hand on his sleeve. "You misunderstand me. I meant, I am sorry to have given you the impression that I do not love you."

He faced her then, not believing what he'd heard, but with such a fierce look of hope in his eyes that she felt a sob catch in her throat. "What did you say?"

She smiled tremulously. "I am sorry to have given you the impression that I do not love you. But I have always heard . . . that is what well-bred young ladies are supposed to do."

He put his big hands on each side of her face, holding her at arm's length, drinking in the sweetness of her words. Then he seized her to him and kissed her, a long, slow, lingering kiss that made the chapel walls spin around her, the ceiling tilt crazily overhead. "Oh, God." He laughed, tracing the hollows of her throat with his mouth. His hand cupped the back of her head, catching in her long loose hair, pulling her against him as he tasted her mouth the way a man who has been in the desert tastes water, drinking love, drinking life. "Why, Genna, why?" he asked her.

And somehow she understood the question. "Because it frightened me. Because it still frightens me . . . that anyone could make me feel this way."

"Oh, my dear love." He drew her back into his arms, long fingers plucking at the buttons of her shirt, and she felt them give way one by one as his tongue plunged between her parted lips, probing gently. "My little dark dove." His hand slipped inside the shirt, covering her breast as he sighed, enflamed with desire. "Genna."

"No," she whispered, bewildered by the swirl of emotion raging through her, torn between fear and longing. "Stop, Alex, I beg you."

"I have waited two endless years to have you," he murmured, his voice low and soft at her ear. "I *beg* you, make me wait no longer." He caught her hard nipple between his fingers, rubbing gently, and she gasped as a flame of hot pleasure shot through her. She pulled away, trembling.

"No, Alex. Please."

"We're betrothed, are we not?" he asked, and smiled. "Or do you still intend not to marry me?"

"I will wed you, I promise. But now, and here . . . in the church . . . this is sacrilege, Alex. We are certain to go to hell."

"Nay, we are going to heaven," he said calmly, and yanked his tunic up over his head. Then he mounted the marble steps to the altar and draped the cloth over the crucifix. "You see? Now He will be no wiser." He came toward her, his flesh, his eyes aglow in the light from the candle. "My wife," he whispered, pulling the blouse from her shoulders, unfastening her wet skirts and letting them fall to the floor.

"No," she murmured again, as he unlaced her corset, thumbs tracing the ribbons of her pale blue veins.

He stepped back, pulling down his hose, unwinding his linen loincloth, standing before her naked, the brand of his desire pulsing between his legs. Genna turned her eyes away.

"Look at me, Genna." She shook her head, shivering. "Look at me!" he commanded, and slowly, unwillingly, she let her gaze stray back. "Look at what you do to me, Genna. Don't—don't be afraid. I need you. Oh, God, how I need you!"

Then his hands were on her, burning her skin as he lay her down on the pile of skirts and blankets, playing over her throat and hair. He tore the corset away and stared down at her white breasts glistening in the candlelight. "So beautiful," he whispered. "God, you are so beautiful." He buried his face against her breast, kissing its tip with fiery ardor. Genna felt a warmth steal over her at his touch, his nearness, as he ran his hands down over her waist and thighs, gentle as a whisper. She put her lips to his forehead, kissing him timidly, twining her fingers in his hair. Her touch made him wild, and he moaned, bringing his mouth up to meet hers, covering her nakedness with his own.

He plunged his tongue between her lips, pushing against her with growing eagerness as he felt her respond. Genna marveled at the feel of his skin against hers, the awesome power she sensed in his long back and legs. He traced the long line of her throat until his mouth once more captured her breast, rimming the dark areola, suckling with wild yearning. He moved his head across her, his gold hair tumbling over his face, and his tongue continued its plundering, his desire heightening as he heard her breath grow shallow and fast. His fingers danced at the edge of her drawers, slipping beneath, playing across the hollow of her belly. He reached lower, brushing the dark curls between her white thighs. Genna gasped as he parted her legs gently, the tips of his fingers grazing softly between, reaching deeper, touching, stroking.

"I love you, Genna." She looked up, saw him kneeling over her, eyes dark with passion, felt him pull her drawers off slowly, over her knees, her feet. Then he stared down again at her small white body, the round, full breasts, the dark wild tangle of her hair. His heart pounding madly, he brushed back the hair from her face, saw her eyes, wide and fearful. He spoke again, his voice tight with need and longing. "Is it all right, Genna? Is it all right, my love?"

"Aye," she whispered, her black eyes huge in the candlelight. "Aye, it is."

He kissed her mouth, achingly tender, and then her breast once more, groaning, before he lowered himself down onto her, cushioning her head with his hand. She shuddered as he entered her slowly, gingerly, biting her lip as unfamiliar pain burst in her belly, and he pulled back quickly, soothing her with his hand. "Stay with me, Genna," he cried softly, and she wondered what he meant until he plunged himself inside her once more. "Stay with me," he moaned, his thighs tight against her, his manhood burning within her like a fiery brand. She swallowed her cry of pain and arched back, tears in her eyes. Once more he withdrew from her, all his muscles straining, his forehead damp with sweat.

"I am with you, love," she whispered, pulling his head down to her and kissing him, her hands on his shoulders, thighs opening beneath him. He grunted, teeth clenched against her lips, pushing into her gently, deeply, so deeply she thought he must feel the stone floor at her back. He hesitated there a moment, withdrew, felt her small hands catch in his hair. His breathing was loud and ragged. And still Genna did not understand.

"Now, Genna. Now." His hands cupped her round white buttocks, pulling her off the floor against him, raising and lowering her as he moved within her, setting the pace of their journey, first slow, impossibly slow, until she matched his movements, her white legs wrapped over his back. Then he smiled, his mouth searing against her, his movements hastening, and Genna was the earth, opening beneath him, swallowing him eagerly, and he was all men, all motion, or else he was the sky. Genna caught her breath as the sensations raged through her, unknown but somehow familiar, like the faces one sees in a dream. And then there was nothing but the yearning, the swift wild ride to completion, the white fire burning within her, and the rasp of his breath at her ear. "Genna!" he cried, clutching her up to him, plunging her down with him, shuddering as she echoed him with a wordless cry. "Oh, Genna." For one long moment he held her there, feeling his hot seed pulse into her, watching her shudder beneath him, love like a fire in his eyes.

At last he released her, laid her back tenderly on the tangled blankets, smoothing her stormy hair. He lay beside her with his head propped in one hand, staring down at her long dark lashes, the fine red mouth that had just let forth those cries of shivering pleasure. She lay still and silent now, her breath growing soft and even, a faint blush yet on her cheeks.

"Alexander."

He leaned close, his mouth brushing her pale eyelids. "Yes, my love?"

She sighed. "'Tis a grievous sin we've committed."

"Aye, I suppose it is."

"And we will burn in hell for it, won't we?"

"Most likely," he allowed.

The white lids fluttered open; her eyes glowed like two live coals. She stretched out her arms. "I feared so. We've naught to lose, then. Come, love, sin with me again."

11

"Only one more week before the wedding—la, you must be skittish as a colt, Genna Fleming!" Ellie Douglas smiled at Genna across the bundle of lamb's wool she was carding. "Fancy his stepping up at the banquet and speaking out for you like that. Every time I think of it I just shiver!" She sighed, her pale eyes wide and dreamy. "Do you think I'll ever find a husband for myself?"

"Of course you will," Genna assured her. "You must be patient, that's all, Ellie, and 'tis just as Papa John used to say: Love comes to us all, sooner or later."

Ellie set down her card and reached for Genna's hand. "Tell me, though, dearie, honestly, aren't you scared to death about your wedding night? My mother's told me how horrid it is, how men are nothing but brutes when they get the—the urge." She frowned, her voice dropping low. "I'm not looking forward to it myself, I know. Just imagine having to put up with *that* whenever he comes for you!"

"Imagine," Genna echoed, with a faint smile.

Ellie shook her head, pulling sticky burrs from the card. "And then come the bairns, and 'tis nothing but mewling and suckling for years and years, and your waist goes, and your teats sag, and he starts to eye the young things again, when 'tis all his fault you got that way in the first place!"

Genna burst out laughing. "You make it sound so dreadful, Ellie, that I wonder you'd even want to find a husband!" She pulled the dried teasel blossoms across the cloth she'd woven, raising up the nap. "There. What do you think of this?"

"It's splendid," said Ellie, admiring the velvety finish. "What is it for?"

"A new saddle blanket for Alex. His old one got torn some-how." Genna blushed faintly. *And* covered with bloodstains, she thought to herself. That had frightened her, until Alex assured her it was perfectly normal. But lovemaking wasn't frightening or horrid, she longed to tell Ellie. It was the most wonderful splendid thing in the whole wide world.

Ellie leaned her head on her hand, eyes shining. "I simply can't get over it, Genna, your marrying the Lord of the Isles. It's just like a fairy tale come true."

"I know," said Genna softly. "That's exactly what it is."

Alex had insisted that they be married as soon as possible after the night they'd spent in the chapel together, and Genna, sharing his urgency, wildly in love, had agreed. As soon as they and Davey rode back to Inverness, Alex and Genna had gone to see the king and queen to ask permission to be wed the following Saturday. James and Joan, not the least surprised, had agreed. His Majesty himself would give the bride away, and Joan had immediately set her own seamstresses to work on Genna's wedding gown. After pouring out cups of wine and offering a salute to the couple, King James had pulled Genna aside and stared down into her glowing black eyes.

"Are you certain, child, that this is what you want?" Genna nodded wordlessly, too filled with happiness to speak. James smiled. "All right, then. I think my young cousin a most fortunate man." His auburn-bearded face grew solemn. "He has shown proof, Genna, that he can be a great lord someday. He has courage, and heart, and a wisdom beyond his years. I only met his father once, when I was a child, but I remember that he impressed me in the same way."

"It would please Alex to hear you say that."

James frowned. "I know some say he reminds them too much of Donald—his pride, his impetuosity." He shrugged, and took Genna's hand. "We will try, together, to keep him from repeating the mistakes of his father. He has already avoided the greatest of those in choosing you to wed." Genna, uncertain what the king meant, nonetheless acknowledged the compliment with a smile.

"I would like him to stay here at court with us," James went on, stroking his beard, "for a year or two at least. I was most impressed with his handling of the clan chiefs. We have much to learn from the Lord of the Isles."

"I know Alex will be happy to accept your gracious invitation."

The king smiled wryly. "Do you? I'm none too certain of that. These men of the Isles are a strange breed; they hate to be away from their homes. However, one advantage of being a king is that even the most gracious invitation cannot be turned down."

Genna laughed. "Then Your Majesty has naught to fear."

"We shall see," said James, his voice thoughtful. "We shall wait, and see. Alexander!"

"Yes, Your Majesty?" Alex joined them, smiling, and put an arm around Genna's waist.

"I believe we should have some sort of tournament to celebrate your nuptials. Do you suppose your clan chiefs would be willing to put on an exhibit of these games I've heard tell of?"

"Golf, perhaps?" Alex asked, grinning.

"No, no, not golf. My entire kingdom is already far too fond of golf. We're not going to repel an invasion of the French by swinging clubs, are we? No, your other games. You—ah —you throw trees, I believe I've heard, and kegs of beer."

Alex bowed, his blue eyes twinkling. "On occasion, we do."

"Good, good. Let us see some of that, then. Perhaps such an exhibition will tempt my own courtiers to spend less time curling their hair and more building up muscle. Shall we say two days hence?"

"Very good, Your Majesty."

"Well, get along then, the both of you. Oh, and Genna . . ." She turned back to the king; his face was set in an expression of fatherly sternness. "No more outings in the woods with him until *after* the wedding, do you hear?"

Genna blushed bright red. "Yes, Your Majesty!" But she saw that his gray eyes were merry.

A tentative knock at the door brought Genna, blushing again at the memory, back to the present. She set down the teasel and cloth and went to answer. Mary Leslie stood framed by the doorway, dressed in sky blue silk and one of the new horned headdresses that were said to be the latest fashion from France. Genna stifled a giggle; to her, they made women look like oxen.

"Good afternoon, madam."

"Oh, dear, I don't want to interrupt your work," said Mary, smiling charmingly as she surveyed the room strewn with wool and fluff. "But I wondered if I might have a word or two with you—alone."

"But of course. Ellie, would you please excuse us?"

Ellie stood up quickly, smiling. "Certainly. I imagine you two must have much to talk about!" She hurried out.

Mary pulled the door shut. Genna indicated a chair. "Won't you sit down, milady? Would you care for some ale, or wine?"

"I think not." Mary settled into the seat, carefully arranging her full skirts, while Genna perched nervously on her nearby stool. She'd not spoken to the Countess of Ross since the night of the banquet, but she remembered all too clearly how the woman's bitter words had unsettled her. Her few brief encounters with Mary Leslie had taught Genna a single lesson: one never knew what to expect.

The countess opened her mouth to speak, hesitated, and then gave a pretty little laugh. "This isn't an easy task, I'm afraid, Mistress Fleming. Alexander has told me that you and he are in love, that you plan to marry quite soon."

Genna inclined her head, smiling. "I hope our plans meet with your approval, milady."

"Well, that is just the point, you see. They don't. Not at all."

Genna stared at the woman, black eyes wide. "Might I ask why?"

Mary tossed back her yellow curls. "Faith, 'tis nothing against you, my dear. I think you're a lovely girl. Very lovely, indeed. But, you see, I made Alexander's father a promise many years ago. And I'd like very much to be able to keep that promise."

"What promise?"

Mary leaned back in her chair. "You never knew Donald, of course, but he was a proud, strong man, very much like Alexander. And he was most proud of his kingdom, his homeland. The Isles. Many's the time he said to me, 'Mary, my dove, if I've one wish in this world, it's that our son be wed to a lass from the Isles." Mary tapped her ivory fan against her palm. "And when he lay on his deathbed, gravely ill, he called me to his side and pulled me very close to him, and made me swear on my life that I would see Alexander did so. 'Don't let our son marry a stranger, Mary,' he whispered. 'Promise me . . . swear it.'" She dabbed at her eyelids with the edge of a delicate kerchief. "You see the position I'm put in, don't you, my dear? Alexander may well believe that he loves you. But how can I go against the final wish, the last mortal request, of my beloved husband?"

Genna stared into the fire that danced in the hearth. "Does Alex know of his father's request?" she asked tentatively.

"Good heavens, no, my dear. I never had reason to tell him. Up until now, he has always been content with his . . . ah . . . his paramours at home in the Isles. Lord, he must have a dozen or so, scattered in his different castles. He never seemed to feel a need to legitimize his children."

"Alex told me that he has no children," Genna said evenly.

Mary raised one pale blond eyebrow in disbelief, then laughed. "Well, of course, my dear, he would say that to *you*. The point is, what am I to do? I made a solemn pledge to Donald that if Alexander wed, it would be to a woman of the Isles. I had hoped that when he returned to Mull a year ago he would forget you. But he is so utterly besotted that you yourself are my last hope. I beg you, will you not tell him that you cannot wed him?"

"Milady." Genna was hurt, and confused. "You must believe that I sympathize with you, that I would never willingly cause you pain." She swallowed, gathering her courage. Was this why the countess had been so cold to her? "But I know how Alex loved and honored his father. And I believe his father would have wanted, above all, for Alex to be happy. I intend to make him happy. I am sorry, but I must refuse your request."

Mary got up from her chair and stood for a moment, her back turned to Genna. "I beg you to reconsider," she said finally.

"I—I cannot, milady. I am too much in love with him."

Mary whirled around, pale eyes narrowed and glittering. "Very well, then. I will give you five hundred marks for your solemn promise not to marry my son."

Genna nearly fell off her stool in astonishment. "I beg your pardon?"

"All right, seven hundred," Mary said briskly, "but not a penny more. All you must do is sign this paper." She drew it forth from her girdle. "It states that you release him from all pledges he has made to you, and that you will not, now or ever, marry him."

Genna accepted the paper she was handed and stared at it in shock. At last she found her tongue. "Is this some sort of jest, milady? Do you honestly believe I would do such a thing?" Her black eyes filled with tears. "'Tis plain you do not

think me good enough to marry your son. But to imply that I
would . . . I would . . ." She bit her lip. "You do not know either me or Alex very well."

"I know everyone has his price," Mary said calmly. "One
thousand marks."

"Why do you hate me so?" Genna whispered, meeting
Mary's imperious blue gaze.

"That is neither here nor there. I love my son, and I know
what is best for him. I will not see his life ruined by this hasty,
imprudent marriage. For his sake, accept my offer."

"I don't think you do know what is best for Alex," Genna
said slowly. "And you cannot know how much I love him, nor
he me." She crumpled the hateful paper in her hand and
tossed it onto the fire. "That is what I think of your offer."

Mary's mouth was tight with rage. "You'll regret that, you
foolish girl. Twelve hundred marks."

Genna felt her own temper flaring. "Madam," she said, her
voice shaking, "I regret that you find the prospect of this marriage so unpleasant. I find the thought of you as my mother-
in-law equally so." She went to the door and pulled it open.
"I'll ask you to leave now."

Mary stood for a moment, the muscles of her jaw working
furiously. Then she swept grandly past Genna and into the
hall. "Wait and see," she called over her shoulder, her tone low
and threatening. "Wait and see if you wed him, girlie. There is
more than one way to skin a cat."

Genna slammed the door shut and leaned against it, feeling
sick to her stomach. What on earth was the matter with that
woman? Why did she have the sense there was more at play
here than a mother's natural concern for her son, more even
than Mary's desire to meet her husband's last request?

Because there had been hatred, malevolence in the countess's cold blue eyes, and something else . . . something like fear.

But why should a great lady like Mary Leslie be afraid of
her? Genna tapped the prickly teasel spines against her cheek.
Should she tell Alex what had happened? Lord, that was no
way to begin a marriage, by complaining about your mother-
in-law. Whenever Alex spoke of Mary Leslie it was with a sort
of bemused regret; Genna knew that the countess had spent
little time with her son and daughter while they were growing
up. He rarely saw her now, Alex had said, unless she needed

money. Mary preferred to spend her time with a gay, wild crowd, with Argyll and his friends.

Genna sighed, thinking wryly that for once in her life she was grateful to have no family to deal with. It would be hard enough adapting to all of Alex's kin. Especially his sister Meggie, who *was* close to Alex. What if she turned out to be like the countess? Well, at least she didn't have to face that hurdle until after the wedding. There simply wasn't time for her to come to court by Saturday. Alex had said that if the king would grant him leave he'd take Genna to Mull for a few weeks as soon as he could, so that she could meet Meggie and all the other members of the clan, and see the Isles at last.

They would have time alone together then, he'd promised last night, as they sat in a windowseat in the corridor just off the Great Hall. Time to talk, to learn all there was about one another. Time to make love for hours on end; Genna shivered with delight, remembering the way his mouth had touched hers then, gently insistent, his breath quick with desire. His hands had slid over her breasts, plucking at the nipples until they grew stiff beneath his fingers, until Genna had begged him, half laughing, half wild with longing, to stop.

"I love you, Genna," he'd whispered. "God, if you only knew how I love you."

"But I do," she'd told him, smiling, tracing those wide, full lips with her fingertips. "The same way that I love you." He had pulled her into his lap, wrapping her in his arms, hands caught in her hair, and kissed her again.

Ellie's head popped through the doorway. "Did you finish?"

"What?" Genna started up from her stool.

"The countess—did she leave?"

"Oh. Oh, yes, she's gone."

Ellie came and sat in the armchair, resuming her carding. "What did she want, anyway?"

Genna hesitated, then laughed, smoothing the nap of the blanket. "Oh, nothing, really. Nothing at all." The chapel bells tolled out three slow chimes. "Good Lord, is it so late already? I promised Alex I would bring him his supper at two!"

"Bring it to him? Where is he?"

"Up in the jousting yards somewhere, making ready for the tournament."

"Are the clan chiefs really going to throw trees?" asked Ellie, wide-eyed.

Genna laughed. "That's what Alex says!" She pulled a short black surcoat over her yellow dress, fastening it at the throat with her brooch, then picked up the basket of meats and bread and ale she'd had Katy bring up and hurried out to meet him. As she ran through the castle yards toward the jousting arena, she saw Mary Leslie and Henry Argyll, their heads close together, meandering along the path to the gardens. I wonder what they're up to, she thought, then shrugged her shoulders and went on.

The vast green tilting yard was empty, and so was the bear-baiting pit beyond. Genna set her basket down and shielded her eyes from the bright afternoon sun that slanted through the surrounding forests. "Alex!" she called, turning in a wide circle. "Alex, where are you?"

"Genna! Is it two already?"

He appeared at the edge of the dark green forest, and she caught her breath at the sight of him, gleaming in the sun. He wore tight brown leather breeches that rode low on his hips, and he'd taken off his shirt and tied it about his waist. His long bronzed torso shone slick with sweat, and his gold hair hung over his shoulders in long dark curls. He grinned when he saw her. "What are you staring at?"

She ran to him, laughing. "You. You look so—so splendid."

He kissed her full on the lips, lifting her into the air and twirling her so that her skirts spun out in a wide bell. "No, love. You look splendid. I look like a stablehand, I imagine."

"A most regal stablehand," she teased him, pushing back his damp curls from his forehead. "I'm sorry I'm so late. I—I had a visit from your mother."

"Oh? What did she have to say? Wait, first come see what I've done." He set her on her feet, then pulled her through an arbor of leafy branches to a clearing beyond. "Well, what do you think?"

"What do I think of what?" Genna surveyed the pile of thick branchless logs on the ground. "There's nothing here but a load of stripped trees."

"Not trees. Cabers," he corrected her.

"What's a caber?"

"A stripped tree."

"Oh, you." She yanked at the thatch of gold curls on his chest, and he winced, jumping back.

"Why, you delightfully vicious creature. How would you like it if I went around grabbing at your chest?"

"King James said I'm not to play in the woods with you anymore." She pirouetted away from him, black eyes flashing, then giggled as he caught her by the waist and pulled her into his arms, clutching her close to him, his mouth lingering on hers.

"Mmm." He licked her ear. "How many more days until we are wed?" His hand slipped over her breast, gently kneading the soft flesh there, as he lavished a long trail of kisses down her throat.

"Too many." She sighed, closing her eyes, drinking in the scent of him, warm and heady and male. She could feel the bulge of his manhood straining at his breeches, the taut muscles of his shoulders rippling beneath her hands. She looked up at him, saw his lazy-lidded eyes gleam, narrowing, and she shivered, knowing what he was thinking. Resolutely, she pushed him away. "But you can wait, can't you?"

He grimaced. "I've been waiting, haven't I? What do you think drove me out here into the wood, cutting trees all day?" But she looked so fragile and innocent, staring up at him, wide-eyed, that he relented. "Well, I can wait a bit longer, I suppose. But much more and King James will find his whole forest laid waste."

"Do you mean to tell me you cut all those trees yourself? Why didn't you have the servants help you?"

He grinned. "I told you. I've been working off lust. And besides, I needed the exertion. This court life makes a man soft."

"Where are you soft?" she scoffed, running her eyes over his lean, strong body.

"I'd rather show you where I'm not," he murmured, taking her hand, pressing it to his breeches.

"Alex."

"I know, I know. What did you ask me? Oh, what's a caber. A caber is a tree like this, twenty feet long, with the branches off." He picked up a long straight-edged axe and idly chipped away some bark.

"And what does one do with it, pray tell? Build a stockade?"

"One throws it," he said, mimicking her supercilious tone.

"Oh, Alex, for heaven's sake."

"No, 'tis true. In the Isles we use the caber toss to tell when a youth is ready to go into battle."

Genna eyed the sturdy logs. "But *how* do you throw them?"

"I'll show you." He scuffed the soles of his boots against a log, hitched up his leather breeches and tightened his belt, then hefted the trunk in his arms. "Come back to the jousting yard; I need more room."

"Alex, you'll kill yourself carrying that thing!" She followed in amazement as he threaded his way through the forest, still clutching the enormous tree.

As they cleared the edge of the wood Genna saw a small knot of courtiers, Henry Argyll in the lead, sauntering toward them across the green lawn, their bright silk doublets and ribbands fluttering in the breeze. Their voices drifted over the grass as they gathered atop a knoll to observe Alex, who was standing the caber on end.

"Why do look there," she heard someone call derisively. "If it isn't the island Hercules."

Alex flushed, reaching up to steady the pole.

"Nay, nay, Lucien," Argyll chided, in his broad affected drawl, "'tis the Lord of the Piles." A burst of raucous laughter rang out on the air.

Genna put a hand on Alex's shoulder. "Come away, love. You can show me later."

"I'll show you now," he insisted, hoisting up the tree trunk and clasping it low against his belt. The muscles in his forearms bulged, and the cords in his neck were like thick ropes as he balanced the log in the air.

"Giving new meaning to the word 'loggerhead,'" Argyll called, sweeping down in a low bow to his friends, "may I present Alexander Mac Donald!"

Genna heard a low rumble as Alex gripped the tree trunk tightly, ran toward the courtiers, bending low, then heaved it high in the air. The caber hung for a moment in the bright sunlight, then landed with a thud, scattering the courtiers who had stood on the knoll but a moment before.

"Oh, well done, well done." Argyll stepped forward, applauding with slow insolence. "My, what quaint customs these islanders have. I reckon they begin with twigs and work up."

Alex's spine stiffened. "What do you want, Argyll?" he called across the yard.

Argyll's fox brown eyes considered him with cool disdain. "Are you addressing me, Your Logship?"

"I am."

"I see." Argyll took another cocky step forward, idly swinging his sheathed sword. "I wonder if you'd be so good as to confirm a point for a history of Scotland that I'm writing. Is it true that you learned about throwing trees from your father?"

"Aye. What of it?"

Argyll knockéd off a dandelion head with his sword. "And your father, did he learn about trees by running like a rabbit to take cover at the Red Harlaw?"

Alex's blue eyes flashed with cold fury. "Bastard," he spat.

Argyll turned to his friends. "Did you hear what this heathen called me? By God, I've a mind to challenge him to a duel."

"Nothing would please me more, you scum."

"Alex," Genna whispered, "you gave King James your pledge there would be no dueling."

"To hell with the king."

"Oh, my, my, my." Argyll arched an eyebrow at his companions. "You heard that? You are my witnesses?" They nodded, laughing. "You know, Mac Donald," he went on, smoothing down his wide ruffled cuffs, "it's good you can manage to get that tree up. From what your betrothed tells me, it's about all that you can."

Alex turned to Genna in shocked disbelief. "What the bloody hell!"

She backed away, frightened by his rage. "Alex, please! You know he is lying!"

"Have you ever noticed," Argyll called coolly, "how much she enjoys spending time in the gardens? Especially at night, it seems. Have you never wondered why?"

"Alex, I swear before God, he is lying!"

"Did she tell you she was a virgin that night in the chapel, Mac Donald? I thought as much. She used that same line with me, and with most of my friends."

"Alex, please." She flinched as he raised up his hand.

Argyll lopped off another dandelion, moving closer. "She's good," he said thoughtfully, "though not so good as some I've

had. Do you know what I do like, though, Mac Donald? That
little shiver she gives before she spreads her legs."

"You deceiving bitch," said Alex from between clenched
teeth. He slapped her across the face, a sharp stinging slap that
dropped her to her knees.

"Oh, Alex, no!" She screamed as he tore off across the
yards toward Argyll, toppling him with a flying hurdle that
knocked the courtier facedown in the fresh green grass. Argyll
scrambled to his feet with a snarl.

"Lucien. Give him your sword."

Lucien obligingly tossed the weapon at Alex's feet. Genna
held her breath as he reached down, his long fingers closing on
the hilt. Argyll pulled on his gloves and brandished his own
sword, daring Alex forward. "Come on, then, you heathen
coward. Let's see if you've ever learned to duel."

Genna watched in horror as Alex sprang toward him, lightning quick movements belying his size. The blades crossed,
clashing with the hard bright clamor of steel on steel. Argyll's
thin face was stamped with confidence as he took his stance,
hand on hip, and broke the deadlock with a laugh. Alex lunged
forward, raining down a hail of driving blows that the courtier
met and countered with slashing force. The yards rang with
the sound of violent thrusts and parries, the scuffle of boots in
the grass and hard, panting breaths. A flock of startled ring-
doves flapped into the sky as the duelists scythed a path
through their hiding place, as Alex grasped his sword hilt with
both hands and slashed out wildly at Argyll's grinning face,
those taunting fox brown eyes.

The sudden sharp blast of a clarion split the air. Genna
drew in her breath as she saw the dozens of riders bearing
down on the knoll, James atop his gray steed in the lead. The
hunting party drew nearer; Argyll stepped back from the fight
and sheathed his sword with a tight, sly smile.

The king stared down over the hillside, fire in his eye.
"Who began this fray?" he roared, his voice like thunder.

Argyll wiped a bit of grass from his boot. "The villain Mac
Donald, Your Majesty. He . . . ah, he made some untoward
comments about you. In fact, he said you could go to hell.
These men here heard him; they'll back me up."

"That's right, Your Majesty," Lucien put in, and the others
chimed in their assents.

"Silence!" James shouted, his beard thrust out like a knife. "Alexander Mac Donald, what have you to say for yourself?"

Alex considered Argyll and his companions with cool steady eyes. Then he met the king's furious stare. "Nothing," he said, and turned away.

"Nothing?" the king echoed, his voice rising incredulously. "The man has accused you of a capital crime, and you've nothing to say? Surely he provoked you somehow! Alexander, I order you to defend yourself!"

Very slowly and calmly, Alexander began to walk away.

"I order you both to kneel and crave my pardon!" the king cried angrily.

Argyll dropped to his knees with alacrity. "Forgive me, Your Majesty, but I sought only to defend your honor..." His words trailed off as he saw that the king paid him no heed; his gray eyes were locked on Alex's retreating figure.

James leaned on his pommel, feeling the thin circlet of gold on his head as heavy as lead. Is this the way it begins? he wondered wearily, eyeing his cousin's magnificent half-naked body, aglow with strength and sweat. With one man's defiance, proud, intractable? Is this the way rebellion begins? He stared down at Alexander Mac Donald and saw the specter of a crown in that wild gold hair; he shook his head to clear away the vision, and saw another: a kingdom on fire.

He felt Joan's hand on his arm, turned, saw her pleading face. "There is more at stake here than you know," he told his wife fiercely.

Joan gestured to Genna, still kneeling in the grass. "And more than you know as well."

The terror in the girl's black eyes, her stark white face, moved James to pity. "Alexander," he called again, more softly. He turned back briefly. "Will you not kneel to me even for her sake?"

Alex looked at Genna, and she saw cold hatred in his steely blue eyes. "Especially not for her sake," he spat, then wheeled about and walked on.

James drew himself up in his saddle, thunder once more in his voice. "Then back to the Isles with you! And let every subject in the realm know that you are a dead man, should you set foot in my dominion again!"

Alex's unhurried pace never wavered as he strode toward the castle gates.

"Your Majesty," Argyll cried, "I demand you have him beheaded! I demand satisfaction."

"Oh, shut up, Henry!" James was anxiously watching the gate. After a moment Alex reappeared, leading Bantigh by her bridle. He cast a last glance back toward the jousting yard, leapt into his saddle, and rode off into the west, into the setting sun.

James chewed his lip, longing to give the order to pursue, call him back, forget, forgive. Joan turned to her husband, disappointment plain in her eyes. "He will not return," she said, "'tis too late." And then added, as a spiteful afterthought, "Your Majesty." She dismounted, handing her reins to a servant, and went to put her arms around Genna, leading her gently back to Inverness.

Mary Leslie sat atop her dainty roan mare, twirling an ivory fan. "Oh, dear, dear," she murmured to those around her. "What a pity. What a perfectly dreadful shame."

"What am I going to do, Davey?" Genna lay on her bed, her face swollen with tears, clutching the bedclothes in her hands. "Whatever am I going to do?"

"Ach, now, Genna, 'tis not so bad as all that," he said with hearty assurance. "This will all blow over in no time, you'll see. Alley'll be forgiven and come right back to court."

"You don't believe that anymore than I do," she told him fiercely. "He'll never come back, not if he believed Argyll's filthy lies! Oh, how could he be so stupid? I hate him!" And she threw herself facedown on the pillows in a new torrent of tears.

"Then just forget him, Genna! Christ, if the man's such a bloody fool as to listen to that weasel."

She drew herself up on her elbows, black eyes flashing. "How dare you say such things about him?" she cried. "And you call yourself his best friend!"

Davey shook his head with perplexity, then burst out laughing. "Well, make up yer mind then, darlin'! Women! Honest to God."

"Just what do you find so amusing?" she demanded. "'Tis your lord the king has banished."

"That's bloody fine by me. I was more than ready to get back to my Meggie. Alley and me never did fit in here, so I say the hell with it. Who needs this old court?" He stuck out his tongue and made an inelegant noise.

Genna started to giggle, hiccuped, and let out a long low moan. "Oh, Davey, he doesn't love me, does he?"

He smoothed back her tangled black hair. "Of course he loves you, darlin'. It's just that red-hot temper of his. He doesn't think things through before he acts."

"Well, I'm proud of him." Genna thrust out her little chin. "Why should he have knelt down to the king? He'd done nothing wrong."

Davey sighed in exasperation. "What would it have cost him, Genna, just this once in his life to give in?" He plucked his cap from the bedpost and twirled it on his thumb. "I'll be off to Mull, then, and try and talk some sense into his big thick head."

"Davey." She raised herself up on her elbows again. "Take me with you."

"Why would you want to go, darlin'? After he shamed you so."

"But don't you see?" She reached for his hand, black eyes pleading. "I've got to tell him Argyll was lying, tell him that I still love him, that I forgive what he did. Oh, I couldn't bear to lose him again!"

"But what about the king, and Joan, and Ellie and Katy? All your friends are here!"

Genna sniffed. "Who needs such fair-weather friends?"

"James won't give you permission to go."

"Oh, hang James! He's a bloody idiot!"

"You're talkin' treason, Genna," said the redhead, but there was a hint of a smile at the corners of his mouth.

"Please, Davey. I'll never, ever, ever ask you for anything again."

He wagged his head. "You don't know what you're askin'. 'Tis at least a week's ride for a man, let alone a wee thing like you, through big dark forests filled with bears and robbers. And wolves."

"I'm not afraid," said Genna. "I won't be any trouble."

"You wouldn't be able to take more with you than the clothes on yer back. You'd have to leave behind all yer fine gowns, yer hats, yer loom."

"Oh, no!" Genna paused, dismayed. "I couldn't bear to

leave my loom behind, Davey." She bit her lip, worried. "There must be some other way."

He rubbed at his chin. "Well, I suppose we *could* take a ship . . . if we could find one headin' that way, of course, and if the captain was willin' to take on passengers."

"That's it!" she cried, black eyes aglow. "I shall sail to the Isles, to Alexander, like Cleopatra to Caesar."

"Darlin'," said Davey, "have you ever been on a ship?"

"Well . . . not exactly." Her enthusiasm faltered, but only momentarily. "I was on a barge once, though, on the River Clyde."

Davey reached forward and cupped her chin in his hand, searching her small, eager face. "Are ye sure this is what you're wantin'? 'Tis no easy life in the Isles, not even for the wife of a laird. There'll be no scores of servants to wait on ye, no gay silk stockings. Yer life will be different."

"I don't care," she insisted, tossing her head.

His voice grew softer. "And you're never going to change Alley, you know. Not ever. There will always be certain things that he puts afore you. Can you live with that, Genna?"

"I'll have to," she said quietly. "Because I simply cannot live without him."

For a long moment he was silent, staring down at her. "All right," he said finally. "If I didn't take you, you'd probably be so rash as to set out on yer own."

"Oh, Davey, thank you!" She flung her arms around his neck and kissed him. "When can we go?"

"I'll head down to the Firth in the mornin' to see about a ship." He saw the start of her pout, and laughed. "Nah, not tonight, Genna. We will both need a good long rest."

"Oh, Davey, I won't sleep a wink!" she said fretfully. But oddly enough, she did.

Part III

The Road to the Isles

12

Genna groaned as the little provisions ship pitched high atop a wave, teetered for a moment on the crest, and then came plunging down with a sickening roll. The air in her tiny cabin below decks was unbearably stifling, dense and stale, but she did not trust her own legs to negotiate the passageway and ladder that would take her above. The last time she'd tried, she'd gotten no farther than the cabin hatch before collapsing back onto her berth, defeated by the awful retching that came with seasickness.

It had been seven days since she and Davey had sailed out of Moray Firth aboard the *Dearg Lomond*, and four since they'd rounded the northernmost tip of Scotland and headed down through the Minch. Davey had coaxed her into coming on deck to catch her first glimpse of the Isles—Lewis, he said it was—and Genna had obediently struggled out of her bed, clinging to him tightly, and followed him up the shaky ladder. She'd tried to pay attention as he pointed out the sharp rocky coastline that just pierced through the dense morning mists, but "Fine, Davey, fine" had been all she could gasp out, the deck heaving wildly beneath her feet, before she begged him, "Please take me back to bed."

"Ooh . . ." Genna moaned again as another wave of nausea swept through her, matching the waves that lapped against the ship's red-painted hull. Wrapping the blanket more tightly over her head, she huddled against the wall, curled up in misery, and prayed for sleep.

"Genna?" Davey's rap at the hatch was hesitant. "Can I come in, darlin'?" He took her pitiable groan for assent and backed into the cabin, a high-sided tray in his hands. "I brought you some nice hot beef broth."

He turned away politely as she vomited weakly into the

167

bucket beside the bed. "Oh, Davey," she moaned finally, "Take it away!"

"You've got to eat, darlin', or you'll fade away to nothin'." He shoved a stool over to the bed with his knee, set down the tray, and scooped up a spoonful of the warm liquid. "Here, open up for me now, there's a good girl."

She shook her head in anguish. "I can't, Davey. I simply can't."

"Poor thing," he clucked, smoothing back tangled hair from her damp brow. "Poor wee thing. I've never in my life seen anyone so seasick. Are you sure you're not with child?"

"I'm not—" She stopped, clutching her stomach as another swell of queasiness swept through her. "Of course I'm not with child. I'm just not used to ships. I think the captain is doing this to me on purpose!"

He laughed. "Diarmot Mac Duff is the finest captain in all the Isles, Genna. We were lucky to find him; he usually ships between the Far Isles and Skye. Nah, I'm afraid you can't blame Diarmot. P'raps Italians just don't take to the sea."

"Oh, Davey, how much longer till we get there? Tell me the truth."

"Any time now, dearie, any time now." But he chewed his lip worriedly; they had at least three more days to sail. And so far the weather had been calm and peaceable; God forbid they should run into a storm!

The ship shuddered beneath a sudden gust of wind, the planks creaking wildly. Genna tugged the pillow over her face with a wretched whimper.

Davey sighed, pulled the pillow away, and swabbed her forehead with a moist cloth, not knowing what else to do. "You must try not to think about bein' sick," he urged her. "Think of happy things. Think of seein' Alley again."

"I don't want to see him," she groaned, writhing beneath his ministering hand. "And I don't want him to see me. Oh, Davey, I wish I were dead."

"Nay, you mustn't talk like that, darlin'. Remember, it was your decision that we sail."

"You didn't tell me I'd be sick as a dog the whole time!"

"Well, how was I to know? Come, sit up and take a bit of broth, and I'll tell you about the time Alley and me won the Portree Races."

"There's only one thing I want to hear from you, Davey Mac Leod, and that's for you to say 'Genna, we're there.'"

"Soon, lovey, soon," he promised, standing helplessly, gazing down at her wan white face and wild hair. "I'll just leave the broth here then, shall I? And come back a bit later, when you're feelin' better."

"I'm *never* going to feel better," she said with conviction.

Davey smiled and went out, drawing the hatch closed gently. Genna pulled herself up on her elbows, stuck out her tongue at the bowl of broth beside her, and curled back up on the bed.

Through the North Minch the *Dearg Lomond* sailed, through the Little Minch and into the Sea of the Hebrides, past Skye and Rhum and around the point of Coll, day and night merging together for Genna into one endless voyage of woe. And then, just as the sky grew pale with light on the tenth morning, Davey came to her cabin and announced, "We're there."

Genna groaned, rolling over. "Go away, Davey."

"No, I mean it! We'll anchor at Tobermory in an hour or so."

For the first time in more than a week he saw a sparkle of life in her dark eyes. "Don't lie to me, now, Davey."

"I'm not lyin'. Come on deck and see for yourself."

Genna dragged herself out of bed, still wrapped in blankets, and grudgingly let him lead her through the passageway and up the ladder again. The dawn sky was overcast and dark, and Genna shivered as she looked across the gray water to the dim, shadowy coastline. "It doesn't look very welcoming, does it?" she said grimly.

Davey laughed. "That's only because it's so cloudy. You'll see when the sun comes out, 'tis the loveliest place you can imagine."

"Is that so? How far to this port you spoke of?"

"Only a few leagues more."

"And how far from there to Alex's castle?"

"Hardly any distance at all."

"How far is 'hardly any distance,' pray tell?"

He looked out over the cliffs. "Oh, ten or a dozen miles."

"Good. We should sail in by midday, then."

"Ah, Genna, I was meanin' to speak to you of that. The captain says he can take us no farther than Tobermory. 'Tis market day there, you see, and he has to unload, and sell his goods."

"But how will we get to Alex's castle if Captain Mac Duff doesn't take us?"

"We'll just have to hire a carriage," he said quickly. "Now, why don't you go below and get your things together, put on a fresh gown and fix your hair?"

"All right." She hesitated, looking up at him. "Davey?"

"Aye, darlin'?"

"I—I haven't been very good company on this voyage, I know. I'm sorry."

"Faith, it wasn't your fault you were ill. You'll be fine the moment you set foot on dry land. Go, now, change your dress."

"I will." She reached up to give him a kiss on the cheek. "Thank you for putting up with me."

"Bosh, 'twas nothin'." But he crossed his fingers as he watched her make her way below. We should have put in to Skye for a few days, he thought. I could have fattened her up a wee bit, put the shine back into her curls. But she'd been in such a rush to get here . . . Well, no sense crying over milk that was spilt. He stood at the stern and watched as the shoreline slipped by in a slow prospect of ocher and dun and gray.

Two hours later Diarmot Mac Duff ordered the sails hauled in as they glided into the sound through the rocky headlands between Mull and the mainland. Davey felt his breath catch as it always did when he saw the trim cottages that rose up from the smooth dark waters of Tobermory Bay, sheltered against wind and storm by the kidney-shaped island of Calbh. He lent a hand with the oars to help guide the ship into place along the weathered docks, then went below to bring Genna ashore. He found her sitting disconsolately on the edge of the bed, bright gowns and petticoats and boots strewn throughout the cabin.

"Oh, Davey," she wailed as he entered, "nothing fits me: What am I going to do?"

"What do you mean, Genna? The dress you have on looks fine."

"Can't you see?" She turned around, pinching her dress tight at the waist in great handfuls. "I look like a plucked chicken! I'm not going to let him see me this way, Davey. I want to go back."

"Back where?" he asked, astonished.

"Anywhere!" Huge tears rolled down her hollowed cheeks.

"Now, darlin'." He sat beside her on the bed, putting his arm around her. "You're every bit as pretty as ever, though 'tis true you could use fillin' out. But I swear to you, Alley will notice nothing amiss. Why, he'll be so happy to see you, he'll think you a vision from heaven."

She sniffed back a tear. "Do you promise?"

"Aye. Now, put yer stockings and shoes on, and yer cloak, for there's a brisk wind blowin', and I'll help you pack up your things." He began to cram the dresses back into her trunks as she dutifully buckled her shoes.

"Tell them to be careful unloading my loom, Davey. And don't crumple that silk; I'll never get it flat! Oh, and have you got a looking glass I can borrow?'

"Ah . . . nah, darlin'," he lied quickly, "'tis bad luck to carry them aboard a ship. Come, now, we want to get to the castle by dark." He hoisted a trunk to his shoulder and followed her up to the deck.

Genna gave the captain a tremulous smile as he helped her onto the docks. "Thank you very much, Captain Mac Duff. It was a most *unusual* experience to sail with you."

"Aye, mum, well, I'm only sorry 'twas so rough a voyage through the Minches for a bit there."

"Was it?" Genna asked blithely. "I hardly noticed."

Mac Duff grinned at Davey. "As you say, mum. Well, Davey, fare thee well. Give my best to the laird, now."

"I will, Diarmot. Thank you kindly for your help."

Davey tossed the bags up into the packed-earth yard above the docks, then helped Genna negotiate the narrow rocky path to the top. Men and women and children were swarming down to the docks to bargain and trade with the captain, and Davey hastily pulled her out of the way of the crowds. "Just sit here with yer baggage for a bit," he told her, lifting her up atop the crates that held her loom, painstakingly dismantled and packed, "and I'll see what . . . ah, what transport's to be had. Back in a moment!" Genna nodded uncertainly and gathered her skirts together in her lap.

A cluster of giggling boys, wide-eyed and unkempt, darted toward her across the yards, calling out in high, lilting voices in a language Genna had never heard. She drew back nervously as they reached out to touch her rich blue velvet cloak with their grimy hands, fondling her long black braids. Most had greenish brown eyes, like Davey, with sun-darkened freckled skin. Genna tried unsuccessfully to avoid their grasping fingers, and scanned the yard anxiously for Davey. But he had vanished into the maze of wattle-roofed huts that were clustered against the hills that guarded the bay.

"Dia's Muire dhuit!" one of the boys piped up. Genna eyed him blankly, then shook her head.

"Do you—do you speak English?" she asked. They laughed, moving closer, watching the movements of her lips.

"Don't any of you speak English?" she tried again, and then, *"Parlez-vous français, peut-être?"* But they only giggled and pointed, still calling out in their foreign tongue.

"Genna!" She sighed with relief when she heard Davey's booming voice, and saw him hurrying toward her across the yard. He clapped his hands at the boys, and they skittered away. "Good old Tom says we can borrow his cart. This must be our lucky day!"

"Davey," she hissed, eyeing the laughing boys, "what language is that they're speaking?"

"The old tongue," he said, surprised.

"Alex doesn't speak it, does he?"

"Of course he does. So do I. Almost everyone still does, here in the Isles." He called out a gay greeting to an old black-clad woman who passed; at least, Genna assumed it was a greeting, for the woman waved back, hurrying down to the docks with a basket of eggs.

"This is like a foreign country, Davey," she said in amazement. "I had no idea."

He looked at her earnestly. "I tried to warn ye, Genna, but ye wouldn't listen. The Isles are what they are. Nothing more and nothing less."

"Even so . . . it's not what I expected."

His voice softened. "Give it time, darlin'. You'll learn to love the place."

Genna stared at the odd wattled huts, the shouting children, the chilly gray sound with the low dark hills beyond. "Perhaps," she said dubiously. It seemed highly unlikely to her.

"Here we are!" Davey called cheerfully, as an ancient bow-legged man led forth a shaggy pony hitched between the well-worn staves of a low two-wheeled cart. Genna eyed the tiny seat for the driver; the pony gave a loud whinny, pawing the ground.

"And where am I supposed to ride?"

Davey patted the piles of peat in the back of the cart. "Right here. It's nice and soft; don't fret. Just hold on to the edge when we make a turn, and you'll be fine." He piled in the trunks and crates, then hoisted her over the steep wooden side and plunked her down atop the bailed turf. Genna sneezed as a cloud of gray green dust rose up around her.

"Bless you," said Davey, clambering up to his seat. He whistled between his teeth and shouted, "Hoy, there, girl, off with ye!" The little horse snorted derisively. Davey cracked the whip. "Hoy, I said!" With a lurching shudder, the cart rolled forward. Genna looked back at the old man; he winked, smiling a wide toothless smile.

"Aren't there any carriages in this village?" Genna demanded, wriggling about amid the crates and peat, trying to find a comfortable spot with little success.

"Nah, who needs carriages?" Davey pushed his cap back at a jaunty angle, jangling the reins. "A man counts himself lucky to have a horse hereabouts these days. 'Tis not like it was in the old times, when Alley's great-grandfather Angus was laird. 'Twas Angus who sheltered Robert the Bruce at Kintyre, and helped him escape to Ireland, savin' his life. Back then the Laird of the Isles and the clan chiefs were forces to be reckoned with. The king of Scotland wouldn't have dared make a law without the laird's approval." He sighed, clucking his tongue at the pony. "Times change. Donald lost more than a battle when he lost at Harlaw. That blasted Duke of Albany was regent for James then, and he proved a harsh victor. The ransom he demanded for Donald's life, and the taxes he levied, sapped the strength out of the Isles. Things are turnin' about some under James now—or were, before Alley decided to be so bullheaded. Plenty of folk still yearn for the old ways. But Alley says 'tis more important that Scotland survive than that the clan chiefs cling to their privileges. A house divided 'gainst itself, he says, is certain to fall."

Genna barely heard Davey's ruminations; she sneezed again, tugging strands of peat from her hair, then knelt and peered out over the cart's splintery side with increasing despair. This was the place Alex told her was paradise, this grim wasteland, colorless and damp and cold? This was the jewel of

the Isles? Who'd *want* to be laird of such a place? she thought
fiercely, ducking an overhanging branch. Nothing but clouds
and gloom wherever one looked—that and the wretched gray
water. She glowered wordlessly as Davey pointed out the
sights to her: Saint Mary's Well, the little Norman chapel beside it, and the lighthouse he called Rubha-nan Gall.

More of the old tongue, she supposed. No one spoke it at
Dumbarton but the very poorest of peasants. And certainly no
one spoke it at court; James's father had ordered its eradication
and the substitution of English as the official language years
ago, as part of his continuing crusade to civilize his people.

Even the clothes of the villagers they passed seemed strange
and outlandish. The men wore loose baggy drawers of gray or
brown wool, coarse gray stockings, and wooden clogs. The
drawers came nearly to their ankles, and over them they wore
huge billowing linen shirts like the ones Alex and Davey had
worn when they danced for the king. The shirts were tied up
at the waist with leather thongs, and the men used the same
sort of thong to pull back their long straight hair. As for the
women . . . Genna sighed as a cluster of girls not much older
than she giggled and waved and called to Davey as he drove
by. They were so swathed in acres of linen—wimples, gor-
gets, tunics, cloaks—that little showed but their gay flashing
smiles and eyes.

They left the outskirts of town and rumbled on into the
forest, following a well-worn cattle trail that skirted the edge
of the sound. "You see, Genna? Isn't this pretty?" Davey
called back over his shoulder. Genna gritted her teeth as the
cart bounced along the rutted stony path, and made no reply.

The cart clicked on, Davey whistling and shouting at the
pony when it tried to stop to nibble at the tufts of grass beside
the road. Tall pine trees towered overhead, their thick heavy
branches only occasionally permitting a glimpse of lowering
sky. The air grew moist and dense and chilly, and Genna shivered in misery as the road wound on and on.

"Best wrap yourself up in that cloak, darlin'," Davey called
as the cart rounded a sharp bend, tossing Genna against the
side with a resounding thud. "I think we may have a bit of a
shower."

"Rain?" she wailed. "Haven't I seen enough water to last
me the rest of my life?"

But Davey was right. Huge raindrops began to patter

through the trees onto the peat and baggage and Genna, and before long she was soaked through to the skin despite the sheltering cloak. She huddled in the bottom of the cart, the scent of damp peat nearly suffocating her, and sought solace by muttering every vile oath she had ever heard over and over again in increasingly imaginative combinations.

Davey had his hands full trying to keep the rickety cart and stubborn pony moving forward at a steady pace. As the rains turned the cattle path to cloying muck, his cheery whistle became more desperate. The left wheel had begun to wobble wildly, making the entire wagon cast to that side, and it was impossible to try to avoid stones and branches he could not even see in the burgeoning swells of mud. "Good girl," he told the pony soothingly, easing her under a rivulet that poured down from the steep hillside above them. He grinned, hearing Genna's faint curses as still more water tumbled into the cart.

He wasn't really surprised, then, when the wheel broke free from the axletree at last. The cart halted abruptly, the wheel spinning for a moment on the roadbank before rolling slowly over the edge into the sound. Then suddenly the whole cart toppled to one side with a mighty crash, landing Genna amid a pile of peat and baggage along the berm. Two trunks of her clothing followed the wheel down into the water, and only Genna's quick desperate lunge saved her loom from the same sad fate.

"Are you all right?" he called anxiously, leaping down from his seat and pulling her upright, making a vain attempt to brush the mud and peat from her cloak. Her braids had come loose in the fall, and her black hair hung over her face and shoulders in a sodden tangled mass. Genna lifted a heavy hank of it from her eyes and stared at him murderously. "Now what?"

Davey had to restrain a strong impulse to laugh; she looked like something from a nightmare. "Well, you have two choices," he said judiciously. "You can ride on the pony with the bags—what's left of them, that is—or else you can walk."

"Isn't there someplace to take shelter, some nearby croft?"

"It's not much farther, now, Genna, I swear it. And look, the sky is clearing! Any minute the sun will come out and dry us."

Genna squinted up at the rumbling sky through muddy lashes. "You lie, Davey Mac Leod," she mumbled. But there was a glimmer of blue in the east, beyond the churning gray waters of the sound. "And what about my trunks?" she demanded, staring down over the cliffside.

"Oh, they're gone, I'm afraid. That water's more than forty fathoms deep. But look at the bright side, Genna, you still have your loom!"

"That's certainly a comfort," she said grimly.

Davey hid another grin. "Will it be walk, or ride?"

Genna eyed the pony; it seemed to be sneering at her. "Walk." She took four steps in her dainty leather shoes before they were swallowed by the clinging mud.

Davey stifled his laughter and unhitched the pony from the remains of the cart. "I think you'd best ride." He perched her atop a folded blanket, and tied the crated loom, her sole remaining trunk, and his bags around her. By the time he'd finished she could barely see out through the towering bundles.

They set off down the road that way, Davey leading the pony by the bridle, Genna clutching tightly to the creature's mane, cursing the lack of a saddle. In another hour's time the skies had turned clear and the sun shone brightly, but what effect that might have had on the desolate landscape was lost on Genna. She was busy swatting away the flies that swarmed around her mud-soaked face.

The woods opened into broad fields of oats and barley, glowing fresh and green in the aftermath of the storm. The road wound steadily downhill, then up again across shifting layers of broken oyster shells. At long last, just when Genna was certain that she could not go another two feet atop that lurching beast, as her buttocks grew so stiff and sore that she nearly wished herself back on shipboard again, Davey stopped and pointed ahead. "There it is, Genna. Aros Castle."

She peered ahead through a patch of scrubby pine trees and saw the blunt stone building that crowned the summit of the hill, its outlines bleak and harsh against the brilliant blue sky. Her startled gaze flew back to Davey. "That's Alex's home?"

"Of course it is. What of it, darlin'?"

Genna stared up at the blackened stone walls overgrown with creeping myrtle and bay, the crumbling towers, the tiny blank windows. "Oh, Davey," she said, dismayed. "But he's a laird, a great one!"

"Aye, that he is. And a poor one."

"Papa John's cows had a barn nicer than that," she said spitefully.

Davey looked back at her with a trace of a smile. "Welcome to the Isles." He pulled the pony through the stunted wind-dwarfed trees that clung to the rocky slope.

From the top of the hill they heard a sudden shout. "'Tis Meggie!" Davey cried, quickening his pace. "Meggie!" he shouted, waving. "Meggie, 'tis I, Davey!"

"Davey!" Genna peeked out through the bundles of baggage and saw a tall slim woman running toward them, her hair shining like gold in the late-day sun.

"Ho, Davey, m'lad!" That was Alex, crashing down the hill after his sister, looking even more splendid than she remembered in a loose billowing shirt and slim dark breeches. Her heart began to beat faster, and she blushed, ashamed of the misgivings she'd expressed to Davey. What did it matter if he lived in a palace or a hovel? He was still her Alexander, her love, and every bit of the miserable journey from Inverness was made worthwhile by this moment, when she saw him again.

Then Genna heard another voice, high and piercing, calling down the hill: "Alley, please! Alley, wait for me!"

Alex stopped in his tracks, waiting as a tall, big-breasted woman with auburn hair picked her way daintily along the path, swirling blue skirts gathered up in her hands. Alex reached out to help her over an outcrop of stone in a familiar, intimate gesture. Genna felt her heart stand still.

Davey had caught Meggie up in his arms and was swinging her through the air, showering her with kisses. "Oh, my darlin', darlin' Meggie, how I've missed ye. Here, let me look at you. Aye, aye, still the fairest flower in the Isles."

"Davey, thank God you've come! Alley's been just impossible to—" She felt his tunic as he clasped her to him. "Why, you're soaking wet! Get on in to the fires this instant. And what do you mean coming here like this, without so much as a message ahead? Checking up on me, were you, to see if I was being true?"

"Nah, darlin', of course not. But wait, there's someone here you must meet."

"Davey!" Alex stumbled up beside his sister, his arm still encircling the waist of the auburn-haired girl. As he drew closer Genna could see that his gold hair was lank and dishev-

eled, his face half-hidden by a scraggly beard. The white shirt
he wore was torn at the shoulder and stained with red wine,
the buttons of his breeches undone. He reached out a hand to
shake Davey's and nearly tripped. "Lord, but 'tis shand to gree
you—I mean, grand to shee you," he cried thickly. "What
brings you to our humble abode? Thish is my cousin Nora.
Nora, here's Davey. She's been keepin' me comp'ny, Davey.
Teachin' me to play chess."

"Uh, Alley," Davey began, making frantic waving motions.

"What in hell's the matter with you? Are you havin' a fit or
somethin'?" asked Alex, laughing uproariously. "Look, Nora,
Davey's havin' a fit. Here, what's all this rubbish on your
horse?"

"Alley..."

As Alex yanked away the bags in front of her, Genna slid
off the pony to the ground. His flushed face went sheet white
as he saw her. "Genna?" he whispered, in shocked disbelief.

"Oh, Alley, I was tryin' to tell you..."

Alex was still staring dumbstruck at the damp mud-drip-
ping creature that stood before him. "My God, Genna," he
said finally. "Aren't you a sight."

Genna aimed a vicious kick at his shin. "I hate you, Alexander Mac Donald!" she shrieked, and ran back down the hillside in her stocking feet, bursting into angry tears.

Meggie glowered at her brother. "Oh, Alley, you pig. How
could you?"

Davey's broad face was furious. "If she looks a sight, Alley,
'tis because she sailed for ten days to get here, sick as a dog the
whole time, and then the cart broke down, and the rain caught
us, and she lost most all she owned in the sound." He paused
for breath. "And then she gets here after all her trouble, and
finds you cavortin' about with this—this—" He pointed to
Nora, speechless with rage.

"*I* didn't do anything," the girl said indignantly.

"Oh, Alley." Meggie was still shaking her head. "You stupid, drunken pig!"

"Well, don't stand there looking at me!" Nora sputtered to
Davey, then gathered her skirts together and flounced haughtily back toward the castle. "And frankly," she said over her
shoulder, "if you want my opinion, he's right!"

Alex stood swaying helplessly, watching her go, then
looked down the slope after Genna. "Oh, Christ," he said,

swallowing. "Oh, Christ, what a bloody mess. I'd best go after her." He took one step down the slope and stumbled to his knees.

"Don't you dare try it!" Meggie cried, eyes flashing. "She'd probably take a dagger to you."

"And she'd have every right to," Davey said darkly, pulling his laird to his feet.

Alex rubbed his eyes with his hands. "You might have sent word you were comin', you know!"

"The poor thing wanted to surprise you."

"She did that, all right," Alex said ruefully, feeling his shin.

"I'll go after her," Meggie announced. "A woman needs to talk to another woman at a time like this. You, husband, see if you can get him back to the kitchens and sober him up." She set off toward the sound with a toss of her golden curls.

Davey looked after her for a moment, then turned to Alex, whose face bore a look of utter confusion. "Chess, Alley?" he asked, the tip of his red beard quivering.

"She's quite good at it, actually."

"Yer cousin, you say."

"Aye, my cousin. Three times removed."

Davey laughed aloud, throwing an arm over his hapless laird's shoulder. "You poor devil."

"'Tis no laughing matter, Davey," Alex said sternly.

"No, of course not. Button up yer bloody trousers." Davey pulled his face straight, glanced sidelong at Alex, and burst out laughing again. "How much have you had to drink?"

"Lost count last week, I'm afraid. You know, Davey, a man's got to do what he can to keep his spirits up."

"I'd settle for keepin' you on your feet. Well, come along, now. I could use a wee dram myself."

Meggie found Genna stumbling blindly along the road to Tobermory, tears streaming down her face, her breath coming in ragged sobs. "Genna, please, wait for me," she called, pulling at the girl's filthy cloak.

"Just leave me alone!" Genna cried angrily, shaking off Meggie's hand.

"Alley didn't meant to hurt your feelings, dearie, he just didn't expect you!"

"I've never in my life been so humiliated!" Genna gasped through her sobs. "How could he say such a thing to me? And in front of that—that—that woman?"

"Please, dearie, come and sit a moment, and catch your breath. You're weary, distraught."

"Well, wouldn't you be?" Genna whirled around to face her. "I feel like such a damned fool!" And she burst into tears again.

Meggie took her arm and led her down to a flat stone by the water's edge, sitting her on it and pulling out a kerchief. "Here, now, wipe your eyes and take a deep breath. That's a good girl. And let it out slowly . . . there. Feel better?"

"No, I don't! Why doesn't anything ever work out the way I plan it? I was going to sail up to Alex's castle like Cleopatra, all shining and beautiful, and he would sweep me up in his arms and carry me ashore, telling me how much he loves me. And instead, I show up looking like a drowned rat, and he doesn't even say that he's glad to see me, just stands there and . . . ohhh!" Her voice trailed off into a wail of despair.

"Well, 'tis not that I'm making excuses for him, now, Genna, but you must remember the man is completely skinked."

"What's that supposed to mean?"

Meggie stared in surprise. "You know, skinked. Addle-pated."

"What on earth are you talking about?"

"Drunk, dear! The man is stone-drunk!"

It was Genna's turn to stare. "But I've never seen Alex drunk before," she said slowly.

Meggie smiled grimly. "Nor had I, till he came back from Inverness. One week past he arrived, with poor Bantigh near run into the ground, and since that time I've not seen him *without* a cup in his hand. Wouldn't speak a word of what brought him back, either, though I figured right enough it had something to do with you."

"It didn't have anything to do with me," Genna said with a sniff.

"No? Then p'rhaps you can tell me why he calls out for you in his sleep. Oh, I've heard him," she said in response to Genna's look of astonishment. "No mistake about it. All day long he's drinkin' and snappin' out at anyone who dares come near him, till he falls asleep by the fire, and shouts out your name."

Genna sat dumbfounded for a moment, then looked into

Meggie's clear blue eyes, so much like her brother's. "Oh, Meggie, what am I going to do?"

"Well, the way I see it, you have two choices," said Meggie, sounding exactly like her husband. "You can take a boat back to the mainland, return to court, and forget all about my brother—"

"And that's just what I'll do," Genna declared, getting to her feet. "I'll go back and wed Henry Argyll. That will teach him!"

Meggie shrugged. "I'll go and send for a boat, then, if you're certain."

Genna sniffed back tears. "Isn't that what you'd do?"

"Who, me? Most likely. But from what Davey's told me of you, I'd expected— Oh, I don't know."

"No, tell me. What?"

"Well, Davey's told me such stories about your spirit, your temper. He said the first time you ever met Alley, you tried to scratch his eyes out and cripple him, too. And then that time he kissed you, Davey said, you near slapped him silly and his ears rang for days!"

Genna's chin jutted out. "So what if I did?"

Meggie twirled her gold wedding band. "I just didn't imagine you as the sort to give up without a fight."

"He's not worth fighting for," Genna said indignantly.

"I don't know if he is or not. All I know is he's not been himself since he came back from Inverness. There's been a desperateness to him."

"He didn't look desperate to me! Who is that horrible woman?"

"What, Nora? Oh, she's just one of our kinfolk. She's been chasing after poor Alley since she was six years old."

Genna sat on the edge of the rock. "Does he—does he keep her, there in the castle?"

Meggie laughed uproariously at that. "Alley? Are you mad? Why would he do that?"

"At court I heard rumors. They say he has a hundred castles, and keeps a mistress in each."

Meggie was still laughing, clutching her sides. "Alley? They really say that?"

"They do," Genna declared. "What is so amusing?"

"Good Lord, Genna, the way our mother runs through money 'tis a wonder Alley can afford the upkeep for one castle, let alone a hundred. And as for keeping mistresses tucked away, why, I don't think he ever even looked at a girl until he met you."

"He's certainly looking now!"

Meggie frowned. "Perhaps he is. I think he's been trying to force himself into forgetting you, Genna. 'Tis like when he came back from Stirling last spring, he got just this way, desperate and wild. He couldn't stand to be alone, couldn't sleep at night, so he told me. He kept seeing you in his dreams. It near broke my heart to see him put up with the likes of Nora. But he's been so unhappy." She took Genna's hand, looked into her eyes. "Lord knows I love my Davey, Genna, and he loves me. But what Alley feels for you is something fierce and frightening. I would not care to love that way, seeing what it's done to him."

"I wish I'd never met him," said Genna, looking out over the sound.

"He's felt the same way about you, sometimes."

Genna plucked at her torn, muddied stockings. "You said I had two choices. What's the other?"

"Well . . ." Meggie's smile was sly. "If it was me that had come all this way to be so disappointed, I'd want to give the fellow a taste of his own medicine before I'd go."

"How would I do that?"

"Oh, I don't know. Maybe get all dressed up in your finest gown, and washed and scented."

"My finest gown's at the bottom of that damned sound." Genna spread out her rumpled skirts. "And I don't think I'll ever get clean again."

"Why, a bit of a bath and you'd be as good as new!"

"Oh, Lord, how I'd love a bath, and to wash my hair out." Genna twirled a mud-caked strand between her fingers longingly. "And now that I've come all this way, I suppose I should stay for a bit. Though I must say my first impressions of Mull have been far from grand."

Meggie pulled her to her feet. "That settles it. You've got to give my island another chance, even if you don't do the same for my fool brother!"

"He was right about one thing," Genna said ruefully. "I must look dreadful."

"You won't when I get finished," Meggie promised. "Just come with me."

She took Genna up to the castle by a path through the woods that led onto the inland gate. With surprise Genna noted that from this approach, Aros Castle wasn't at all forbidding. In fact, it was charming, with wide casements overlooking the forests and fields, neatly kept outbuildings, and a yard within the walls filled with carefully tended flowers— corn poppies and cowslips, thrift and foxgloves—that nodded in the shadows of stately hazel and birch trees.

"Oh, Meggie, how beautiful! Your gardener must have Adam's touch."

Her pretty face, like a soft, rounded version of Alex's, flushed with pleasure. "Thank you. I . . . I do all the work myself. Alley and Davey laugh at the time I spend on it, but I enjoy it. And with them away from home so much, it gives me something to do. Besides, I must keep up my end of the prophecy."

"What prophecy?"

"When I was christened, the seeress foretold that if the gardens at Aros Castle ever fell into disorder, great grief would come to the Clan Mac Donald."

Genna looked over at Meggie suspiciously, sure that she was being gulled, but Meggie seemed perfectly serious. "You don't—you don't actually believe such things, do you?" she asked hesitantly.

"Of course I do! The seeress is hardly ever wrong. If you spend any time at all in the Isles, you'll find that out."

The chamber Meggie led her to was a surprise as well: spacious and airy, hung with bright tapestries, with a magnificent view of the sound and the mist-shrouded hills of Morven beyond. A pale moon was just beginning to rise above the treetops, and Venus peeked out of the dark violet veil of the sky like a warm bright beacon. Genna felt her spirits lift as she saw the glitter of the moonlight on the water.

"You see, there are certain compensations to life here," Meggie said softly, standing beside her at the casement. "Every time I see the night sky, or watch the sun come up through the mists . . . " She laughed. "But listen to me going on so, with you still standing in your muddy things. Here, take off that cloak and gown, and I'll get some hot water for your bath. Althea! Thea!" she called down the corridor.

"Aye, Mistress Meggie?" asked the huge round woman who came lumbering up the stairs.

"Thea, this is Genevieve Fleming. Genna, Althea is my strong right arm, and the finest cook in the Isles. Thea, send up some hot water, would you?"

Genna saw a warm sparkle in the housekeeper's brown eyes as she made a sort of half bow, half curtsy, hindered somewhat by her great girth. Her gray hair was drawn back in a tight bun, the way Taggert had worn hers. But where Taggert's features had been stern and forbidding, Althea's were merry and blithe. It was plain to see from the easy manner in which she and Meggie spoke to one another that the housekeeper considered herself every bit a part of the family.

"Pleased to meet you, mum. Gor, what a mess you are."

"Thea, have you seen my brother?"

"Young Master's down in the kitchens with Davey, completely underfoot as usual, both sopping up quantities of ale. Would this be the young lady, then, that he's moaning over?"

Meggie winked. "Aye, but don't you tell him she's here."

The woman's crinkled brown eyes considered Genna kindly but thoroughly. "Needs fattening, don't she?" she observed, pinching Genna's arm. "My, what a tiny little thing! See how lovely her skin is, Mistress Meggie. So would yours be, if you'd keep out of the sun."

"All right, then, Thea, just send up the water, and have Hoban tote up her baggage. And not a word to Alley, remember."

"Meggie Mac Donald, what mischief might you be plannin'?"

"You'll see soon enough," Meggie promised, pushing her toward the door.

After soaking for nearly an hour in the warm, violet-scented bath Althea poured her, Genna felt almost human again. While she lathered her hair with rich fatty soap and rinsed it, Meggie went through the sole trunk that had survived the broken cart, pulling out garments and holding them up before a looking glass. "What wonderful clothes you have, Genna!"

"I had a great deal more before they all fell into the sound. There's naught in that trunk but my riding clothes and night things."

"But they're so beautiful!" She seized on a sheer creamy gown, embroidered with pale roses at the throat and hem.

"Oh, this is just the thing for you to wear to supper; 'twill drive poor Alley wild!"

"It's a nightdress, for heaven's sake!"

"So? He won't know that. We'll put a lot of pettiskirts beneath it, and tie up the waist with a sash. Now, how do you wear your hair?"

"Just plaited into braids. Really, Meggie, you can't be serious."

"We'll leave it loose down your back, and tie up just a bit at the crown."

Genna stared. "I can't wear my hair down in public, Meggie! 'Tis a breach of manners. The queen would banish me from court!"

Meggie arched an eyebrow. "The queen's not here, though, is she? That's another advantage of life on Mull, Genna. We make our own rules of manners—within reason, of course."

"Of course," Genna echoed weakly. But Meggie's carefree mischievousness was infectious. By the time Genna had dried her hair by the roaring fire, working through the tangles with a borrowed comb, the idea of wearing a nightgown to supper had begun to seem intriguing rather than insane.

"I'll have Thea wash up your things," Meggie said briskly, piling up the muddy bundle. "What's this?" She carefully unclasped Genna's gold and pearl brooch from the collar of her cloak.

"Oh, just something my parents left to me. It's rather out of fashion."

"Nonsense, 'tis beautiful! Look at that gold-work. You don't see things so finely made anymore."

"That's what I used to try and scratch your brother's eyes out," Genna recalled wryly.

"All the more reason to wear it tonight. Now, slip into your gown." She pulled the creamy dress over Genna's black head, tied a pale green swath of silk at the waist, and brought the edge of the sash up over the right shoulder from the back, fastening it with the brooch. Then she stood back to survey her handiwork. "What do you think?" She turned Genna to face the glass.

Genna stared at her reflection, chewing her lip. "I don't know, Meggie. Somehow it just doesn't seem proper." But she twisted to the side, admiring the loose flowing lines of the skirts, the way the tight sash accentuated her narrow waist and the curves of her hips. Her heavy ebony hair rippled in the firelight, reaching almost to her knees, and the rich gold and milky white pearls of the brooch seemed to have taken on added luster in the soft, clear island air.

"Well, I think you look absolutely breathtaking. Wait here a moment while I run to the kitchens and tell Thea there'll be one more for supper."

"She already knows," said Genna, puzzled.

Meggie laughed and kissed her forehead. "Aye, but Alley does not!"

"Meggie"—she turned back from the doorway, and Genna blushed—"thank you for—for coming after me. Whatever else may happen, it was worth the trial of getting here just to meet you."

"I imagine you had some doubts about me, having met my mother at court." Meggie giggled at Genna's guilt-stricken face. "No need to look that way; I don't blame you a bit. That's yet another advantage of living here: I see so little of Mary. She never has managed to understand how she gave birth to a runagate like me! I'm glad you're here." She waved cheerfully, then skipped off down the stairs.

Genna eyed the figure in the looking glass with fascination, touching the sash, the gleaming brooch, twirling in a circle to watch the play of the firelight on her hair. I truly do look different, she thought with amazement, somehow other-worldly. She smiled, and the reflection smiled back, mysterious and alluring, as unlike the bedraggled girl who had ridden up to Aros that afternoon as two creatures could be. She giggled. That talk of Meggie's about the seeress and her prophecies must have made an impression. She could not remember ever having felt so... *bewitching* before. Her dark eyes were agleam as though with some hidden secret, and her ghost-pale face, her shoulders, glowed like ivory against the ethereal gown.

Alex loved to take down her hair, to let the heavy strands run through his fingers like silken ribbons, twine them around his shoulders and throat. Or at least he'd said he had. Genna thought again of the scene on the hillside, and bit her lip. He certainly hadn't looked miserable or bereft to her, with his arm tucked cozily about Nora's waist, and his breeches undone. At the thought all her confidence vanished; the face in the mirror was once more that of a forlorn waif.

She couldn't go through with this, she couldn't! A taste of his own medicine, Meggie had said, but that taste was too bitter for Genna to swallow. What was the use of teaching him a lesson when her heart was broken, her trust in him so completely destroyed that neither could be made new again? How was she supposed to flirt and tease, as Meggie had laughingly instructed, when her pride had been battered to death?

Deep down within her breast a spark of temper flickered, flared, and then began to blaze with fury. The flames in the hearth leapt and danced in a gust of wind, reaching higher and higher. Genna stared into their depths and for a moment imagined she felt their power course through her, filling her with such heat and light that she could have danced as well.

Then the stacked logs groaned and collapsed in a flurry of crackling sparks. The strange sensation of omnipotence left her, but when Genna glanced once more in the mirror she could see that the flames still smoldered in her eyes.

13

Meggie found Davey and Alex in the kitchens, working hard at making a dent in a huge cask of ale. Alex stumbled to his feet when he saw her. "Did you catch up to her, Meggie? What did she say?"

"Aye, I caught up with her." Meggie smiled coyly and bent down to give Davey a kiss. "Hello, my love. How much of that ale have you had?"

"Enough to hear Alley say fifty times that if Genna doesn't forgive him, he'll go and drown himself in the sound. Faith, don't tease him, Meggie, I'm afraid he might mean it. What did the wee thing say?"

Meggie turned to Althea, standing stirring her pots at the hearth, red-faced from the heat. "There will be one more for dinner, Thea," she announced. "Please set Master Davey's place beside me, and put Mistress Fleming next to Sebastian."

"Very good, mum," the housekeeper said with a nod.

"Sebastian?" cried Alex indignantly. "Why, that lecher will have his fingers on her knee before the meat course!"

"What's sauce for the goose," Meggie murmured. "Oh, and, Thea, do put Cousin Nora beside my brother. They seem to be getting along so awfully well."

Davey threw back his head and laughed. "Come here, Meggie, lass. Great God in heaven, how I've missed ye."

"And I've missed you, pet," she said softly, perching on his lap, her arm around his neck.

"Now that," said Althea from the hearth, "is the sort of talk it does my heart good to hear. 'Tis a pity some certain other young men don't take a lesson from it."

"Why don't you mind your own damned business, Althea?" snapped Alex.

"There's some of us who know how to do that better than others, wouldn't you say, Mistress Meggie?"

"I would, Althea. I certainly would."

189

* * *

"Ready?" asked Meggie.

Genna took a deep breath. "Meggie, if 'tis all the same with you, I think perhaps I'll just have my supper up here."

"Oh, no you don't—not after all the work I went to getting you clean! Come along, now." Laughing, she took Genna's hand and led her down the long stone stairs, through the billeting room, and up another stairway to the arched entrance of the banquet hall.

The scene there had been set; the castle's finest pewter and silver glowed in the light of dozens of tallow candles placed along the length of the huge carved oak table. Peat and heather crackled in the fireplace, a lutist plucked out soft chords in the gallery, and the score of kinsmen and -women that made up the household were already seated. Alex held back Nora's chair as she fluffed her skirts around her, then grimaced at her coo of thanks.

"'Tis naught," he said curtly, inwardly cursing his sister.

Nora giggled, toying with the low-cut neckline of her gown. "Why, if I didn't know you better, Alley Mac Donald, I'd swear you'd had too much to drink. Your manners are perfectly frightful!"

"Shut up, Nora, won't you?"

She stared openmouthed for a moment, said, "Well! Of all the nerve!" and then clamped her lips shut tight.

He took his seat at the far end of the table, scowling down at his hands. A sudden murmuring of voices made Alex glance up at the archway; he started from his seat with a sharp catch of his breath as Genna entered behind Meggie, her dark eyes downcast, the pale dress shimmering, her magnificent hair tumbling over her shoulders like a sheer black waterfall. In the flickering candlelight she reminded him of the spirit he'd seen slipping through the trees at Dumbarton, the image he'd pursued in his dreams—half woman, half child, enchantingly, achingly lovely, but impossible to catch and hold.

Meggie clapped her hands together. "Everyone, this is Genna Fleming, a very good friend of mine who has come to visit. I trust you'll make her welcome. Sebastian, I've put her beside you; I hope you don't mind."

Alexander's darkly handsome second cousin sprang to his feet. "Mind? Why, bless you, Meggie, for thinking so well of me as to seat me beside an angel! Mistress Fleming, please, come and sit down."

"Thank you kindly, sir." Genna smiled up, black eyes sparkling, as he guided her to her chair.

Sebastian groaned. "Ah, the voice of an angel as well. Tell me, I beg you, what possessed you to come down from heaven tonight to share our humble meal?"

Genna's long black lashes swept her cheeks. "Oh, I just happened to be flying by when my poor wings grew so weary I feared I'd drop into the sea. Fortunately, I just managed to reach Meggie's garden."

He touched his wine cup to hers. "Let us drink, then, to whatever fair wind brought you this way." He drained the cup, still staring at her over the rim.

"Oh, for God's sake," snapped Alex, "if you two have finished making cow's eyes at each other, could we eat? Davey, ask the blessing."

"Very well, Alley. Let us pray." Davey began the benediction in Latin, and Alex felt a sudden pain rip through his heart as he remembered the night in the chapel at Urquhart, the tears in Genna's eyes as he took her, and the way she had whispered, "Come, love, sin with me again." He glanced down the table surreptitiously and saw her sitting demurely, hands folded in solemn devotion, palms together. Those hands that had caught in his hair, pulling him close to her, as her white body writhed beneath him. Suddenly, Nora rubbed her long shin against him, interrupting his thoughts. He thrust it angrily away.

Never in his life had he seen anything so beautiful, he thought, sneaking another glance at Genna, feeling his loins heat with the urge to make love to her, carry her up to his big bed and tear that sheer white gown from her breasts, see her red lips part in ecstasy as he thrust into her again and again.

"Amen," said Davey, and the others echoed him. Alex looked up from behind his tight-clenched fists and realized that everyone was waiting for him. He dropped his hands abruptly, clanging his plate against the table, and felt his color rise.

"Amen, amen!"

Meggie arched a pale gold eyebrow in Genna's direction. Genna flashed her a beatific smile, and turned to Sebastian.

"Tell me, if you would, sir, how you are related to our

hostess. She has said a great deal about you, but there is still so much I don't know."

"I cannot wait to satisfy your curiosity," Sebastian said smoothly. "Where would you like me to begin?"

"For the love of God," Alex swore softly, and stabbed with his knife at the huge pink salmon Althea set before him. It stared back with a vacant fishy grin.

"What an adventure Genna and I had in getting here," Davey told the household, taking a deep draft of ale. "And what a thrashing I'll have for Tom the peatman when next I see him!" Before long he had everyone laughing merrily at the mishaps they'd encountered between Tobermory and Aros. Everyone, that is, except Alex, who ate silently, sullenly, occasionally glaring at an oblivious Genna with furious blue eyes.

Sebastian wiped away tears of hilarity as Davey told of sitting aboard the cart and feeling it list farther and farther to the side as they skirted the sound in the driving rain. "I'm surprised you didn't just turn about and go home after such an introduction to our island," he told Genna, patting her small white hand.

"Faith, had it been up to me, I would have," she said, laughing. The sound was like silvery bells.

"I'm terribly glad you came on," he murmured, leaning toward her. Genna smiled up from beneath thick black lashes.

"Indeed, so am I."

Alex's knife fell to the stone floor with an angry clatter.

"What did you do with the cart, then, Davey?" called fat, jolly Uncle Liam.

"Left it there in the bloody ditch," the redhead said ruefully. "And don't you just bet when I go back to Tom and tell him what happened, the cadger will stroke his grizzled chin and say"—he mimicked the old man's lilting accents—"'Gor, Master Davey, Bessie and me hae been pullin' that cart behind us for nigh on fifty year, and never once is the time a wheel's gone out on us. Ye mustna hae been handlin' her aright.' And then he'll want me to buy him a new cart!"

"Why not?" asked Meggie, smiling at her husband. "He gets a new one that way every year or so!"

Sebastian leaned back in his chair, laughing, refilling Genna's cup with wine. "Lord, but it's grand to have Davey back among us. There's been too little merriment hereabouts of late." His arm draped nonchalantly over the back of Genna's chair, brushing her bare white shoulder, her rippling hair. "How long will you be staying with us, angel?"

Genna smiled shyly, black eyes wide. "I'm not really certain, Sebastian. Not more than a few days, I would think."

"Perhaps we can convince you to stay longer."

"Perhaps you can," she allowed.

He leaned closer, his arm tightening around her. "If you've not made plans for the morrow, I'd be honored to show you some of the sights on the island. There's a spot along the River Forsa with a view of the sound that will take your breath away."

"I'd love to see it," said Genna.

"She's not going anywhere with you tomorrow, Sebastian," Alex growled.

His cousin looked up with surprise. "And why not, Alley, if she's wanting to?"

"I have made other plans for our visitor."

"And what might those be?" Sebastian demanded, his dark beard out-thrust.

"She and I are going to be married."

There was a moment of startled silence at the table. Then Sebastian gave a short bark of laughter. "What a jester you are, coz."

And Nora put an anxious hand on Alex's arm. "What in heaven are you talking about?"

"I'm not jesting." His blue eyes were dark and angry. "The lady and I are betrothed. We'll be wed on the morrow."

"Well, that's just grand then, isn't it?" Davey said heartily, to no one in particular.

Genna pushed back her chair with a loud harsh scrape. "If you don't mind, milord," she told Alex, the civil words belying her fury, "I beg a word with you. In private."

He glanced around the table with a wide grin. "Some final plans to be made, no doubt. You know how peculiar women get at a time like this."

"*Now*, milord!" Black eyes flashing, she stood abruptly and stalked out into the corridor.

Alex spread out his hands and shrugged, grinning indulgently as if to say, "Who knows?" But his heart was pounding as he followed Genna's slim, straight figure through the arched doors.

"Alley!" Nora cried petulantly, jumping to her feet. Davey shoved her back into her chair.

"How *dare* you?" came Genna's rage-filled voice from the passageway. Meggie got up quickly and closed the heavy doors.

"I?" hissed Alex, glaring down at her. "How dare you carry on like that with that fool Sebastian, letting him fondle you that way? Why didn't you just jump right into his bloody lap and have done with it?"

"How are your chess lessons progressing, milord?" she snapped.

"Would you please lower your voice? Everyone will hear you." He grabbed her elbow to pull her farther down the hall.

"And what if they do? You had no right to say we were going to be married."

"I've thought it over, Genna, and decided to forgive you."

"Forgive *me*? Forgive me for what?"

"You're still very young, and I can understand how a man like Argyll may have turned your head. But I'm willing to marry you anyway," he said nobly, with a pained, brave smile.

"You— Oh, you bastard! I swear, I'll kill you!" She smacked him across the face. "There's the one I owe you, and here's another! Oh!" She kicked him in the shins, the ankles, pommeling him with her fists. "How could you believe his lies, you vain, stupid man?"

Alex wrestled with her wrists. "Are you telling me you never lay with him?" he demanded.

"Of course I never lay with him, you bastard!"

"Then how did he know about the night in the chapel?"

"How should I know? Maybe you bragged about it while you were in your cups!"

"I didn't tell a soul! That is—" He started. Had he mentioned that night to Mary? No, surely not. But the king had known of it, too. Ach, anyone might have talked, a stable-hand, or even Davey.

"I'm sorry," he began again, more gently. "Pray you, forgive me. When Argyll started in on my father, I couldn't think straight."

"Couldn't think at all is more like it."

"I love you, Genna."

"How can you love me when you don't even trust me?"

"I love you, damn you! And you know that you love me."

"I believed once that I loved you. Now I see the situation is changed."

"What are you talking about? Nothing has changed between us."

"Everything has changed," she said bitterly. "'Hello, Davey, this is my cousin Nora.'" She found she was shaking with rage. "Little wonder you're so quick to think others untrue! Why should you give in and kneel to King James when you knew she'd be right here waiting for you? Oh, you were simply inconsolable with losing me, weren't you, Alex? Tell me, do you whisper those same sweet things when you make love to her, tell her how lovely she is, how precious to you?"

"That's enough, Genna!" he roared. "You've said your piece; now I'll say mine."

She turned her back with an angry stamp of her foot. "I'll listen to none of your drunken lies!"

"I have never been more sober in my life, I assure you. There is nothing quite like seeing the woman one loves behaving like a harlot to induce sobriety."

"Talk about the pot and the kettle! Being loved by you is apparently not a terribly exclusive honor."

"I have never loved any woman but you."

"Nora would be most surprised to hear that, I'm sure."

"I've never spoken those words to her. I've never spoken them to anyone in my life, except for you."

Genna whipped around to face him, tears filling her eyes. "Then you're a most peculiar man, for you show her you love her without telling her, and tell me the same without showing me!"

His arms were around her suddenly, pinioning her against him, his lips searing hers with a need that took her breath away. His hands roved over her shoulders, down her back, cupping her buttocks and lifting her up so that she felt the hot brand of his desire against her gown. And still he kissed her with wild, dizzying fervor, his tongue seeking hers, tasting its sweetness, burning her with his fire.

"It's no use denying it, Genna," he told her, mouth at her ear. "You have belonged to me from the first moment I saw you, and I to you. You're in my blood, my soul; I can no more live without you than I could without air."

"Let go of me, damn you."

"Never, Genna. Never again. You proved you loved me when you followed me here!"

"I proved only what a fool I could be!" She wrenched away, her fists clenched. "I followed you here because I believed you to be a man of honor, a man who would give up everything—the king's favor, the woman he wanted—for honor's sake. I loved you for that, Alex, loved you with all my heart. And all the time you were here with that woman, making a mockery of my love."

"Ask her, Genna," he said softly, staring down into her huge dark eyes. "Ask her, if you don't believe me. God forgive me, I tried to use Nora to forget you. But I could not make love to her. I could not even bring myself to kiss her mouth."

He reached out gingerly to caress her cheek, twisting a long strand of black hair in his fingers. "You looked just so that night in the chapel at Urquhart, standing before me so angry, so frightened. Do you remember, Genna? Do you remember how you lay beneath me, gave yourself to me all through that night?" His hands caught in the cascade of her hair, twining, entangling; he pulled her head back and touched his lips to hers, tenderly this time, with all the aching love that he felt for her.

Genna willed herself to go limp and lifeless in his grasp, steeled herself against the flood of longing his touch threatened to unleash, prayed furiously to a God who had surely abandoned her, to let her feel such need for him, have his hands on her feel so *right*.

He released her abruptly, holding her at arm's length, his blue eyes fathomless. "God, you are so beautiful, Genna. You look like a gypsy goddess, a spirit of night."

"You told me that I looked a sight." A tear slid slowly down her cheek.

"No," he said gravely, "I said you *were* a sight. You looked as though you had come a very long way on a ship." He wiped the tear away with his fingertip. "And then were stuck into a peat cart." He tipped her chin up to him solemnly, as if touching a wild bird. "And then got caught in a fiendish rainstorm." His mouth brushed her temple, warm and winning. "And then tumbled down into the mud, and rode ten miles on a stubborn pony without a saddle." His hand pressed the small of her back, rubbing tenderly, sweetly. "And then found your lover frolicking in the sun with another woman. That is what you looked like."

She nearly smiled. "I must have looked dreadful."

"You were a sight," he repeated. "The most precious sight these poor eyes will ever see. I could not believe that after what I did to you, you would still . . . might still want me."

"Oh, Alex." She leaned against his chest, drinking in the scent of him, warm, male, clean. "How could you not believe I would want you?"

"Because I took Argyll at his word. Because I shamed you. And because I have naught to offer you but a name that is tainted now, and a life that is strange and harsh."

"But it's your life, Alex." She tugged at his long gold hair, forcing his gaze to meet hers. "How could I choose any other?"

"I prayed each night . . . that you would come after me," he whispered.

"And now that I have?"

He kissed her. "Now I know there is a God. I love you so much, Genna."

"Enough to marry me tomorrow?"

He met her teasing black eyes. "Enough to take you this minute." He lifted her into his arms, her hair sweeping the stones at his feet.

"Then, prithee, take me back in to supper," she murmured in his ear, and giggled at his look of dismay. "I had no stomach to eat for more than a week aboard that thrice-damned ship. The salmon you were so lethally dissecting is even more attractive to me at this moment than you."

He raised one dark gold eyebrow in mock anger. "Are you saying my kisses aren't food enough for you, my love?"

"For a first course, perhaps, my love." She wrapped her hands in his hair, drew his mouth down to hers.

Meggie hushed everyone at the table as she peered through the keyhole. "Althea!" she called then.

"Yes, mum?"

"We shall need a wedding breakfast in the morning."

"Very good, mum," said Althea, without a trace of surprise.

14

Alexander Mac Donald, Lord of the Isles, emerged with his new bride from the little stone chapel, laughing and ducking low beneath a hail of flower petals and birch leaves. A shout went up from the retainers and neighbors gathered in the courtyard, and a single green-clad piper filled all the soft morning air with the stately strains of "The Road to the Isles." Alex obliged the repeated demands of his household and led Genna along the traditional circuit of each doorway in the castle, giving his bride a kiss in each to ward off any mischievous spirits.

Davey and Meggie watched, hand in hand, as the newlyweds shared their first sips of wine as husband and wife, and it was impossible to tell whether Alex's sister or his best friend was smiling more broadly. "She looks beautiful, doesn't she?" Meggie asked fondly, admiring the shimmering splendor of Genna's long black hair, and the brilliant flush of excitement on her cheeks.

"No more so than you did when we were wed," said Davey, and kissed her. "Wherever did you find such an appropriate dress on such brief notice?" The bride wore a long flowing robe of royal purple velvet, its bodice and waist embroidered in gold with the emblems of Alex's kingdom, a galley under full sail, and a garlanded sword.

"'Tis the dress Mother wore when she married Father. I'd forgotten it was still here until I came across it in an old trunk last night."

"You let Genna wear Mary Leslie's wedding gown, darlin'?"

"Well, why not? Don't you think it suits her?"

"Aye, but . . . I don't know. It seems a wee bit unlucky, considerin' how unhappy yer mother was here."

"Oh, for heaven's sake," scoffed Meggie, "you're as bad as

Thea and her silly superstitions. It's only a dress, and a lovely one at that. Mother always has had exquisite taste in clothes."

"If you say so, darlin'." But as Davey watched Alex give his bride a long, lingering kiss in the stable doorway, he felt a tingle of apprehension play down his spine.

Meggie gazed up at him with clouded blue eyes. "You think I did wrong to give it to her, don't you?"

"Of course not, Meggie," he lied. "As you said, 'tis only a dress."

When Alex and Genna had fulfilled their obligation to tradition, everyone gathered in the big timber-beamed hall for the wedding breakfast Althea had prepared. There was smoked fish, haggis, tongue, eel, and a whole roasted ox, its flesh scented with garlic and costmary, that had been turned on a spit all night long by dogs pulling ropes, watched over by a sleepy-eyed boy with a stick. There were pasty pies, dumplings, custards, blancmange, and more kinds of cakes than Genna had ever seen before in her life: oat cakes, cream cakes, sponge cakes, griddle cakes, rock cakes, almond cakes, and five huge gold-crusted berry pies. "Good Lord, Thea," Alex exclaimed, looking over the sumptuous spread, "how did you ever get all this ready so soon?"

"Haven't I been waiting for this day for nigh on twenty-four years?" the cook demanded, and clasped him in a huge hug. "My Young Master Alley, wed at last." She dabbed her eyes with an apron edge. "Faith, how I wish your father could be here to witness this day."

"And what about Mother?" asked Alex, gently teasing.

Althea pulled away from him, her wide brow furrowed. "You should bless your lucky stars she's not here, Young Master. That woman brings naught but rue and woe wherever she goes. And as for you, Young Mistress"—she fixed Genna with a baleful stare—"'tis tempting the fates that you be, wearing that gown."

"Oh, hush, Thea," said Alex, bussing her leathery cheek. "'Tis a bonny gown."

"And a bonnier bride," Sebastian added, coming up to clasp Alex's hand and give Genna a swift chaste kiss. "I knew 'twas too good to be true when Meggie set me beside you last night. Blessings to you both. May you live forever, and die in your bed."

"Thanks, coz, that's a fine wedding wish. Come, now, sit

and have your breakfast. And you, Genna, you'd best eat up as well. 'Tis the last peaceful meal we're likely to have for some time."

"You call this peaceful?" Genna asked, laughing as she took in the crowds of people elbowing their way to the huge table, calling out greetings and jests and well-wishings.

"I do," he said, and kissed her fiercely, tenderly, tilting up her chin with his finger. And for that moment, there might have been no other beings in all the world.

He pulled away with a look of regret to answer Davey's shouted question: "Will ye be takin' Genna to Iona, Alley?"

"Of course! We'll need to get a blessing from Father Gervase."

"And who is Father Gervase?" asked Genna, feeding her husband a perfectly ripe strawberry.

He caught her hand between his lips and ran his tongue along her palm, making her giggle. "Sweet," he murmured.

"The berries?"

"You, wife." He sat back in his chair and pulled her onto his lap, imprisoning her there in his strong sure arms. "What were you saying?"

"Who is Father Gervase?"

"The abbot at Iona. Davey and I had our schooling there together."

"You'll like him, Genna," Davey assured her. "He's a jolly cheerful man, not a bit like some of your priests."

Father Alban, who had performed the wedding mass, overheard him and clapped him a mocking blow. "I'll show you jolly and cheerful, laddie," he boomed. "Come along outside to the yards."

"He is nearly as nice as our own jolly, cheerful father," Davey amended quickly, with a wink at Genna. Mollified, the priest scooped another big helping of haggis onto his trencher.

Genna tugged at Alex's saffron yellow *leinechroich*, the billowing tunic the islanders wore for celebrations and battle. "Iona is an island, isn't it?" she whispered.

He glanced down at her, amused. "Aye."

"Then you must get on a ship to get there."

He laughed. "Who would believe the Lord of the Isles would marry a woman who cannot stand the sea? Don't worry, my love, 'tis a very short trip, and I'll be right there beside

you. Here, taste a bit of this wine. Meggie and Althea make it
themselves from the cherries that grow in the garden."

Genna sipped the sweet crimson wine, like distilled sunlight, then she looked up as a sudden burst of low buzzing
sound drifted through the arched doorway. A dozen yellow-
skirted pipers filed in slowly and stood at the far end of the
hall, playing a slow solemn tune. Genna cocked her head, listening to the odd high melody that danced in and around the
drones, watching the pipers puff out their cheeks as they
played. "Who are they?" she whispered to Alex.

"The Mac Crimmons of Skye. Hereditary pipers to
Davey's clan. He must have sent for them for the wedding."

"What is the tune called?"

"'Over the Sea to Skye.' Do you like it?"

"I love the sound of the pipes." She settled deeper in his
lap.

"We'll make an islander of you yet, my love," he whispered.

"But how could Davey have got them here all the way from
Skye overnight?"

"We savages have a rather advanced system of communicat-
ing from island to island," he told her, grinning. "I'll show it to
you sometime." Genna wrinkled up her nose at him and listened as the pipers played.

Their tribute finished, the Mac Crimmon pipers filed out
the same way they had come in, silently, one by one, while the
music hovered behind them, clinging to the ancient stone
walls, hanging from the rafters, filling Genna's heart long after
they'd gone. She looked out over the noisy, cheerful throng of
guests, felt Alex's big hand curl over hers, and knew a sense of
contentment, of belonging, that was stronger than any she had
ever known before.

When the last bits of roast ox and cake had been gobbled
up, and the men leaned back at the table, glutted with rich
food and wine, while the women chattered in the corners
about this wedding and every other they'd seen, Alex led
Genna into the high-ceilinged presence chamber and sat beside
her on the simple carved bench that passed for his throne. In
came a steady stream of the island's crofters and their families,
bearing what gifts they could to their laird and his bride: a
basket of woodcock eggs, a tiny squealing piglet, a new goose-
down pillow, a cask of home-brewed ale, a brace of pigeons, a

polished stone. Alex thanked each one in the same grave tone, sometimes in English, mostly in the old tongue, asking after their households.

Genna felt a catch in her throat as she watched her husband greet his subjects, saw his solicitude for their welfare, and she recalled with a sudden flush of embarrassment the way she and Argyll and so many others had taunted him at court. Maybe he isn't the richest laird in Scotland, she thought fiercely, nor his castle and plate the finest. But he's rich in love of his people, and that is not measured in gold. She reached for his hand and saw his grateful, half-shy smile.

"Not what you expected, I suppose," he said softly, as a ruddy-faced tanner laid a beautifully finished hide at their feet.

"Nay, 'tis far more wonderful than I expected," she answered, and was rewarded with another smile, this one pleased and surprised.

At the end of the long line of gift givers came an ancient, wizened woman, hunched over like a weathered tree, her long hair grizzled and wild. She hobbled up to the throne with impossible slowness, bracing herself on a staff of curled beechwood, her tattered black cloak sweeping the stone floor.

The hall grew suddenly quiet, the crofters' wives pressing forward, children darting behind their skirts. Genna looked at Alex questioningly, then back at the crone. In the midst of the sea of deep wrinkles that webbed her face Genna could see a pair of bright, shrewd gray eyes.

"The seeress," Alex murmured, then stood and bowed to the woman. He spoke briefly to her in the old tongue, indicating his bride, smiling. The seeress nodded and smiled back, a gaping black-toothed smile.

"She's going to make an augury," Alex told Genna, with a hint of apology. "It's customary when a laird is wed. I hope you don't mind."

"Mind? Of course not." Genna's dark eyes glinted with laughter. "Is this the same seeress that told Meggie about her gardens?"

"Aye." He put his finger to his lips.

"You must promise to translate every word that she says for me," Genna whispered, leaning back on the bench.

She watched in amused fascination as the seeress opened the purse that hung from her belt with crabbed, shaking hands, pulled out a lump of chalk, squinted up at the casements, and then drew a circle on the stone floor where two shafts of sunlight crossed. Then she drew a Solomon's seal within the circle, tapped her staff at its points, held the purse to her forehead, and mumbled a long string of ominous-sounding Gaelic. Genna bit down on her hand to stifle the giggle that threatened to erupt as she scanned the rapt faces of the sturdy crofters. As if anyone could believe such nonsense in this day and age, she thought, and glanced at Alex beneath her lashes. To her surprise he too bore that same look of keen attentiveness, his blue eyes narrowed beneath his crown of gold hair.

Still mumbling, the old woman touched the purse with her thin, tight lips, crossed herself, and spilled its contents into the circle on the floor. Out fell a dozen round polished pieces of agate, and the glistening sun-bleached bones of a bird.

The seeress passed her palms over the jumbled pile of bone and stone seven times, eyes clenched shut, her entire withered body rocking almost imperceptibly from side to side. The big room was so still that Genna could hear the woman's faint rasping breaths, even imagined for a moment that she could make out the sound of the heart beating inside that hollow shrivel-dugged chest.

Then, head thrown back, eyes wide open and staring intently at Alex, the woman began to speak in a loud deep voice. The words poured out of her in a torrent, like water bursting over a dam, a deluge of harsh strange sounds that died away slowly to a trickle and then to silence. When she'd finished, the crofters crossed themselves to a man and began to whisper among themselves.

Alex barked a question at her; the seeress shook her head and mumbled something beneath her breath.

"What did she say?" Genna demanded, pulling at Alex's sleeve. Did she only imagine that he hesitated for a moment before he answered?

"The usual sort of thing. Beware of the man who rides the black horse, and the woman who shares his bed."

"She had to say more than that, Alex! She went on forever."

"Hush, I'll tell you later. Now she's going to make another prophecy, for you."

Genna watched as the seeress gathered up the agate and

bones and repeated the ritual. Once more the hall grew deathly still. The stones tumbled to the ground with a clatter, in a pattern that to Genna seemed not a whit different from the one before. The woman waved her hands over the circle, eyes once more closed, bobbing ever so slightly from side to side.

She opened her piercing gray eyes, stared down at the floor, and then stared at the bride. Genna had a sensation of heat, of fire, as the woman's unwavering gaze bored into her.

And then, without another word, the seeress gathered her portents back into her purse, stood with a creak of her knees, and turned to go.

Alex bolted up from the bench and called out to her sharply, commandingly. The old hag paused, leaning heavily on her staff, said a few words, and turned once more for the door.

Alex spoke again, his voice this time entreating. The old woman faced him again with obvious reluctance, her eyes on the floor. Genna shivered despite herself as the seeress uttered a single halting sentence. Then she made her slow, hobbling way to the exit, the crofters drawing back from her as she passed.

Genna stood as well, the rich purple velvet cascading around her, black hair shining in the bright slanting rays of the sun. "What is it, Alex? Is something wrong?"

He stepped down from the bench and scuffed away the marks on the floor. "No, my love," he told her, but his voice sounded unsteady. "The witless old fool must be losing her gifts, or she's had too much new wine to drink. She said that she would not—that she could not—read your signs." He shrugged. "It happens, sometimes."

"Is that why everyone here is staring at me?"

Alex lifted her down from the dais, his big hands circling her waist. "No. They are staring because you are the most amazingly beautiful creature they have ever seen." He pulled her into his arms and held her there for a moment, his chin resting against her soft hair. Then, "Come, wife," he said cheerily. "We have much dancing to do!"

The celebration continued all through that day, and when twilight fell the castle yards still throbbed with the music of the drums and pipes. Ale and wine flowed over the cobblestones, and Genna laughed to the point of tears as she tried to follow the intricate steps of the reels and jigs and hornpipes that everyone was eager to teach her. She took a turn with all the men, from the fourteen-year-old shepherd who approached her falteringly, blushing to the roots of his hair, and held her hands as though they were made of glass, to gnarled old Tom, the peat man, who whirled her through the yards with gay abandon and concluded their round with a hearty pinch to her buttocks.

"Having a good time, my love?" asked Alex, finally managing to reclaim her for himself a brief instant.

"Very," she told him, black eyes aglow in the torchlight.

"They like you," he said, with evident satisfaction.

"I like them." She stood on tiptoe to give him a kiss.

"Come, let's away to bed," he said suddenly, and pulled her toward a stairway. But Meggie and Davey and Sebastian surged toward them, dragging them back, laughing at their dismay. Sebastian offered an arm to each of the ladies, and led them both in a high-stepping *pas de trois*, while Davey and Alex adjourned to the steps of the chapel for a much-needed sip of ale.

"Well," said Davey, tipping his tankard against his laird's, "they say the greatest happiness grows out of the deepest woe, and this proves 'tis true. Here's joy to ye, Alley."

Alex wrested his gaze from his bride and met Davey's eyes. "I'll never be able to thank you enough for bringing her here."

"Bosh, t'weren't nothing I did. The wee darlin' would have swum here on her own if she'd had to. All I did was find us a boat. I must say, I never will know what she sees in ye, Alley, you pig-headed bumpkin."

"Charm," said Alex, waving his tankard. "Intelligence. Not to mention my good looks." Davey choked in his ale, sending a fine spray of foam high into the air.

"You left out modesty, m'lord."

"So I did."

Davey darted a look about, then, satisfied he would not be overheard, leaned closer. "I'm surprised to see Sebastian back here. Did he bring you news?"

"Nothing concrete." Alex frowned. "Looking for one redheaded scoundrel in Ireland is like looking for a virgin at court. There's no shortage of candidates, but—"

"But the real thing is hard to find?" Davey grinned wickedly. "A fine analogy comin' from you, you deflowerer."

But Alex still wore a look of concern. "If only I had the time to go after Ranalt myself, Davey, I'd feel much better."

"Ach, now, ye know Sebastian and Conn are as good as any men in the Isles at trackin'. Didn't they nearly sight him last year at Rathlin?"

"Almost isn't good enough, Davey, not after what he tried to do to Genna. Do you know what puzzles me? Where he's getting the money to live on. I've put his lands and house under attainder. No one in the Isles would dare give him shelter or aid."

"Forget it, man, at least for this day. I'm sure Genna knows you're doin' all that ye can." Davey saw the sudden flush of Alex's face and groaned. "Oh, no, Alley. Don't tell me ye haven't told her."

"I keep meaning to," Alex said faintly. "But it never seems to be the right time."

"Then *make* the right time, Alley, before ye regret it. 'Tis no way to start out a marriage, keepin' secrets from yer wife."

"What's this?" Meggie danced toward them, her arm twined through Genna's. "Is Davey giving you advice on wedlock, Alley? Don't listen to a word he says."

"And why not, lass?" Davey demanded, pulling her into his lap.

"Because you're a terrible husband, Davey. You're never at home for more than a week at a time, and you don't like my cooking, and you steal the covers at night."

"All due respect, m'love, but yer cookin' ain't fit for swine swill. And at least *I* don't snore."

"Davey Mac Leod, are you implying—"

"Implyin', hell, lass. 'Tis little wonder I don't stay home more, when I can't get a decent sleep nights. I keep dreamin' I'm sawin' cabers!"

"You bald-faced liar! Perhaps you'd like me to show Alley and Genna that spot where you're so ticklish." Her fingers dug into the flesh of his thigh, just above the kneecap, and Davey convulsed in a paroxysm of moans.

"Not—not ticklish!" he gasped. "I'm not ticklish!"

"It seems to me, Davey," Alex said gravely, "that was one secret you should have kept!"

The moon rose over the sound and fell away beyond the mountains, and the first rays of the morning sun were filtering through the birch trees before the pipers, giddy with ale, finally dropped off to sleep where they sat, and the Lord of the Isles was grudgingly permitted to gather his bride in his arms and carry her off to bed.

She nestled against him as he bore her through the long, silent halls and up the stairs to his chambers, his heart pounding in anticipation. He laid her down softly on his big feather-stuffed mattress, then turned away to yank off his leinechroich and breeches. "I thought they'd never let us go," he called over his shoulder, laughing at his memories. "Did you see old Tom trying to play the pipes, so drunk he could hardly see? And Althea and Hoban dancing, him jumping about in terror she'd step on his toes? And Meggie and Davey—"

"Husband." She'd come up behind him and wrapped her small arms about his chest, fingers catching in the golden curls there. He could feel her breath, cool and sweet, at his back.

"Wife." He turned to face her. "A fine old word."

Genna blushed as she felt his nakedness against her, his upright manhood pressing at her thigh. Without thinking she started to push it away, and gasped as it seemed to leap at her slight touch. Alex let out a low, deep groan.

"Oh, wife, do you know what restraint it took not to come to you last night? To think of you sleeping but a few rooms away?"

"I did not sleep much," she confessed shyly.

"What did you, then?"

She smiled. "Listened to Meggie tell me all of your faults. Prayed . . . that I would make you happy."

"You've already made me happier than a man has any right to be." He ran his fingers along her white throat, feeling her tremble. "I could have murdered Meggie for insisting on her damned proprieties."

"Would you I'd told her what a lecher you are? That you'd already taken my maidenhead?" She laughed, a little nervously. "It makes it sound as if you robbed me of something, and yet I feel only the richer for it."

She was unbearably timid and excited at once, not quite able to believe that after so long they were finally together, alone together, with a lifetime of love to share. Genna was aching for him to take her, to teach her more of the wild sensate lessons he'd begun at Urquhart, to awaken in her the mysteries she had only glimpsed thus far. In the faint, shimmering light of dawn Alex's hair, his flesh, his eyes were aglow with pale fires. She felt awed, oddly chastened by the power she knew she held over him.

He must have sensed some of her uncertainty, for he bridled his urge to begin his lovemaking at once and kissed her lightly before going to the huge fireplace to stir the embers there. He glanced back, saw her still standing in the center of the chamber looking vaguely apprehensive, and he felt a rush of warm solicitude. As he'd feared, the last time he had been too hasty, had hurt her. He would have to be patient, exquisitely gentle. He would have to allay her shyness . . .

"Would you like a cup of warmed wine?" he asked softly.

"No. No, thank you. I've had quite enough to drink."

"Are you certain? I'm going to have one."

"Well, all right, then."

He busied himself with setting the kettle on the fire, fetching two pewter chalices from the cupboard across the room, finding a ladle. Alex noticed her dark gaze sweep over the furnishings, and, seeing the room through her eyes, looked about him anxiously. "I know, Genna, 'tis not the most cordial chamber in the castle." He eyed the far wall, hung with his father's shields and battleaxes, and the tapestries of sundry gory combats. "It could use fixing up, I suppose," he said diffidently. "I could get you some rush mats for the floor, if you'd like, a few comfortable chairs." He gave her wine, his hand barely brushing hers. "For now, you can sit on the—on the bed."

"I like the room as it is. 'Tis so much like you. Rugged, and spare. And handsome."

Alex felt his cheeks grow warm. Christ, were they to trade pretty compliments through all that was left of the night? She was so unspeakably beautiful, so softly tempting. He struggled for self-control. It was his fault, after all, that she was frightened. If he'd not let his passion get the best of him the last time, she'd not be so hesitant now. But, dammit, she was his wife!

"Genna." His voice was low and impassioned. "Will you not take off your gown?"

She bit her lower lip. God, how he loved her innocence! He was about to explode with need.

"I can't, milord," she murmured. He met her eyes, saw them sparkling with tears.

"Oh, Genna." The words burst from him like a torrent. "I

know we have not spent much time together, do not really know one another as yet, but you must trust me, believe in me. I'm sorry that I hurt you the last time; I swear it won't happen again. You must never feel afraid or shy when you are with me, must never be ashamed of your nakedness. We are man and wife now, for God's sake! Take off your dress!"

"I cannot, milord!" Her shoulders were shaking, her black eyes shining, but not with tears, he realized suddenly. With laughter, instead. Had her fear made her lose her wits? He grasped her wrists.

"What is it, Genna? What is the matter?"

She fell against him; he could barely make out the muffled words: "Meggie sewed me in!"

"She *what?*"

"Well, there wasn't time to change all the buttons, Alex, and your mother's waist was so much bigger, and her breasts and shoulders. You see, milord, I cannot undress!"

"You mean you aren't—I didn't—you weren't?"

"Oh, Alex." Genna reached up on tiptoe to kiss him. "Could you please find some way to undo me? I cannot bear to wait much longer; you will have to tup me like a tavern wench, under my skirts!"

Relief flooding through him, Alex grinned and demanded, "What do you know of tavern wenches?"

"What do *you* know about them, at that?"

He turned her about, examining the seams of the velvet gown, searching for an entrance, but Meggie's handiwork defied him. "She did a bloody good job of it too, didn't she?" He gritted his teeth as his hands ran over her breasts, as the nipples stiffened beneath his fingers. "I've a mind to tear it apart."

"No, Alex, please; 'tis too fine a gown."

"'Tis too fine a nuisance is what it is." His eyes caught on the gleaming edge of an axe on the wall. Genna followed his gaze, and shuddered.

"Put that thought right out of your head, you barbarian!"

"Don't you trust me?"

"Not with that thing, I don't."

"Here, then." He caught up the dagger he carried in his boot, and flourished it before her. "Will this do?" Too late he saw the wince of remembrance on her face. "Oh, Christ, forgive me, love."

Her small hand closed over his, gripping the hilt. She smiled. "No, go on, love. I do trust you."

"Genna." His mouth descended on hers as he lifted her off her feet and carried her to the bed. She sank down, softness swallowing softness, and he knelt over her, the knife in his hand. Like a whisper she heard the keen blade sever the seam between her breasts, thread by thread; he followed each cut with a kiss, his breath hot and quick. She lay perfectly still, unmoving, as his long fingers parted the cloth, as he sliced down the bodice to the waist, and then lower, all the length of the gown to the hem.

Then his arm encircled her waist, lifting her to him as he slid the heavy sleeves back over her shoulders and off, and flung the wedding dress to the floor. Beneath the gown she wore a soft, sheer cloud of pale saffron batiste, trimmed with needlepoint lace. Tenderly he pulled it over her head, her ebony hair spilling over its edge like teasing black flames. He eyed the lawn corset and drawers that still served as foils. "Last layer, I hope," he grunted, tossing the knife across the room. He unlaced the corset ties with fumbling fingers, nearly cursing with eagerness.

The sight of her rose-tipped breasts against that sea of black hair was a spur to his senses; he buried his face in their sweet perfection, his mouth and tongue stroking the nipples to hardness with deliberate slowness. Genna sighed as she felt the strong welcome weight of his head upon her, as his long legs sprawled over hers. She caught her hands in his hair, pulling his mouth up to hers, quivering as his hand slid over her belly, down her thighs. It rested for a moment on the soft mound between her legs, gently pressing. Alex thrust his tongue between her parted lips, tasting eagerly, then traced a long line of heated kisses down her throat to her breast again. She marveled at the trembling responses of her body, her soul, as his big thumbs drew ever smaller circles on her flesh, closing in on the tight red prizes his mouth would claim. She opened her eyes, saw that he was watching her, his blue gaze dark with love and longing, and she smiled, then caught her breath as he rolled to his side and pressed the whole great length of his body tight to her, so that she felt once more the throbbing pulse of his manhood at her thighs.

"Oh, my love," he whispered breathlessly, drawing back to let his eyes roam over her near-nakedness. She blushed at his unabashed enjoyment of her body, and he laughed, pressing his lips to the deep vee between her breasts. "So that is where those becoming stains of color begin! I had always wondered."

Against her will her eyes were drawn down the length of his hard-muscled body. He saw her wide-eyed stare and smiled. "Touch me, Genna," he challenged her. She drew away, shaking her head.

"Here." He took her hand and guided it slowly downward, over his flat, hard stomach, the hollows of his loins. Wanting desperately to please him, Genna swallowed her fear and let his hand do the leading. He let out a slow, deep groan. "Am I hurting you, my love?" she whispered anxiously.

"Hurting me?" Alex tried to laugh, but her touch was making him wild with need. "Great God, no, I assure you." With more confidence she reached for him again, and met his gaze with surprise when he pushed her away. "No more, or I fear I'll spill my seed to no purpose." He wrapped her in his arms and rolled her onto her back, in a shower of kisses. He untied the string of her drawers and slipped them over her hips and knees to her ankles, then tickled her toes with his tongue.

Genna could feel a half-remembered warmth unfurling in her belly, a sweet flow of honey between her legs as he cupped his hand over the dark curls at her thighs and began to rub his fingers against her with exquisite gentleness, back and forth, around, down into her quivering sheath and then out again. She opened eagerly to his touch, her skin tingling, alive beneath his hand. She let out a shivering moan as his probing fingers caressed, stroked, delicate as feathers. He intensified his movements, listening as her breath grew quick and shallow, his urge to take her close to overwhelming in its strength.

At last he could wait no longer; he withdrew his hand, staring down into her widening eyes as he knelt between her legs, forcing them open, and thrust with his swollen manhood at the portal of her womb. Her muscles constricted, tightening around him, against him, and he pulled back, panting, teeth clenched, and thrust again. Inch by inch he pressed onto her, into her, until she gasped and shivered and pushed at his shoulders, begging him to wait. He did, but for no more than a moment; his need for her had become a raging tide that could not be stilled.

"Trust me, love," he urged her, his voice tight with hunger, and though she trembled beneath him, she lay quietly, content that he should take his pleasure from her.

Again he entered her, plunged deep within her, and to Genna's astonishment and Alex's delight a fire seemed to take hold low in her belly, flaring with a suddenness that made her cry out in surprise. Her hands slid over his buttocks, clasping him tightly, welcoming his eager thrusts, whetting his tumultuous need. Every fiber of her being was aflame with passionate fury; she writhed beneath his piercing shaft, arching, straining, unashamed, filled only with wild longing. He quickened his movements, pushing, driving, pounding, then calling her name with a shudder as he felt his semen burst forth with shattering force. Genna matched his cry with her own, trembling with ecstasy as the seed of his love poured into her womb, as the fire within her blazed to unbearable brightness, consuming all thought, all will.

It seemed as though hours passed before either moved; then Alex roused himself with a sigh and tumbled onto the bed beside her, smiling into her shining eyes. She reached over and stroked his cheek with her fingers, pushed strands of gold hair back over his shoulders. He kissed her. "How do you feel?"

"All warm and content—and sleepy." She traced the line of the scar at his temple. "Tell me something," she whispered.

"Aye?"

"Will it—will it always be like that, so wondrous and unexpected?"

"I hope so. I'll do my best."

She nodded with satisfaction, curled tight against him, and fell sound asleep.

He propped himself on his elbow, looking down at her, watching the steady rise and fall of her breasts, struck anew by her fragileness, the delicate bones of her high cheeks, the hollows of her throat. He thought of the children they would give to one another and hoped they would have her dark beauty, her magnificent eyes. He loved her so much at that moment that it frightened him: he wanted to shield her, protect her from the hurts the world could inflict on her, spread his love over her like a sheltering cloak and draw it tight.

The words of the old woman's prophecy for him still lingered far back in his mind: "I see bale and woe in the bones for you, Yer Lairdship. I see you kneeling in shame before a great king, naked, your sword in your hand. From two women will the woe come down to you: she that bore you, and she that stands by your side. One shall be blameless, but the other is cursed. I see a hail of fire and brimstone, and the greatest danger of all from the man on the black horse, and the woman that shares his bed. I see death in the bones, Yer Lairdship."

"Whose death?" he had asked then.

The seeress shook her head. "That, not even I can tell."

He shrugged impatiently, staring down at his wife, so innocent and quiet in sleep. It was nonsense, all of it. Look what she'd said about Genna. And he'd had to beg for that much; she hadn't wanted to speak a word. "Don't ask, Yer Lairdship," she'd muttered, turning away.

"I command you," he'd told her.

"Nay, I'll not say."

"Please. In the name of God."

Reluctantly, eyes on the ground, she'd turned back. "An empty womb," she'd whispered. "Doom for your father's house..."

Alex shivered, drawing the quilts up over Genna, pulling her closer against him. The seeress had been wrong before. She had been wrong about Donald. She'd prove wrong about Genna as well.

"Sleep, love," he murmured, burying his face in the flood of her black hair. He kissed the nape of her neck and she stirred, her hand seeking his. Alex smiled, there in the chill light of morning. "Good day, wife," he whispered, and in moments was fast asleep.

15

Wherever they went on Mull, Alex and Genna were feted and feasted and urged to "stay over just a wee while." As a result, it took them nearly a week to make a circuit of the southern half of the island on their journey to Iona. They set off first along the road beside the sound to Salen and Craignure, then spent two nights with the Clan Mac Lean at Duart Castle. The company there was merry, and Genna was sorry to leave, but Alex promised old Fergus, the chief, that they would pass that way again soon enough.

Still farther south, along the rocky shores of Loch Usig, they came to the castle at Moy. Genna was enchanted with this great house, nestled close against the clear blue waters of the loch, with the imposing bulk of Ben Buie rising above like a faithful guardian, its green crests shrouded in mist. Alex told her the legend of Eoghann a'Chinn Bhig, who had challenged his father for possession of the lands between the loch and Craig and lost, and now wandered the shores of Buie as a ghost, still mounted on his black steed, carrying his head in his hand.

"Perhaps that is the man on the black horse that the seeress warned you to beware of," she teased him.

"If so, 'twill be easy enough to avoid him; I have only to stop drinking," he told her, grinning. "No one yet has seen the headless horseman without having had a few too many tots of ale."

"You never have told me what else she said, Alex. If I didn't know better, I'd think you were keeping secrets from me."

"I told you it was all nonsense, and so it was," he said firmly. "Next thing I know, you'll be seeing ghosties and goblins and getting visits from the sith."

"From the what?"

"The little people. Don't tell me you've never seen them."
She shook her head slowly. "Well, watch out if you ever do.
They wear green hats and coats and skirts, and live in the
ground."

She eyed him suspiciously. "You're making this up."

"Oh, no I'm not. Watch what you say, for the sith are kind
to those who are kind to them, but they make trouble for those
who treat them badly. They can cure any disease, and they
play the pipes, and they eat heather and silverweed. Have I
left anything out? Oh, yes. They travel on eddy winds, and
cannot go below the high-water mark."

"Oh, for heaven's sake."

He leaned over her, blue eyes glinting. "They make love to
human women," he hissed in her ear, tickling her rib cage.
"The old village women pour milk into the ground every night
to feed them. And when we have a baby, you must lay birch
branches over its cradle every night, or the sith will steal it
away."

"Is there anything else I should know about them, pray
tell?"

"If you ever meet up with the sith," he whispered, "you
must never, ever mention Friday by name. You must call it the
'Day of Yonder Town.'"

"And what will happen if I don't?"

"I'll tell you what happened to someone else. Stop laughing! This is a true story. Once there was a hunchbacked man
from Tobermory who came upon the sith while they were
dancing beside their temple in the woods. They invited him to
join in the dance, and so he did. And as they danced they sang
a song that named all the days of the week: 'Saturday, Sunday,
Monday, Tuesday, Wednesday, Thursday, Day of Yonder
Town.' Now, fortunately, this was a very clever hunchback
who knew not to mention Friday. At dawn the sith disappeared into the ground, and Taig, the hunchback, found that
his hump had disappeared, too. He hied himself back to Tobermory, excited as could be, and met another hunchback
along the road. 'Why, Taig,' cries the other hunchback, 'what's
become of your hump, my good man?' So Taig told him all
about his meeting with the sith, and the other hunchback determined to visit their temple as well. The next night he goes
to the place Taig told him, and finds the sith all dancing in a
circle. 'Mind if I join you?' says he, and they bade him wel-

come. He hears the song they're singing, and thinks, 'Well, that's simple enough.' And he bellows out, 'Saturday, Sunday, Monday, Tuesday, Wednesday, Thursday, Friday!'"

"What happened?"

"The sith all vanished in a great puff of smoke. And the hunchback went back to Tobermory with two humps, his own, and that of Taig as well!"

"I must work to learn this tongue of yours, I see," she said ruefully, as they parted company from a red-haired shepherd and his wife who had met them on the road. Not a single word of their excited conversation with Alex had been intelligible to her.

"I'll teach you." He leaned down from his saddle to give her a kiss. "Here is a start: 'A chumain's a stor.'"

She repeated it slowly, tasting the unfamiliar rhythms. "And what does it mean?"

"'My love and my treasure,'" he told her, blue eyes blazing. "And by God, Genna, that is what you are."

The sun shone each day, the pipes played each night, and Genna could not recall having ever been so happy, so utterly content. It was hard for her to believe she'd first thought of Mull as a dark, dreary place, for with Alex as her guide the more she saw of the island the more she loved it, loved the verdant valleys, the tall cloud-ringed mountains, the impossibly clear blue lochs and the pounding sea. She loved its people as well, sturdy ruddy-faced men, gracious laughing women, and the children, wide-eyed and giggling, who came out of their cottages to see their laird and his lady pass. But above all she loved her tall, handsome husband, loved to watch him as he ate and drank and jested with his subjects, or settled a local dispute patiently, wisely, or judged whose cider was best at the tapster's inn.

And she loved him best when he carried her each night to their borrowed bed and awakened in her, wildly, passionately, all the sweet joys of intimacy.

From Loch Buie they went east to Kinloch, and rode along the sandy shores of Loch Scridain to Bunessan, where they stayed at the village inn and saw white seals frolicking off the piers, and what Alex told Genna was a whale. She watched in awe as the huge creature spouted a stream of sparkling water into the air, and laughed at the bright-colored puffins swooping down over the sea from the high cliffs across the loch.

They came at last to the cool white beach at Fionnphort, and stood hand in hand gazing out over the dark blue water to the holy island of Iona. "There is the abbey," said Alex, pointing to the cluster of low gray buildings that rose up from the grassy plains on the distant shore. The scent of the sea was cool and spicy as the wind blew over the waters, riffling through Alex's sun gold hair.

"For nearly a thousand years that land has been hallowed," he said in a near-whisper. "My father lies at rest there, and his fathers before him for fourteen generations. And it is there I will rest when I die."

Genna glanced up at him; his blue eyes were dark and solemn. "And I beside you." She clutched his hand. "But that will not be for a very long time."

He smiled and wrapped her in his arms, burying his face in the soft dark clouds of her hair. "A very, *very* long time," he agreed. Then the ferrymen swarmed up over the strand, clamoring for the honor of carrying His Lairdship across the sound, each claiming his boat as the swiftest or safest or most comfortable. Alex laughed and chose one at random, then distributed pennies to the others, promising them future rides. They went back good-naturedly to their games of dice and draughts, waiting for other pilgrims, while Alex swept Genna off the sand and waded out to the ferry, settling down on the bench in the bow, holding her in his lap. The ferryman tilted his blue cap back on his head and pushed off from the beach with a lurching scrape of his oars.

"How do you feel, love?" Alex asked anxiously, watching her face turning faintly green.

Genna swallowed, clutching the sides of the tiny boat. "Not . . . terribly well."

"Seasick, is she?" the ferryman called cheerily. "Faith, I used to be the same way till I learnt how to handle the sail and oars. 'Tis only what we don't understand that frightens us, ain't that true, milord?"

Alex agreed gravely that he had always found it to be so. The ferryman beamed in satisfaction. "Following that, then, Yer Lairdship, supposing I give Her Ladyship a bit of a lesson in sailing?"

"I think that's a splendid idea. What do you say, Genna?"

"I really don't think it will—"

"Good, very good, then," the ferryman said, nodding.

"Now, this here, milady, is an oar." He pulled it from the water with a loud splash, nearly smashing a low-flying gull. "And this is the sail. Square, you see. It runs up on this pole here, which we seafaring men call the mast." He winked. "'Tis naught but a pole, though, in truth. These here ropes are the halyards. See how I can use 'em to haul the sail up and down?" He demonstrated with great fervor, making the little boat rock wildly from side to side. Genna stifled a groan. "And the sail hangs down from the yard, and is connected to the boom. I use the boom to steer us— Whoa! Duck, milady!" Genna dove for the bottom of the boat as the heavy length of wood came careening toward her head. The ferryman grinned at Alex. "Has the true reflexes of a sailor in her, don't she, milord?"

Biting his lip, Alex allowed as how she did.

"Aye, then, you see, milady? This here paddle at the back —we call the back of the boat the stern, and the front the bow, don't ask me why. We seafaring men like to make up our own names for things so as to confuse you landsmen more readily. Where was I, now? Oh, this here paddle is called the rudder, and I uses it to steer us. Say we was heading for that big rock over there." He luffed to catch the brisk breeze, pulling at the sail, adjusting the rudder, and to Genna's horror the boat whipped around and soared toward the reef at lightning speed. The ferryman leaned back with his hands folded over his knees, still grinning widely. With a low wail, Genna covered her eyes. "No, no, milady, watch now!" She peeked out from between her fingers, saw the rock rushing to greet them, and buried her face again. At the last possible moment the ferryman shouted "Duck again!" and tacked, bringing the bow hard about and reversing the boom. "There, you see, milady? 'Tis as simple as that."

Genna tugged Alex's sleeve, and he leaned over obligingly. "Tell that maniac," she hissed in his ear, "that if he doesn't take us back to shore *this instant*, I'm going to get hold of his bloody oar and break it right over his head!"

"You're not still feeling sick, I'll wager," he told her, grinning.

"I'm too terrified to be sick!"

"Then what have you got to complain of?"

"Alex . . ."

"Oh, very well. My wife is, ah, in awe of your skill, Captain. But we are rather anxious to get to the abbey. Perhaps you could finish your lesson on our return trip?"

"But she hasn't even learnt what we call the rudiments, Yer Lairdship!"

"Nay, I understand that, Captain, but she says she'd like time to reflect on all that you've taught her so far."

"Oh. Oh, aye. Well, then. Comin' about! Duck, milady!" Once more the boom sliced the air overhead.

A white-crested wave lifted the boat and carried it onto the pebbly shore. Alex hurried to deposit his wife on dry land before she had a chance to make good her threat against the ferryman, who beached his craft, settled into the shade of a rock, and pulled out a flask. Alex tossed him a handful of coins.

"Blessings on you, milord!" he called, with a wide grin. "I'll wait right here for you, and give some thought to what else milady might need to know!"

Alex knocked at the front door to the abbey, while a still shaky Genna leaned against him, torn between laughter and anger. After a moment the door swung open to reveal a tall, beefy tonsured monk. As he stood in the shadows Genna thought he was quite a handsome man, aged thirty-five or so, with a wide brow, deep-set eyes, and a pleasant flattened nose. As he ushered them inside, she looked more closely at him, and hurriedly looked away. The monk had a dreadful set of scars carved across each cheek, long and dark red and shiny against his smooth pale skin.

"We've not seen Your Lordship here for some time," the monk remarked without surprise. His voice was flat and monotonous, without expression. "Not since your father's burial."

"I've been away too long, Brother Martin." Alex stood in the cool, vaulted entranceway and eyed the polished tile floor, the dark paneled walls. "The place looks splendid. You must work very hard at maintaining it."

"Thank you, Your Lordship. But I fear the repairs I've made have been of a cosmetic nature for the most part. The more serious problems—a roof for the chapel, the leaks in the sacristy—will have to wait until we receive more contributions." He shrugged. "I do what I can. Go and sit in the garden, and I'll tell the abbot you're here."

Alex took Genna's hand and led her through the narrow

hallways and into a sunny courtyard, while Brother Martin vanished within.

"Alex, what happened to that poor man's face?" Genna whispered, after making certain the monk was out of earshot.

"He used to be a cattle thief," Alex told her matter-of-factly. "The scars are for his first offenses. He's missing two fingers from his right hand as well, for later crimes. By law he should have lost the whole hand, but Donald had hopes of his reforming."

"Your father did that to him?" she asked, aghast.

"He did it to himself," Alex said grimly. "He knew the penalties for stealing."

"Oh, but still, it seems so harsh a punishment."

"He would have been hanged had he committed his crimes on the mainland. Is that more humane?"

Genna bit her lip, picturing the angry wounds. "What is he doing here?"

"After his fifth crime, Donald had no choice but to order him hanged. But my mother apparently took pity on him, and pleaded for his life. She suggested he be sent here, where he might do some good. That must have been, oh, five or six years past. He has served Father Gervase most faithfully. He is adept at accounts and figures. And they say he makes bloody good cider, as well. Look, here are Father Gervase's gardens." He opened a gate in the courtyard wall.

"Oh, Alex, how lovely!" Genna surveyed the sun-flooded herb garden with delight, sniffing the pungent air. The flagstone walkways were lined with neatly tended bushes of rue and catmint and thyme, and against the old walls spilled vines laden with soft full-blown roses and cranesbill and celandine. Sweet violets nodded their heads in a shadowy corner, and hundreds of bees buzzed lazily back and forth against the sparkling blue sky.

"Alexander! Is that you, my son?"

Genna turned and saw Brother Martin leading a thin, stoop-shouldered man with a shock of snowy hair through the garden gate.

"Your Holiness." Alex knelt at the old man's feet and kissed his gnarled hand.

"It has been too long since we saw you here." The abbot rested his fingers for a moment atop Alex's golden head. Then

Alex rose and took his arm, leading him to a bench along the ivy-draped wall.

"How are you, holy father?"

"The Lord has not yet seen fit to take me to him," the abbot said, sighing, "so how should I complain? But some days it is hard, my son. Some days it is very hard." He gasped in air, then grasped Alex's hand. "A single sentence from you would do more to ease my aches and pains than all of Brother Martin's concoctions. Have you heard the call, Alexander, and come to answer it? Have you come to join the order at last?"

"I've answered a call of a different kind, holy father," Alex said gently.

The abbot cocked his white head suddenly, listening, and Genna realized with a start that his lively brown eyes, surrounded by wrinkles, were blind. "Is someone here with you, Alexander?"

Alex smiled, gesturing Genna forward. "My wife, Your Holiness. Genevieve. Genna, this is Father Gervase."

"Your wife." Genna knelt to kiss his hand, and after a moment's hesitation the abbot reached out to trace her features with his crabbed fingers. "So you've married, instead. A pretty thing, is she?"

"Aye," said Alex, grinning at his wife. "Very pretty."

Father Gervase grunted. "She would have to be, to entice you away from a life of peace and joyous contemplation here."

"It was you yourself, holy father, who taught me a man must follow his own heart."

"Aye," said the abbot, grimacing, "I suppose I did. But I had always hoped— Well, no matter. If she is pretty, then she must have some of my violets." He leaned over to scrabble among the plants below the bench. "Brother Martin, where have you hidden my violets?"

"I put them over behind the cresses," the monk said smoothly, "do you not remember? You hoped they would set seed more favorably there."

"Did I? Hmph! I did, did I? Well, I suppose I did. What would I do without my Brother Martin, Alexander, now that I am old and blind? Well, what is this under my chair, then?" He rubbed the leaves between his fingers.

"Nightshade, holy father, and wolfsbane."

"Ugh! Well, we can't give that to a pretty lady, can we? Pick her some violets, Martin. Don't dawdle so! Genevieve, come and sit beside me." He patted the bench. Brother Martin cast a rather rueful look over his shoulder, and went to gather violets.

"Now, then, how long have you two been wed?"

"Only for a week, Your Holiness," Genna said shyly.

Father Gervase threw back his head and laughed; the sound was surprisingly hearty coming from a body so frail. "Only a week! Then you've still much to learn about one another. Do you know he is stubborn, and willful?"

"Oh, aye, I know that," said Genna, smiling slyly at her husband.

"He and Davey, that red-haired demon— Ach, 'tis a wonder we lived through their years with us. Teaching those two their Latin was a trial I'll never forget."

"Davey sends you his love, holy father," Alex put in. "You know he and Meggie were married at Lammastide past."

"Aye, aye, we had word of it. How is your sister Margaret?"

"As lovely as ever."

"With child yet, is she?"

Alex shook his head, grinning. "Not yet. Soon, though, God willing."

Father Gervase fixed him with a blank, intent stare. Of course, 'tis far too soon for your wife to have conceived."

"Of course," Alex said easily, while Genna blushed to the roots of her hair, grateful the abbot could not see.

"Come autumn we must send Margaret some of our vervain seed, Brother Martin. Make a note of it. A bit of that in her wine will have her bearing in no time. And speaking of bearing, how is your mother, Alexander?"

"The same as ever, holy father."

"You must pray for her, my son. I will pray as well." His hand groped forward, and Alex grasped it. "Have you been to the graveyard?"

"Nay, we came to see you first."

"Say a prayer for Donald there for me. I don't get around and about now so much as I did. I've had to put the tending of the graves into Martin's care."

The monk handed Genna a nosegay of violets. She smiled up at his mutilated face, wondering briefly how he liked tending the grave of the man who had ordered him marred that way. The stumps of his fingers brushed her arm. His broad peasant features were utterly impassive.

"Holy father," he said in his flat voice, "you must take your rest now."

"Ah, Martin, my dear Brother Martin. I don't deserve the vigilance you show me." The abbot pushed himself up from the bench. "Will you join me for supper, Alexander, you and your new wife, after you've shown her the island? I believe I can find us a drop of wine that hasn't been consecrated. Not that that ever stopped you or Davey."

Alex's blue eyes twinkled. "I swear to you, holy father, we never touched that wine."

"Aye, aye, and I'll live to be pope someday. Get on with you now, while I have my nap." He turned in Genna's direction. "God grant you his peace, my child. You'll need it, married to such a one as this!" Then Brother Martin came forward soundlessly and led him slowly back into the abbey.

"Christ, how swiftly he ages," Alex said softly, watching the stooped figure hobble through the gate.

"Little wonder," Genna teased, "if he had to teach you and Davey your Latin!"

Alex frowned. "His eyesight is gone completely, too. Five years past he could see to Tiree on a clear day. Strange how the Lord seems to take what a man holds dearest. Reading and tending his gardens, those were his chief joys. Well, at least he has Brother Martin to serve as his eyes." He shrugged. "I forget that we all grow older."

Genna took his hand and squeezed it. "Come. Show me your father's grave."

He led her through the garden gates to the ancient burial place, called in the old tongue *Reilig Oiran*, where fifty kings of Scotland lay at rest, and sovereigns from Ireland and Norway and Denmark, as well.

"Look, here lies Somerled, first Lord of the Isles," Alex told her, pointing out a small stone carved with runes. "He was high king of Norway, and sailed here to claim the Isles as his own. And here is Angus Og, my great-grandfather, who fought with the Bruce." He moved along the row of stones. "Here is my grandfather John, who married Margaret Stewart, King James's aunt. She is buried at Perth now. But this is the grave of John's first wife, Amy Mac Ruarie. My uncle Ranalt's mother."

"Yet *another* uncle?" Genna laughed. "Did I meet him at the wedding?"

"He was not there," Alex said quickly. "He has not been home to Aros in years and years. There was bad blood between my father and him."

"Over what?" Genna asked curiously.

"It's a long story," Alex said, his voice reluctant.

"Well, if you'd rather not tell me."

"It's no secret. It's just—well—Ranalt was John's eldest son, and John named him his tanist."

"His what?"

"His heir, his successor. Whoever is laird chooses from among his male relatives the one he wants to succeed him as laird. That person is called the tanist."

"Was Ranalt laird before your father?"

"No. A little while before John died, Ranalt was accused of a crime committed at Portree, on the Isle of Skye."

"What crime?"

Alex hesitated, looking away. Then, "There was a girl," he said, "the daughter of the clan chief, Mac Leod—one of Davey's aunts. She was raped and murdered."

"My God! And did Ranalt do it?"

"No one knows. But John must have thought so, for he changed his mind about having Ranalt as tanist. At the autumn meeting of the chiefs that year, my father was sworn in instead."

"It doesn't seem right that Ranalt should have lost the lairdship just because of suspicion!" Genna said indignantly.

"Not only the lairdship." Alex's face was grim. "Before all the trouble started, my mother had been betrothed to Ranalt. When he fell out of favor with John, she married my father instead."

"Do you know why?"

"I asked her, once. She said that whether Uncle Ranalt was guilty or no, she didn't think she'd be able to sleep at night wondering whether the man that lay beside her might be a murderer."

Genna shivered. "I don't blame her. But little wonder there was bad blood between your father and Ranalt."

Alex nodded. "I tried to patch things over when I was made tanist for my father. I named Ranalt's son Euan as my successor. I didn't see why he should suffer for the sins of his father. Of course, I didn't know then—"

Her black eyes slanted up at him. "Know what?"

"Nothing," Alex said quickly. "I mean, I didn't know that I would meet the most beautiful girl in all of Scotland, and fall madly in love with her, and want to have eighty-six babies by her." He leaned down and kissed her. "At this year's autumn meeting of the chiefs I'll change my tanist. I'll want our eldest son to rule after me."

Genna returned his kiss, then said thoughtfully, "So he did find someone to marry him, then, after all."

"Who?"

"Ranalt. If he has a son, I mean."

"Oh, aye, soon enough after. He wed some lass from one of the Far Isles. None of us ever met her. She died giving birth to Euan. When Meggie and I were very young, Euan once came and spent the summer with us at Aros. But I haven't seen him now for twenty years." He flushed slightly. "Davey has never liked it much that I named Euan my tanist. The Mac Leods still swear 'twas Ranalt who killed his aunt. But I felt sorry for Euan, and I think Mother must have been a bit guilty over dropping Ranalt for my father. 'Twas she who first suggested I make Euan my heir." He shrugged. "'Tis all ancient history, anyway. Look, here is Donald's headstone." Like those of the other Lords of the Isles, it was carved with the galley and garlanded sword, and it bore an inscription in Gaelic.

Genna stared down at the small gray stone, surrounded by tufts of green grass. "What does it say?"

Alex leaned over to trace the words with his finger, translating. "'At peace lies he who recks the worth of peace.'" His voice caught. "God, how he regretted marching against Buchan and Albany at the Harlaw. He made me swear years ago that I'd put that inscription on his grave."

Genna clutched his hand tightly, gazing out at the long rows of tombs that traced her husband's history, which she still understood so little about. "I wish I might have known him," she whispered.

"You would have loved him. He would have loved you as well."

Genna hesitated, but asked the question. "He would have forgiven you, then, for marrying me?"

"Forgiven? What are you talking about?"

"Because I do not come from the Isles."

He eyed her as though she were daft. "Of course he would have. He did the same when he married my mother. What on earth makes you say such a thing?"

"Oh . . . I don't know." Genna had no wish to spoil the afternoon with any more talk of Mary Leslie. Besides, she sensed that discussing this uncle Ranalt was somehow painful for Alex. She had asked enough questions for one day. "Come, let's pray for his soul." And they knelt together in the cool green grass.

After a few minutes Alex pulled her to her feet, grinning, his mood of introspection past. "I still have so much to show you. We had best get started, or we'll be late to supper!"

He led her all around the abbey grounds, showing her the great stone crosses of Saint John and Saint Martin, erected and carved with runes by the earliest monks on the island, who, led by Saint Columba, had kept the flickering light of Christianity burning in the west of Scotland while all the rest of Britain was overrun by pagan Norsemen. Then they wandered over the low hills to see the wattle-and-daub huts of the hermits on the seaward shore.

"They've taken vows of silence," Alex whispered, as she watched the cowled men tending their garden patches, or walking by the water's edge. "They join the abbot for meals and services, but most of the day he and Brother Martin are quite alone." He chuckled at a sudden memory. "Davey and I once set a beehive in one of their huts, to see if the monk would cry out. But he never did, though he came running out with bees swarming over him and jumped straight into the sea."

"Oh, Alex, what an awful trick to play!"

"It was, wasn't it?" He grinned lopsidedly, looking like a ten-year-old. "I have one more spot to show you." He pulled her along toward the hills and up a steep rocky trail.

The path led to a high round hill with a flattened top; near the summit, beneath a bower of larch trees, a set of sharp stone outcroppings blocked their way. "What now?" asked Genna, staring at the sheer wall of rock.

Alex winked, then wriggled one of the tall stones around to the left. "Milady." He bowed, ushering her over the threshold. Wonderingly, Genna stepped through.

"Oh, Alex"—she turned back to him, black eyes shining—
"what a beautiful place!"

Beyond the stone wall lay a small cave, enclosed on three
sides by rock. The far end opened onto a grotto filled with tall
ferns and deep green moss, the smooth carpet broken only by
the nodding heads of tiny wild flowers and the occasional iri-
descent wings of a dragonfly.

Alex wedged the stone door back into place and came to
stand behind her on the edge of the natural platform made by
the rocky cliff. He wrapped his arms tight around her waist. "I
used to come to this cave all the time, years ago," he said
softly. "Not even Davey could find me here. I would look out
over the water"—he gestured toward the blue ocean, dotted
with tiny far-off islands—"and I would think, someday I will
be laird of all this, and much more besides."

"Did that thought make you happy?" she asked, smiling up
at him.

"On the contrary." He laughed. "It frightened me to death.
Sometimes it still does."

Genna could picture him, a tall, gangly, flaxen-haired boy
crouching here on the green moss, staring out over that vast
expanse of water, the misty islands, afraid of his future, unsure
of himself. And then she remembered the way he had looked
as he greeted his subjects at the wedding, wise and grave as he
accepted their gifts, calling each by name, asking after their
welfare. She nestled close against his broad shoulder. "I think
you are the finest lord the Isles will ever see," she whispered.

His blue eyes were far-off and sad. "Nay, Genna. I might
have been, perhaps, but not now. If only I were more like my
father."

"King James himself told me how much you reminded him
of Donald! He said you had courage, and heart, and wisdom
beyond your years."

"Oh, yes, he is one of my greatest supporters, is James,"
Alex said bitterly.

"He may change his mind."

"You know him better than that. I don't blame him for
banishing me; I don't even blame Henry Argyll. But I curse
myself for my stubbornness, for not being able to swallow my
pride." He sat on the springy moss, pulling her into his lap.
"Perhaps Father Gervase is right, perhaps I should have joined

the order. God has a way of teaching humbleness here on this island. He might even have taught it to me."

"I would have been sorely disappointed to follow you here from Inverness to find you'd taken your vows," Genna teased gently, turning to face him, twisting her hands in his hair.

"What, of poverty? You've seen Mull, Genna, and the rest of my islands are even more beggarly."

"That wasn't the vow I was thinking of," she whispered, and tugged his mouth down to hers.

He kissed her hungrily, tasting the honeyed sweetness of her red lips, exploring her mouth with his tongue. Genna reached to unfasten the buttons of his doublet, slipping her hands beneath his white shirt, loving the feel of his warm skin against her palms, and the crisp curls on his golden chest.

"Wife," he murmured, with mock sternness, "don't you know this is a holy island? What would the abbot say if he found us thus?"

"He'd say we were fulfilling our vows," Genna said with a giggle. "Did you not promise to love and cherish me?"

"I did." He drew in his breath as her small hand slipped downward, across the smooth plane of his stomach, and lower still.

"Well, then?" She reached into his breeches, her fingers soft as they stroked him.

"Watch out," he warned, his breath coming faster at her touch, "or I'll take you here and now." He groaned as she ran her fingertips along his swollen shaft.

"That is just what I mean for you to do."

His hands fumbled at the buttons of her blue gown, pulling it down from her shoulders, then tearing away the lacy shift beneath so that her white breasts tipped with rose pink buds came free from their bindings. He buried his face against her, his mouth tracing circles against the sweet pale flesh until he captured one nipple between his teeth and suckled fiercely, making her moan with pleasure. His hand fumbled with the fillet in which she'd bound her hair, pulling it loose, and a cascade of ebony curls spilled out over the green moss, aglow with the late summer sun. He moved his lips to her earlobe, teasing her with his hot breath, his hands still playing over her breasts. "It was thus that I saw you at Stirling," he whispered, "there in the moonlight, your white throat, your black hair." He kissed her with fevered intensity, his need for her raging like a fire. "My love, my wife . . ." He reached beneath her skirts, hands roaming upward along her thighs, soft as roses. Before Genna realized it he had slid her drawers down over her feet, throwing them aside on the moss, and brought his head down, kissing her breasts as his long fingers tantalized between her legs, spreading them open to the sky as he searched out the sweet bud hidden there. His gold head moved lower still, and she cried out, suddenly afraid as his mouth brushed against her belly, buried beneath a tumble of linen skirts.

"No, Alex, what are you doing?"

"Hush," he said softly, soothing her with his hands. "There is so much yet to teach you, Genna. Trust me." But she shivered despite his assurance as his tongue flickered against her, probing inside her, as his lips closed softly on her hard sweet bud.

"Oh," she gasped, and reached down to pull him from her.

But his mouth was moving more quickly now, his tongue eagerly exploring her warm wetness, and she gasped again as a tremor of need pulsed through her, her legs parting to welcome his hunger for her. He felt her hands tighten on his hair as he circled his tongue against her, as she began to move with him, slowly, and then faster, faster, until she cried out sharply, shuddered, and was still.

When he raised his head he feared for a moment she would be angry. She lay pale and faint against the cool green moss, eyes tightly closed. But when she raised her lids he saw that her eyes were huge, dark and glowing. "Oh, Alex," she whispered, her voice slight and breathless. "Oh, my dear love, I had no idea."

He laughed, pulling himself up beside her, cradling her head in his arm. "That is but one more thing," he said, kissing her forehead, "that a man does to pleasure his wife."

But his need for her was still unslaked, and the sight of her lying there against the dark green moss, so small and disheveled, lips parted, made his manhood pound for release. He kissed her again, felt her shiver in his grasp as he pressed tight against her, his brand throbbing at her belly, flush with fire. He reached to pull down his breeches, then knelt between her legs, his mouth teasing at her breasts.

"You will surely kill me with loving," she whispered, but as he entered her she felt the familiar quiver of desire, as well. He pushed deep within her, marveling at the sensation, the slippery-quick tightening of her flesh. Then he pulled out and drove into her again, and again, his breath harsh and ragged, and Genna felt the sky opening overhead as he cupped her buttocks with his hands and tilted her toward him. Like a raging tide he ebbed and flowed within her, his pace quickening until they were one body, one movement, hearts pounding wildly as he rode her with passionate abandon, until at last he plunged so deeply that she cried out, lost in the sharp wild fire that burst from his groin. She felt his seed pour into her womb, heard him cry out her name, then he lay atop her like a dead man, drained of all feeling but love.

She held him there, his mouth at her breast, reveling in his warmth, his closeness, until at last he raised his head to look at her. She smiled at his adoring gaze. "You know, Alexander, we must not make this a habit," she told him, and bit her lip.

He laughed. "So far I have made love to you in a chapel, on an island, and in a number of my subjects' beds. How I long to get you home to Aros and have you all to myself!"

"Wherever you are, my love, that is my home." She looked out over the sparkling sea at the setting sun; the skies were ablaze with crimson and violet and gold. "I love you, Alexander Mac Donald."

"I love you, my little black gypsy." He sat up, leaning his back against the moss, and she found her drawers and slipped them on, then rested her head on his knees.

"I am going to close my eyes now, just for a moment," she said. "Don't let me fall asleep, or we'll miss our supper."

"I won't let you fall asleep," he murmured, then smiled over her dark head as her breath grew soft and even. He kissed her black hair, warm with the sun's dying rays, and wrapped her more tightly in his arms.

It amazed him how quickly she had come to trust him utterly, to lay her fate and future in his hands the way her head lay in his lap. He thought with a grin of the prickly flashing-eyed girl in the woods at Dumbarton, calling him names, lashing out with her brooch. He thought suddenly of Ranalt, and sighed. He hated to go on hiding the truth about Red John's murderer from her. But how would she react if she learned of the secret he had kept from her all this time? What if the knowledge of that secret destroyed the precious trust she had in him?

Wasn't it better for everyone if he kept that secret just a little while longer? The time would come, perhaps, when he would tell her. Surely, with Ranalt hiding in Ireland with Jamie Stewart's gang, she had nothing to fear from him. If she asked about Ranalt again, then he would tell her. Or in the autumn, when he called the clan chiefs to Islay for the meeting to change his tanist. That would be time enough . . . time enough then. His eyelids began to droop, his breathing matching the sweet sound of Genna's heartbeats. There would be time enough then . . .

Alex awakened with a start. He lay on hard ground in pitch darkness, and someone was calling his name. "Genna!" He stumbled to his feet, eyes vainly trying to pierce the darkness. "Where are you, Genna?"

"Alexander!" Her voice was a loud unearthly wail, and he ran toward it blindly. Suddenly she was in his arms, writhing wildly, still screaming his name.

"Genna!" He took her by the shoulders and shook her. "I'm right here, my love! What is it?" He reached for her face and found it wet with tears.

"Oh, Alex, is that you?" She was trembling like a bird in his grasp. "Thank God! Where on earth did you go?"

"I didn't go anywhere! I was lying right next to you, sleeping. What possessed you to wander around in the dark like that? You might have fallen from the cliff—you might have been killed!" He crushed her in his arms.

"It must have been a dream." She clung to him as he lifted her up and carried her back to the cave. "Oh, Lord, what a horrible dream!"

"What was it? What happened?"

"I was walking by the seaside, it was night, just as it is now, and I had lost you—oh, Alex, I couldn't find you anywhere, though I screamed your name again and again! And all around me the mists were swirling, and the waves pounding, and there was a terrible storm, the wind was tearing at my clothes, and the worst of it was that I knew you were in danger, in terrible danger, but I couldn't find you to tell you!" She sobbed against his shoulder; even the memory of the despair she'd felt in the dream was terrifying.

"Hush, now, it was only a nightmare. It was only a bad dream, Genna darling. How could you lose me? I'm never going to leave you."

"But I *had* lost you! I can still see it so clearly, the mists, and the sea, and that awful driving storm."

He smoothed back her tangled black hair. "Hush, now, there is nothing to be afraid of. I will never, ever get lost, you silly, precious thing."

She stared up at his face in the darkness. "Oh, but if you did, Alex . . . if you ever did, I would die." She kissed him fiercely, her arms around his neck. "Make me a promise, my love, a solemn oath."

"Anything."

"If I ever should lose you somehow"—she put a finger to his lips as he started to protest again—"just promise, if that should happen, to meet me here, on this island. I'll know where to look for you, then."

He started to laugh, but quickly bit his lip. "All right, Genna. I promise.

"Swear it!" she commanded, pressing his hand against her fast-beating heart.

"I swear," he said solemnly, and sealed it with a kiss. "And now, if you are satisfied, I should like to go and have my supper."

"You won't forget, will you?"

"Nay, love. I won't forget."

Father Gervase was already seated at the table in his receiving room when they arrived back at the abbey. Brother Martin stood at his side, keeping his plate well filled.

"Forgive us, holy father," Alex told him, helping Genna into her chair. "We fell sound asleep while watching the sunset. I'd forgotten how beautiful the view is from up on those hills."

"Humph!" said Father Gervase, gnawing at a wing from the fat brown capon the monk had carved. "You never were one to be on time for supper, so I started without you. Brother Martin, give Genevieve a glass of your cider. And get Alex some wine."

Moving efficiently despite his missing fingers, Brother Martin poured out a brimming cup from the pitcher on the table and set it before Genna, then went to the sideboard for the wine.

Genna sipped at the cider and found it surprisingly robust, heady with subtle spices. "Why, Brother Martin, this is extraordinary," she exclaimed, taking a deeper swallow.

"Thank you, milady." He laid neatly carved slices of breast meat and roasted turnips on her plate.

"I've been telling Martin for years that his cider is the only reason any of the brothers stay here, haven't I, Martin?" the abbot said fondly.

"Yes, Your Holiness." The monk deftly separated a drumstick from the capon and extended it to Alex on the point of his knife. "You prefer the dark meat, Your Lordship, as I recall."

"So I do. Your memory is as extraordinary as your cider."

"Have a cup, my son, won't you?" Father Gervase urged.

"No, thank you. I'm not much of a one for cider."

"You take after your father in that, then; he never could abide the stuff." There was a faint clink as the carving fork slipped from Brother Martin's hand.

"Well, I'd like some more," said Genna, draining her cup. "May I ask what's in it?"

"You can ask," said the abbot, with a wheezy laugh, "but he won't tell you. It's a deep, dark secret, I'm afraid; he won't even tell me. Never told another soul how to make it, have you, Martin?"

"Not a soul," he echoed. "Sorry, milady. But we all have our secrets, don't we?"

She met his disinterested eyes. "I suppose we do."

Alex and the abbot were soon laughing together over tales of the old days, while Genna giggled into her cider cup. "What was the very worst trick he and Davey ever played?" she asked Father Gervase at one point. He considered it briefly, leaning back in his chair.

"The worst? I would have to say it was that Christmastide when I was punishing them for something, I can't recall what, and would not let them go home. Do you remember, Alexander?"

"Indeed I do."

"They took two pews from the chapel," the abbot continued, "and lashed them together, with a sail made out of a habit."

"We used Brother Padraic's," Alex said, "since it was the biggest we could find."

"Aye, he was a fat one, was Padraic, God rest his soul." Father Gervase crossed himself and laughed. "Talk about cider drinkers, that man could outguzzle Bacchus. Well, he's gone on to his reward."

"But what were you trying to do?" asked Genna.

"They were making a boat, you see," the abbot explained. "To sail them across the sound."

"Oh, no, Alex! How could you?"

"It wasn't so bad as all that," he assured her, eyes twinkling. "After we'd dragged the bloody things all the way to the water, we discovered they didn't float."

"Two Hail Marys for blasphemy, Alexander," the priest said absently. "I came upon them up to their waists in the freezing water, sputtering and cursing, with Brother Padraic's habit dragging atop them like a shroud."

"You dove right in to save us, though."

"Aye. And made you say acts of contrition till your beads wore thin!"

"That you did," Alex said ruefully. "My fingers burned until Eastertide."

"It was a blessing of God," the abbot said sternly, "that you both didn't break your necks." Abruptly he stopped. "Forgive me, my son. I meant nothing by it."

Alex shrugged, but Genna had seen the sudden flash of pain that crossed his brow. "I know, holy father. 'Tis naught."

Genna looked from one man to the other, uncomprehending. Brother Martin swiftly passed her a platter of cheese.

"So," said Father Gervase, more heartily than seemed necessary, "I hear you attended the Parliament at Inverness, Alexander. Tell me what went on there."

For a time they spoke of political matters, while Genna nibbled at a thick slice of black bread spread with soft ripe cheese and wondered about what the priest had said. Alex told the abbot nothing of the circumstances surrounding his return to Mull, and she knew from the quick glance he shot her that he preferred she not mention them as well.

It was very late when they'd finished eating. Alex stretched out his legs, smiling at his wife across the littered table. "How it takes me back, holy father, to sit and sup with you. Back to the days of my youth."

"Those were simpler days then, weren't they?" The abbot folded his gnarled hands over his stomach. "So many gone now, who once shared meals with me. Your father. Padraic. Brother Samuel. So many dead and gone . . ."

Genna noted with concern that his voice had grown weaker, his voice more rasping, and gave Alex a pointed look.

"That long walk we took this afternoon has exhausted me, Alex. I fear I am about to fall asleep in my chair. I have stuffed myself like a pig." And despite her earlier nap she did feel weary, her head sort of muddled and thick.

He took the hint quickly. "Aye, we have imposed on you for too long, holy father. I hope our ferryman has not given up on us and started back."

"If he has," the abbot wheezed, "there are still plenty of pews in the chapel!"

"Father Gervase." Alex pulled out his purse and emptied it on the table. "Here are a few hundred marks for the abbey. I'll send more along when I return home. And if there is anything at all that you or the brothers have need of, you must let me know."

"What's this?" The abbot reached toward the pile of coins and pushed it back. "We have no need of more money. Your stipend to us is more than generous. We have all that we want, Brother Martin, do we not?"

"Forgive me, Your Holiness," the tonsured monk said quickly, "but I took the liberty of mentioning to His Lordship that the roof of the chapel needs mending. And the scribes have need of parchment, and ink."

"Why said you nothing of these matters to me?" the old man thundered.

Brother Martin rolled his eyes at Alex, with a tiny shrug. "But I did, Your Holiness. Just a few days past."

"You did? You did? Hmph. Well, perhaps you did. Still, you ought not to have spoken to Alexander. You know how generous he is to us already."

"I only thought, Your Holiness—"

"Never mind, then," Alex put in hurriedly. "I know it will not go to waste."

"But you must use your money to buy some pretty gewgaws for this pretty wife of yours, Alexander! I insist. Take it back. Go on, I say! Take it!" He began to cough, and Brother Martin stepped forward quickly, pouring cider and holding it to his thin dry lips.

Alex looked over Father Gervase's head to the monk, scooped the coins up into his purse, and handed it to Genna with a wink. "One favor before I go, holy father. Will you hear my confession?"

"Will I hear your confession?" The abbot pushed back his

chair with renewed vigor. "Gladly, my son! Without you and Davey here, my penances have been most tame! Come into my cell." He moved with the ease of long practice past the table and into the small sleeping chamber beyond. Alex followed, closing the door.

Genna looked up at Brother Martin, still hovering by the sideboard, and extended the purse. "I know Alex wanted you to have this."

"Thank you, milady." He slipped it into the folds of his robe in a swift, clean motion. "Perhaps so as not to perplex the father, you ought not to mention it again. You can see how his mind tends to wander."

"Of course," she said kindly. "He is an old dear, though, isn't he?"

"He certainly is." He saw her still smiling at him, and involuntarily his fingers scrabbled toward his face, as though to shield his scars.

"Don't, please." Genna reached up impulsively for his hand. "You should not be ashamed; you have made so much of your life."

"Have I?" For the first time there was a spark of emotion in that low, flat voice, a flash in his green eyes almost of laughter. It made Genna wince. Then, just as quickly, his face and voice were again impassive. "It heartens me that you think so."

"I—I did not mean to offend you."

"No offense is taken."

"Brother Martin." Genna toyed with the edge of the tablecloth. "Could I ask you a question?"

"Of course, milady."

"When Alex and Father Gervase were talking about that Christmastide, with the church pews, and Brother Padraic's habit . . ."

"Yes, milady?"

"Father Gervase said something about Alex and Davey breaking their necks. And then he apologized, and Alex looked hurt for a moment. Do you know why?"

"Aye, milady." He stared at her with something akin to amusement. "Because of his father."

"What about his father?"

"That was how Donald died. Did you not know that?" He did laugh then, a not entirely pleasant sound. "My goodness. There is still much that you have to learn about one another, isn't there? Donald was thrown from his horse on the road to Tobermory, these two years past. His neck was broken. They found his body the next day."

"Found his body?" Genna echoed, puzzled, remembering Mary Leslie's tale of her husband on his deathbed. "But I thought—"

His green eyes bored into her. "What did you think?"

The cell door opened. Alex smiled at his wife. "Ready to go now, love?"

"I—I suppose so. Let me bid farewell to Father Gervase."

Alex held a finger to his lips. "He has dropped off to sleep. I fear now that I am married my sins are not nearly so entertaining." He leaned down to kiss her. Through his tangle of golden hair Genna caught a glimpse of Brother Martin's face, taut and suddenly cunning. The scars on his cheeks stood out like two fresh wounds.

"Brother Martin." Alex turned, extending his hand. "I can't tell you how much it means to me, to know that you are looking after him. Remember, if there is anything at all you need . . ."

"Thank you, Your Lordship. It is my honor and privilege to serve him, I assure you. Let me see you down to your boat."

He picked up a lantern from the sideboard, then led them back through the narrow twisting corridors to the abbey doors, out to the strand. Alex slipped an arm around Genna; she felt suddenly bone-weary, her feet as heavy as lead. Brother Martin stood on the dark beach, his lantern held high in the air, as Alex helped Genna into the boat. The ferryman poled off into the fathomless black waters, his oars splashing like fish as he dipped them below the surface. A pale half-moon was rising in the east, casting a shimmering trail of glitter across the sound.

Alex unfastened his cloak and spread it over Genna's knees. "So," he whispered, "what did you think of Iona?"

"It's beautiful," she murmured sleepily.

"And Father Gervase?"

She curled tight against him. "I can see why you love him so. But that Brother Martin . . ."

"He just takes a bit of getting used to," Alex said with a laugh. "Father Gervase has done a remarkable job of reforming him."

Genna raised heavy eyelids and stared back over the glistening water to the rocky strand. The monk still held the flickering lantern aloft. His pale face, marked with the jagged reminders of his sins, shone like a jaundiced reflection of the moon.

"Now, milady," the ferryman began, his voice with a faint trace of a slur. "Here's how you takes your bearings from the stars and moon. Sirius, that's the dog star, is always the brightest spot in the heavens. He's that sturdy-lookin' fellow up there." He pointed with an oar, nodding his head. The little boat rocked on the breeze, the sail a white gash against the dark sky.

The lantern on shore went out with a soft low hiss, plunging the strand into darkness. Genna shivered.

"*Seóthó, a thóil*," Alex sang softly, wrapping his wife in his strong arms, and the boatman chimed in:

> Hush, my darling, hush, my fair one;
> Cry no tears today.
> Know instead
> That from this bed
> I never more will stray.
>
> I that thought myself the hunter
> Find myself misled,
> For the charms
> Of your white arms
> Entangled me instead.
>
> Hush, my darling, hush, my fair one;
> Never will we part.
> Your sweet sighs,
> Your tender eyes
> Have tamed this wild hart.

"Ach, 'tis a pretty song, that," the boatman murmured, pulling at the lanyards. He looked at the sleeping woman, and smiled. "Aye, a mighty pretty song."

16

"*Ta gaim*," Genna muttered to herself. "I come. *Teim*, I go. *Do thanag*, I came. *Do chuas*, I went. Oh, damn." She threw the list she held down on the bed with a sigh. "Why didn't I marry a nice plain Englishman?"

"Genna!" Meggie poked her head through the bedchamber door.

"*Cad ta vait?*" Genna asked tentatively, and giggled. "If you can understand that, Meggie, I'll give you sixpence."

"I understood perfectly. I wanted to know if you'd like to come fishing with Davey and Alley and me."

Genna consulted the paper. "*Tá dúil agam ann anocht cosúil tine chreasa.*"

"Well, actually, a simple yes or no would do. Did my brother make out that list for you?"

"Aye. Why do you ask?"

Meggie laughed. "I thought as much. What you just said was, 'I desire it tonight like a burning fire.'"

Genna blushed beet red. "Lord, no wonder Uncle Liam looked at me so strangely when I asked for the butter at breakfast! What a devilishly hard language this is."

"Forget your lessons for this day, and come to the loch with us. Davey woke up with a burning desire for salmon. And there won't be many more days this fine now that October is nearly over."

"Let me just put on my boots, and I'll meet you all at the stables."

"Wonderful!" Meggie smiled and clattered off down the stairs.

Genna tucked her growing pile of phrase lists into a drawer, pulled off her slippers, and buckled on her kid-leather boots. Her gaze swept over the big high-ceilinged room, still lined with arms and trophies of battles, and her loom, set incon-

241

gruously in a corner. She had not spent much time at weaving lately! Alex's birthday was in mid-December, less than two months away, and she'd not even begun the cloak she wanted to make him. But how could she sit at the loom when there was so much else to do? Each day seemed to bring some new visitors here to the castle, and even when there were no so-journers the halls were filled with relatives, with aunts and uncles and cousins and their laughing children, dozens of children who tormented Althea and Hoban with mischievous tricks and made life hell for the hounds and the cats.

Alex had worried at first that the noise and commotion would prove too much for Genna, but she adored the haphazard life here, the steady streams of guests, the gay, informal meals at which one nearly had to shout to be heard. Each day some new crisis had Thea threatening to leave for a nunnery, and each day Alex and Meggie and Davey would coax and cajole her with promises and kisses and lavish compliments until the housekeeper would blush with pleasure, say, "Go on, get off with ye, now," and cheerfully set about making supper for three dozen hungry souls.

"*Sa bhaile,*" Genna whispered to herself, "home. *My* home." One of the first phrases she'd asked Alex to teach her, and still the one she liked best.

"Genna!" Alex's shout carried over the steady din that rang through the corridors and all the way up the stairs. She hurried out to the courtyard to join the others and found him already fastening Rannoch's bridle and bit. "Hello, my love," he said, swinging her into the saddle. "You look absolutely breathtaking." His eyes ran over her full teal skirts and lingered on the tight bodice of her rose linen jacket. Her hair was tied up in two long glossy braids, and her nose and cheekbones showed a faint sheen of brown from a summer spent in the sun.

Althea, hauling saddle pouches stuffed with food and wine out to the yards, clucked her tongue when she saw Genna. "Best march back inside and get a hat, Young Mistress, or you'll have a face full of freckles one of these days."

"And I will love every single one of them," Alex told the housekeeper, laughing. "My God, Thea, what did you pack for us? These weigh a ton."

"Just a little somewhat to keep body and soul together. Now, mind you, Davey Mac Leod, don't you be bringing me back those wee spawn you caught the last time. Anything less than a foot long t'ain't worth my bother."

"Yes, mum," said Davey, giving Meggie a hand up to her horse. "Funny thing, you know. That's what Mistress Mabel down at the bawdy house used to say."

"You cheeky devil!" cried Althea, snatching Meggie's crop and pursuing him through the yards. Nimbly he avoided her reach, leapt onto his horse, and spurred through the gates, sticking out his tongue. The others followed, laughing helplessly.

They set off on the forest trail to Loch Frisa, passing the wide-hatted crofters who were scattered through the common fields tilling for winter wheat and scything oats. The crisp autumn air was filled with the sweet green scent of hay, and Genna drank it in eagerly, head tilted back toward the sky. *"Dia's Muire dhuit!"* the farmers called out as their laird and his lady passed, and Genna knew enough now to answer, "God and Mary to you as well!"

This was Genna's favorite trail on all the island. As it wound steadily northward to the loch the blocks of green and gold fields gave way to dense forests of oak and pine, which in turn opened onto the hilly pastures where sheep grazed, the gentle tinkling of their bells sounding high and sweet and clear. Through the tangles of bittersweet and ferns beside the road one could catch swift glimpses of black-tailed stoats, still clothed in their brown summer coats, or even a shy red deer.

Then clumps of graceful white birches appeared, and beyond their windswept branches lay the crystal blue waters of the loch, shining bright in the sun. Davey jumped down from his mount and pulled out his rod and creel, wading in to his knees in his tall boots. "Alex, where is your gear?" asked Genna, seeing only the bags Althea had packed tied to Bantigh's saddle.

"I thought I'd leave the fishing to Davey, since he's the one with the hankering for salmon. Meggie, we'll see you before too long. Save us something to eat."

She nodded, already settling down beside her husband on the shore. Davey was busy skewering bait on his hook, and did not even spare a wave. "Come on," said Alex, grinning, taking Genna's hand. "I want to be alone with my wife."

They wandered along the banks of the lake, Alex ducking low beneath the broad pine branches that hung down over the water. A few hundred yards ahead the path crossed a stream that tumbled down a hillside; Genna gathered her skirts in her hand to step from stone to stone to cross, while Alex splashed right through the shallow currents. Beyond the stream the path bent sharply to the right, around a small sheltered cove that the lake had carved from the woods. When they reached that point Alex stripped off his tunic and shirt and wrapped them in a ball on the grass, then began to tug down his hose.

"What do you think you're doing, love?" asked Genna, idly gathering a bunch of yellow-cupped celandine and winding them into her braids.

"Going swimming. Care to join me?"

She looked up to see that he was stark naked. "Put your clothes back on, for heaven's sake, husband! What if someone sees you?" But she could not help but admire his beautiful golden body, the rippling muscles of his chest and arms and loins.

He plucked at her bodice buttons. "Come bathe with me."

She pulled away from him, laughing. "Honestly, one would think you didn't get enough of it in your bed at night!"

"I'm shocked at you, Genna! I invite you to go bathing, and find you've naught but venery on your mind."

"And you haven't, I suppose?"

He pushed her down in the warm grass and kissed her, teasing her lips with his tongue. "I want to see you naked once more in the sunlight, before the winter comes."

"And if someone else should just happen to walk by this way?"

"He will see a young couple in love."

She sighed as his long fingers worked at the buttons. "There is simply no reasoning with you, husband."

He slipped the shirt down over her shoulders, nuzzling at her white breasts. "Not when it comes to you." He worked his hands back to her waistband, unfastening her skirt and the petticoats beneath it in one swift motion, then pulled off each piece of clothing with deliberate slowness, devouring her with hungry blue eyes. "So beautiful," he murmured, as she lay before him naked at last. He pulled her to her feet, holding her tight against him, unbraiding her hair. Then he swept her up into his arms and walked toward the water.

Genna felt his erect manhood push at her buttocks, and

giggled. "Make up your mind, please. Do you want to go bathing or make love to me?"

"Both," he whispered, his mouth at her ear. He stepped off the shore and into the clear lake, nibbling at her white shoulder, one big hand fondling her breast.

"Brr!" Genna shivered as the water touched her dangling toes. "Alex, 'tis far too cold for me!" But he plunged below the surface with her still in his arms, and the chilly splash took her breath away. They rose to the surface in a flurry of bright bubbles, Genna sputtering and gasping for air.

"You might at least have given me a chance to get used to it!" she cried, when she'd caught her breath at last.

"You can't get used to loch water; you have to just jump right in." He was standing on the reedy lake floor, the water lapping at his shoulders, long hair dripping down in his eyes. She brushed it away with a laugh as he pressed her against him, their bodies sleek and wet, and aglow in the sun. She wrapped her legs around his waist and leaned back, her black hair floating out over the water. "Move a wee bit lower," he murmured, then drew in his breath as she obediently shifted down, and his manhood slipped between her thighs. He ducked his head and sucked at her hard pink nipples, sliding back and forth, teasingly gentle, until she clutched at his shoulders with a little moan.

"Oh, Alex, you are making me wild." The slick movement of his manhood, the hot bright sun on his skin, the drops of water that clung to his lashes . . . He is like a god, she thought, so potent and shining.

"What do you think you are doing to me?" He pulled her toward the bank and lay on his back against the reeds and bracken. She sat straddling his loins, pushing back long strands of wet black hair. Her round white breasts shimmered before him; he licked the lake water from her nipples as she set her hands on his shoulders.

"What now?" asked Genna, as his breath began to come faster.

"Whatever you wish, love." His hands closed over her firm buttocks, and she felt him enter her, drive up into her. She slid upward along his shaft, then down slowly, pushing against his chest.

"Does that please you?" she whispered, seeing his eyes close, his mouth tighten.

He groaned. "Oh, Christ, Genna, it pleases me." She tried again, feeling awkward and unsure, but knowing from his quick rasping breath that he liked what she did. She leaned forward, pressing her breasts against his slippery chest, tracing his throat with kisses as she continued to slide up and down. Then suddenly she found the rhythm, as his hands pressed the small of her back, molding her to him, plunging her onto him as curious bottleflies buzzed through the air around them, blue wings flickering in the sun. He stifled her cries with his mouth as they came together in a furious burst of passion, as his manhood strained deep inside her, throbbing with release. She fell against him, panting for breath, mouth curving in a smile as she thought of her secret, of the new life already growing in her womb.

"What are you finding so amusing?" Alex demanded, pulling her damp hair away to stare into her sable eyes.

"You. Us. . . . This." She indicated the lake and trees and sky with a wave of her hand, then wriggled up to sit on his stomach. "What a wanton you have made of me, Alex. How would I ever live without you now?"

He ran his hands over her pale shoulders and breasts, drinking in the warm glow in her eyes. "I love you, wife."

"And I you, husband." But she saw the flicker of concern that crossed his face, and lay down once more across him, her mouth touching his. "What is it? Something is troubling you."

He kissed her with slow, lingering gentleness, his hands caught in her hair, trying to commit to memory the exact way she had looked a moment ago, her proud, high breasts, the delicious curve of her back, the red lips that parted to welcome his tongue.

"I must go away for a time," he told her softly. "I have summoned a meeting of the clan chiefs at Finlagen, on Islay."

"Away. . ." Genna paused, trying to conceal her dismay. "For how long a time?"

"A fortnight, a month at the most."

"Is it because of something that Sebastian told you? You and he spent nearly two hours closeted together the other day, when he returned."

"No, no. It is simply time for the autumn meeting of the chiefs. Davey will be coming with me. I've put it off too long already, my love. I've been neglecting my work because of you." He felt only a twinge of guilt as he lied to her.

The news Sebastian brought had been good. Ranalt was no longer in Ireland. Conn had followed his tracks to Machrihanish and Knapsdale, and a man of his description had seized a packet boat at Oban, killing the captain and replacing the crew with waterfront ruffians. But Sebastian had brought a clear description of the vessel, and Alex would pass that on to the clan chiefs, ordering them to seize the ship should it appear in their districts. This time Ranalt would not slip away. But just in case something went awry, he did not want to raise up Genna's hopes only to dash them down again.

"There are tributes to be collected," he went on, "disputes to be heard, laws to be changed."

"What laws?"

"My tanist, first off. I want to be sure any son we have will succeed me as laird instead of Euan. I should have taken care of that months ago."

She longed so much to tell him then of the child she was carrying, but she held her tongue. If she did, he might insist on staying here on Mull to be with her. And much as she would miss him, she did not want him to neglect his duties for her. The lairdship was too important to him. There would be time enough to tell him when he returned from Islay. The news would only make their reunion all the more joyous.

"When do you leave?"

"Tomorrow."

"Tomorrow! Why didn't you tell me sooner?"

He pulled her close to him. "Because I knew you would be sad. And I cannot bear to see you that way. Forgive me?"

"I suppose I must," she said, pouting. "So that's what all those flares were that I saw on the hilltops two nights past."

He nodded. "We use the torches to carry signals from one island to another. I can summon the clans from as far away as Lewis in a single night. The chiefs from the Far Isles are already under sail."

"Then I can see it is too late to try and dissuade you from going," said Genna, smiling wickedly as she leaned forward to kiss him. "A month?"

"At the very most," he promised.

She traced the veins in his throat with the tip of her finger. "It is not too late, however, to pursuade you to hurry back."

Genna and Meggie saw their husbands down to the sound the next morning and aboard the long carved galley that would carry them to Islay. Sebastian had already departed for Oban in another ship, to pick up Conn and continue the search for Ranalt and his purloined packet. Alex was in high spirits, certain that his troublesome uncle would soon be in his hands. "Now, don't let this wife of mine mourn and waste away while I'm gone," Alex cautioned his sister, giving her a kiss farewell.

"Who, me? Not likely," Genna scoffed. "It will be one long holiday for me. I'll sleep until noon, grow fat and saucy, and not bathe once until you return."

"Then I won't need to worry about my lecherous kinsmen coming near you."

"Well, perhaps one bath," she allowed.

His mouth tickled at her ear. "God be with you, my love, until next I see you."

"And with you." She smiled up at him, fighting back tears. "I will be waiting right here when you return."

"Yer Lairdship, we'll miss the tide," the galley's captain warned.

Davey kissed Meggie soundly and clambered into the boat. "Come along, Alley, and don't look so mournful. It gives the rest of us poor husbands a bad name."

"You're right. Farewell, Genna! Farewell, Meggie!" He leapt into the prow as the oarsmen began to row. The sail unfurled with a loud flap, catching the wind, and Meggie and Genna stood on the shore waving wildly for as long as the ship could be seen.

Genna bit her lip as her tears spilled over. "Oh, Meggie, does it ever get any easier to bid farewell?"

The gold-haired woman looked off across the calm blue waters, then shook her head. "Each time I see Davey off, I get the most awful sensation in the pit of my stomach, thinking that I might never see him again." She shrugged and took Genna's arm. "There is nothing to do about it but trust in God until they return. Come back inside now, or you'll catch a chill in this early air. You've got to take care of that wee one you're carrying!"

"How did you know?" Genna demanded, wide-eyed.

Meggie laughed. "Althea told me. She says you've been sneaking down into her kitchens at all hours of the night, hungry as a jaybird, and stealing pieces of cake."

"I thought I'd covered my tracks better than that," Genna said ruefully. "She didn't say anything to Alex, did she?"

"Of course not. Are you waiting to tell him until he comes back?"

Genna nodded. "I was afraid he might think he should stay here with me. And I know he has work that he must do."

Meggie kissed her forehead. "You're very noble, Genna Fleming. Well, this news should certainly put the seeress into a temper."

"Why is that?"

"Oh, I don't know," Meggie said quickly. "No reason."

Genna looked at her curiously, but the blue eyes that met hers were innocent and clear. "Meggie," she began, but just then Althea bustled out from the kitchen doorway, a length of wool in her hands.

"Shame on you, Young Mistress," she scolded, "going down by the water so early, without even a wrap. A fine mother you'll turn out to be!"

"Speaking of mothers," said Meggie, "I suppose we must write to mine, and tell her she's due to be a grandmother."

"Oh, please, not just yet," begged Genna, shivering as she remembered Mary Leslie's strange hatred for her.

"Too late." Althea smiled smugly. "I sent a message to my Hannah three weeks past and gave her the news. And if I know Hannah, I'm sure she's spread the word to Old Mistress."

"Thea's daughter, Hannah, is my mother's chambermaid," Meggie explained. "And just like our Thea, she's an awful gossip."

Thea put her fists on her wide hips. "I am *not* a gossip, Meggie Mac Donald. 'Tis just that there's some news, good and bad, that demands the telling."

"And I don't suppose the thought that Mother might be less than delighted to have everyone at court know she's old enough to be a grandmother ever even crossed your mind, eh, Thea?"

"Hoo, haven't you got a suspicious nature?" Althea clucked her tongue, but there was a bright twinkle in her eye.

"At any rate," said Meggie, "'tis all taken care of."

"Yes, I suppose it is." Genna shivered again in the cool autumn air.

Althea tucked the wool over Genna's shoulders with a disapproving stare. "Now, didn't I tell you? Come along inside to the fire."

Genna let the housekeeper lead her into the kitchen and sit her down at the long trestle for a bowl of hot broth. She had already begun to miss Alex, but the thought of the wonderful news she would have to tell him when he returned helped to raise her spirits. He would be so proud, so pleased. But the seeress would be in a temper, Meggie had said. Why would that be, Genna wondered, watching Althea ladle out the soup.

"Thea," she said impulsively, "what did that seeress prophesy about me at the wedding?"

The housekeeper paused with the ladle in midair. Then, "Whatever are you talking about, mum?" she asked, and set the bowl before Genna with unsteady hands. A bit of the broth slopped over onto the table, and she wiped it up hurriedly with her apron edge.

Genna eyed her sternly. "Now, Thea, didn't Alex say you were to obey my every order?"

"Aye, mum, he did, but—"

"Well, I'm ordering you to tell me what that woman said!"

"Oh, she's naught but a crazy old hag, a lunatic. Nobody ever pays her no mind."

"I don't think that's true, Thea. I think you believe in her powers. Don't you?"

"P'raps." The housekeeper's one was noncommittal.

"Well, if it's about me, don't I have a right to know what she said?"

Althea glanced around the deserted kitchen apprehensively. "I'd really rather not say."

"That's obvious," Genna said dryly, "but I'd rather you did. Please, Althea." She reached out an imploring hand.

Althea hesitated a moment longer, her passion for gossip warring with the promise she and all the household had made to Alex. Then she pulled a stool up close to Genna's and sat down, wagging her head. "All right, then, mum," she whispered conspiratorially, "but if any asks you, you did not get it from me. Did Young Master tell you anything at all?"

"Just something about 'Beware the man on the black horse, and the woman that shares his bed.'"

"Oh, there was much more to it than that, mum. Now let me see if I can get it right." The housekeeper rubbed her nose. "First off, she says, says she, 'I see bale and woe in the bones for you,' she tells him. And then, 'I see you kneeling in shame before a great king, naked, your sword in your hand.'"

"He didn't tell me that part!"

"Wait, there's more. 'From two women will the woe descend,' she says, 'from the one that bore you, and the one that stands at your side.' That's you, you see, mum."

"Me and Mary Leslie," Genna murmured thoughtfully. "Well, go on."

"She said one of the women was blameless, and the other was cursed. And then, milady, comes the part about the black horse. 'I see fire and brimstone,' she tells him, 'and the worst danger of all from the man on the black horse, and the woman in his bed.'"

"What meant she by that?"

"Who knows, mum? And then"—she leaned even closer—"she said she saw death in the bones, but whose death, she couldn't tell."

Genna shuddered. "How awful! What right does she have to say such things?"

"Well, she's the seeress, mum," said Althea, as though that explained it all. Her brown eyes narrowed. "And when it came time to read your signs, mum, she refused to say even a word, just looked at the charms and got up to go. Then Young Master, he says, 'What do you think you're doing?' And the old witch looks him up and down, and 'I'll not do it,' says she. 'By God, you shall,' says Master. And then: 'Doom,' says she, 'that is all I see for your bride. An empty womb, and the fall of your father's house.'"

"Why, that's silly," said Genna. "I'm already with child."

Althea crossed herself and said nothing.

"No wonder Alex wouldn't tell me her prediction," Genna went on, laughing. "What a deal of rubbish. The fall of his father's house, indeed."

The housekeeper put a finger to her lips. "Hush, milady! You mustn't mock at the seeress! Her powers are great, and her auguries are never wrong."

"Never?" Genna asked teasingly.

"Never," Althea repeated, lips pushed out. "Oh, I know

there's some as thinks she was wrong what she said about Old Master, but I'm not one of 'em."

"What said she about him?"

The reply was the merest whisper. "That he'd die of murder."

"Why, then, she has been wrong! Alex's father fell off his horse."

"Maybe so," Althea hissed, eyes narrowed. "And maybe not."

Meggie came in just then, rinsing dirt from her hands at the pump and drying them on the cloth Althea hurried to bring her. She stared at the housekeeper's flushed, guilty face with amusement. "Goodness, Thea, you look like a pup caught flat in the henhouse. What on earth have you two been up to?"

"Talking of old times," the woman said quickly, with a warning glance at Genna. "We was just talking over old times."

"*I'd* rather talk about the future," said Meggie, her blue eyes shining. "Genna, when will the baby be born?"

"At the end of May."

"God willing," Althea said darkly.

"Now, none of your usual doom and gloom, please, Thea," Meggie said, and laughed. "I was thinking perhaps we could clear out Mother's old apartments to make a nursery. 'Tis close enough to Alley and Genna's rooms, but not *too* close. And 'tis nice and sunny, or so it used to be. Thea, for heaven's sake, don't make such faces!"

"You know I don't like to touch her things, nor even look at 'em," Althea said stubbornly. "That there room's been closed off for years, and that's how it should stay."

"Thea," Meggie said gravely, "thinks my mother is the devil incarnate."

"Not himself, p'raps, but she knows the old gentleman well enough."

"I wonder you let your daughter wait on her, then," said Genna.

"Work's work." Althea folded the towel she held with grim methodicalness. "It lets Hannah be near her husband at court, and there's something to be said for that."

"Amen," Meggie put in ruefully. "If my husband doesn't start staying home more, I'll never have children of my own."

"Faith, girl, you'll be carrying in no time." Althea laid her work-reddened hands on Meggie's shoulders.

"That reminds me, Meggie. When we were on Iona, Father Gervase said he was sending you something this autumn to help you conceive. Vervain, I think he called it."

"There, you see?" Althea said triumphantly. "And just as soon as Master Davey gets back, you'll have all winter to work at it."

Meggie giggled. "It isn't work, you know, Thea."

The housekeeper waggled her finger. "Don't get saucy with me, young lady. I know well enough what I'm talking about. Didn't Percy and me bear six bairns altogether, God rest his soul? You don't get that many youngsters by spinning tops."

"You don't?" Meggie stared, wide-eyed. "So that's what Davey and I have been doing wrong!"

Althea snapped the towel at her. "Smart thing, I ought to slap your bottom."

Meggie scrambled out of reach. "I'll go and get started on that nursery."

"I'll help," Genna offered.

"Thea?"

The housekeeper sighed. "All right, then, but don't say I didn't warn you. Let sleeping dogs lie, that's what I believe in. But Mistress Meggie must have her way."

17

Mary Leslie's room at Aros Castle had been vacant since her husband's death. A thick layer of gray dust covered all the furnishings, and the draperies and bedding gave off a sour, musty smell as Althea unlocked the doors and stepped aside.

"Phew, what a mess!" Meggie flicked a rag across a desktop, sending puffs of dust into the air.

Genna sneezed while pulling the heavy draperies back from the casements. "But what a beautiful view from here, Meggie!" The room was high up in the north tower, and looked out over the gardens to the hills beyond.

"Old Mistress hated it," said Althea from the doorway. "Hated everything about this island, she did. Couldn't even wait for Old Master to be buried over on Iona before she hightailed it out of here."

"Now, Thea." Meggie laughed, embarrassed. "The poor woman was distraught, in shock."

"Bullfeathers. If she'd stayed, she'd have danced on his grave."

"She truly did hate it here," Meggie said thoughtfully, bundling up the old draperies. "Said all the noise and commotion played havoc on her nerves."

"That one don't have no nerves," said Althea bitterly. "Nor no heart either. Why, two weeks after your brother was born she was packing up to go back to court, to her dancing and fancy friends. Did the same a fortnight after you were delivered too, Mistress Meggie. And I don't think she'd have ever come back if Old Master hadn't insisted she spend each summer here. La, the fights there were over that!"

"It must have been very hard for you, seeing so little of her," Genna said softly.

Meggie smiled. "Not really. It all seemed perfectly normal

255

to Alley and me. We had a father who loved us dearly, and if our mother spent less time with us than most do, well, that was better than having her stay here, hating it so. Father more than made up for Mary."

"If she'd spent more time here, perhaps she would have come to love it, as I have."

Althea snorted. "Not that one. Not in a million years."

Meggie stood in the center of the chamber and looked about with bemused dismay. "I hardly know where to begin. Thea, come help me move this bed."

It took the three of them, working together, nearly two weeks to clear the moldy carpets and furnishings from the room, wash the walls and floors, and make the place habitable again. As they worked Meggie tutored Genna in Gaelic, or told her the island's legends. In return Genna recounted stories of her life at the court of King James, and taught Meggie the snatches of French that she knew. Althea, walking along the passageways, would hear them giggling together and singing, and the sounds warmed her heart. "Now, that's what a happy house sounds like," she would mutter to herself approvingly. "That's the sounds a soul loves to hear."

Meanwhile, the days grew shorter, the nights colder, as autumn slipped quickly toward winter. The flowers in Meggie's garden were taken by the first frost, and each morning thick hoar mists rose from the sound to shroud the hills. Genna and Meggie took two afternoons off from their labors in the nursery to help Althea press cider and wine and set the kegs to ferment in the low-ceilinged cellar off the kitchens. Althea sipped a bit of the cider mash from the tip of a spoon, wrinkling her nose, shaking her head.

"I might say what I say about Mary Leslie," she told Genna, "but that woman made a wicked cider one autumn. Had a bit of a spicy taste to it, like cloves or nutmegs. I asked her for the receipt, but she wouldn't give it away. I've been trying ever since to copy it, but I still can't get it right."

"You just hate it that Mother was better at something than you are," said Meggie.

"Poor Hoban was near brokenhearted when she went back off to court without leaving that receipt," Althea recalled with a grin. "For a while there I thought I could stop locking this cellar to keep him out of it." Meggie and she rolled the last barrel down the planks they'd put over the ladder, and then the housekeeper drew the bar back across the sloping doors, securing the lock with a key she kept on a chain about her neck. She winked. "He adjusted to the taste of mine again, though, without too much trouble. Now I'm back to keeping the key right here." She tucked it into her bodice again.

Genna's tiny waist had begun to thicken considerably as she entered the third month of carrying the child, and Althea watched her like a hawk lest she try to move some piece of the sturdy furniture or take too heavy a load of rubbish to the yards to be burned. So while Althea and Meggie stood on stools to hang the new curtains she'd woven for the baby's room, it fell to Genna to rummage through Mary's wardrobe and her old oak desk to see if there was anything worth saving. The wardrobe held nothing but old kerchiefs and scraps of lace and feathers, but the drawer of the desk was crammed with pages of parchment.

"What do you suppose these are?" she asked, holding up a sheaf of the papers.

Althea frowned, pulling a small forest of pins from her mouth. "Mary's notebooks, I'd wager. She was always trying out different possets and potions and such to keep herself looking young. I tried to tell her she'd do harm pouring all that stuff down her gullet, but would she listen? Not she."

Genna leafed through the pages, peering at the thin, spidery handwriting. "Maybe her cider receipt is in here, Thea."

"Aye, and maybe there's worse stuff in there, too. Like conjuring tricks, and magic spells."

"It's a handsome desk, Meggie, don't you think so?" Genna ran a finger over the carved wooden legs. "I could use this in my room."

"I'll get some of the boys to bring it down for you."

Althea nearly fell off her stool. "Are you mad, Meggie Mac Donald? Burn the thing and be rid of it! Who knows what evil ferlies may lurk inside!"

Meggie rolled her eyes to the ceiling. "Land sakes, Thea. If you want, we'll have Father Alban exorcise it."

"Laugh if you will, Mistress Meggie," said Althea, through pursed lips. "Don't say as I didn't warn you, though."

Genna had Hoban set the desk in her bedchamber, beneath the window. Its smooth flat top was just the right size for laying out patterns for weaving, while the spindled back of the chair that went with it was perfect for balling yarn. And sometimes, late at night, when she was restless and lonely, she would sit and stare out over the hills, and watch for the dawn. For even in a castle filled with friendly faces, she found, a new bride without her husband can feel very much alone.

It was on one such night, when the winter winds howled and moaned through the halls, making the candles flicker, that she opened the drawer again and pulled out Mary's papers, desperate for anything that might take her mind off worrying for Alex. Pulling out a page at random, she began to decipher Mary's rude scrawl. "Willow seeds for sleeplessness," she read. "The willow is the moon's own tree. Gather at the fullness thereof and mix with the wild wall lettuce. Seethe with the juice of violets, and set in a black cloth beneath the pillow at night."

And this: "Plump roots of orchis do provoke to lust and stir up nature; the flowers of the dogstone by signature do the same. Boil with sowbread and white pepper for an amorous philtre."

That might come in useful someday, thought Genna, grinning to herself. She set the page aside and began the next.

"Thornapple in a cup of new wine will bring on visions of swarming rats. To induce the falling sickness, give seeds of the peony, fifteen or sixteen of the black seeds in a portion of goat's milk, for the goat is the devil's own mistress, and on its back witches ride."

She shivered, wrapping her robe more tightly about her shoulders. It was one thing to laugh at such nonsense during the day, and quite another while alone in the dead of night. She turned the page over hurriedly. The sheet beneath was written in a different hand, bolder, easier to read.

"For Mary Leslie," it began, "in humble gratitude, and with hopes that I may someday repay your kindnesses to me. Take ten pecks of ripe apples, and put three times through the press. Add crushed cloves, three whole nutmegs, and press again. Add berries of dwale, one half peck, and press the last time. Barrel and age six months."

Genna stared at the page in surprise. Could this be the receipt that Thea had mentioned? She glanced at the signature at the foot of the page. "Br. Martin Chalmers, Iona, *anno Domini* 1425."

Well, that was odd. She could have sworn the monk told Alex he'd never given his receipt away. And yet here was a copy addressed to Alex's mother. She looked again at the date. It was the year before she had met Alex. Such a long time ago; perhaps Brother Martin had simply forgotten.

She yawned as a sudden gust of cold wind through the shutters nearly guttered the candle flame. Realizing that her feet were freezing, Genna set the cider receipt aside and returned the rest of the papers to the drawer. As she put out the candle and jumped back into her bed, an image floated up in her mind: the flat, scarred face of the monk, mouth twisting as he told her how Donald had died.

Again the winter winds rocked the castle. The old stones shuddered and groaned, each with a plaint of its own. The handle to the chamber door creaked, and Genna sat up abruptly. Were those footsteps she'd heard in the hall?

The shutters rattled wildly in the window. With a laugh at her own superstitiousness, Genna got up to fasten them more tightly. Meggie had been right when she'd said these Isles could make one believe in the seeress, and ghosties. Next thing she knew she'd be setting birch branches over the baby's cradle, and wasting good milk in the ground. She unhooked the shutter latch and reached to be sure the oiled cloth was pulled down tight.

As she raised the edge of the cloth to straighten it, Genna saw the moon, huge and stark white, nearly full as it rolled along the crest of a distant hill. That same moon shone down on Alex tonight, wherever he might be. She leaned on the sill for a moment, whispering a prayer for his hasty return.

As she opened her eyes some movement against the pale glowing stillness of the moon arrested her sight. Across the hilltop a horse and rider were passing, showing clear and black as coal.

She blinked, rubbing her eyes, and that quickly the figure had disappeared. The man on the black horse, thought Genna, then tossed her head in wonder at her silliness. The horse could have been red or green or purple, but of course it looked black, standing out against the moon that way.

She fastened the cloth and shutter and padded back to her bed with a hearty yawn.

She awoke the next morning while the sky was barely light, feeling utterly ravenous. Putting on a warm robe and slippers, she made her way down to the kitchens, where the fires at the hearth were already roaring away.

"Well, aren't you up early, Young Mistress!" Althea greeted her. "Come and sit where 'tis warm, and I'll bring you some porridge and jam." Obediently Genna drew up a stool to the table, and as the housekeeper bustled to bring her breakfast she toasted her toes before the hearth. "Here's some milk for you, now, and your biscuits, and blackberry jam." She eyed the pot she held. "Blackberry jam, that was Ranalt's favorite too when he was a young thing."

"Alex's Uncle Ranalt? Did you know him, Althea?"

"Knew him as well as I'd want to, a long time ago. You know, both he and Old Master used to court Mary Leslie. Oh, la, 'twas a score of years back. How I prayed that Ranalt would take her—those two deserved one another! But when Master John made Donald his tanist, didn't Mary drop Ranalt in the wink of an eye? Hmph," she sniffed, "and Donald was fool enough to take her. Well, he lived to regret it, didn't he? I might have told him he would."

"Do you think Ranalt killed Davey's aunt, Althea?"

"Damned right I do," the housekeeper snapped. "That one was a bad seed from the day he was born. And as for that son of his, Euan, well everyone else might pretend as they might, but 'twas clear as day to me the boy was feebleminded. Praise be Young Master's got a bairn coming now to take Euan's place as tanist. We'd have been the butt of jests from here to Otterburn with such a one as Euan as laird!"

"Morning, Genna; morning, Thea." Meggie strode into the kitchen and plopped down on a chair. "What's for breakfast?"

"What is it with you two today? Can't wait to be served in the hall with the others? Think I've nothing better to do than wait on you hand and foot?"

"I thought I'd ride down to Salen to see if there's news from Davey." Meggie crammed a biscuit into her mouth. "Wanted to get an early start."

"Oh, Meggie, let me come with you! I'd adore a ride. I've been cooped up inside forever."

"Absolutely not!" Althea said in horror. "Bouncing that babe you're carrying from here to creation! What can you be thinking of?"

"I'll go ever so slow, Althea, I promise!"

"Over my dead body will you go at all! So long as I'm in charge here, young lady, you'll spend your lying-in doing just that."

Genna looked pleadingly at Meggie, but she shook her head. "Thea's right this time, Genna. 'Tis too long a ride, and too cold a day."

"Oh, but Meggie—"

"Here." Meggie pulled a flat parcel out of her bodice. "I nearly forgot. Hoban says this was left for you last night."

As Genna slit open the seal with her knife, she suddenly remembered the cider receipt. "Thea," she said slyly, "would you let me go with Meggie if I was to tell you how Mary made her cider?"

"Gor, go on, girl. How would you know such a thing?"

"The receipt was in her desk after all. I left it out on top; I'll go get it."

"Sit and eat," said Althea, pushing her firmly back into her chair. "I'll go." She heaved herself up the back stair.

"What's in the letter?" Meggie asked curiously.

Genna scanned the contents hurriedly. "It's from Iona. Father Gervase is sending Brother Martin with your vervain seed. He'll be at Tobermory at noon on the first of December."

Meggie looked up. "But that's today."

"So it is. Well, it looks as though I'll be going out riding, after all. If I leave right now, I can easily be there by noon."

"Oh, no you don't. I'll go. The seeds are for me, after all."

"But, Meggie—"

"No, Genna. And that's final."

"Please? I promise I'll be careful."

"No!" Meggie's voice was unusually sharp, and Genna looked over to her with surprise. A glint of tears shone in the woman's blue eyes. "Oh, Genna, don't you know how blessed you are to be having that baby? Do you know what I'd give for a babe of my own?"

"Oh, Meggie, I'm sorry," Genna said with dismay. "I didn't mean— Of course, you are right. Give my best regards to Brother Martin."

Meggie swallowed the last bite of her biscuit. "That's bet-

ter." She went and kissed Genna's forehead. "I will. You behave yourself while I'm gone, now, you hear?" She skipped
out through the kitchen doors.

Huffing and puffing, Althea came back down the stairway,
the cider receipt clutched in her hand. "Now, then." She eased
herself onto a stool. "What's all this about cider?"

"Didn't you read it?" asked Genna.

"Can't read," the housekeeper said shortly. "Never bothered to learn. You tell me what's in it."

"Ten pecks of apples," Genna told her, "ripe ones, it says,
put three times through the press."

"Hmph. Nothing so special about that."

"'Add crushed cloves, three whole nutmegs, press again.'"

The housekeeper nodded. "Aye. And what else, then?"

"A half peck of berries of dwale."

"Of what?"

"*D-w-a-l-e*. I guess that's how you say it. Don't you know
what it is?"

Althea's brown eyes were wide as saucers. "Witchcraft,"
she whispered, and crossed herself, shivering. "Didn't I tell
you that woman is a witch?"

"What in God's name are you talking about?"

"Dwale—dwale's a deadly poison, child! It makes men lose
their sight, and lose their minds as well!"

"Oh, Thea." Genna was getting a wee bit tired of the
woman's strange notions. "That's the silliest thing I ever
heard. Why would Mary poison her own cider?"

"I could tell you some things," the housekeeper crooned,
clutching the crucifix at her throat. "Oh, I could tell you some
things, all right."

"Well, don't bother," Genna said crossly, pushing back her
stool. "I'm going upstairs to weave. Do you know, I had
wretched dreams all last night, thanks to your carrying on?"
She stalked out the door.

"Still," Althea whispered to herself, "there are things I
could tell you. Saints preserve us." She eyed the receipt on the
table as though it were a live snake, then stuck it through with
a knife and carried it to the fire. The letter that had lain beneath the receipt fluttered onto the flames as well. "Damn,"
she muttered, and made a grab for the parchment. But it flared
on the coals, and had burned to ashes before she could reach
out her hand.

* * *

Genna fought back a wave of nausea that rose as she walked up the stairs. The porridge she'd eaten was like lead in her belly. She took off her robe and pulled on a warm woolen shirt, then stepped into an old brown riding skirt Meggie had given her when her own clothes had grown too tight. But now even the skirt no longer fit her. She struggled to draw the ends of the cloth together, then finally gave up and fastened them loosely at the waist with her gold and pearl brooch, grimacing at how wide her middle had become. From the courtyard below she could hear Meggie call to Hoban for her horse, her gay voice carrying above the usual clamor of wagon wheels and hounds and the clank of the blacksmith working. She could afford to be gay, Genna thought morosely. She wasn't stuck here inside all day long, growing fat as a cow. She could go to Tobermory and meet Brother Martin and anyone else she pleased.

She sat at her loom and began to work, pushing the shuttle to and fro with a vengeance, slamming the batten back to tighten the threads. Not until she paused to roll up the finished woof did she notice that the last two rows of the intricate chevron pattern she was making were upside down.

She cursed and began to unravel the threads. Christ, what a mess! She must be going blind as poor old Father Gervase. Soon she would need someone like Brother Martin to lead her around and look after her. She tore at the weft yarn with angry fingers, thinking of the monk's dreadfully scarred face, his disfigured hand curled around a cup of cider as he gave it to the abbot.

Abruptly she stopped. The thought that had flown into her head was laughable, absurd. In fact, it was mad.

She pictured the abbot's sightless brown eyes, and Brother Martin's crabbed, blunted hand on the cup, Althea's hushed voice running through her mind: "Dwale—dwale's a deadly poison . . . it makes men lose their sight, and their minds as well . . ."

Genna stifled a giggle. She was getting as bad as Althea! Why would Brother Martin want to poison Father Gervase, cause him to go blind? He owed everything to the abbot. Why, if Mary Leslie hadn't suggested he be sent to Iona, he'd be dead now, hanged for a thief. Instead, he was saved, reformed, had a position of honor and responsibility, looking after the abbot, running the abbey, tending to the gardens, the accounts...

And growing nightshade and wolfsbane in the gardens, tampering with the abbot's violets.

A thin tingle of apprehension ran down Genna's spine. She tried to shake her uneasiness off, tell herself that her imagination was getting the best of her, but she kept thinking of that mutilated face, the undercurrent of satisfaction in the monk's voice as he told her how Donald died on the road to Tobermory. The road that Meggie was riding even now, riding in Genna's place.

She tried to rewind the yarn, but her hands were shaking. Annoyed at her foolishness, she nonetheless grabbed her cloak from the wardrobe and pulled on a hat. The one sure way to put her mind at ease was to follow Meggie, to ride with her to Tobermory to see the monk. Now, if only she could get past Althea to the stables without having to explain what she was doing! After she'd just scolded the housekeeper for her superstitions, she hardly wanted to confess her own.

She opened the door and peered out into the corridor. For once it was empty, not even a stray cat prowling. She ran to the front stairs, tiptoed down them, then slipped out into the yards.

"Morning, mum!" Hoban greeted her at the stables. "Haven't seen you out here in quite some time."

"Saddle Rannoch for me, will you, Hoban? And hurry."

"Yes, mum. Right away, mum." But the white-haired stablemaster moved as slowly as ever, checking the harnesses, tightening the girth.

Genna cast an anxious glance over her shoulder. "Honestly, Hoban, you're slower than sap. Give me that bridle."

"I'll take my time and do it right, thank you, young missy! Guess that letter must ha' been mighty important news, eh?"

"Genna! Genevieve Fleming, get back here!" Althea's piercing tone could have splintered wood. "Hoban, don't you dare let her take that horse! Hoban!"

Genna shoved the stablemaster aside, caught the stirrup in her boot, and, only half-seated, galloped through the castle gates. Althea's outraged shouts pursued her past the first bend in the road.

"You want as I should go after her, mum?" Hoban asked the red-faced housekeeper.

Althea spat in the dust. "Nay, let her go, then, the head-strong little fool."

Genna followed the same winding trail she'd ridden the day before Alex and Davey left for Islay, through the fields, now barren and deserted, and the bare-branched forests of oak. Rannoch's hooves rustled through the fallen leaves that covered the road, startling scattered flocks of wild pheasants into the cloudless blue sky. As the road wound upward to the loch Genna began to feel more and more foolish. They said that of times pregnant women had odd fancies and notions, didn't they? That must be what was wrong with her. The chill December wind cut right through the cloak she wore, and the clasp of the brooch pinched her waist. The road was deserted, the day too cold and harsh for travel. Meggie would laugh herself silly when she heard what had brought Genna after her. No, more likely she'd be furious to see her at all. The only sensible thing, thought Genna, was to turn back to Aros right now.

"Genna! Is that you?" Meggie was suddenly standing in the road before her, looking cross and disheveled. "Some bloody idiot left a rope tied right across the highway, can you believe it? My horse has pulled up lame."

Genna slid down from her saddle. "Are you all right?"

"All things considered. I twisted my ankle a bit when I fell. What in hell are you doing here, anyway? I thought I ordered you to stay at the castle."

Genna laughed. "Oh, Meggie, I really must be going soft in the head. Wait until you hear this."

A twig snapped, loud as thunder, beyond her shoulder. Genna whirled around, startled, and saw two black-hooded men atop huge black horses. They had paused some few hundred yards down the road, and now as they advanced through the trees she saw the bright-edged daggers they held glisten and flash in the sun.

"What in God's name." Meggie's hand flew to her throat as she stood frozen, staring. Rannoch let out a long, high whinny and reared up, pulling the reins from Genna's grasp.

She lunged for them desperately, but the frightened horse nickered again and plunged off into the underbrush. Genna cursed and grabbed Meggie's hand. "Come on," she urged, pulling her down the road toward the lake. "Run, Meggie, run!" They caught up their skirts in their fists and ran.

"Help!" Genna screamed for all she was worth. "Please, someone, help us!"

"There's no one to hear you," Meggie whispered tremulously, as the hoofbeats of their pursuers drew nearer still. "Oh, Genna, I'm afraid."

"Don't be," Genna told her firmly. "They are only robbers, looking for gold. Faster, Meggie, faster!" Her heart pounding madly, she pulled her toward the clearing by the lake.

At its brink Meggie stumbled, her ankle giving way, and stared up at Genna with wild blue eyes. "You go on," she urged. "I cannot run any farther. Go on, you must get away!"

"I'll not leave you!" Genna cried fiercely, then turned to face the masked brigands, one arm around Meggie's trembling shoulders. "Who are you?" she demanded. "What do you want?"

They pulled up on their horses, taken aback by her defiance. She saw their pale eyes glittering through the slits in the hoods they wore.

Then the taller man leapt down from his horse and grabbed Genna by the hair, tugging her toward him. She tried to cling to Meggie, but his strength was too much for her. "Let me go!" she screamed, twisting in his grasp like a wildcat, clawing for his eyes.

"Let her be!" Meggie screeched, coming to her senses at last, taking her cue from Genna. She jumped at the attacker, seeking to tear the mask from his face. There was a sharp loud rip as his hood split down the back—and then a long in-drawn breath from Meggie as she saw the man's bright red hair and hard gray eyes.

"You shouldn't have done that, Meggie, my girl," he said, with genuine reluctance. Meggie backed away toward the lake edge in disbelief.

"Ranalt?" she whispered, her voice high, incredulous. Genna screamed as she saw, looming over Meggie, the face of the man who had murdered Red John.

"You shouldn't have done it, I tell you," said Ranalt, still advancing on Meggie. He glanced back at his accomplice. "Well, don't sit there like a stone, for Christ's sake!" he snapped. "Take care of that one!"

Genna started as she felt a hood thrown over her face and

drawn tight at the throat. "Meggie!" she cried in terror, gasping for breath, unable to see. "Meggie, where are you?" There was no answer but the sound of her captor's voice.

"Hush, now, be quiet," he urged her. Genna shuddered as she recognized that odd, high, singsongy voice.

"Meggie!" she screamed again. "Meggie!" Ruefully, Euan Mac Ruarie clapped his big hand over her face.

"There, now," he murmured, as she fought for air a moment longer, then crumpled to the ground in a small, still heap. "There, now, that's better, isn't it?" Pleased with himself, he gathered her up in his arms and slung her over the saddle of his horse.

18

Alex and Davey were weary but merry as their galley glided toward Aros Castle. The two-day sail from Islay had gone well despite the threatening advances of winter. The meeting of the clan chiefs had gone even better. Alex had confirmed the first male offspring of his marriage to Genna as his tanist, with the blessings of the chiefs, and had sent four galleys of men out under Sebastian's leadership to help track Ranalt down. They were to start at Oban, where he'd commandeered the ship, and work north through each of the islands. The man would have to be a sorcerer to slip their hands this time.

The galley rode silently through the Sound of Mull past the point of Salen, running under full sail. Though the hour was early the sky was already pitch-dark, the blackness cut only by the sharp bright pinpoints of stars. The full moon would not rise above the hills of Morven until the night was nearly half through.

Davey sighed and rubbed his eyes with his fists. "'Tis glad I'll be to be home at last, and see my Meggie." He stared out over the rippling black water. "I'm gettin' too old for all this travelin' about, Alley. 'Tis time you bred up some sons to take with you instead."

Alex grinned in the darkness. "You don't mean that, Davey. You'd itch like a dog with fleas if you were stuck in one place for the rest of your days."

"Faith, I'm not so sure of that, Alley." Alex was surprised by the earnestness in his friend's voice. "I've seen about as much of the world as I care to. I figure I'm ready to settle down and make Meggie happy. You know how bad she wants bairns. Two years we've been wed now, and naught to show for it, what with me always runnin' from one place to the other. I haven't been fair to yer sister, Alley. I'm going to make it up to her."

"Ach, 'tis your tiredness talking, Davey. That and all the mead you've poured down your gullet these past weeks."

"Nay, I mean it, my travelin' days are over. I'm going to set my feet up by the fire, bounce babes on my knees."

"I'll believe that when I see it."

"You just wait, then," said Davey stubbornly. "Just you wait and see."

Alley laughed and leaned back in the bow, rearranging his cloak for a pillow, wondering if Davey was sincere. The old chiefs he knew—Iain Cameron, Angus Mac Pherson, Cato Duffy—only grew wilder and fiercer as they aged. None of them was content to curl up by a fire with grandchildren in his lap, or give up a life of adventure for the woman he loved.

Look at the way they'd reacted to the news that his banishment was still in effect, with Angus and Iain clamoring to take up arms against the king, force James to capitulate. And while they were at it, Brian Mac Intosh had suggested, they might fight to have golf reinstated as well.

He'd managed to stave off their bloodthirstiness again this time, with flattery and humoring and vague promises, but who knew for how long? He wondered how his father had kept the chiefs reined in. By all accounts the Harlaw had sobered them considerably, but as the memory of their defeat there gradually receded, the eagerness for war was flaring anew. The petty skirmishes and feuds they carried on with one another were a poor substitute for all-out battle, and now that the king had curtailed even that recreation, the Lord of the Isles was going to be hard-pressed to maintain peace.

Alex sighed, watching the first silvery rays of moonlight pierce through the clouds over Morven. There had been rumblings among a few of the chiefs that Alexander Mac Donald was afraid to do battle, that his calm acceptance of his banishment was girlish and weak. Iain Cameron, besotted with mead one night, had suggested as much to His Lairdship, then quickly backed down when Alex offered to take on any man there, bare hands against axe, to prove himself. Damn, why was it so bloody hard to make them understand? "There is no shame in being a man of peace": Donald had taught him that, and he still believed it. How, though, did one convince the clan chiefs, who were ready to take up arms over a game of golf?

"Look, Alley!" Davey nudged his elbow. "The lights are on in the towers. Do you think they're waitin' up for us?"

"How could they be? They had no way to know we would come tonight." But the thought sent a sudden rush of warmth running through him despite the chilly night winds. Genna waiting, there in the bedchamber, clad in her long pale night-dress, with her ebony hair unbound. She would hold her small white arms to him. "My love," she would say, that slow smile igniting her eyes. "Welcome home."

"Faster," he told the oarsmen. Davey laughed, the sound ringing from water and rocks.

"Seems to me," he said slyly, "that you're ready to stop wanderin' as well!"

As the galley drew up to the dock and dropped anchor, they saw Althea's bulky figure come stumbling down the hill. "Oh, Master Alley, Master Davey, it is you!" she cried, bounding onto the wharf. "Thank God you've come at last!"

"What's the matter, Althea?" asked Alex, leaping from the boat and whirling her around in a dance. "Where's my wife? Why isn't she here to greet me?"

"Or mine?" Davey demanded in mock anger, lugging their baggage to the shore.

"I don't know where they are!" Althea wailed, and burst into a torrent of tears.

"What do you mean?" asked Alex, holding her at arm's length, trying to see her face in the shadowy darkness.

The housekeeper wrung her hands in her apron. "They went off yesterday morning, and no one has seen them since! Oh, Master Alley, I didn't do anything wrong. I told Young Mistress not to go."

"Go where, Althea?"

"Nobody knows!" She grabbed his hand, pulling him toward the castle. "Mistress Meggie was going riding, and Young Mistress wanted to go with her, but I wouldn't let her, you see, owing to her condition."

Alex halted, thunderstruck. "Condition? What condition?"

"There, now, I've gone and given away her secret," sobbed Althea, "but I've been so fearful for them, gone all day and all night, and all day again."

"Genna was—with child?"

"Aye, aye." Althea nodded, the tears streaming down her round face. "Oh, I just know something dreadful has happened!"

"Where's Hoban? Hoban!" Alex bellowed into the yards. The stablemaster stumbled up, face flushed with drink, and fell to his knees at Alex's feet.

"It's not my fault, Master!" he whimpered, covering his head with his hands. "I didn't know about the child. I never would have let her go."

"But where did they go?"

"Who knows? Mistress Meggie, she rode off first, and then Young Mistress comes out all in a rush, and shoves me aside and rides off, too! Nearly yanked my arm from its socket, such a rush she was in. I says to Althea, I says, well, it must have been somethin' in the letter."

"What letter?"

"Why, the one what came for Young Mistress the mornin' she left!"

Davey shook the man's shoulders furiously. "What did it say?"

"How should I know? I gave it to Mistress Meggie, and that's the last I saw."

"Thea? Did you see a letter?"

She hesitated only an instant, then said, "Young Mistress —she burned it." God knew she was in enough trouble already; no sense telling the master what else she'd done.

"Hoban, in what direction did they ride?"

The stablemaster raised his terrified face. "I don't know, Master Alley, God's troth! They just took off like that, one after t'other. I thought nothin' of it. Christ ha' mercy, I thought nothin' of it till the horses came back!"

Hot fear suddenly twisted in Alex's bowels. "Their horses came back? Without them?"

Hoban nodded miserably. "Aye, last night at sundown, with their bridles trailin'. Mistress Meggie's had pulled up somethin' awful lame." He clutched at Alex's knees. "Please don't kill me, Master Alley, I beg ye."

"Of course I'm not going to kill you, Hoban. Get up off the ground."

Davey turned to Althea. "Did you send out parties to look for them?"

"Oh, aye, we did that. Searched all day long, all over the

country. Neddie Coulter, he says he saw some tracks high up on the Tobermory road, but then the night fell, and they said 'twas too dark to see."

"Go fetch them again!" Alex roared. "Light the tower torches. Get every man here, and tell them to bring their hounds."

"But they've looked everywhere, Master Alley!"

"Tell them to look again!" he snapped. "Hoban, get Bantigh and Drummond saddled. Move, man!" The stablemaster skittered away. "Thea, where did Neddie see those hoofprints?"

"Close by the loch, on the seaward side. But it couldn't have been the mistresses, for he said there was four sets of tracks there."

"Send him up the road after us as soon as he gets here. Get something that belonged to each of them, Thea. A shirt, or a shoe. Give them to Neddie." Hoban led the horses out of the stable. "Come on, Davey, let's go!"

But though he and Davey searched along every inch of the road for miles, shouting at the tops of their lungs, not a sign of Genna or Meggie could they find. As they neared the clearing that gave onto Loch Frisa, Alex reined Bantigh in with a heavy sigh.

"If there were any tracks, 'tis likely we've run right over them. What do you think, Davey? Should we go back for Neddie, or wait?"

Davey shrugged. Alex could just make out his taut, drawn face in the light of the moon that filtered through the pine trees. "Hard to say. P'raps someone else has already found them by now. P'raps they just left their mounts untied, and had to walk home."

"It wouldn't take Meggie this long to get back to Aros. She knows this island better than either of us." Alex peered into the shadows of the pines.

"Why don't you head on back, then Alley, and fetch Neddie and the hounds?"

"I don't like to leave you alone here."

"Oh, bosh," the redhead said, more confidently than he felt. "Mark my words, they're warmin' their heels back at Aros already. Go on, why don't you, and see?" No matter how desperate Davey's concern was for Meggie, he knew Alex must be even more upset. Meggie did know the island. And besides,

His Lairdship had just now learned he was to be a father. "Go on, then," he said sternly. "Ten marks says you find them both cosied up to the fire."

Alex hesitated, then grinned. "You're on. But if they're not, I'm coming right back here with Neddie. Be careful, Davey." He wheeled Bantigh around in a flurry of crackling leaves.

"I will. Oh, and Alley . . ."

He looked back over his shoulder and saw Davey's teeth flash white in the gloom.

"Congratulations . . . Papa."

Alex grinned again. "Thanks." Then he spurred Bantigh into the night.

Davey sat listening as the great white horse's hooves thundered down the road, and stared out over the calm smooth surface of the lake that was just beginning to glisten with moonlight. Above the tall, ghostly pines he could see a bank of dense clouds. As the moon slipped behind it he sighed, urging Drummond forward.

"Just goes to show you, old friend, what happens when you keep away from yer woman too long. 'Tis just as I told Alley, this is it for me. From now on, I'm stayin' home!" He clucked his tongue. "Might as well have one more look around here. Meggie!" he shouted, his voice echoing eerily across the water. "Genna! Meggie! Can ye hear me, darlin's?" He turned the horse to the right, toward Dervaig, following the white-frosted strand. "Meggie! Genna!" he shouted again, and heard the hills answer far across the loch. He shivered as a gust of wind ruffled its unbroken surface, eddying the crisp fallen leaves.

Then Drummond reared up with a terrifying whinny, nostrils flaring as her hooves sought the sky. "Hush, there, girl!" cried Davey, yanking at the reins. "'Tis naught but a bit of wind, you silly thing. Hush now!" But the horse would not be soothed, though Davey ran a comforting hand over her mane. She bucked again, frantically, as the clouds that had shrouded the moon glided silently away, and pale silver light flooded over the treetops, illuminating every blade of grass, each fallen leaf with a ghostly white glare.

Davey reached out again for Drummond's curling mane, then stopped as he saw the tangle of cloth that lay at the water's edge, half-submerged by the lapping lake. A bit of gold hair shone in the shimmering moonlight.

"Meggie!" The word was an indistinguishable wail of terror

and anguish. Davey tumbled from the horse's back, not heeding the deadly hooves that sliced through the air. "Oh, sweet Christ, my darlin' Meggie." He gathered her into his arms, felt the cold stiff weight of her limbs, looked into her vacant blue eyes.

"No!" he screamed to the sky, the night, the stars, his heart rending open. "No, God damn you!"

He pulled the tumbled gold hair from her face, kissed her pale mouth, shivering at its coldness. "Oh, Meggie," he crooned, clutching the frail corpse against him, tears streaming wildly down his face. "There, there, my darlin' sweet Meggie. Hush now. Go to sleep, now. I will make everything all right."

Part IV

19

"For the love of God, tell me *why*," Genna pleaded, into darkness, into silence punctuated by Euan's sibilant breath. Again she tried to sit up, wrenching at the ropes that bound her, struggling against the choking hood.

Euan stared down regretfully at the small body lashed to the cot. "I'm sorry, mum, but I can't. I have my orders, you see."

"Then tell me where you are taking—" Genna broke off to fight down a knot of bile that rose in her throat. Euan listened timidly as she gagged in agony.

"Best save your strength, mum, 'tis a long sail we're taking. If I was you, I'd lie back quiet and rest."

Rest? Genna thought bitterly, collapsing back in exhaustion. How could she rest? If she stopped fighting, talking, arguing even for a moment, stark terror seized her, and the cold hard grip of despair.

For a long time there was no sound in the hold of the ship but the creaking of the sails above and the man's whistling breaths. Genna alternated desperate prayers with vain attempts to loosen the thongs at her wrist. Anything to keep her occupied, keep her from dwelling on her seasickness and her fear.

She had thought when Davey brought her to Mull aboard the *Dearg Lomond* that it was impossible to be any more ill and still live. She knew now that she had been wrong.

After hours had passed, the whistling ceased. She heard the scrape of a chair on the cabin floor and the grating rasp of a hatchway opening. Footsteps receded down the passageway. "Meggie!" Genna hissed, straining her ears for an answer, any answer. "Meggie, are you there?" But except for the lap of the waves against the hull, no sound came in reply.

Sweet Christ, Genna prayed, have mercy upon me. Have mercy on Meggie, dear God, and on my child as well.

The footsteps hurried back down the passageway, followed by more footsteps, heavier, and voices. The hatchway opened and shut.

"What in hell is the matter with you?" Ranalt growled at his son. "I give you one simple task to do—watch over her—and the next thing I know you're sneaking up on deck!"

"She's not going anywhere, Father. And besides, I wanted to see the gulls."

"See the— Christ, what a bloody idiot. When I give you a job to do, damn you, do it!"

"But, Father—"

Genna heard someone coming closer. "Please," she whispered, "please, tell me why you're doing this. I beg you—" She ended in a heavy scream of pain as a harsh hand wrenched at her breast.

"I'll make you beg, little missy. Don't think I've forgotten you." His mouth brushed the hood at her ear. "I never did get to conclude my business with you, so long ago. Do you remember?" Genna lay motionless, terrified, recalling the ruthlessness with which he'd tried to rape her, and then murdered Papa John.

His fingers jabbed at her thighs. "I said, do you remember?"

"Aye," Genna whispered, "I remember."

"Good, then. See that you do." Once more his cruel hands clawed at her breasts and she heard him pant with eagerness.

"Father, can't you stay down here for a while?" Euan asked plaintively. "I do want to watch the seabirds."

"Shut up, you sniveling idiot." Ranalt knew he could not face the temptation of being alone with the girl. He remembered those wide dark eyes, the way she'd looked at him at Dumbarton, defiant and angry, and the silky white skin of her shoulders, her breasts. God damn Mary Leslie, he thought furiously. If not for her, he'd teach the black-haired beauty a lesson or two right now. He'd begin by jamming himself into that pretty little thing. She would learn to beg then! But Mary . . . Mary was waiting for them. And there would be hell to pay from her if she found out he'd raped the girl. Not that she would have minded him hurting her. It was the idea that he lusted after another woman that would make the countess wild with rage.

For an instant he considered having his way with her despite Mary, then tossing her overboard. His tongue flicked over his lip, savoring the idea. Then, reluctantly, he rejected it. Mary was too smart to fall for any tale he might make up to explain his prisoner's disappearance.

There would be time enough for all that later, he told himself, smiling. When Mary left them to go to Mull. There'd be days and days in which to amuse himself then . . .

"My husband," Genna murmured.

"Aye, what about him?"

"He'll kill you for this."

"Will he?" Again he leaned over her, a quiver of laughter in his voice. "You pathetic fool, on whose orders do you think I came for you?"

"You're lying," Genna whispered, but a paroxysm of fear swept through her.

Ranalt laughed. "He's tired of you, wench! You've served your purpose. He wanted to make certain King James never learned that he and I were at Dumbarton. He needed to get you far away from the court. But now—now he'll play the grieving widower for a bit, and then you'll be forgotten. He wanted me to kill you, but I thought it might be amusing to get to know you first. If you're a good little girl . . ." Again his fingers played at her breasts. "Who knows? I might be persuaded to spare your life."

"Liar!" Genna cried, writhing beneath his touch. "Oh, Christ, I know you are lying!"

"Am I?" he asked in that same cool, wry tone.

"Father, please don't hurt her," Euan began again. Genna shuddered as she heard a mighty smack.

"Shut up! For once in your life, shut up and do as I tell you!"

"Yes, Father," Euan said faintly. "I'm sorry I made you angry. I'll do as you say."

The hatch slammed shut once more. Genna felt tears of hopelessness spring in her eyes. She tried with every fiber of her being to reject Ranalt's taunting words, but one awful fact remained: Ranalt Mac Ruarie was the man who had murdered Papa John. And Alex had known that, all along.

Could it be true that he had never loved her? That he had

only used her, coldly, calculatingly, to protect his uncle from the king? Had he been so determined to save Ranalt that he'd married the only witness who could ever make certain his uncle lost his head?

No, her heart told her. It could not have all been false, not the way he held her, kissed her, made love to her. No one could convince her that her husband, the man whose child she carried, the man she knew better than any other being on earth, could so deceive her.

But husbands and wives did not keep secrets from one another, especially secrets as horrible as that. What reason could he have for hiding his uncle's identity from her, if not to protect Ranalt? Genna searched her soul there in the dark hold, seeking through her heart-rending grief for any slim ray of hope.

Those few times she'd heard Alex talk of Ranalt, what had he said? That there was bad blood between his uncle and Donald. Surely he would not go to such lengths to save the neck of someone his beloved father had disavowed!

But what about Euan? Alex had told her himself that he'd made Ranalt's son his tanist. And it had been Euan who'd attacked her in the garden at Stirling, with Alex looking on. Alex must have known it was his cousin there . . . and that meant his show of jealous anger had all been a sham. Oh, Christ, could it be true that he'd sent Ranalt and Euan to snatch her away from Mull? Of course he would have chosen a time when he himself wasn't at Aros. That way there would be no questions about how he could have let his wife be kidnapped from beneath his nose.

Alex would never do such a thing, she tried to assure herself. But he would if he had never loved her. A man who could play the role of devoted, trusting husband as well as he had was capable of anything.

Good God, this way lies madness, she thought desperately, trying to subdue the awful fears and suspicions that whirled through her head. The ship shuddered, hull groaning, in a sudden gust of wind. Genna writhed on the cold hard cot, her seasickness forgotten, consumed by the far more torturous disease of doubt.

The sound of Ranalt's heavy footfalls, the squeal of the hatch door, raised her back up from her torpor. "How is she?" she heard him growl.

"I—I think she's in pain, Father. Couldn't we take that hood off her?"

Ranalt stared at his son with disgust. "What the bloody hell is it to you if she's in pain?"

"But, Father, she cries out."

"Then hit her, you fool." Ranalt stared grimly down at the cot. "I don't want those sailors to know she's on board. If there's so much as a peep out of her." He leaned over and pulled the hood down more snuggly around her head, then wrapped an extra tie around her forehead to keep it in place. Genna cried out in protest, and Ranalt clamped his hand down over her mouth. "Didn't you hear what I said? Not a peep out of you or else.

"You see how simple it is?" Ranalt demanded of his son. "I don't want to hear any more noise from down there, or I'll really give her something to scream about—and you as well!" The hatch slammed shut again, and the cabin was silent except for Euan's wheezing breath.

But the words Ranalt had spoken gave Genna her first tiny glimmer of relief. There were sailors on board, sailors who Ranalt was afraid would find her. If she could only make her way to them. And Euan felt sorry for her, pitied her. Could she play on that pity to win her freedom, her life?

She would have to be cunning, and careful. She began to count to herself, slowly, one number for each painful breath. When she'd reached one thousand, she let out a whimpering moan.

"What—what is it?" She could sense him hovering over her anxiously. "Hush, now, be quiet, or he'll hear you and hurt you again."

Genna waited a few more seconds, then thrashed weakly from side to side, making gurgling noises in her throat.

"Oh, Lord," Euan whispered, "whatever's the matter? You're not going to die, are you? He'll beat me for sure if you do."

Genna gulped in one last huge mouthful of air with a shuddering groan, then lay perfectly still, holding her breath. She felt him lean over her, and fought with every ounce of will not to flinch from his touch. His heavy hand grabbed at her breast, but he was only feeling for her heartbeat. Please, God, she prayed soundlessly, her head spinning, now! Now, or I shall have to let out my breath!

Euan yanked the hood from her head with a sudden jerk. Genna took advantage of the movement to gasp in air.

"Lady?" Euan's voice was tentative, hushed. "Lady, can you hear me? What's wrong?"

Hesitantly, Genna fluttered her lashes, opened her eyes. "Where—where am I?" she whispered.

"On a boat." Euan peered down at her ghost-pale face, those haunted black eyes, and smiled. "I'm glad you're not dead, for there would have been hell to pay then!" He glanced back toward the hatchway nervously, then held a water skin to her lips. "Here, drink some of this. But for God's sake, don't tell Father!"

Genna sipped eagerly at the spout, felt the cool water course down her parched, gritty throat. Heaven . . . but now what? She gave him a sweet, tremulous smile of thanks.

"Here, take some more but slowly." He rested the bag on his shoulder and let a slow trickle stream from the spout. His aim was off at first, and the water splashed down over Genna's bodice and waist. "You'll get the cramp if you drink too fast, you know. I had cramp once. I thought it was the end of me. I shouldn't want you to get cramp."

"You're so terribly, terribly kind," Genna murmured. Euan's face creased in shy delight, and again the stream of water fell onto her clothes.

"I wish Father could hear you say that. He only ever calls me bad names."

"I can't see why! I think you are wonderful."

A slow flush of red crept over Euan's cheeks and down his thick neck. "Well. If you're feeling better, I've got to put that hood on before Father comes back."

Now, Genna thought, I must come up with something now, before he puts that damned thing back on me. But all she could think of was water, sweet, clear, cool water, pouring down her throat, splashing over her clothes.

"Wait, please!" He looked at her curiously, the hood stretched over his big hands. "I'm afraid that I have to . . . have to . . ." She summoned up her own pink blush. "Dear me, I'm so terribly sorry, but I have to . . ." She lowered her thick dark lashes. "You know . . ."

"I do?" Then Euan's neck turned a deeper red. "Oh. You mean—"

Genna nodded, eyes still delicately downcast. Euan pon-

dered the request, his brow creased. "Father didn't say anything about that," he said finally. "I'll have to go and ask him."

"Oh, no, please." He hesitated, gazing down at her. "It's
just that, well . . . you're so much nicer than he. He always
hurts me when he comes down here. And I'm afraid he might
say no, and then I would ruin my dress."

"That would be a shame," said Euan, "for there aren't any
other girls on board for you to borrow from." But then he
shook his head. "No, I'm sorry, I'll have to ask Father. I can't
bear it when he's angry with me."

"But I'll be quick as a wink!" Genna pleaded. "Just untie
my hands, and I'll go right there in the corner. He'll never
even know, I swear it. Oh, Euan, please." Fat round tears
welled up in her eyes.

"Oh, no. Oh, for God's sake, don't cry, then." Euan wrung
his big hands together in distress. He knew what it was like
when women got started crying. Wasn't that what Mary
always did when he disappointed her? "Please, just stop crying!" The tears spilled over, tumbling down her snowy cheeks,
and she let out a little sob. "Oh, all right then!" Euan hissed,
tearing at the ropes that held her wrists. "But for God's sake,
hurry!" Genna hid her smile of triumph as he yanked the
knots free. She swung her legs over the edge of the cot and
stood, then sat down again, heavily. Her legs were stiff and
uncooperative, her head spinning wildly from the pitching of
the ship.

"Go!" Euan hissed. Summoning all her strength, Genna
got up from the bed and hobbled across the cabin, crouching
in the corner by the hatch. Euan's pale eyes followed her prog-
ress nervously. Genna gathered up her skirts, then raised her
gaze to his with a timid smile.

"Could you—" She bit her lip. "Would you mind terribly
looking the other way for a moment?"

"What? Oh. Oh, certainly." Color rising again, Euan
turned his back.

Genna darted for the hatch, pushed it open, and stumbled
over the threshold into the passageway and slid back the bolt.

"Hey—hey!" She heard Euan's frantic shouting, and the
pounding of his fists on the door. "Hey, you had better come
back here!"

Shaking with excitement, rejoicing, Genna forced her
numbed legs to carry her forward toward the ladder that

showed down the passage in a flood of bright blinding sunlight. Behind her, Euan had forced the hatch open. She heard his shoulder crash against the sturdy wood, and his boots as they pounded on the planks. "You're going to be sorry!" he shouted. Never, thought Genna, her hands clawing out toward the ladder, feet flailing to find the rungs.

Through the opening atop the ladder she could see birds! Birds wheeling against the glory of a clear blue sky! One hand closed over the top rung, grasping the deck above.

Then birds and light and sky were blocked by Ranalt's bulky figure. Genna stared up into his glittering narrowed eyes. His heavy boot swung toward her, caught her in the throat, tearing her scream away. She saw his twisted smile looming over her as she tumbled back to the deck below.

He followed down the ladder with a loud clatter. Crumpled in a skewed heap at the ladder's base, Genna felt an impossible searing pain shoot through her belly, her womb. "No," she whispered, unbelieving, and then more loudly, "No!" as Ranalt advanced with his fists clenched tight.

But he strode right past her to where Euan stood shaking, cowering, kneeling by the passage wall. "Please, Father, no," he whimpered in terror. "She tricked me, Father! Please—" He shielded his face with his hands.

Ranalt struck out at him in a blind rage, raining down blows with his huge hammy fists, kicking out with his hard-toed boots. "You half-witted fool," he snarled, punctuating each word with a furious blow. "You monkey! You unspeakable idiot!"

"Father!" wailed Euan.

"Don't call me Father! Don't remind me I spawned you, you mistake of nature, you miserable cur!"

Genna heard a loud thud, and then silence. She raised her agonized eyes from the planks of the deck, and saw Ranalt's boots draw near. She lifted her chin and stared him right in the eye, hands clasping her belly. A thin stain of blood spread out over her riding skirt.

"Go on and kill me," she said steadily, bitingly. "You cannot possibly hurt me more than you have already."

"No? We'll see about that." Ranalt grinned as he unleashed his belt. "Beg me now, bitch. Go on, let me hear you plead with me." The belt lashed out, the buckle shearing her skin.

Genna clenched her teeth together, refusing to cry out, refusing to plead as he wound up the belt once more. She stayed silent for a long, long time before Ranalt, bored and restless, hitched the belt around his loins and kicked her back through the hatch.

Sunlight, and a trickle of water. The soothing chaos of seabirds chattering, far off, high in the sky. A sharp scent of salt, like the brine from herring, borne on air so frigid that it made her scalp tingle. And beneath, above, surrounding it all, the endless pulse of the waves.

Genna raised herself up on one elbow, crackling bedstraw, pushing back hair from her eyes. The casual gesture sent a stab of pain down to her toes. Surprised, she stared at her arm and saw the angry purple welts that striped it, and the coppery brown of dried blood.

Half-dazed, she moistened her dry lips and eyed the surroundings. Ancient green-mossed stones made up the walls, overhung by a low-beamed ceiling of knotty pine. The room contained only the pallet she lay on, but there was barely space even for that. She reached out a hand and touched the wall; the stones were rough-hewn, pocked with mildew, so old that they threatened to crumble beneath her fingers. The oldest sections of Dumbarton Castle, the Great Hall and the close defenses, had been built more than five hundred years before. This stone was even older than that.

Grimacing in pain, Genna rolled to her side and saw a broad wood door, half-open. From the room beyond she could make out the sound of low, indistinct voices. She hauled herself to a sitting position, slowly, awkwardly, and realized with a start that she was naked except for her linen shirt. Her white legs bore huge yellowing bruises—the marks of a whip.

Her first instinct was to cry out, but then the memory of Ranalt's malevolent grinning face rose up in her mind. She strained in an effort to recognize the shadowy voices, to distinguish his among the murmur, but they were too far away. She moved to push herself off the bed, and saw the puddled blood that lay, thick and dark, coloring the bedding between her thighs.

She knew with a flash of certainty that she had lost her child. She recalled the fall down the ladder, the brutal beating she had endured. She remembered praying to be delivered by death, thinking it a pity she could not explain to Ranalt that she could barely feel the lashings, the kicks he enjoyed administering. Nothing he did could come close to touching the pain she suffered from knowing that Alex had betrayed her, had delivered her into that demon's hands.

She stood up, pale and shaky, and moved to the casement, narrow, deeply edged, carved into the distant wall. If she stood on tiptoe, she could just see through the opening. There was nothing outside but a bleak windswept beach, treeless, barren, and beyond that the white-crested sea. Stout-breasted plovers ran down to meet the tide, screeching with laughter, and then scurried back again.

Her head began to throb wildly from the thump of the sea on the strand. Genna collapsed to her knees with a low moan. The voices in the next room ceased briefly, and then started in once more.

Inch by inch, Genna dragged herself across the icy floor to the doorway. After ages, centuries, she reached the jamb and peered through the crack between door and wall.

Her heart leapt in joy when she saw the gold-haired woman who sat with her back to the door at a low slatted table. "Meggie!" she started to cry, but the word caught in her throat as she heard the woman's brittle metallic laugh. Meggie had never laughed that way in her life.

"I *told* you I wasn't upset about Meggie," the woman told Ranalt, who sat hunched over the table across from her, a candle's dim light playing over his red hair. "What's done is done, and there's no undoing. As usual, you reacted stupidly."

"What would you have had me do, then?" Ranalt demanded, scratching his beard. "She'd seen me, I tell you. What else could I do?"

"It never would have occurred to you, of course, to bring her here."

"Why? You can't stand the sight of her."

"I might have found a method of making use of her. She is no good to anyone dead."

Genna leaned against the wall, her empty stomach heaving. Dead—was Meggie dead? Had Ranalt actually murdered his own flesh and blood?

Then Ranalt leaned forward, clasping the woman's hand in his two coarse paws. "Tell me, then," he said softly. "How have I angered you, my pet?"

Mary Leslie rose from the table with a violent scrape of her chair, turning to face the doorway. Genna stuffed her fist into her mouth in horror as she saw the countess's sculpted features and haughty blue eyes.

Mary Leslie. Meggie's mother. And she had not a word of reproach for her daughter's killer. Genna bit down on her fist, forcing herself to swallow her fear and listen to what was being said.

"Because of Euan!" the countess cried, voice rising, eyes flashing in fury. "You had no right to beat him!"

"He's an idiot, Mary, a stark raving idiot!"

"Don't call my son an idiot!" Mary screamed, turning on him, slashing out with her open palm. The slap left a bright red splotch against Ranalt's pasty cheek.

Genna swayed against the door jamb, unable to believe what she'd heard. Euan . . . Euan Mac Ruarie . . . Mary's son? *And* Ranalt's son? How could it be? God, was the whole world turned upside down?

Mary's tone fell to a low, vicious hiss. "He is my firstborn, Ranalt, and I love him. He is a good son. He does as he's told."

"That's just the problem, Mary, he does what he's told! That whey-faced bitch in there told him to untie her, and so he did!"

"That was not Euan's fault. I know the girl, she's deceptive, scheming. Anyone might fall for her tricks."

"I agree, my pet! And that is why you must let me stay here to look after her."

Mary stalked behind his chair and stood over him, a thin, tight smile on her lips. She brought her long white hands to rest on his face, caressing, teasing, until his eyes closed in anticipation. Then she twined her fingers in his beard and jerked back his head. "Do you take me for an idiot as well, my sweet?" she demanded, staring into his startled gray eyes.

"I swear to you, Mary—"

"I swear to you, Mary," she mimicked, pushing his heavy head forward. "I know you, Ranalt Mac Ruarie. I know your lustful thoughts, your corrupt desires. They cost you your lordship when you couldn't keep your hands off that chippy of a Mac Leod. That's where all our troubles began. If I left you here with that girl, you'd be between her legs before my boat raised anchor."

"You're wrong," Ranalt muttered, slapping her fingers

away, resting his chin in his palms. "I am only thinking of what is best for all of us. I don't trust Euan alone with the girl."

"Why?" Mary asked mockingly, coming around the table. "Afraid your son might prove more of a man than you are?"

His pale gaze never wavered from her face as he answered, "You are such a doting mother with Euan, Mary. It would not surprise me to learn you have already compared our merits."

Mary laid her hands flat on the table, inclining toward him. "What unspeakable filth there is in your mind, my darling."

Ranalt shrugged, staring into her eyes. "It is one thing to have unspeakable thoughts, my pet. And another to perform unspeakable acts."

Genna watched in horror as Mary's strained features relaxed into a beckoning smile. "You know, that is what I love most about you, dear, sweet Ranalt. You always bring out the best in me." Her hands roved up to her bodice, tugging it down. "Kiss me, my darling."

Ranalt grasped her breast in his mouth, pulling, biting. Mary sighed and threw back her head, eyes closed in ecstasy. Her long arms curled about his neck, drawing him closer. Ranalt groaned, low in his throat, and pulled her over his knees.

Genna turned away from the door, sick in her stomach, sick to her heart. She could smell the evil permeating the room, the house, the entire world, as her husband's mother and her husband's uncle made loud, grunting, bestial love on the floor.

In sad desperation, Genna covered her ears with her hands and began to pray. "Hail Mary, full of grace, the Lord is with thee . . ." But the comfortable soothing phrases rang hollow as a bell, and though she repeated them faster and faster, all she could hear were Ranalt's bitter words: "It would not surprise me to learn that you have already compared our merits . . ." Surely he didn't mean— Oh, sweet blessed Jesus, what manner of woman was this, who shed no tears for the death of her daughter, who would commit such sin with her son? "Holy Mary, mother of God, pray for us sinners." Genna choked on the mocking words.

After a long time, the grotesque moans and squeals from the next room subsided. Tentatively Genna peered through the crack once more. Mary was calmly fastening the buttons on her bodice as Ranalt wiped his mouth with the back of his hand.

"So"—Mary sat once more at the table, her back to Genna —"it is understood, then, what you will do."

Ranalt rubbed his ragged beard with the hem of his shirt. "I still think it would be better if I stayed here."

Mary's fist slammed down on the table, making it rock madly. When she spoke her voice was iron-clad. "I have waited too many years this time to see your base, carnal hungers ruin my plans again!"

"Your plans, Mary? Why must it always be your plans?"

"They've worked out so far, haven't they?"

Ranalt stared down at the table, then raised his gaze with a weary sigh. "Mary, Mary," he murmured softly. "Why not let it rest now? Do you remember the way it used to be, long ago, when we were young? We could go away someplace, to Ireland, to England. I'm growing tired of making plans and then more plans. Don't you ever get tired, my pet?"

"Never," Mary spat, the word thick with loathing. "Never will I rest until I have my revenge on Donald, see his line destroyed and Euan installed as Lord."

"Donald is dead, Mary! For God's sake! Is not the knowledge that you had that crazed monk murder him enough for you?"

Mary stood with a swish of her skirts. "You never will understand, Ranalt, will you? I might have been queen. *Queen*," she cried, her voice filled with longing and rage. "Queen of all Scotland. But your brother failed me. One tiny setback at Harlaw and he came trotting home, tail between his legs, prattling of justice and peace. And Alexander is exactly like him. I tried to convince him to defy the king long ago. But he is his father's son, God damn his soul."

"Lord knows Euan doesn't take after me," Ranalt muttered.

"Euan will serve us well, once he becomes lord. From there, it will be but one short step to . . . king."

"Pah. The boy's no more fit to be king than to be a swineherd."

"My Euan is a good boy." Mary's eyes gleamed. "He always does exactly as his mother says."

Ranalt opened his mouth to speak again, shrugged, and was silent. Mary came and rested her cheek against his fiery hair. "Trust me, my darling," she murmured. "Trust me, and do as

I ask. You go on to Uist and fall in with Duffy's men. Once Alexander is dead, you will lead the army of the Isles."

"What makes you think they'll follow me, Mary?"

"Oh, don't you worry about that. They'll follow you."

Ranalt nodded with slow resignation. "I'll go to Uist. How long do you think this will take?"

"A month, perhaps. I'm in no rush. Remember, I have waited a long time already. But meanwhile, we sail on the next tide."

He looked up with just a hint of eagerness. "I feel like strangling the girl to be done with it, Mary. Then Euan could come with me."

"What, and risk battle?" asked Mary, appalled. "He might be killed!"

Ranalt stared at her curiously for a moment. "So might I, for that matter."

"Oh, not you, my darling," Mary said quickly. "You're far too wise and brave and clever to die. No, we'll leave the girl here and Euan can guard her. Besides, you know how much he hates to be alone. He can stay right here, far out of harm's way, and you can come and fetch him when Alexander is dead."

"I tell you, you take a risk leaving him alone with her."

Mary spread out her long white hands, gesturing around her. "What do you fear, my darling? That she'll escape?"

Ranalt's pale eyes glinted. "Your point is well taken. I bow, as always, to your better judgment." He threw back his head and laughed.

Mary chimed in shrilly, delightedly. The stone walls threw back the sounds in a howling echo, like hounds from hell.

Genna heard the whining creak of another door opening, and shrank back against the wall. Euan's odd high voice demanded querulously, "What's the jest, Mother?"

"There is no jest, my darling." Mary got up and led him to her seat at the table. "Now, my dear one, you know that your father and I must go away from here for a little while."

"But not for very *long*," Euan chanted, as if it were a lesson he'd learned by rote.

Mary beamed at him. "That's right, darling, not for very long. Now, do you understand all you're to do?"

Euan leaned his red head on his hand, smiling up at his mother. "I must keep the fires going, and gather driftwood. I must carry the keys to that room." He indicated the door behind which Genna was hiding with a nod. "I must keep them with me at all times." He paused, brow furrowed in concentration.

"And?" Mary prompted gently.

"And I must . . . I must . . . ah—"

"Christ, Mary, this will never work!" Ranalt moaned in disgust.

"I must go to the tower each day, at evening and morning, and look for sails!"

Mary shot Ranalt a look of triumph, then leaned down to kiss Euan's brow. "That's right, my dear one. And if you see them?"

"It means you are coming to get me! And then I shall be laird at last!"

"Very good, Euan, darling. What a wonderful good boy you are."

Ranalt grasped his son's wrist across the table, twisting it harshly. "Now, you listen to me, and you listen closely. If you botch this in any way, if you make a mess of it, I'll have more than a box on the ear to give you when I see you next."

"Mother, he's hurting me!" Euan cried. "Make him stop!"

"I'll give you something to whine about, by God, if you let that girl in there make a fool out of you again!"

"She won't," Euan whimpered. "I swear it."

His father stared at him, long and hard. "See that she doesn't, or you'll regret it. I promise *you* that."

"Enough, Ranalt!" Mary said sharply. "I tell you, all will be well."

Ranalt raised one red eyebrow. "I hope so." He stood up and stretched, lazily, nonchalantly. "I'll just have one more look at the girl."

"You'll do no such thing. Come, the tide has changed. We must be going."

He cast a regretful glance at the doorway and sighed. "Very well, my love. Euan. Be careful."

"Aye, sir."

Mary clasped her son in a fervent hug.

Genna felt her heart warming, though the air was still so cold she could see her breath. Alex hadn't betrayed her, he did love her! It was Mary Leslie's scheming that had led Ranalt to kidnap her, and to murder Meggie. Oh, damn it all, she thought angrily, if only I had been brave enough to tell Alex about the money she offered me, and that she lied to me about how Donald died.

It is too late now to fret about such things, she told herself sternly. Alex is in terrible danger. I've got to escape and warn him, right away.

Mary and Ranalt were leaving her alone here with Euan. She had only to wait until they sailed away, and then she could make her break for freedom, run as fast and as far as she could until she reached someone she could trust. She held her breath, watching, waiting.

"I'll come out to the dock to see you off," Euan offered.

His mother kissed him fondly. "All right, dear, if you like. Come, Ranalt, or we'll miss the tide." Her arm circling Euan's wide waist, she waited until Ranalt preceded her through the door and then followed, smiling up at her son.

Genna peered cautiously into the outer room, making certain it was empty. Then she scrambled to her feet, ignoring the warnings of her aching muscles, and darted to the open door.

The three figures were moving slowly across the strand, heading for the ship that swayed at anchor off the rickety wharf. Genna looked to the right and then the left. Beyond the little cottage in which she stood she saw a sloping seawall, extending out to the calm blue water on either side. It was twice her height, but Genna was certain she could scale it. She watched in tense anticipation as Mary and Ranalt boarded the ship. Euan stood alone at the end of the dock, waving a kerchief as the white sails billowed in the breeze.

Now, she whispered to herself. I must go now. She took a deep breath and crept through the door.

Hugging the side of the house, keeping out of sight of the dock, she tiptoed around the corner. The cold wind that whipped down over the wall was so strong that it nearly punched her down on the sand. She gritted her teeth, forcing her way forward. Beyond that wall lay hope, salvation for Alex. Behind her lay nothing but the cold crashing depths of the sea.

She took a last glance back at the ship. It was pulling away from the wharf on the ebbing tide, the sailors scrambling in the rigging, the captain shouting hoarse orders. Euan was still waving madly, calling farewell to his mother. She reached for the wall and began to climb, searching out crevices with her frozen fingers, bare feet and knees scraping raw on the stones. Ten feet, eight feet, six feet. Each perilous inch seemed a mile. She cursed as a stone pulled loose beneath her hand, leaving her dangling by a fingertip. But she was nearly there. She grasped the stone overhead and pulled herself to the top with a triumphant cry.

Impatiently she thrust long strands of wind-tossed hair back from her eyes and stared ahead, at her road to freedom. At the foot of the wall the pebbly beach ran for a hundred feet more, lying dark beneath a huge black shadow. At its end, the white-crested waves thundered onto the shore.

In disbelief Genna stared up at the towering structure that cast the long shadow across the sand. Its beaconless windows stared back impassively, like cold blank eyes.

Genna stood atop the wall, scourged by the stinging wind, and slowly turned in a full circle. In all directions there lay nothing but water as far as she could see.

20

Mary Leslie stepped onto the wharf at Aros, wrapping her coat of soft white fitchet more tightly around her, and grimaced up at the castle's walls, suppressing a shudder. Christ, she'd forgotten what a dreary, dull place this was. Well, once Euan was lord they would move the seat of power to some civilized place, someplace *not* in the Isles. And then, later, there would the castles at Edinburgh, and Stirling, and Perth. Just this one last time, she told herself firmly, and then you are free of Mull forever. This one last time, and soon all of Scotland will be yours.

The thought warmed her heart. She beckoned to the captain with a limp gloved hand, hoisted her skirts, and began the ascent up the hill to the gates. The captain stumbled after her, a trunk and bag under each arm.

A cold pall of silence lay over the grounds that were wont to be bustling with activity, and the gates were bolted from inside. "Knock," she commanded the captain. He set down her baggage with a grunt and plied his red knuckles against the wood.

Mary stood, one foot tapping impatiently, arms folded over her chest, and waited. There was no sound from within. "Knock again, you fool. Louder."

The captain glanced at her, grinned inwardly, and attacked the planks with furious energy. "Ho, there," he shouted, "open these bloody gates, God damn you! Ho, do you hear me? Open up, I say!" Anything to make certain she wouldn't set foot back on the ship.

Mary rolled her eyes skyward with a sigh of distaste.

But the uncouth racket had results. After a moment old Hoban drew back the bolts and opened the gates just a crack, peering through. "Go away," he muttered to the captain. "We're having no visitors. Leave us in peace."

Mary stepped forward, elbowing the captain away. "Stand aside, you drunken ass," she told Hoban angrily. "I have come to see my son."

Hoban's rheumy eyes focused on the fur-wrapped figure, and his jaw dropped, showing a singular absence of teeth. He yanked open the gates. "Sorry, milady, but all the household's been sent away. There's no one here but him and Master Davey. And I had no word to expect you."

Mary swept grandly past him with a toss of her head. "Had it been up to me, you would have been put out to pasture years ago, Hoban. Take my things."

"Yes, milady." Hoban bobbed in a terrified bow. "Right away, m'lady." He hurried to relieve the captain of the bags.

The captain looked after the Countess of Ross and spat on the ground. "Good riddance to bad trash," he told Hoban with a wink. "That 'un's enough trouble to make an honest man of me, almost. Enjoy her visit." He turned and headed back to the commandeered ship as quickly as he could.

Mary strode down the long snow-covered path toward the Grand Hall, frowning at the stalks of dead flowers and shrubs that cluttered the gardens. "Why hasn't all this been cleared away, Hoban?"

"No one has the heart to touch Mistress Meggie's garden," he stammered, his eyes filling with tears.

"Well, I want it clean by tomorrow morning," she ordered. "It depresses me to see such a mess."

"Mum, you'll have to come 'round to the kitchen doors. Them ones there have been nailed shut."

"My God, the whole place is like a mausoleum," Mary muttered. "Very well, then. Don't drag those bags in the snow!"

Hoban staggered after her, swamped with baggage. When Mary reached the kitchen doors she stood again and waited, tapping her toes. Hoban pulled up, panting, and looked at her. "The *door*, you old fool," she said tartly. Hoban hesitated, started to set the bags down, thought better of it, and turned the latch with his nose. Mary entered, brushing snow from the hem of her cloak, without a nod of thanks.

Althea looked up from the long kitchen table at which she sat, shelling dried beans. Her once-merry eyes were red-rimmed and filled with bleak resignation. Her mouth curved downward as she saw who had come through the door. She half turned to wipe her hands on a bit of toweling, surreptitiously crossing herself.

"So sorrow leads on to sorrow," she said, her voice thin and weary. "Hoban, take her things upstairs."

Mary heard a soft whimper, like the cry of a wounded dog, and her cold blue eyes surveyed the room. In the far corner by the hearth, hunched up on a stool, sat Davey Mac Leod, his red hair tangled and wild, staring into the fire.

"Hello there, Davey," said Mary.

Althea went to stand beside him, one arm circling his shoulders protectively, the other smoothing back his hair. "He can't hear you," she said dispassionately. "Even if he could, he wouldn't answer. He hasn't spoken since we laid Mistress Meggie in the ground. Not one word." She rested her cheek against his bowed head.

"Fancy that." Mary eyed him curiously, coming around in front of him, waving a hand before his face, then snapping her fingers. "Davey!" she called. "Davey!"

There was no flicker of recognition or of life in his hazel eyes. "I told you, he can't hear," Althea said bitterly. "Leave him be. He's not a puppy to make do tricks."

Mary met the housekeeper's venomous glance and smiled, slowly. "You haven't changed one whit, have you, Althea? You still can't bear to have me here in your house. I've news for you, it's my house, not yours. And I don't care to have you sitting in judgment of me the livelong day."

"'Tis not my place to judge you, Mary Leslie, the Lord will do that. But this house has seen grievous sorrow since the day you first put foot over the threshold. You may have fooled Old Master with your soft ways and smiles, and Young Master, too. But you never fooled me."

"What a fat impertinent hag you are, Althea. Tell me, where is my son?"

The housekeeper's voice fell to a near-whisper. "Go away from here," she beseeched, still cradling Davey's head against her broad chest. "Go away from here before you bring us any more woe."

"I have come," said Mary, clearly, haughtily, "to comfort my son. I order you to tell me where I might find him."

Althea hesitated, struggling against the custom of centuries to defy the countess's command. Her shamed glance fell to the floor. Bred to serve, trained to serve, she served now, though with reluctance. She reached out to take Mary's cloak. "He is in his chambers. I'll see you up."

"I'll see myself." She started out, turned again to Davey, and clapped her hands together as loudly as she could. He never moved. "Remarkable," Mary murmured. Then she swept across the kitchens and through the hall to the stairs.

Althea clasped the crucifix that dangled from a ribbon around her neck and mumbled a prayer, watching her go.

Alex was lying on his back atop the tall white bed he'd once shared with Genna, staring up at the ceiling above him. Mary had to rap three times at the chamber door before she heard him call softly, "What is it, Thea? Davey again?"

She pushed open the door and went in. When she saw Alex she gave a little pitying cry and fell to her knees on the floor. "Oh, my poor dear boy," she crooned, clutching at his hands, showering them with kisses. "Oh, my son, how my heart is broken, broken! Poor darling Meggie!"

"Mother." He swung his legs over the side of the bed and kissed her cheek. "I did not expect you to come here."

"Didn't you *know* I would come the moment I heard the awful news? My little baby girl, laid in the cold ground. Oh, I tell you, it was the worst day of my life when they brought the news to me. What a bitter, bitter cross it is, to follow your child to the grave. Oh, woe is me!" She burst into loud sobs, carefully obscuring her eyes with a handkerchief.

"There, Mother, there," Alex soothed her, pulling her tight to his chest. "You must not carry on so. What's done is done. Our Meggie is in God's hads."

"But so young, so young and so fair!" She wiped her eyes one last time, folded the kerchief, and assumed an expression of sad, brave forbearance. "But you are right, my darling son, as always. She has gone to a better place now." She sniffed and looked up at him. "What is ailing poor Davey? I saw him just now in the kitchens; he looks dead himself."

"Well might he be." Alex went to the window, looking out over the bleak winter landscape. "I fear he's gone mad, Mother. Ever since he . . . since he found Meggie."

"What do you mean?"

"He carried her back from the loch in his arms, chafing and rubbing her hands, kissing her face. He—he put her body by the fire. He kept saying, 'There, now, Meggie my love. We must get you warm now, put some color into those pretty cheeks." Alex swallowed. "He would not let us near to shroud her for four days. Just kept her there by the fires, fending us off with his dagger while he swore all she needed was a wee bit more warmth."

"My God, how perfectly dreadful," said Mary, fascinated. "And then what happened?"

"Eventually he grew so weary that Hoban and I disarmed him. Father Alban said the requiem, but Davey wouldn't go to the chapel. He tried to jump into the ground when we set in the coffin, and we had to shackle him. He hasn't spoken since then."

"That's what Althea told me. My, my, my, what an awful shame." She came and stood beside him at the window, patting his shoulder. "You know, I was absolutely astonished when I got word that Meggie, our little Meggie, had drowned. She was always so clever in the water. Don't you remember, Alexander, how your father taught her to swim when she was only a babe? 'That Meggie's got fish blood in her,' he used to say."

Alex laughed shakily. "I remember. But the water was freezing cold. You know these lochs in winter."

"Still, it did seem strange to me," Mary mused.

"We started to dredge the loch right away, but the next week it froze over." He rubbed his forehead with his thumb and forefinger. "That is the worst part of all this terrible grief, Mother, that I shall have to wait now until spring."

"Wait until spring for what, Alexander?"

"To finish the dredging."

"But why are you dredging?"

"To—to find Genna's body, of course."

Mary's blue eyes grew enormously round. "You think— you think that she drowned?" she asked, her voice hushed. "My God, you poor boy. Do you really mean you don't know?"

"Know what?" Alex grasped his mother's arms, white-knuckled, wild-eyed. "What do you know about my wife?"

Mary turned away, her shoulders sagging. "I never dreamed, Alexander, that I would be the one to bring this news to you. I forget how remote, how isolated these islands are. For all I know, you won't even believe the news. But I've brought proof with me, indeed I have. Letters, letters that they threw at me while they laughed in my face. Letters that he wrote to her."

"Letters?" Alex felt a catch in his heart, remembering the letter Hoban had told him of. "Damn you, Mother, tell me! What do you know about my wife?"

"All right, then!" Mary pushed his hands away and faced him. "You need mourn no longer for that cheap brazen hussy! She is plenty alive, and staying at Inverness."

"Inverness?" Alex repeated incredulously. "What is she doing at Inverness?"

Mary's mouth twisted. "Living and sinning with Henry Argyll. And boasting to all who will listen that the child she's bearing is his!"

That night the torches blazed from the peaks of Ben More and the heights of Ben Buie. The watchers at their posts atop the steep cliffs of Coll and Scarba saw the flickering signals, and hastened to light their own brands. From station to station, island to island, the message flared out: "The Lord of the Isles summons you. Glenshiel, in three days' time. Bring mounts and arms."

Mary Leslie stood beside her son in the tower at Aros, watching the far-off lights. "I am proud of you, son," she said softly. "It is just what your father would have done."

"That bastard may have my wife and welcome," Alex muttered fiercely, "but by God, he'll not claim my bairn for his own."

"You know, Alexander, I cannot help but wonder..." Her voice trailed off, and she looked up at him with wide blue eyes. "Those letters date back months; she and Argyll must have been plotting this for some time. I cannot help but wonder whether they were responsible for Meggie's death."

Alex stared at the fires in the distance, his face drawn and haggard. He thought of the dripping sweet love notes she'd shown to him, addressed to "My little tiger cat." And then— oh, God, he thought of Genna's smile, the kisses she gave him. "No," he said finally. "She would not be a party to murder."

"Oh, but darling, a woman who would steal a child, abandon her husband, an adulteress—surely such a woman would not shrink at murder."

"I don't know what to believe!" Alex cried in anguish. "I only know that Henry Argyll is—a dead man."

Mary clutched his hand, pressing it to her cheek. "I fear for you, Alexander. The moment you cross that sound, a price lies on your head."

"Two thousand men of the Isles march with me. Let King James or anyone else try to stand in my way."

"Inverness is well defended," Mary mused, half to herself. "And Argyll is vice governor."

"Not one stone of that castle will be left standing when I am through."

In the kitchens Althea made butter, red-faced from the effort. "There's more here than meets the eye," she muttered to the unheeding Davey, punctuating each word with a thump of the churn. "Young Mistress wasn't the sort to run off; she worshiped Master Alley. If he wasn't so all-fired angry, he'd see that himself. I smell a rat here, indeed I do. Mark my words."

From Eigg to Rhum to Skye the torches carried the summons, from Jura to Islay. The clan chiefs smiled grimly in the chill winter darkness and tightened their shield grips, sharpened their swords.

Davey stared deep into the red and gold flames that danced in the fireplace.

Alexander came down from the tower and stood in his chambers, tall and unbending, while Mary laced up the greaves of his mail and buckled the silver belt over his saffron tunic. The garlanded sword and galley gleamed in the candlelight.

"Here's for luck," said Mary, kissing his taut mouth. She tucked her linen kerchief into the band of his sleeve.

"Thanks." Alex took the sword and shield that had been his father's down from the wall. They felt oddly heavy. He slipped the sword into his sheath and stalked down the long steep stairs.

The men of Clan Mac Donald were waiting, ready for war, in the castle yards. At the wharf the long flat barges that would carry them to Morven rocked on the ebbing tide. No one asked the Lord of the Isles where they were headed, on whom they were marching. All would be explained at Glenshiel, when the clans had gathered. For now it was theirs to follow wherever he led.

Old Hoban brought Bantigh, white-maned and stamping, out from the stable gate. Althea stood at the kitchen door, clutching her crucifix, and watched as Alex straddled the spirited steed.

Through the gates, stooped and wizened, unnoticed, the black-garbed seeress came creeping, leaning on her gnarled staff.

At a signal from Alex the clansmen aligned their horses, ready to gallop down to the sound. The seeress raised her staff and brandished it over her head. "Turn back, Alexander Mac Donald!" she cried, her voice a bone-chilling wail. "The day of woe draws nigh!"

The warriors hesitated as her warning swirled on the wind. Alex alone spurred his mount through the gate, never once looking back.

"Damn that meddlesome fool." Althea heard Mary's barked curses and turned from the doorway. The countess's face was frightening, contorted with rage.

The clansmen still waited, uncertain. Then Hoban came and thrust at the hag with his broom.

"Be gone with ye," he shouted, "ye raving harpy! Get ye gone from here!" She vanished into the shadows beyond the gate.

Laughing, calling out jests about one another's qualms, the clansmen followed their laird to the sound.

Mary Leslie smiled sweetly. "I'm absolutely famished, Althea. Bring up some bread and cheese to my chambers, right away."

"After I feed Master Davey," Althea told her, from between clenched teeth.

"Now." The countess's eyes were narrowed and glittering.

Althea's were just as flinty. "When I finish with Davey, I said."

"Let me come to the tower with you, Euan."

Euan Mac Ruarie shook his head and tucked a handful of oats into his rolled-up sleeve. "Nope."

"Please? Just this once? I won't bother the birds, I promise."

"Father said absolutely not." He stared down at her, the keys dangling from his big hand. "Do you like birds, Genna?"

"Oh, Euan, I love birds, don't you? Big birds, little birds, scrawny ones and fat ones." Genna's voice caught as she found herself repeating the words Alex had spoken to her, his blue eyes aglow with laughter, such a long time ago. A million years . . .

Each day on the island was precisely the same as the one before. Euan brought her oatmeal for breakfast, oatmeal at midday, oatmeal for supper. He let her sit by the fire in the main room of the cottage for her meals, and sometimes into the evening, if he felt lonely. He chattered about what it might be like to be laird, and how much he loved the ocean. And twice a day, when he went up to the tower to look for sails, he fed his birds.

And each time he mounted those stairs Genna's heart stopped beating, terrified that he would see those sails, that Ranalt would arrive, with the news that Alex was dead. Tears of forlorn despair welled up in her eyes. She felt so utterly helpless, so alone, so afraid.

"Oh, now, for heaven's sake, don't start crying again." Euan chewed his lip worriedly, twirling the keys. "How about if I give you one of my blankets? Or would you like some oatmeal? Something to drink?"

Genna forced a sad smile. "I'm sorry, Euan. It's just that I would like to feed the birds with you so badly." She sighed and turned to face the wall.

The long string of marks she'd made there to tally the days was a grim reminder. Four weeks she had been cooped up here on the island, while Mary and Ranalt were free to carry out their deadly plans. But Mary had said it might take her as much as a month to seal Alex's fate, however she meant to do that. There might still be time to warn him, save him. If only she could get to that tower, and seek out the nearest land! The island was no more than a skerry, a rocky isle thrown up out of the sea, but it had a lighttower. And if there was a lighttower, didn't that prove there had to be land somewhere nearby?

What she would do if she did sight land Genna did not consider. For now it was enough to pursue one goal at a time.

"I'd *like* to let you up there, but I promised Father."

"I won't tell him, I swear I won't!"

Euan pursed his thick lips. "The last time you swore me a promise, you broke it. You shouldn't have done that. You got me into a lot of trouble, you know."

"I know. I'm sorry."

Euan reached out tentatively and put his hand on her hair. "You are very pretty, Genna, do you know that?"

"Thank you, Euan."

He twined the long dark strands between his fingers. "I would never do anything to hurt you."

"I hope not, Euan." Genna shivered, suddenly apprehensive. He was such a strange creature: the body of a man, the mind of a child. What did he long for when he touched her that way? Did he even know?

"Do you remember the time that I kissed you in the garden, Genna? The night that the doggy died?"

"No," she whispered. "I don't. But I know that you hurt me."

"I'm sorry. I would never want to hurt you." She inclined her head, accepting the apology. "I liked it, though. When I am laird, Genna, perhaps you could marry me. And then we could always live together, just as we do now."

"If I promise to marry you, will you take me up to the tower?"

"Oh, I don't know. I still don't think I'd better."

"But if we're to be husband and wife, then we must share everything together. It wouldn't be fair if you were the only one who got to feed the birds."

"Is that so? We share everything?"

"Everything." She nodded firmly. "Every single thing."

"Well, then." His broad face creased in a delighted grin. "I suppose it wouldn't hurt to start sharing. Come along." He unlocked the tower door and led the way up the stairs.

Genna's legs were stiff from disuse, and halfway up the steep winding stairs she had to pause, leaning against the wall, to catch her breath. Euan peered back at her face in the shadows. "I could carry you, if you'd like."

"I'll be fine," she assured him. She gritted her teeth and resumed the climb.

The stairs led up to a blank-walled chamber cluttered with cast-off goods and clothing that looked as though they hadn't been touched in years. A smell of moldy wool permeated the close air. Genna looked about in shocked disappointment. "There aren't any windows, Euan! How can you feed the birds?"

He laughed, a childlike conspirator. "The doorway is hidden. Here, behind this pile of cloth." He flung aside a mass of mildewing draperies to reveal a low narrow door.

It opened with a creak of rotting hinges. Genna shielded her eyes from the sudden blaze of white sunlight, and then squeezed through. Four more stairs went up in a semicircle, into the lightkeeper's cell.

She stood blinking for a moment, adjusting to the harsh glare. Euan took her elbow and pulled her toward one of the recessed casements. "Look, isn't it lovely? Nothing but blue so far as you can see!"

Genna peered through the window and felt her heart sink. For miles and miles around she saw only the endless rolling waves. In desperation she ran to the other openings, but the view from each was the same. She leaned out over the ledge and stared at the patch of rocky sand below.

"Ocean, ocean, ocean." Euan hugged himself with glee. "I love the ocean."

"I hate it," Genna said fiercely, feeling tears spring in her eyes. How could there be not even a glimpse of land in all that wide blue sea?

Euan leaned out from the casement beside her and whistled, and a flock of hungry chattering gulls appeared instantaneously, beating their wings against the wind as he tossed oats high in the air. They screeched and dove, fighting each other for the grain, as Euan laughed and called them by name.

"That big white one, I call him Jack. Do you hear him saying hello to you? Hello, Jack! Hey, boy! The one with the stripes on his wings is Stripy. And that pretty little black bird, I named her after you, Genna. I hope you don't mind."

"I don't mind, Euan. I think it was very nice of you." Her voice caught in a little sob as she watched him whistle between his teeth and fling the oats over the sill.

Euan looked over and frowned, seeing her tears. "What's wrong, Genna? Are you angry at me?"

"Of course not. I'm just sad."

His face brightened. "When I'm sad, Genna, I go to that

room below and play with the clothes. I dress up like a king. I'm going to be king, someday. Did you know that?"

"I fear you will," said Genna, staring out over the sea.

He shook the last bits of oats from his sleeve and tossed them to the gulls. "That's all for tonight, fellows. I'll see you in the morning." The birds flapped at the casement for a few seconds more, then wheeled and swooped away. Euan considered Genna's tear-streaked face, then grabbed her arm. "Come on, let's go and play king."

He led her back to the tower room and began to pull cloaks and tunics out of a corner. He wound a moth-bitten tapestry around his shoulders, and set a cap with molted ostrich plumes on his head. "See, Genna, now I'm the king! Bow to His Majesty!" Euan gathered the threadbare tapestry around him and perched on a low wooden bench. "This is my throne. When I really am king, I'll have a far finer throne than this, of course. This is nothing but an old church pew."

"So it is." Genna ran her finger over the carved arm. What did that remind her of?

Euan bounded up again. "There are all sorts of things up here to play with. Here's a dress you can wear to be my queen!" He flung a bundle of diaphanous silk toward her. It caught a wisp of wind that whistled up the staircase and hung, suspended, on a shred of sunbeam.

They took two pews from the chapel and lashed them together, with a sail made out of a habit . . .

"What did you say?" asked Euan.

"Nothing. Nothing! Let me see that throne." But it was ancient, rotted; it crumbled to splinters at her touch.

"Look at this old wine cask," Euan exclaimed. "It's so big you could take a bath in it!"

"What a clever idea, Euan," Genna whispered, testing its staunch oak staves. And the cask she could roll out to the wharf.

But what good would it do to set herself afloat in a barrel on the ocean? She might as well just kill herself by jumping out of the tower. Or swim, for that matter.

But what if she had some way of guiding herself? Hands shaking, she began to paw through the discarded clothing. This was too small, that too worn, another unraveled into threads as she tested its strength.

"I say, what's this?" Euan had discovered a new item. Impatiently she turned to look.

"My God." She stepped forward, unbelieving, and touched the polished breastbeam. "Sweet God in heaven. It's a loom."

"Well, that's no use, is it?" Euan rubbed his nose and sneezed. "I surely would like to take a warm bath, Genna. Wouldn't you?"

"I think it would be wonderful. I swear, you are such a smart man, Euan. Why don't you carry the cask downstairs, and I'll bring the loom."

"Why should we take that old loom?"

Genna looked up at him, black eyes glinting. "If you are to be king, Euan, you need a proper mantle. A beautiful robe, in gold and purple, with the emblems of the Lord of the Isles. I'll make it for you on this loom."

"You will?" Euan eyed the decrepit implement dubiously. "But there isn't any wool here. What will you weave it from?"

"I can use these old clothes and hangings. All I'll have to do is unwind the yarn."

Euan frowned. "I don't know, Genna. Father might get angry with me"

"But just imagine what a wonderful surprise it will be when they come back here and find you already dressed as a king!"

Still he hesitated. She put a hand on his arm, her black eyes pleading. "Please, Euan."

"Oh, all right. Since you are going to be my queen."

"Oh, thank you, Euan!" She reached up and gave him a kiss on the cheek.

Euan froze, staring down at her. His gray eyes were suddenly narrowed, glittering, like his father's. "Once you are my queen, I'll be able to play the secret game with you, won't I?"

"What game is that?"

"The one that Mother taught me. I'm not supposed to tell anybody about it, though."

Genna shivered, seeing a vein twitch on his forehead. "How do you play the secret game, Euan?"

He plucked at the sleeve of the shirt she wore. "First, you take off all your clothes."

Genna swallowed the hard, tight knot of her loathing. Mary Leslie had taken her toll on this son as well. Poor simple Euan. She made her voice bright, winning. "Of course we will play that game, Euan. But not until you are king."

"I suppose that's fair. I'll take the loom down; 'tis too heavy for you to carry. Why don't you bring the draperies you need?"

Genna turned to gather them up, her hands trembling as she piled the helter-skelter rags together. Please, God, she prayed, more fervently than she had ever prayed before in her life. Don't let Ranalt return before I am finished. Give me time enough to make a robe for Euan. Time enough to weave . . . a sail.

21

Henry Argyll was feeling rather pleased with himself.

It just goes to show you, Henry my boy, he mused, leaning back in the chair before a roaring fire, always go with your instincts. You knew that offer was sound the moment you heard it. Five hundred marks just to pick a fight with her son, and pen some pretty letters. Hah! It was the easiest money he'd ever made. It had allowed him to grease enough palms to be touted by those close to King James for the post of vice governor here, and then to provide a handsome christening gift for the new little princess. That had given him the chance to gain James's ear, and gently remind him of the Argyll family's long service to the crown.

Vice governor now, but soon governor. Even finer lodgings. More money to skim from the king's coffers. It was so easy to find ways to cheat the crown. His idea to dismiss half the guards at the castle, for example, was brilliant! Why should he pay two hundred men to drink and gamble and wench, when he could pay one hundred and pocket the savings himself? And use it to drink and gamble and wench. Women were more than willing when a man had a fine suit of clothes, a bit of change in his purse.

Lord, but women were stupid. Good for what they were made for, and nothing more. He laughed uproariously, smoothing down his velvet doublet, gazing in satisfaction at his luxurious paneled study. And he had Mary Leslie to thank for it all, God bless the scheming bitch.

He stretched out his long arms, reaching to jangle the bell that hung by the chair. What had she gotten out of their bargain, he wondered. She couldn't possibly be as satisfied as he was, that was sure.

Behind his shoulder he heard the door to the chamber open. "You certainly took your time getting here, Calum," he said petulantly. "I nearly froze to death waiting. Warm me some wine, and be quick about it. And throw another log on the fire."

Through the richly curtained casements a burst of garbled shouting floated up from the yards. "Good God, Calum, what is that racket? Another of your damned peasant holidays?" He turned back his broidered cuffs with slow disdain, waiting for an answer. When none was forthcoming he raised one eyebrow and picked up his cane. He'd teach that impertinent boy to be civil, damn him.

The huge gloved hand that reached from behind the chair to wrench the stick away did not belong to Calum. Argyll watched in stunned fascination as the hand snapped the thick wood like a paltry twig.

"Who—who is there?" Argyll demanded, voice quavering, as there spread in the pit of his stomach a cold sour dread.

"Hello, Argyll," Alex said softly. Argyll froze at the sound of the calm low voice. Alex tossed the broken cane into the fire.

Argyll twisted about in his chair, his coppery eyes widening. "Mac Donald? Is that you?"

Alex bowed from the waist with offhanded elegance. "The same."

"I—I hadn't heard that King James had pardoned you."

"He hasn't," said Alex, slowly pulling off his gloves.

Another shout burst forth from the courtyard. Argyll pushed himself up from his chair and took a step toward the casement. "What's going on out there?" he demanded, his voice rising in a nervous squeal.

"My men have surrounded your walls. Your guards are our prisoners. I have two thousand soldiers waiting for my signal to torch the castle."

"T-t-torch the castle? Good God, are they crazy?"

"I wouldn't say crazy. But they are . . . rather eager to begin."

Argyll licked his lips. "Mac Donald, can't we be reasonable? I know we've had our differences in the past. You probably blame me for your banishment. Well, you may be right! But all that is long past, long buried. Let's just let bygones be bygones, what do you say? Forgive and forget?"

Alex's broad fists tightened ominously. "Where is she, you adulterous bastard?"

Argyll looked into Alex's steel blue eyes, then down at his hands. He swallowed. "Ad-d-dulterous?" he stammered. "Where is who?"

One fist darted out, closing on the velvet of his doublet. "Don't toy with me, swine."

"I don't know what you're talking about, I swear it! For whom are you searching?"

"Where is my wife?" Alex roared, knocking him out of the chair with a swift hard kick. Argyll scrambled away along the floor, sideward, like a crab.

"How would I know where your wife is?"

Alex's boot connected solidly with the pit of Argyll's stomach. The vice governor stared up with terrified eyes. "I don't know your wife," he gasped, clutching himself sickly.

Alex crouched over him. "Suppose I slit your filthy throat, then, and go through your castle room by room, looking for her myself."

"On the cross of Christ, Mac Donald, I never even heard that you'd married!"

Alex hesitated, seized by a pang of doubt. Argyll was too great a coward not to relinquish Genna at the price of his life. Or was he? "You lying dog. My own mother told me she'd seen you together, showed me the letters you wrote."

Argyll stared openmouthed for a long moment. Then he began to laugh. "Your mother? Your mother told you? Oh, you poor benighted fool."

Alex gripped the man's throat. "What do you mean?" he demanded furiously.

Argyll was clutching his stomach again, this time from laughter. "Your mother is a whoring she-bear! Only you would be idiot enough to believe a word she said!"

Alex's fist whipped against his face. "You'll burn in hell for that!"

"Mary Leslie will be right there beside me, if I do!"

Alex began to hit him, slowly, methodically, his great strength multiplying with his rage. When Argyll's hysterical laughter stopped at last, Alex went to the doorway. Iain Cameron and Angus Mac Pherson stood there waiting, side by side, dressed alike in leinechroich and untanned boots. The fever of anticipation made their dark eyes glow like those of the prophets. Alex smiled at them grimly. "Search the castle. Ransack it room by room. As you go, put each to the flame."

* * *

"Altheeeah!" Mary Leslie's petulant cry echoed through the empty hallway of Aros Castle. About to slide a tray of scones into her brick-walled oven, Althea hesitated, set it down, picked it up as the voice called again, and finally threw the whole tray to the floor with an angry oath. Sure it was that good Saint Paul had said vassals must serve their masters. But equally sure, he'd had no such master as Mary Leslie in mind!

She went to the foot of the stairway, hands on hips, and bellowed, "Whatever it is you want, you can get it yourself!"

Mary's elegant white-clad figure appeared on the landing. "I don't believe I understood you aright, Althea." Her blue eyes were narrowed.

"Oh, you heard me aright, Mistress Feathers and Lace. Whatever it is you want, you can get your dainty little butt out of bed and get it yourself!"

The Countess of Ross advanced down the stairway with slow sure steps. There was a bright patch of red high in each of her cheeks. "Now, you listen to me, you base-born scullion, and listen well. When I tell you to jump, by God, the only thing I want to hear out of you is 'How high?'"

"Ach, go jump in the sound," Althea spat. "I've put up with your high-blown ways for a month now, and frankly, that's more than enough. There'll be no more scraping your boots or washing out your dainties by these hands. Scullion though I may be, I'm too good for that!" And Althea turned her broad back and strode into her kitchens, her heart beating furiously, but her shoulders held high.

"Too good? *Too good?*" Mary's voice was an outraged roar as she followed. "You're not good enough to empty my chamber pot, you fat turd!"

"I was good enough to nurse your bairns when you couldn't be bothered, and to look after your poor husband that you kept deserting as well! Unnatural, that's what you are, Mary Leslie. Never once in your life did you think of any other creature but yourself!"

"Get out of this house!" Mary thundered, pointing to the doorway. "Get out, and don't you ever come back!"

Althea turned to her, dark eyes blazing. "And happy I'll be to go! But before I do, there's a few things I'll say."

"And what might those be?" Mary's gaze was amused, imperious.

Althea advanced until the two women stood nearly nose to nose. "I know you for what you are, Mary Leslie, an evil witch. I've watched you make life hell for those around you for twenty-five years. You didn't marry Old Master because you loved him. You married him because he was made tanist in Ranalt's place."

"So what if I did? There's no law that says a woman must love a man to wed him."

"Nay, but there's laws against fornication."

Mary laughed. "Go on. I find this quite droll. Are you accusing me of fornication? With whom?"

Althea's voice fell. "Three years past, my cousin Hattie's husband died up at Dingwall, and she came back here to live with her mother, at Tobermory. I went to visit her there. She told me that that last summer before you married you got pretty fat yourself, Mary Leslie. She said if she didn't know better, she'd have sworn you were carrying a bairn."

"Prattle. Servants' gossip," Mary said disdainfully.

"That's what I thought too, milady, but Old Master didn't. The day after I mentioned it to him, he sent Master Alley off to find Ranalt Mac Ruarie. And then he set off for Tobermory, to see Cousin Hattie himself. But he never made it there, did he, Mary Leslie? He fell off his horse that night, and he broke his neck."

Something hard, metallic, clicked in Mary's eyes. "So it was you who told Donald about me. I might have known, you conniving busybody."

"It was. And I've held my tongue about it for too long now. Whether 'tis my place or not, I'm telling Master Alley when he gets back."

"He's not coming back, Althea. I've made certain of that. Alexander has to die, just as Donald had to."

Althea took a step backward. "Then the seeress was right. You murdered Old Master!"

"Not I. A certain young man with his own grudge against my husband, but I told him how. He strung a bit of wire across the road by the loch there. Poor Donald fell right off his horse. And after that, he never knew what hit him."

Althea crossed herself. "Mistress Meggie—her horse was lamed, too."

Mary nodded, her pale eyes glittering. "So it was." She picked up a butchering knife from the table. "Your tongue is

entirely too long, do you know that, Althea? It's so long, in
fact, that I'm going to blunt it a bit."

Althea's brown eyes had grown suddenly enormous. But as
Mary stepped toward her, she realized Althea's gaze was not
focused on the knife.

She glanced over her shoulder, suspecting a trick. Quick as
lightning, Davey wrapped his hands around her long white
neck.

Althea fell back against the table, swooning. Davey smiled
at the countess, tightening his hold. "So you murdered my
Meggie, did you?" he growled, his voice raspy from long silence.

"No," Mary gasped, "not I! It was Ranalt, Ranalt."

Davey smiled, without amusement. "What shall we do
with her, Althea? Strangle her? Drown her? Or maybe just
burn her for the witch she is."

"Oh, Master Davey, sweet Jesus, you gave me a fright!
Like seeing a soul come back from the dead, it was!"

Davey was still staring down at the countess, his wrath
taut, controlled. "She was all light, all virtue. An angel. You
just couldn't stand that, could you? You could not bear to have
such goodness near you, on earth with you."

Mary smiled cunningly. "Go on. Kill me. I've gained my
ends. Alexander is marching on Inverness at this moment.
Once he strikes there, King James will hunt him down and
murder him for me. His wife and her child are dead. Euan will
be lord."

"She's lying, Davey! She told Master Alley that Genna was
at Inverness!"

Mary reached into her purse with one thin hand. "Oh?
Then tell me, where did I get this?"

"Master Davey, 'tis Young Mistress's brooch!" Althea
reached out and took the love knot, her fingers trembling.

"My God," said Davey, disbelieving. "You've murdered
her, too." He yanked back her head, curling his hands, pressing her throat, relishing the way that she gasped for breath.

"Master Davey," Althea whispered, "wait. Think of your
immortal soul."

"That's right, Master Davey." Mary's voice was choked but
mocking. "Then your angel Meggie will be in heaven. And
you and I will have until time ends to spend with one another
in hell."

"It cannot be a sin to kill such a one as you." But Davey's grip relaxed, just for a moment. Mary twisted out of his grasp and pinned the knife she still held to Althea's throat.

"Now," she said calmly, "I am going to Edinburgh to see my son beheaded. If you'll just move aside."

Davey took a step forward. Althea screamed as the blade sliced against her chin.

He backed away with slow reluctance. Mary yanked the key to the cider cellar from Althea's bosom and gestured to the low cellar doors. "Down there. You first, MacLeod, you pathetic innocent." Still holding the knife to Althea, she opened the lock.

Davey pulled the doors up and clambered down the ladder. Althea followed, trembling, turning back once for a last look at Mary. "Have you no mercy?" she asked of that pale twisted face.

For answer Mary slammed the hatch shut. In the darkness Althea and Davey heard the bars snapped to, and the grind of the key.

Euan stood at Genna's shoulder, watching in fascination as the handmade shuttle flew back and forth between the outstretched threads. "Aren't you hungry, Genna? It's time for supper."

"You go ahead, Euan, I'll eat later."

"But I made us a nice thick porridge."

"I said, later!" She bit her tongue, leaning forward on the breastbeam, her head on her arms. "I'm sorry. I didn't mean to shout at you."

"That's all right." He reached out tentatively to touch the length of fabric that hung from the warp beam. "It's beginning to look like a cloak now. I like the ship on it best." He rubbed the cloth between two thick fingers. "But why are you making it so heavy?"

"It's a winter cloak, Euan. It will keep you good and warm." With a sigh she sat back and picked up the shuttle again. God, it seemed she'd been weaving forever, and still she was only half-finished. But if she worked all through the night, perhaps by tomorrow noon, she'd be ready to try.

She needed a mast to hold the sail up, and rope to lash the mast to the cask. And something to spread the sail out at the bottom. What had the ferryman called that? The boom.

The shuttle flew back and forth with lightning speed. Genna's mind was working just as fast. She would have to take food along, and water. The cask was watertight; at least, it hadn't leaked when Euan had taken a bath in it. If it floated— it *had* to float—she would be all right.

Be all right? cried a small voice in her head. What are you talking about? You don't know anything about sailing. You don't know where to sail *to*. You don't know what you're doing at all.

Well, it's better to be busy than to sit and wait and do nothing! she argued back. When Ranalt returns he'll kill me anyway. At least this way I have a chance.

Some chance, the voice continued. Setting out on the sea in the dead of winter in a bathtub. You're as simple as Euan.

Grimly she thrust the voice away and continued her plotting. She could take the water skin Euan kept by the doorway, and a sack of oats as well. A plank from the trestle table could be the mast, and the beam of the loom would serve for the boom. All she had to do was finish the sail, find some rope, roll the cask down to the water.

Oh, that should be easy. The voice intruded again. You've finally got Euan to trust you a bit, and now you're going to throw it away on this crazy scheme? You're going to die for certain.

I'll be dead anyway when Ranalt gets back—raped and tortured and murdered. Shut up, won't you, and leave me alone?

Five and a half weeks since Ranalt left here, the voice ran on, unheeding. Alex is dead already. You are wasting your time.

"Euan," she said desperately, "tell me a story. Sing me a song."

"I'm eating," he said through a mouthful of porridge. "You had better eat, too."

"Do you know if there's any rope up in the lighttower?"

"Rope?" He eyed her warily over the edge of his porridge bowl. "I don't know. Why?"

"I need some to measure you for the cloak. I don't know how long to make it."

"Oh! Wait, I'll go up and see." He set down his supper and unlocked the door. "Don't you move, now, do you hear me?"

"I won't." He disappeared up the stairs.

He came back down a moment later with a thick coil slung over his shoulder. "Will this do?"

"Oh, that's perfect! Now, you stand right here, and let me see." She stood on tiptoe to stretch the rope from his head down to the floor. There was twice that much. Surely that would be enough. For appearance's sake she measured his shoulders and waist.

"All right?" he asked, twisting to see her.

"Wonderful. How clever of you to find it."

His broad face glowed. "I'll just take it back up if you're through."

"No, leave it here, please. I might need to use it again."

He shrugged and picked up his porridge, sitting on the table by her side, watching the quick sure movements of her hands. "I like it here with you, Genna," he told her. "You're hardly ever cross with me. And you don't call me horrid names." He swallowed a huge mouthful. "I wish we could stay here like this forever, just the two of us."

"So do I, Euan." Genna swallowed a mouthful of guilt. "But what about being king? Aren't you looking forward to that?"

He dismissed it with a wave. "It will be all right, I suppose. Mother wants it more than I do. I'm really only trying to make her happy."

Genna set down the shuttle for a moment and met his strange pale eyes. "What makes you happy, Euan?" she asked him softly.

"Being here with you. Feeding the birds. Being away from Father." He paused, his eyes clouding; he seemed to be reaching back in his mind. "I remember once, a long time ago, my uncle Donald. Do you know my uncle Donald?" Genna nodded. "I stayed with him for a summer. Alley and Meggie were there, and Donald let me watch the sheep. Every day I went up with the men to the hills, and they gave me my own flock, five of them!" He smiled suddenly. "I gave names to them all, I remember. Blackie, and Whitey, and Fred . . ." His voice trailed off. "I liked it there in the hills. But at the castle it was different. I wasn't allowed to call Mother Mother. Sometimes I forgot, and she hit me." He met her steady black gaze, his voice filled with pride. "But Donald said I was a good shepherd. One of the best, he called me. I still remember. 'Euan,' he told me, 'you are one of the best.'"

Genna turned back to her loom, a sob caught in her throat.
Poor Euan, why couldn't Mary and Ranalt have left him there
in the hills, with his Whitey and Blackie? Why did they have
to drag him into their treacherous schemes? She wiped away
the bitter tears that welled in her eyes.

"Genna? What's the matter, Genna? Please don't cry; you
know I can't stand to see you cry."

"I'm sorry, Euan. I'm not crying. There is something in my
eye, that's all. Would you like to go back to Aros and have a
flock of sheep of your own again?"

"Would you be there, Genna?"

"I'd be there."

He smiled. "I'd like that a lot."

By the following afternoon, the cloak was finished. Genna
borrowed Euan's knife to cut the warp threads from the frame,
while he clapped his hands and nearly danced with excitement.

"Oh, Genna, it's—it's—" He paused, speechless. "It is
nearly as pretty as you are," he finished haltingly. "The
sword, and the ship, and the different colors." He sighed happily, reaching out his hands. "Can I put it on now?"

Hating herself, Genna pulled it away. "First we must have
your coronation."

"What's that?" he demanded, wrinkling his nose.

"Your crowning. You go up the stairs to the tower, and
when you hear me call 'His Royal Majesty, Euan Mac Ruarie,'
then you come down."

"But what about my cloak?"

"When you come through the door, I'll lay it across your
shoulders. And I'll put the crown on your head."

He nodded, comprehending, his eyes shining. "Here I go
then, up the stairs."

"Oh, and Euan, you must leave the keys here."

"What for?"

She laughed. "Oh, Euan, don't be silly! You know a king
never carries his own keys. He has a royal key bearer."

"He does?"

"Of course! You knew that, didn't you?"

His brow knotted, then cleared. "Of course I did. I just
forgot." She held out her hand; he pulled the key ring from his
belt and relinquished it.

"Now, don't come down until you hear me call 'His Royal Majesty,'" she cautioned.

"'His Royal Majesty,'" he repeated. "I like the sound of that."

Genna pushed him toward the tower door. "Go on, now." He lumbered up the twisting steps.

God forgive me, thought Genna, as she pushed the door closed gently and turned the key.

"Now, Genna? Now?" She shut her ears to his anxious shouts as she unlocked the door to the cottage and heaved the tub over on its side. She rolled it down to the edge of the wharf, then dashed back inside for the cloak and her mast and the knife. One more trip brought the beam of the loom, blankets, and a water bag. She assembled it all on the frigid rocky beach and began to work. Her fingers fumbled with the heavy line as she lashed the staff to the edge of the tub, then threaded the rope through slashes she made in the sail. Next she lashed the beam to the mast, and tied the sail there. The heavy cord rubbed against her fingers, numb with the cold, making them bleed. At any moment she expected to look up and see Ranalt's ship approaching the wharf.

Damn, why was it taking so long? The beam wouldn't hold to the mast, the sail flopped and tangled in the wind. Genna cursed and tied it again, forcing herself to work slowly, carefully. She gave it a tug, and the bright-colored sail billowed, rippling on the seaward breeze.

Genna dashed back into the lighttower, grabbed a sack of oats, and set the knife back on the table. She didn't want to take anything with her that Euan might need.

Through the tower door she heard his increasingly plaintive voice. "Why am I locked in, Genna? I don't think I like this game."

"Just another moment, Euan. Now you must go to the top of the stairs and count as high as you can." God, how high could he count? "And then count back down again, backward. Then come down the stairs, very slowly and grandly, and open the door."

"Oh, all right." She heard his boots clunking on the stairs. Hands shaking, she unlocked the door.

Then she flew back to the wharf, threw the oats and water into the tub, and shoved at it in desperation. It refused to budge even an inch. Oh, sweet Christ, not after all that work and planning. She couldn't fail now! She closed her eyes, thinking of Alex, and shoved again. Nothing. Her hands were riddled with splinters from the rough wood, her head pounding louder than the waves, and the chattering songs of the seabirds seemed to mock her efforts. She braced her bare feet against a railing, gritted her teeth, and edged the heavy cask forward with her shoulder. There was a loud shuddering scrape, and the tub plunged off the wharf and into the sea.

Genna leapt in, caught the rope, and tugged at the sail. The heavy cloth hung for a moment, motionless, useless, and then filled with a mighty flap.

Euan pushed open the tower door. "I can't count any higher, and I'm tired of waiting. Where's my cloak, Genna?" With a growing sense of dread he saw the sunlight pouring in through the cottage door.

"Genna! No!" He rushed down the strand toward the tub that was receding from the wharf with dizzying quickness. "Genna! Don't leave me! Genna, come back!"

"I'll come back for you, Euan, I promise!" she shouted, then covered her ears against his anguished wails. She tried to tell herself that he'd been a party to Meggie's death, to Mary's plotting, but in her heart she knew he was innocent, and it ripped at her soul. She forced herself to focus on steadying the cask in the water, kept her eyes on the unfurling sail.

On the rocky shore Euan stood with his arms outstretched, beseeching. "Come back," he whispered, "don't leave me. Please don't leave me alone."

But the beautiful rippling sail only taunted him, dancing ever farther way. Euan turned and raced for the tower, stumbling up the long stairway, crouching to squeeze through the door. He leaned out from the casement, hurt, bewildered, the harsh winds whipping his hair.

The sail moved toward the horizon, dipping and swaying. High above the mast, against the blue sky, seabirds flapped and screeched and dove.

Gone. She was really gone, then. He was alone, would be alone until Mary and Ranalt returned. Alone all day long, with nobody to talk to. Alone through the long cold nights.

But perhaps they were already on their way for him! Hurriedly he ran to each window and peered out. He saw nothing but the beautiful sea, and the endless sky.

They would come for him soon, though. Mother had

promised. In the morning, maybe, or tomorrow evening.
Their ship would glide up to the dock, and he'd rush out to
greet them. Mother. Father. What would they say when they
found that the girl was gone?

He frowned uneasily. Father would be angry. Father would
beat him, hurt him, and call him terrible names.

It wasn't my fault, though, he would explain. She tricked
me! But that had not stopped Father from hurting him there
on the boat. Father would call him an idiot, stupid. His face
would get red and tight, and then the hurting would begin.

Euan searched the sea for the sail, the bright sail that was to
have been his cloak. It had been so pretty. She had been so
pretty. And now they both were gone. He slumped down in a
ball on the stone floor, hiding his face in his hands.

He stayed there for a long time. The sun slipped down in
the sky till it touched the sea's edge. The horizon glowed,
ablaze with red and gold fire.

A seagull alighted on the sill and began to chatter. Wiping
his eyes, Euan reached in his sleeve for some oats. The gull
hopped closer, its head cocked to one side. "Here, little birdie," called Euan, whistling. "Come and sing for your supper."
The bird eyed him with a bright blank stare.

"Come on, little birdie," Euan urged again. "Don't be
frightened. I won't hurt you, I promise. I've never hurt anyone." He reached out his hand, palm up, offering what he had.

The gull shied at the sudden gesture. "Don't leave me,
birdie!" Euan cried in a loud high voice.

But the seagull soared away with a flap of its white wings.
Euan ran to the casement, shouting, leaning over the edge.
"Birdie, come back!" He crawled out onto the sill, salt tears
streaming. "Birdie!" The seagull screeched, making circles
against the fiery sky.

Euan looked down at the rocks below, then over the wide,
empty ocean. He thought of a far-off green hill, and the sound
of sheep bells in the quiet morning air.

He knelt on the ledge, gripping its edge with his hands as a
gust of wintry wind swept over him. He shivered; night was
coming. He thought again of his father.

And he flew.

22

It was an eager, high-spirited army of islanders that rode away from the smoking rubble of Inverness and into the heights of the Muir of Ord. The dungeons from which King James had freed their chiefs such a short time ago had been demolished, the wine cellars had been easy to locate, and Henry Argyll's household goods had proven surprisingly luxe. The negligent, underpaid guards put up little resistance, and as a result the only casualties had been among the first group to locate the wine casks, and most of those wounds were self-inflicted, consisting of headaches and stepped-on toes. True, Iain Cameron had fallen down a staircase, but equally true, he ought not to have been in the maidservants' quarters. And if His Lairdship's wife had not been found in the castle, well, that meant only that some other fortress must be sacked. All in all, the army of the Isles agreed, thundering through the mountains and glens toward Loch Lochy, it had been a most satisfying raid.

For Alex, though, the ride was one of bitter anger—at Genna, at Argyll, at himself. The vice governor must have hidden his mistress away someplace. But where? Perth? Stirling? Edinburgh? If I hadn't lost my temper with Argyll, Alex thought grimly, I might have wrung the answer out of him. Instead, he had beaten him senseless, and left him there in the castle to burn.

At least Argyll would enjoy Genna's favors no longer. Perhaps now that her lover was dead, Genna would come back to him.

But did he want her back? No, he answered to himself, his jaw set firmly. The child, yes, but the mother, no. Never again. Not if she went down on her knees to plead with him, implore him, staring up at him with her huge midnight eyes.

It was strange, he thought, that of all the household at Inverness not one man or woman claimed ever to have seen Genna there. But Mary had been so certain, had even described to him the way his wife and Argyll hung on one another, laughing and kissing, reveling in the way she had played the Lord of the Isles for a fool. And he'd read the letters with his own eyes; even to think of them made his blood boil with rage. In those long, loving letters Argyll thanked her for the nights she'd spent with him at Stirling and Inverness, going into all too accurate detail. No one but a lover would know about the scar on the inside of Genna's knee, which she'd gotten in a fall as a child, or that her favorite place to wear scent was in the hollows of her throat.

But why had Argyll laughed even as he was beaten, laughed uncontrollably at the mention of Mary's name?

The brief January days made for very short marches. As dusk settled over the moors like a threadbare blanket, Alex reined Bantigh in and issued the order to make camp. Heavy snow-filled clouds were gathering overhead as he summoned the clan chiefs together beside a blazing bonfire.

"How is that ankle, Iain?" he asked, watching the old man hobble to his place.

Cameron winced, lowering himself to the ground. "Better, faith. Better."

"Gettin' too old for fightin', are ye, Iain?" Brian Mac Intosh taunted him, grinning.

The white-bearded warrior's eyes flashed. "'Tis fightin' keeps the bones young, and the heart staunch. There's naught wrong with me that another good battle wouldn't cure." He shifted his gaze to Alex. "Well, Yer Lairdship, where do we head next? To Edinburgh, do ye think, to tackle King James?"

"I've got no quarrel with the king," Alex said shortly.

Angus Mac Pherson rubbed his nose with a knobby finger. "Nor none with Argyll, it seems, since yer wife wasn't there." He eyed Alex shrewdly. "'Tis but five days' march to Edinburgh. We could strike while the iron is hot, while t'advantage is ours."

"My quarrel is not with the king," Alex repeated, staring into the roaring flames.

"Oh, Argyll, the king, 'tis all one and the same," Cameron muttered impatiently. "They are not islanders, Alley. They do not respect our ways."

"They take our land, our money, our soldiers," Mac Pherson said, his beard thrust out.

"They take our golf away," Mac Intosh added darkly.

Old Cameron whetted the blade of his sword on a stone. "Now they take our wives as well. I tell ye, Alley, ye cannot stand for it. Yer father would never have stood for it."

"Donald would never have stood it in a million years," Mac Pherson echoed, his eyes aglow in the dark.

Alex gazed across the fire at their fierce shadowy faces. "I made a pledge to the king, swore an oath to him. So did all of you as well."

Cameron spat loudly into the fire. "There's yer pledge," he barked, as the flames hissed and jumped. "He tricked us into those oaths, plain and simple. He coerced us into pledging our privileges away."

"He is our lawful king."

"By whose law?" Mac Pherson demanded, getting to his feet, pacing angrily beneath a slow swirl of snowflakes. "By what right does his claim take precedence over yours?"

"He's the heir of the Bruce, and of Wallace."

"And so was yer grandmother Margaret." Cameron glared at him. "Don't be a damned stubborn fool, Alley. Can't ye see that this is our chance?"

· "We could break him, Alley." Mac Pherson's voice was grave, solemn. "The men of the moors would join us. We could march on Edinburgh with a troop of forty thousand."

Cameron chuckled. "He'd run like a rabbit to see us comin', I wager. The town would be all yours, Alley. The town, and the throne."

"I gave him my word I would serve him."

Mac Pherson snorted. "And see what it gets ye, Yer Laird-ship? He sends ye from court with yer head bowed in shame. And his lieutenant filches yer wife."

Alex looked up at Mac Pherson's grim, grizzled face, and then over to Cameron. "Iain, give me your best counsel. What would you have me do?"

"I give you the selfsame counsel I'd give any man who'd been so dishonored." Cameron gripped the hilt of his sword. "March, that's what I say."

Alex sighed. "We'll put it to a vote. God grant you wisdom. Duffy, what say you?"

"March," Duffy barked.

"Montrose?"

"I say march."

"And you, Mac Kenzie?"

"March."

From all round the circle came the same response. Alex pondered the vote for a moment, then stood up, buckling his silver belt. "This must be the first time in three hundred years that all of you have agreed to any one thing." He laughed, "Very well. We'll march."

"Alley!"

Alex stared out into the darkness, disbelieving. "Davey! Is that you?"

The redhead rode his horse into the circle of firelight. "Alley, for God's sake, I've got to speak to you right away!"

"Well, get off that horse and sit down! Christ, 'tis fine to see you, Davey! And just like your old self again."

Davey swung down from the saddle. "I've got something to tell you, Alley."

"Go on and speak, then! And you may as well cast your vote too so long as you're here."

"What I have to say is for your ears only, Alley." He pulled him into the shadows, away from the fire.

"Good God, what is it?" Alex asked, and laughed. "Your news can't be any hotter than mine. We've just voted to go to war against King James."

"Alley, you've got to listen to me. You're not goin' to believe what I have to tell you, but I swear on my immortal soul 'tis true." And he blurted out what Mary had said to Althea about Donald's death.

Alex stared at him. "My God. You really have gone crazy, Davey, do you know that?"

"I haven't! I tell ye, she boasted of killing yer father! And she said it was Ranalt who murdered Meggie."

"Murdered Meggie? Meggie drowned."

"That's not the worst of it, Alley." Davey pulled the brooch from his purse. "Mary had this with her. She told us Genna is dead."

Alex stared down at the heavy gold love knot. "You're lying! I don't believe you! Genna ran away to be with Argyll. Mary showed me the letters he wrote her!"

"Think, man!" Davey grabbed his shoulders. "Mary could have asked Argyll to write those letters, or paid him!"

"But what about the letter that came the day Genna ran off? The one she burned?"

"She never did burn it, Alley. Thea did. She was just afraid to tell you. Genna left the letter lying right there on the kitchen table."

"No," Alex whispered, backing away. "It can't be! Why, for God's sake?"

Davey stared him straight in the eye. "Whose word but Mary Leslie's do you have that Genna ever was at Inverness? I don't know the whole of it, Alley, but I know Mary wants you dead. She's waitin' at Edinburgh, waitin' to see you beheaded. And that's just what will happen if you go to war against the king."

Alex shook his head, clutching the brooch he held. "My God." His voice was like brittle glass, shattered. "Genna dead —and Meggie—and Donald? There's no reason! There's no reason she'd do such things!"

But even as he fought to deny Davey's words an image rose up in his mind, unbidden, long buried. Donald, back from his defeat at the Harlaw, sitting on his bed at Aros, trying to explain to Mary what had brought him home. "Three thousand men, three thousand *lives*, Mary, young lives, good lives! How can you ask me to shed still more blood over money, over land?"

And Mary facing him, her blue eyes flashing: "I don't give a damn how many lives it takes, Donald! That land is mine by right. I'll get it, and more!"

Donald rubbed his forehead with a weary hand. "Not with my help you won't."

Mary had slapped at him then, clawed out at him, red with fury. "Coward!" she'd shouted, "miserable crawling coward! I should have married your brother, by God!"

Donald pushed her away. "He's a rapist and a murderer, Mary."

Mary laughed, her blue eyes like slits. "He is twice the man you are."

Donald stood up then, grabbing her hair, pulling her toward him, his face contorted with pain, and rage. "I swear to God, Mary, if I ever find that you laid with him—"

"What?" she taunted, tensed like a cat. "What will you do to me—coward?"

Donald raised his immense fist. Alex, cowering unseen in the doorway, had not been able to help himself; he let out a strangled sob.

Donald turned, saw his son by the door. "Alexander," he'd said softly, "go down to the kitchens. Tell Thea to give you a biscuit, and milk."

"Yes, Papa," Alex had whispered, bobbing his head.

"Son." He turned back. "Shut the door."

"Yes, Papa." He could feel the cold iron of the latch in his hand, saw the small cruel smile of triumph on his mother's pale face.

Davey reached out to touch his shoulder. "Forgive me, Alley. But don't you know I'd die myself before I'd tell you such things, if they weren't true?"

Alex knelt and buried his face in the clean cold snow. "All those years ago," he whispered into the earth. "How could any soul hate that much?"

But he knew she had, knew it with terrible, utter certainty, knew it as surely as if he had heard Mary say it herself. So much suddenly made sense where there had been no sense before. Mary leading him into the garden at Stirling, while Genna lay there. Mary astride her gray palfrey at Inverness, watching as he was banished with that same small smile. Mary and Ranalt . . . No wonder his uncle had been able to elude him for so long.

At long last he got to his feet, brushing snow from his clothes. "The clan chiefs. I must go and tell them there will be no more warring." He walked slowly back into the circle of firelight, saw their glowing, expectant faces. He stopped.

"What is it?" asked Iain Cameron. "Bad news, Alley?"

Alex inclined his head. "My wife is dead. Your men are dispersed. Return to your districts."

"What's that?" "Are ye mad?" A clamor of indignant howls filled the night air. "What about the vote, then?" "What about our rebellion?"

"There will be no rebellion! Go back to your homes!"

"But, Alley, why?" Iain demanded.

From the shadows at the edge of the circle a tall man stepped forward, his face hidden by a long hood. "Because His Lairdship is a coward," the figure said coolly.

Alex looked him over slowly from head to toe. "Who is it that accuses me of cowardice?"

Ranalt pulled back the hood with a cocksure grin. "I do. Will you make something of it?"

"Why, you murderous bastard," Davey began. Alex put a hand on his arm.

"Let him say what he will. No man here will give him credence."

"No? How certain are you of that?" His gaze swept over the astonished faces of the clan chiefs, then back to Alex. "You called for a vote, and the vote was taken. Unless you abide by that vote, you are not worthy to be laird."

"And you are?"

"Not I. My son, Euan. Your tanist."

"He is my tanist no longer."

"Your wife and your child are dead. By law, the right reverts to Euan. I claim it for him."

Davey lunged for him. "'Twas you who killed her, you lyin' cur!"

Alex pulled him back, his jaw set, eyes solemn. "No, Davey, wait. Let the clan chiefs decide who their laird will be, Euan or me."

"But, Alley, tell them about Mary, about Donald."

"No. None of that matters. Whom will they have as laird?"

"Well, then." Ranalt flexed his hands. "I am ready, with Euan's blessing, to march this night against the king at Edinburgh. Who is with me? Iain? Angus?"

Cameron hesitated, looking up at Ranalt, then to Alex, uncertain. "Come, come," Ranalt said smoothly. "Rich rewards are waiting. Or perhaps you prefer to crawl back to your islands in shame, and practice archery for the king."

"Alley—"

"I'll make it easier for you, Iain," Alex said wearily, unbuckling the silver sword belt that bore the emblems of his dominion. He met Ranalt's hard gray stare. "Take it and welcome. It has brought me nothing but sorrow." He threw it to the ground at his uncle's feet, then surveyed the chiefs. "God have mercy on all of you, you poor blind fools."

Eyes glittering, Ranalt stooped for the belt and flourished it over his head. "To Edinburgh!" he shouted. "Follow me!"

The clan chiefs let out a ferocious roar: "To Edinburgh!" The troops heard the shout and echoed it, running to saddle their horses and gather their gear. Ranalt leaped atop his black stallion, sword in hand, to lead the charge. Within minutes the encampment had been emptied; the soldiers rode in a surging rollicking mass across the barren moor. Only the bright scattered flares of their bonfires gave hint to what had once been there.

Alex crouched down to warm his hands on the coals. "Do you know what the worst of it is, Davey?" he said conversationally. "I killed a man for no reason. I killed Argyll."

"Alley, there was no way for you to know."

He went on, not even listening. "And as I hit him, he laughed at me. He lay there, laughing. He knew my mother better than I ever did."

The snow began to fall in earnest, sputtering onto the fires. Alex whistled, a single high, clear note. Bantigh came charging over the hard-frozen moor, mane flying, her head held high, nostrils flared at the prospect of battle. Alex considered her curiously for a moment. The huge white war-horse whinnied, pawing the ground.

"You too, old friend?" Alex ran a hand over her mane, stroked her flank. "Are you too so ready to desert me? Go on, then." He slapped her sharply. "Go on, follow the pack!"

Bantigh started away, balked, snorted. "Go on!" Alex shouted, picking up a rock and feinting a throw. "Get off with you, damn you!" She let out a long, plaintive whinny, then bounded away.

Davey watched in silence as she vanished over the hills. Then he said softly, "What will you do now?"

"Go to Iona."

"Why, whatever for?"

"To pray. I have an uphill climb ahead of me. It seems unlikely God will welcome a murderer into heaven. One can but try."

"But what about Ranalt, and Mary? What about your lairdship?"

Alex shrugged. "'Revenge is mine, saith the Lord.' Leave me be, Davey. Follow the others. Leave me alone." And then his cool demeanor shattered suddenly. "Oh, God in heaven, Davey, how I loved that girl."

Davey linked his arm through his laird's. "I know you did. Let's be on our way."

Through the swirling snow they heard loud hoofbeats pounding. Bantigh loomed up out of the darkness, eyeing Alex warily. She made a wide circle and sidled toward him, nuzzling his hair.

"Some friends 'tis not so easy to rid yourself of," observed Davey.

Alex looked at him. The snow fell, mingling with tears.

23

Two days, and still no sight of land. Genna tried to stretch her cramped, weary legs and groped for the water skin. One third gone. Four more days, or five at the most. If the cold didn't take her by then.

She cupped her hands and tried to scoop out the frigid water that had splashed over the edge of the cask. That task finished, there was nothing at all to do except sit, and wait. Sit, and watch the unbounded sea that lay before her. Sit, and watch, and think.

For all she knew she might be headed in the wrong direction, toward the voids at the end of the earth. During the brief hours of daylight she tried to keep the tub pointing south, between the arc the sun made rising and setting. But all through the long, bleak nights she was at the mercy of the wind and the waves.

There was so much time to think. Time to consider what might have happened if Alex and Davey had not left Mull, if Thea hadn't written to her Hannah, if the letter from Brother Martin had never arrived. If she had never met Alex, or followed him to Mull . . . Were those few brief months of happiness together worth all this cost?

Yes, her heart cried, yes. She remembered the words he had whispered to her once: "You have belonged to me from the first moment I saw you, and I to you. You are in my blood, my soul; I can no more live without you than I could without air." If she died on this foolhardy voyage, at least she would have known such love in her lifetime. When the cask washed up on some far-distant shore, weeks, months from now, and some curious fisherman's wife saw the wasted body that lay within, she would see a smile on its face.

Unless—what about seabirds? she wondered idly. Did they eat carrion? Would they swoop down on her if the boat neared land? What if she was too weak to fight them off? They would pick her flesh away, pluck out her eyes, and leave nothing but a dry dusty pile of sun-bleached bones.

Genna shivered. Don't think of that! she told herself sternly. Think of Alex, remember his love for you. She tried to summon up his proud, stern face, but saw only a grinning death mask, a skull with gaping holes where there once had been clear blue eyes. If Mary had her way, Alex was already dead now.

Genna blinked away tears salty as the ocean, and thought of the seeress, grim and black-shrouded. "Doom, that is all I see for your bride. An empty womb, and the fall of your father's house..." She had been right. Genna stared out over the endless waves, and saw snowflakes drift from the swollen clouds. What use was it to challenge fate? The stones and the bones had spoken, and laid out the future. She might as well let the gulls come and devour her alive. She felt unbearably weary, so cold that no fire ever could warm her. The snow fell more quickly, the wind lashing at the sail, spinning the cask like a silly top. Genna curled up tight in the bottom of the tiny boat, head buried in a damp frozen blanket. She crossed her arms over her breasts and began to pray. Oh, Alex, if you are still alive, somehow, someplace, know that I love you, have always loved you, and that I saw your face before me, had your name on my lips at the hour of my death.

Diarmot Mac Duff guided the *Dearg Lomond* around the north tip of Coll and into the Sea of the Hebrides. "A rough passage, Cap'n," his first mate grunted.

"Aye, Geordie, it is." He eyed the gathering clouds with a deep frown. "And rougher to come, if I'm not mistaken."

"Should I give the order to tack, head back to Coll?"

Mac Duff sighed. "I suppose we must. These winter storms—better to be safe than sorry. Though I hate to lose another day."

"Better a day than a ship, eh?" asked Geordie, grinning.

"Always the philosopher, aren't you?" Mac Duff grumbled. He scanned the ominous gray horizon with resignation. "Very well. Give the order to— Ho!"

Geordie spun around. "What is it, Cap'n?"

Mac Duff shielded his eyes with his hand, his keen sight

once more sweeping over the waves. He shook his head. "Nothing. I thought for a moment— Wait, there it is again!"

"There's what?" Geordie gazed out over the bleak empty sea. "I don't see nothin', Cap'n."

Mac Duff pointed with a work-worn finger. "There, hard to starboard. But I cannot make out what it is."

Geordie peered more closely, then laughed, turning away. "Faith, 'tis naught but a child's toy! Look at the size of it."

"Aye, but..." Mac Duff strained to pierce the growing darkness. "I could have sworn I saw something, there on the sail."

The mate cleared his throat. "Ah, Cap'n. If we don't head for port right now, we'll be caught in the storm."

"Very well. Give the order." But still Mac Duff stood at the stern, staring over the sea.

Geordie cupped his hands, shouting up to the rigging. "Make hard to port, mates! We're headin' back to the Isles!"

As the ship swung about, lines creaking, the thick clouds lifted for an instant, and the pale shivering sun shone through.

"Belay that order!" bellowed Mac Duff. "Put around once more to starboard! Make haste!"

Geordie turned to him questioningly. "What is it, Cap'n?"

Mac Duff shrugged and gave a half-embarrassed laugh. "I don't know, Geordie. But I could swear I saw the laird's marks there upon the sail, the sword and the galley." He grimaced. "I'll not sleep tonight if I don't set my mind at ease. Just sweep a bit closer."

"By God, I believe you're right." Geordie squinted at the sail that bobbed in the distance. "Bejesus, ain't that a queer thing. Bring her about!" he shouted. "Make hard for that sail!" The *Dearg Lomond* slipped through the roiling waters, bearing down on the doll-sized boat.

"What do you see?" Mac Duff called to the watch in the shrouds.

"It's empty, Cap'n. Nothing at all inside 'er."

Mac Duff shook off a vague disappointment. The men must think him stark mad. "Geordie, go down there and cut the sail away. 'Tis a fair piece of work; we can make it a gift to poor Alley Mac Donald when next we see him. To remind him of when he was laird."

Geordie eyed him askance for a moment, then rolled out the windlass. "Give me a hand here, Robby, Gerard. Though if you ask me," he added in an undertone, "the cap'n's been too long at sea." Knife between his teeth, he clambered down the winchline and into the cask. As he landed he felt his foot light on something soft, something firm yet giving. Curious, he groped beneath the ragtag bundles of leather and cloth.

His hand brought out a hand, small, cold, deathly white. With a terrified scream, the mate scrambled back up the lines. "Cap'n, Cap'n! There's a ghostie in there, Cap'n!"

Genna heard the loud voice shouting, heard it from a million miles off. Dreaming, she sat up slowly, the blankets falling from her shoulders, yawning as the cold air hit her.

Geordie saw the tiny black-haired figure rising up through the snowstorm, screamed again, and fell into the sea.

Captain Mac Duff stared in utter disbelief at the small bedraggled woman. "Great God Almighty." That wan face, those haunted black eyes... He swung down the ropes. "Robby, toss a line to Geordie!" he cried, gathering the frail white-clad body up in his arms.

"Mistress Fleming?" he whispered uncertainly, brushing away the tangles of her jet-colored hair.

Genna lay back in his strong grasp, eyes closing wearily. "Captain Mac Duff," she whispered. "Now *that* was what I'd call a rough sail."

"But what in God's name made you think you could do it?" Mac Duff looked across the table to Genna, still shaking his head. "Those frigid seas, the harsh weather, the reefs—why, that bloody lighttower is nigh on a hundred miles away!"

Genna took another sip of warmed wine. "If I'd known then what I know now, I probably wouldn't have tried! But I had no choice, I'm afraid." She leaned toward him. "What do you know of my husband?"

Mac Duff stroked his chin. "I don't know what to say, milady. He summoned the chiefs more than four weeks past to march on Inverness. I heard at Portree that they'd sacked the castle."

"Inverness? Why in God's name went he to Inverness?"

"Why, because of you, milady! He'd had word you were living there." He flushed. "With a fellow named Argyll."

"Oh, sweet Christ." Genna slammed her fist down on the table. "Mary Leslie's lies. How could Alex believe such a thing?"

"Well, mum, he'd been under such strain, with his sister drowning."

"Meggie didn't drown." Genna's mouth was taut. "Ranalt Mac Ruarie murdered her. And now he and Mary are going to murder Alex as well, so that Euan will be laird."

"They won't have to murder him, milady. Alley has already given up his lairdship."

"He what?" Genna stared, openmouthed.

"Well, the way I heard it, mum, the clan chiefs decided they'd had such a good time burning Inverness that they wanted to march on to Edinburgh. The laird—I mean Alley —he wouldn't go with them. So they took off anyway, with Ranalt Mac Ruarie as leader in Euan's name. The king's army beat the stuffing out of 'em a week past, at Glencoe. The chiefs are all in prison at Edinburgh, waitin' to be beheaded."

"My God! But where's Alex?"

"No one knows, mum. He just vanished, there on the moors."

"Where would he go? There must be someplace." Mac Duff watched as her white brow furrowed, then cleared. "Of course! To Iona!"

"Why would he go there, mum?"

"He made me a pledge, once; how I pray he remembers." A thought struck her suddenly. "Oh, Christ, I forgot— Brother Martin! Captain, you've got to take me to Iona at once!"

"Now, mum, I'm sorry, but that's not possible. We have to put in at Coll, to ride out the storm."

"There's no time!" Genna reached out and grasped his hand; he felt the chill, desperate fear there. "He's not safe on Iona, Captain. His fate is depending on you!"

"Oh, now, mum, I don't know. I'm not much of a one for fate and depending and what-not. I'm a plain seafaring trader, 'tis all I am."

Genna got to her feet. "Very well, then. I'll thank you to launch me again in my boat."

Mac Duff stared. "Your boat? That miserable leaky tub won't last three minutes in this storm!"

She shrugged. "You leave me no choice. I'm not going to sit here and do nothing while my husband is being murdered."

"Murdered?" His jaw dropped. "You're serious, aren't you?"

"I certainly am."

Mac Duff sputtered for a moment, then let out a loud barking laugh. "Alley Mac Donald got himself a real mule when he got you—beggin' your pardon, mum. Very well, then. Iona it is."

Genna swayed on her feet and grasped the edge of the table; her head was spinning wildly. Mac Duff sprang up and helped her back into her chair.

"Aye, going to sail off again then, were you? You can't even stand," he grumbled, but there was admiration in his eyes. "You stay right here and rest, and I'll go give the order to change course." Genna put her head down on her arms, unbearably, achingly weary. The captain laid a gingerly hand on her thick tangled hair. "Aye, that's it. Rest now. I'll get you safe back to your laird."

24

"I'd hoped you and Father Gervase would talk some sense into his thick head, Brother Martin!" Davey paced across the floor of the abbot's outer room, hands clasped behind his back. "He can't give up the lairdship to Euan; that's what Mary Leslie sought all along!"

"I've spoken to Alexander at great length," the monk said calmly. "It is his decision to join the order. He has a multitude of sins to expiate."

"Mary's sins are not his sins!" Davey cried angrily.

Brother Martin smiled enigmatically, the scars standing out on his cheeks. "I don't mean her sins."

Davey barely heard the man, he was so incensed. "Let me see Father Gervase."

Brother Martin shrugged, his palms uplifted. "He is ill; he cannot be disturbed."

"Then tell me where I can find Alley."

"Alexander is in retreat, at prayer. Making his peace with God."

"I never would have brought him here had I known this would happen." Davey's voice was bitter.

"'All they that take up the sword, by the sword shall they perish.'" Brother Martin tapped his blunted hand on the table. "Words to remember, my boy. Won't you have some cider?"

"I don't want your bloody cider! I want to see Father Gervase!"

"Impossible. I'm afraid I must ask you to leave now. There is nothing more that you can do."

"Martin?" The word was a querulous whisper from behind the inner cell door. "Martin, why have you locked me in here? Who's there with you?"

"Locked him—" Davey's green brown eyes widened as he

stared at the monk. "My God, what are you up to?" He sprang toward the cell door.

Brother Martin raised his hand, showing the edge of a knife. "You should have gone while I gave you the chance. Now I am going to have to ask you to stay. Here, in this chair." He pointed toward it with the knife. Davey hesitated.

The monk whetted the blade on the stump of a missing finger.

Gingerly, Davey sat.

The monk drew off his rope belt and looped it around Davey's wrists and over the chair back, then tied the ends securely together, testing it with his teeth. He grunted with approval. "There."

"Where is Alley?" Davey whispered.

"I told you. Praying. In the hills. He is probably growing quite sleepy by now, though. The cider I gave him should be nearly gone."

"But if he falls asleep in this storm . . ."

Again the monk smiled. "It will be the sleep of the dead." He went to the table and poured out a cup from the pitcher. "I do wish you'd try some. I believe this is my finest batch yet."

"Martin!" The handle to the cell door rattled. "Martin, I demand you let me out of here!"

"What's the matter, holy father?" the monk called back, grinning. "Run out of prayers?"

"Father Gervase, are you all right?" Davey cried.

"Davey! Davey, my son, is that you? Thank God! Brother Martin is sorely troubled."

"Brother Martin is *troubled?*" The monk roared with laughter. "Not any longer, you shriveled old fool. Brother Martin is free, free at last from your mewling and whining, from the stink of your incense and candles. Brother Martin has a purse filled with ten thousand marks that he's taken from your bloody crawling pilgrims." He ran the point of his blade along Davey's cheek. "And that ought to be enough so that the ladies will look at him, don't you think? Look at him, and overlook these . . ." He brought his mutilated face within inches of Davey's, the pink satin of the scars shining in the lantern light.

And at that moment Genna appeared, framed in the door from the corridor, stamping snow from her boots. "Oh, Davey, there you are at last!" she cried. "Where is Alex?"

Brother Martin turned. She saw the knife in his hand.

"Ah," he said, tongue running over his lip, "here's a lady! I can ask her myself. Tell me, dear, will you not kiss me? Wait, better still, come hither. Make love to me."

Genna looked at Davey. The words burst from him like shot: "Run, Genna! For God's sake, run!"

She ran through the empty, echoing hallway, through the deserted chapel, the kitchens. "All gone," she heard Brother Martin calling after her as he followed. "All the busy little bees flown back to their hives. All gone except you, and me."

Somehow she found a door, undid the latch with wild hands, and fled from the abbey out into the storm. Night had fallen, and the snow still swirled up in great wide swaths across the strand. Brother Martin's loud, cackling laughter pursued her into the darkness. "Alex," her thumping heart seemed to call out, "find Alex." From the sea a thick white mist had blown up, so dense that it nearly choked her, while the winter winds roared over the rocky shores, tearing at her hair, her cloak.

"Alexander!" she screamed into the night. The suffocating mists fillled her lungs with their gripping cold. Then she thought of Donald's grave.

The waves thundered onto the strand with implacable savagery, yet even through the frenzied sounds of sea and storm Genna imagined she could hear Brother Martin's laughter. She clapped her hands over her ears and pressed on, blinded by snow, whipped by the winds, still screaming Alex's name. The storm caught the word and twisted it, drawing it out into a wisp, a thin shivering sigh.

In the tiny cave high in the hills above the abbey, Alex struggled to close his mind to the storm's cacophony and continued to pray. "Thy kingdom come, thy will be done, on earth as it is in heaven . . ." And if thy will it was that Genna should die, and Mother and Ranalt live, and be victorious— well, then, thy will be done.

"You must purge yourself of all regrets, all your former desires, Alexander," Brother Martin had said. "The devil will test you, as he did our Savior. He will take you to a high mountain and show you the world, will offer you that which you hold most dear in return for your soul. This is what Father Gervase instructed me to tell you: not until you have proven stronger than such temptations can you truly be free.

Go up into the hills now, and pray for forgiveness, that you might be cleansed."

Feverishly Alex clutched his beads and began the rosary again. Though he could not see the jet black beads in the darkness, he knew their color. It had once shone in Genna's eyes. It might have shone in the eyes of their son.

Sorrow overwhelmed him once more and he buried his face in his hands.

The sound floated out of the storm, a faint sighing summons. His name, who called out his name? He started up from his knees.

Through the howl of wind and snow it came again, high and unearthly. Surely that was Genna's voice! He stood and pressed his ear to the rock that served as a door.

"Alexander!"

He set his shoulder against the rock to push, then stopped abruptly. This was what Brother Martin had warned him of! The devil's temptation, using what he held most dear... "Be gone with you, spirit of evil!" he shouted. "Be gone with you; leave me in peace!"

"Alexander!" The spectral summons whirled on the wind, beckoning him into the storm. It was a trick of the wind, or a trick of the devil. He heard a scrambling at the stones overhead, like the claws of a wild beast, the hooves of a demon. With grim resolution Alex stopped up his ears, his heart, and groped at the throat of his robe for his beads.

His fingers closed instead on the brooch he still carried with him, the gold and pearl love knot that was all he had left of his wife. He heard his name again, and the prayer that he whispered became one of hopeless longing: "Take me as well, dear God. Oh, dear Father, take me, that I might be with her again."

A gust of cold wind burst through the cave's gaping mouth. A few steps beyond that opening lay the towering cliffs, their depths shrouded in mist and darkness, beckoning him onward. Alex shook his head angrily, reached for the flask Brother Martin had given him, and took a long draught. The thick, sweet cider warmed him to his toes, made him feel content and drowsy. He swallowed more.

"Alexander!"

He jerked his head up. Was he sleeping, dreaming? There in the mouth of the cave a figure appeared, calling through the

storm's wild clamor, reaching out its hands. Eerie white mists
swirled toward him, then parted to show his beloved's face,
her wide black eyes, amid a torrent of wind-ravaged hair. Her
thin, imploring hands floated on nothingness; she was a
wraith, a spirit, and her voice was the voice of the dead. Alex
felt his grief, forlorn, inconsolable, welling up in his heart, and
knew that he no longer cared which she might be, angel or
demon. "By God," he muttered, "if I must condemn myself to
hell, I will do it. Christ forgive me, if I could but touch you
one last time."

He stumbled toward the spirit, reaching for its hands,
straining, yearning. Out of the shadows another image loomed
up, bulky and black.

"Alexander! No!" Brother Martin's voice was stern and forbidding. "She's a demon sent to torment you! Fight her, Alexander!"

"Oh, Alex, my love." She stepped toward him and his
fingers locked on flesh that was cold as death.

His hand traced her pale mouth. He groaned. "Lead me on
to hell then, but I'll have one kiss." His mouth closed over
hers, furious with longing, abandoning his soul for that moment of splendor, for the taste, the scent of her, warm once
more on his tongue.

"Alex, he's trying to revenge himself on your father!" She
struggled to free herself.

"I would almost believe you were real," he murmured.

"For God's sake, Alex."

With a roar like a lion Brother Martin sprang at them, the
knife in his hand. The blade slashed through the cowl of Alex's
robe and pricked his chest. With the instinct born of long
training he thrust Genna aside and faced his assailant, all his
senses on guard.

"I've got you now, you bastard," the monk snarled, grap-
pling him to the ground. "We'll see how you like to be marked
as a scoundrel, and a thief." He slashed out again with the
knife. Alex ducked, leapt at his knees, and wrestled him to the
floor of the cave. The two cowled figures shifted and scrambled across the stones, one gaining the advantage and then the
other, all the time moving closer and closer to the edge of the
cliff. In the grim freezing dark Genna could not seem to move
to help, could not even tell which was which.

They sprang apart for a moment, panting, their cold breath

hanging white in the air. Then there was a sudden flash of the knife; the two men grappled together with renewed fury. Genna heard a flurry of pebbles falling and then a sharp crack as the cliff face crumbled and gave way.

With a scream like a hell-dog's howl, one huge black shape toppled over the edge, falling with a mighty crash into the raging sea. Genna watched in stunned horror as the remaining figure turned toward her. His hands reached up to his cowl, slowly drawing it back.

A tumble of golden curls spilled out. Alex shook his head, running his fingers through his hair. Then, "Genna," he whispered.

She was in his arms in an instant, laughing and crying while he clutched her to him with all his might. "Oh, Alex," she sobbed, "I was searching, searching in the storm, and I couldn't find you."

"I thought you were dead! Mary told Davey you were dead!" He kissed her with passionate abandon, hands caught in her wild black hair.

"And you believed her?"

He drew out her brooch. "She had this with her."

Genna wrapped her hand around the gold, still warm from its place near his heart. "I never thought I would see this again." She smiled up at him, her dark eyes bright with tears.

"And I thought I would never see you again." He kissed her once more, with lingering tenderness. Then, "Tell me, Genna, the child, what became of our child?"

"I'm sorry, my love. The child is dead."

He turned from her, letting out a low moan of hopelessness. "How can you call me your love? After all that my kin have done to you—all the way back to your poor Papa John. I never had the courage to tell you that, I kept it secret, fearing it would make you hate me." He laughed grimly. "How much more you must hate me now."

She went and stood before him, took his hands in hers, staring into his anguished blue eyes. "No, Alex. No. I love you . . . more than I ever have."

"My sweet, darling Genna. What have I ever done in this life to deserve you?"

"Well, once, a very long time ago, you saved the life of a spoiled, ungrateful child."

He laughed shakily. "Was that what I called you?"

"Oh, and much worse. You said I was an ugly, scrawny little beast."

"I must have been blind, then," he whispered, pulling her into his arms.

"My God, Alex, Davey! I nearly forgot!"

"Where is he?"

"Brother Martin had him trussed up back in the abbey. And Father Gervase—"

"Let's go." He swept her into his arms, pulled his cloak over both their faces. Genna settled against him with a sigh, clutching her brooch in her fist. Alex pushed open the rock that barred the entrance to the cavern, and a burst of snow-flakes and howling wind enveloped them.

Genna thought she had never, ever felt so warm.

Father Gervase sat back in his chair, his face a puzzle of wrinkles. "But why did Mary have Ranalt kidnap you, Genna? That is what I do not understand." They were seated around the table in his outer cell, making a meal of bread and honey and wine that Genna found in the kitchens. Alex had poured every drop of Brother Martin's cider into the abbey's sewers and listened, his jaw tight, while Genna explained.

"Because I was with child. If the child lived, then Euan would not become laird."

"But she barely knows Euan!" Alex objected.

"He's your half brother as well as your cousin, Alex," Genna said gently. "He is Mary and Ranalt's son."

"He can't be!"

Genna nodded. "He is. He was born the year before Donald and Mary were wed."

Davey nodded too, slowly. "The baby that Thea found out about from her cousin in Dingwall. The one she told Donald about."

"When did she tell him?" Alex demanded.

"In the spring, these three years past."

"When Father sent me to bring Ranalt to him . . ." Alex's blue eyes were far-off and sad; he remembered again the scene between Mary and Donald he'd witnessed as a child. "Mary must have known that if Father learned the rumor was true, he'd divorce her, or even have her imprisoned."

"And so she murdered him," Davey realized out loud, "with Brother Martin's all too willing assistance."

"You told me, Alex," Genna reminded him, "that it was Mary who first suggested you make Euan your tanist."

"But why didn't she just go ahead and kill me as well?"

"She was waiting," Davey explained, "waiting until the hubbub over Donald's death died down. She knew well enough that people like Thea believed in the seeress's predictions. She was biding her time."

"The king nearly did the job for her after you quarreled with Argyll at Inverness," Genna told him. "It must have been a bitter disappointment to her when he banished you instead. I wouldn't be the least surprised if she was behind that incident as well."

Alex looked at Genna. "The man in the garden at Stirling —was that her doing?"

"Aye. It was Euan, following her orders." Genna's black eyes filled with tears. "Poor Euan, I believe he has suffered as much as any of us. He never wanted to be laird. He wanted only to please his mother, and to keep Ranalt from hurting him any more."

"But once he was laird," said Davey grimly, "Mary would rule the Isles through him. And use the clan chiefs and their men to win back the lands Donald would not fight for after the Harlaw, maybe even win the crown."

"My God." Alex was still struggling to grasp the scope of his mother's deceptions. "What an incredible plan! How could she have believed it would work?"

"It might have," said Davey. "*If* you had not met Genna."

"The one factor Mary never considered," Father Gervase murmured thoughtfully, "was that you might fall in love. Poor woman, I wonder has she ever loved anyone or anything herself?"

"But how could she ever have conceived such evil?" Alex said in wonder.

Father Gervase pushed back his chair. "'And the serpent said unto the woman, Ye shall surely not die: For God doth know that in the day you eat the fruit of that tree, then your eyes shall be opened, and ye shall be as gods.'" He sighed. "We have all been blind." He got up slowly and hobbled toward the doorway. "Pardon me, my children. I should like to go and pray."

When he had gone, Alex sat quietly for a moment, his head bowed. "Where is Euan now?" he asked at last.

"I had to leave him there in the lighttower, in the Far Isles." Genna put her hand over his. "Captain Mac Duff has sailed to fetch him. He will bring him to Edinburgh to meet us."

"Edinburgh?" he repeated in astonishment. "Who is going to Edinburgh?"

"Why, you, and me, and Davey, of course. To see King James."

"You've forgotten that I am under sentence of death if I leave the Isles."

"Well, yes, but if you explain—"

"To say nothing of the fact that I burned the king's fortress at Inverness, and murdered Henry Argyll. There is no way in hell that I am going to Edinburgh so that the king can more conveniently behead me! After all we have been through, I'll not make you a widow so soon."

"But if you explain to the king, Mary and Ranalt will be convicted of treason!"

"To hell with Mary and Ranalt. And to hell with King James."

"Oh, but Alex, what about the clan chiefs?"

"They made their bed," he said darkly. "Let them lie in it now."

"Alexander Mac Donald, how can you say that when 'tis your fault that they rebelled?"

"What would you suggest I do about it?"

Genna leaned across the table. "Have you forgotten the words of the seeress?"

"What words?" He scowled.

"'I see you kneeling in shame before a great king, naked, your sword in your hand.'"

"For the sake of those damned old fools? For their sake you want me to prostrate myself before the king like some common thief?"

Genna's dark eyes flashed. "Oh, I see. And instead you're just going to sit there and let them die."

Davey hurried over to the door. "I believe I'll just be seein' if the holy father could use a bit of help with his prayers." As he left the cell he reflected wryly that the battle at Harlaw had likely been no more fierce than the one that was about to begin.

Alex folded his arms over his chest, his eyes flinty-hard.

"You told me you don't even believe in seeresses and prophecies, said it was a pack of nonsense. Why bring all that up
now?"

"Meggie said to me once that if I spent enough time in the
Isles, I'd come to believe. I don't know whether that old
woman can really see into the future, Alex, but I do know this:
every word she's spoken has come true. Your father's murder,
the woe that would come to you because of your mother and
me, the empty womb, the fall of your father's house. The only
prophecy left unfulfilled is that you kneel in shame before the
king."

"You're actually suggesting I do so because of some mad old
hag's visions? Don't you know who I am?"

"I know bloody damned well who you are. I married you,
remember?" She glared at him, ticking off on her fingers.
"You're the man who left a helpless girl alone in a forest because she piqued your pride. The man who left me to be attacked by Euan at Stirling because of your vanity. The man
who handed his lairdship over to a murderer because your
mother had made a fool out of you. And now you're going to
let those clan chiefs die because of that same stupid, stubborn
pride!"

He stood unmoving, his jaw set. "I am what I am, Genna
Fleming. If you can't accept that, then maybe our marriage
was a mistake."

"I couldn't agree more!" She stood up and stalked to the
door.

"Get back here, damn you!" he thundered. "Why can't we
discuss this like two sane, reasonable people?"

"Because you happen to be neither of those things!" Genna
shot back, her hand on the latch. "You're vain and selfish and
obstinate. In fact, you're a great deal like your mother!"

Alex's face was dark with fury. "Go on. Walk out that door.
But don't expect me ever to take you back."

"Oh, don't worry, I won't," Genna said sweetly. "Because
before I would *come* back, you would have to admit you've
been wrong. And we both know that's the one thing you'll
never do!"

He threw open the door, the veins in his forehead bulging.
"Get out. And don't bother begging me to change my mind. I
can get along without you, without anyone. I'll stay here with
Father Gervase and become a monk."

Genna stared up at him, eyes darting fire. "Well, you won't be a very good one! You're so bloody conceited you probably think it's beneath you to kneel down to God!"

She watched as a series of contrary emotions passed over his stern, rugged face: fury, obstinacy, acknowledgment, and then slowly, grudgingly, a hint of laughter. He reached out an unsteady hand to stroke her cheek. "You know, you are absolutely right, Genevieve Fleming," he said softly. "I'd make a terrible monk. You *are* right, and I am wrong. Have you anything else to say?"

She rested her hand against his. "I remember you once were a splendid Lord of the Isles." She smiled, and the glow of her joy lit up the spare dark room.

He leaned down to kiss her, holding her as though she were a delicate precious flower, the touch of his mouth like a promise. His arms tightened, pulling her closer, lifting her into the air.

"Ahem"—Davey cleared his throat in the doorway—"I seem to have a penchant for interrupting you at this. But the storm is finished, and there's a ferry waiting. What should I tell the skipper?"

Alex moved his mouth from Genna's, just for a moment. "Tell him the storm is finished."

"He knows that, Alley." Davey's grin was as wide as the sea.

"Go tell him again," the Lord of the Isles said over his shoulder, kicking the door closed, carrying Genna to the hard narrow cot against the wall.

Alex set his wife down on the edge of the pallet, then knelt before her, unbuckling her heavy boots, rolling down her stockings, bending to kiss her white feet.

She put her hands in his thick, tawny hair, trying to raise him up. "My love, what on earth are you doing?"

"You want me to kiss the king's feet, don't you?" he growled in mock anger. "Well, leave me alone, then. I am practicing."

Epilogue

Holyrood Chapel, Edinburgh
Palm Sunday, 1429

Though the early morning air still held a hint of winter's chill, the royal chapel at Holyroodhouse was filled with a multitude of worshipers, making it seem hot and close. King James ran a finger under the collar of his green velvet doublet, impatient for the mass to begin. Queen Joan, seated beside him on a throne to the right of the altar, smiled and patted his hand. "Calm yourself, my darling. The falconer can wait until the service is ended, and so can you."

"A perfect day to hunt," His Majesty grumbled, "and 'tis like a bloody oven in here. Just look at the crowds, will you? It's going to take forever. Where's the bishop? Why doesn't he get started?"

"There are an extraordinary number of people here," Joan mused. "'Tis almost as though they expected something to happen."

"It will if that bishop doesn't start soon," James muttered. "The king will get up and leave!"

Joan smiled indulgently and squeezed his hand, then looked out to the first row of pews, where Genevieve Fleming, looking tiny and darkly exotic as ever in a flame red gown of velvet, knelt in fervent prayer. It had not taken long for her to enlist the queen's help when she'd appeared at Edinburgh Castle the night before. Joan had listened openmouthed to the tale of murder and lust and betrayal she and Davy Mac Leod spun out, then had cried and promised to do her best when they explained the boon they craved. Davey knelt beside Genna now in the chapel, his usually merry face tense and apprehensive. As though she felt the queen's gaze on her, Genna suddenly raised her solemn black eyes to the throne. Joan winked reassuringly. Blushing, Genna hastily glanced back down.

351

The faithful were still filing into the huge high-vaulted chapel, spilling out from the packed pews to line the narthex and aisles. James mopped at his damp brow with a kerchief and cursed as his crown slipped down over his eyes. "Darling!" Joan rebuked him, in a tone of shock. She scanned the crowds once more, looking for Mary Leslie, and saw her glide in through the north porch doors, looking neither to the right nor left as she took her seat demurely just below the chancel, her face nearly hidden by a huge horned hat.

The bishop appeared at last at the end of the long center aisle, surrounded by priests and incense bearers and choristers. A flourish of trumpets sounded from the gallery in the tower. James groaned, covering his ears. "Remind me to have whichever of those fools is off pitch beheaded, will you, Joan?"

"Yes, dear," she said mildly, "whatever you say."

With a sort of lurching shove the procession toward the altar began, led by a towheaded boy bearing the crucifix. The trumpets faltered, regrouped, began again. "The third beat, you idiots," James muttered, thumping out the time on the arm of his throne. "One-two-*three*-four, one-two-*three*-four . . . Are they deaf, for God's sake?" Braziers swinging defiantly on two and four, the incense bearers made their proud way up the aisle.

The boy with the crucifix reached the altar at last, genuflected, turned right, and kept on walking. "What is he *doing?*" James hissed angrily, watching the receding figure.

"'Tis the Palm Sunday processional," Joan whispered back. "They go three times 'round the church."

"Oh, for the love of God."

"Exactly."

James cocked an eyebrow at his queen, sighed, and settled back in his throne.

Two more full, slow circuits completed at last, the long string of celebrants led off once more from the rear of the chapel. But this time as they passed the crowds seemed to part in waves, staring over their shoulders, eagerly whispering, nudging neighbors with their elbows. "What is going on now?" James demanded, straining up in his seat. Even the bishop, whose eyes should have been fixed on the cross before him, was peering back toward the narthex with something akin to alarm.

Wearing only a white cloth wrapped over his loins, Alex-

ander Mac Donald knelt at the end of the processional line and
began the long journey toward the throne, moving forward
one knee at a time. His long gold hair flowed over his naked
shoulders, gleaming in the candlelight, and clasped before him
in both his hands he held the sharp silver tip of his sword. The
hilt duplicated the cruciform lines of the cross, casting a long
shadow on the stone floor behind Alex as he approached the
altar, his face impassive, deep blue eyes trained on the king.

"Good God." James stared at the supplicant. "'Tis Alex
Mac Donald! How dare he show himself here? Guards!" He
leapt up and signaled to his sentries. "Seize that man! Behead
him at once!"

Alex's voice rang out, echoing through the sanctuary. "Hear
me out, Your Most Gracious Highness! I come before you,
naked and humbled, to crave your pardon for the offenses I
have committed against the throne."

"My pardon?" James's voice squeaked with astonishment,
and he hurriedly started again. "There will be no pardon for
you, you scurrilous traitor! I have gibbets set up in four towns
to receive your body—once I've drawn and quartered it!"

"I freely admit my transgressions against Your Majesty. I
am all that you have called me, and far worse. No man here
deserves more the fate that you have decreed for me. Yet,
trusting in your generous and loving kindness, I come to you,
sword in hand, and sue for forgiveness. I pray you, in the
name of God and of Scotland, show mercy unto me!"

James stared down at his cousin, at his splendid unclothed
body, the mane of gold hair, his unreadable blue eyes. Even in
that position of contrite disgrace he had an unmistakable air of
royalty about him. James shook his head impatiently, recalling
the vision he'd seen once of a crown atop that imperious brow.

"Guards! Take him away! Execute him without delay!"

James felt Joan's hand on his arm, had an odd disquieting
sense that he'd played this scene out before, and had been
found lacking. But he, the king, was not the one kneeling for
judgment! Angrily he turned and met Joan's passionate pleading gaze.

"Another time," she whispered, "you regretted your treat-
ment of him."

"That was before he burned my castle at Inverness," James
snapped, "and rallied the clan chiefs against me!"

"James, have I ever given you bad counsel?" He hesitated,

shook his head. "I give you this counsel now. Forgive Alexander. A great king must know when to punish, and when to forgive."

"I will seem a weak old fool if I forgive such outrageous insurrection!"

"You will regret it to the end of your days if you do not hear what he has to say."

"What could he possibly say?" James demanded furiously. "What could possibly excuse his actions?"

"Love," Joan whispered, pointing to where Genna knelt in her pew, watching, waiting. "Love for that woman, his wife." The entire assembly was silent, motionless, watching as the queen took James's hands in her own and held them to her face. "If you tell me you cannot believe that, accept that, dear James, I cannot help but wonder whether you truly love me."

For a long moment the king stared into her solemn shining eyes, bright with challenge. He looked down at Genna and to Alexander, and then at last back to the queen. He balanced his crown, his kingdom, his very life against the love he had for her. And then he granted the prayer that he read in her eyes.

He walked slowly down the three stone steps to where Alex knelt patiently, the sword blade clasped in his hands. The king reached out and felt the smooth cool weight of the hilt in his palm as he drew it from Alex's grasp.

Then he reached down with his other hand, pulling the Lord of the Isles to his feet. "In the name of love, I pardon you, Alexander Mac Donald," he announced. The crowds that packed the chapel began to shout and cheer. James stepped forward and embraced his cousin, kissing him on both cheeks, though not before he hissed in his ear, "But you'd better have some damned good explanations for me!"

"Thank you, Your Majesty. I have. But right now, would you excuse me?" And as the king watched, dumbfounded, Alex bounded over to the pew where Genna was waiting, smiling as the tears streamed down from her wide dark eyes. He lifted her over the rail, her red skirts swirling, and kissed her with wild abandon, knocking her cap from her head.

"Alex!" she hissed, blushing madly. "This is neither the time nor the place."

"Hush, love," he told her, grinning. "For once I am right, and you are wrong." And to the delight of the congregation, he kissed her again.

Joan stepped down from the throne to stand beside her husband, beaming up at him. "Thank you, darling," she told him softly.

"You know, Joan, I have the distinct impression that Alexander's appearance here this morning is not a total surprise to you."

"As always, my darling, you are right. Shouldn't you rescind his banishment, so long as he's here?"

James peered down at her suspiciously, then shrugged, turning to the exultant crowds, raising his voice. "Hear ye! Know from this moment that I, James Stewart of Scotland, rescind my banishment of the Lord of the Isles, and the price on his head. So be it. Bishop, may we please begin?" Taking Joan's hand, he started back up to this throne.

"One minute, Your Majesty." Mary Leslie's voice was a coiled whip. "That man is not the Lord of the Isles."

"Oh? Who is?" James asked curtly.

Mary left her pew and sauntered forward, her cold eyes glittering. "His cousin and tanist, Euan Mac Ruarie."

"She's wrong there, Yer Majesty," Davey Mac Leod called, clambering out of his seat to stand beside Alex and Genna. "'Tis true that woman conspired with Ranalt Mac Ruarie to trick Alley out of his lairdship. But Euan Mac Ruarie isn't fit to rule."

Mary was staring openmouthed at the jaunty redhead. "Y-you!" she stammered finally. "I left you locked in that cider cellar."

"Aye, well, you ought not to have upset poor old Hoban when you were leavin' that day. You struck him so hard that he needed a drink," Davey told her, grinning. His face was grim, though, as he turned back to the king. "Your Majesty, this woman confessed to me that she was guilty of the murder of her husband and of her daughter, my wife. Now she'd like nothing better than to have you behead her son."

"My son is guilty of treason," Mary snarled. "I agree he should be beheaded, Your Majesty, for your safety and that of the kingdom."

"Do I understand you areight?" the king asked her. "You *want* me to behead him?"

"He's a traitor! I do!"

"Your Majesty, I've something to say!" Henry Argyll strode

to the front of the church, glaring at the countess. "If you ask me, Mary Leslie, this has gone far enough."

Alex was staring at Argyll as if he saw a ghost. Genna tugged at his sleeve. "You didn't kill him, Alex. You didn't even hurt him very badly—even if he deserved it."

"Your Majesty," Argyll went on, "just one year past this woman offered me five hundred marks to engage her son in a duel. I'm ashamed to say that I took it."

"Liar! You wretched liar!" Mary screeched. The heads of the rapt crowd were moving as one from speaker to speaker; this was far more interesting than any mass might have been.

"I may be wretched, Mary, but I'll not be a party to murder. I speak the truth, Your Majesty. She paid me to quarrel with Mac Donald at Inverness."

"And she and Ranalt Mac Ruarie kidnapped me," Genna put in. "It was thanks to them that I lost the child I was carrying."

King James put a hand to his forehead, somewhat bewildered. "Bring Ranalt up from the dungeons," he told the sentries. "I'll hear what he has to say."

All eyes were on Ranalt Mac Ruarie as the sentries half dragged, half carried him to the front of the chapel. He took in the odd assortment of characters standing before the altar warily, then brought up his red-bearded chin and stared at the king. "Who dares to accuse me of murder?" he demanded haughtily.

Genna stepped forward. "I do. And of kidnap and treason as well."

"Pah." Ranalt turned away disdainfully. "The word of one deranged woman? You can't seriously expect me to answer the charge."

Mary Leslie's pale eyes glinted. "Two women, Your Majesty." She fell to her knees before James, clutching at his hands. "I confess that I may have done wrong, that I was foolish. But it was this man who hatched the plots against Alexander and you, Your Majesty, I swear it! He told me what to do, and I did it. He planned it all."

Ranalt stared at her in disbelief, then grabbed her hair, pulling her around to face him. "Try to pin it all on me, will you, Mary? Is this to be the thanks I get for following after you for twenty-five years? For fathering your child, doing your dirty work? You double-dealing bitch, do you think that

I'm willing to hang for you as well?" He pushed her to the ground in a heap. "I'll be the dupe for her no longer, Your Majesty." He eyed his former lover with disgust. "It's over, Mary, can't you see that? It's finished." He turned back to James. "She had her husband murdered because he'd found out about our son."

"He's mad, Your Majesty," Mary gasped. "I swear, I don't know what he's talking about!"

A low murmur began in the rear of the chapel, and swelled to an uproar. Diarmot Mac Duff, still dressed in his captain's garb, was making his way up the aisle, a blanket-wrapped bundle in his arms.

"Oh, no!" Genna saw the sorrow in his expression and ran down the aisle to meet him, her hand at her throat.

"We were too late, milady," Mac Duff told her with regret. "We found him at the foot of the tower, all dashed to bits. He must have fallen somehow. I'm sorry. We bought him back just to make sure someone could identify his clothing."

Mary Leslie raised herself up on her knees, realizing what the blanket contained, her eyes wide with horror. Now she crawled slowly toward Mac Duff, one hand outstretched. "My baby," she whispered, pulling at the blankets. "Oh, my baby . . . Euan!" The name was a howl of despair. Mac Duff relinquished the body to her, and she gathered Euan's smiling face against her breasts.

Ranalt stood stone-faced, watching, but even Alex felt his heart wrench as he heard his mother keening for her first-born child. And Genna put a timid hand on the woman's shoulder. "I'm so very sorry."

Mary looked up at her, eyes glittering with venomous hatred. "Sorry . . . what do you know of sorry?" And before anyone realized she'd moved, she scrambled to her feet and wrenched Alex's sword from a startled King James. "I'll show you sorry," she spat at Genna, advancing on her, brandishing the sword over her head. "What was the sense of it, what was the sense of any of it, if my baby had to die?"

Every soul in the chapel was spellbound, rooted, immobile. Not even a breath could be heard as Mary swung the huge sword in a high flashing arc. Genna stood alone before her, incapable of flight, transfixed by the insane rage in those flinty blue eyes.

How Alex covered the distance so quickly he could never

say afterward. He only knew that he saw the sword flash, and somehow he moved.

His big hand closed over his mother's fingers, and almost tenderly, he tugged the blade from her grasp. "Come, Mother," he said softly, putting his arm around her shoulders. "Come, now. It is time to bury your son."

"My son . . ." Mary seemed to crumple, to age visibly as she bent over Euan's corpse. "He was a good son, my Euan. He always did . . . exactly as his mother told him . . ."

Alex beckoned the sentries forward. "Would you take her to her rooms now? Watch over her. Be gentle." Two of the guards stepped forward gingerly and carried the countess away.

"Oh, Alex."

He turned to Genna and held her tight against his chest as she cried. "There now, my darling. Ranalt was right. It is finished. She'll trouble us no more." Genna shivered as he smoothed back her hair and smiled sadly into her night black eyes.

The king coughed meaningfully, and Alex and Genna looked to him. "Not quite finished, I'm afraid," James said sternly. "There is still the matter of punishment." He gestured to Ranalt. "What would you suggest I do with your uncle? Shall I have him drawn and quartered and hung on the gibbets in your stead?"

Alex shook his head slowly. "I would ask you to spare his life, though he spend it in prison, if he will confess one last thing."

"What's that?" Ranalt asked wearily, his head slumped forward on his chest. Seeing the plain evidence of Mary's madness at last had drawn the fight out of him.

Genna stepped forward. "That it was you who murdered Red John Stewart."

"What?" the king demanded in amazement.

Ranalt nodded, avoiding his eyes. "Aye, 'twas I who killed him. I rode with Jamie Stewart's men."

"I'll hang you for that alone, you cur!" James shouted.

"If it please Your Majesty," Genna began, her hand clutching Alex's tightly. The king raised an eyebrow. "Let him live out his days in prison, I beg you. Even the worst of felons deserves the chance to make peace with his soul."

"Hmph." James glared at the couple. "And I suppose you believe the Countess of Ross should be spared her life as well."

"You saw her yourself, Your Majesty," Alex said softly. "The poor woman is demented. If her punishment were up to me to decide—"

"Well? What?" James demanded impatiently.

"Send her to the priory at Incholm," Alex suggested. "Let the sisters of Saint Agnes care for her. I do not think that she will live very long."

The king considered him curiously. "A strange sort of lord you will prove to be, Alexander Mac Donald, if you show such mercy."

Alex bowed, smiling. "Even so did Your Majesty show mercy to me."

James stared; Queen Joan giggled. Flustered, the king turned again to his guards. "Bring up those accursed clan chiefs from the cellars, while we are at it. I suppose I must pardon them, too. Perhaps I should just declare a general amnesty, eh, cousin? Is that what you'd like me to do?"

Alex grinned. "If it would please Your Majesty—"

"Well, it does not please me!" James thundered. "There has been entirely too much pardoning and mercy around here today. I am going to miss my hunting. And the mass hasn't even begun." He waggled a finger at Alex. "You're not going to get off scot-free, young man, not after the mess you made up at Inverness. You owe me eight thousand pounds for that."

"I'll gladly pay for the damage to the castle," Alex said gravely. Genna shot him a quick glance, remembering.

"Damn right you will," James grumbled, only slightly appeased. "And I think a term in prison might serve you well, too!"

"Oh, now, James," Queen Joan protested, staring up at him. And a disgruntled murmur arose from the enthralled congregation.

"Well, I say he shall go to prison!" James insisted, gazing around defiantly. "Am I not still the king?"

"Of course you are, darling," Joan assured him. "But, really—"

"Yer Lairdship!" Iain Cameron ran down the aisle of the chapel as fast as his old legs would carry him, Angus Mac Pherson close behind him. The chiefs threw themselves down at Alex's feet. "Oh, Yer Lairdship," Iain cried, "fergive us fer bein' so foolish! That Ranalt's a madman! He don't know the first thing about running a war." He considered more closely the feet before him, then slowly peered up. "Sweet God in heaven, Alley, you're near naked! What kind of outfit is that to wear into a church?"

The crowds around them erupted in peals of laughter, the sound spreading all through the chapel in great rippling waves. Alex pulled the startled Iain upright and hugged him. "Of course I forgive you, you damned old fool. Aren't you going to greet my wife?"

Iain gaped at the smiling Genna, blinked his eyes, and gaped again. "Well, God be praised, milady," he sputtered finally.

And Angus echoed him: "God be praised!"

"*If* I might be permitted to speak?" James bellowed indignantly. "This *is* still Scotland. And my wife has told me I am still king."

Alex hurriedly shushed Iain and Angus and turned back to the king, his hand in Genna's. The laughter and cheers of the crowd slowly died away.

"Now, then." James straightened the crown on his head with dignity. "I am prepared to pronounce sentence on Alexander Mac Donald, Lord of the Isles, for the sacking and burning of Inverness Castle, as well as for . . . for . . . for other things." Sensing the lameness of his finish, he roared even more loudly. "I sentence you to imprisonment at Tantallon Castle for your crimes against the crown. And your wife will go to prison there as well."

A disbelieving gasp rose up from the onlookers. Alex and Genna simply smiled at one another, still holding hands.

"Hrmph," said James. Queen Joan tugged at his doublet. "Well, what is it?" Frowning, he leaned down to listen as she whispered in his ear. His brow cleared slowly, the frown changing to a satisfied smile. He nodded. "I repeat, you and your wife are to remain imprisoned at Tantallon—until you conceive a child."

The crowd was silent for a moment, considering the implications of this sentence. Then the men present began to applaud wildly, laughing and whooping. The women—some of the women—cheered as well.

"Your Majesty." Alexander was striving unsuccessfully to

restrain his grin of delight. But he could not help it; he began to laugh. "That's not a judgment; 'tis a blessing!"

Genna curtsied demurely. "I will do my best, Your Majesty, to see that our stay there is not overlong." Her eyes met Joan's, saw the bright twinkle there. She tried to express her thanks, but Joan waved her back.

"Guards!" King James barked. "Take them away to begin their sentence. And now, for God's sake, may we please get on with this mass?"

Alex stretched out languorously across the soft feather bed at Tantallon. It was nearly mid-morning, he saw through the unbarred window, and bright sun was glistening on the calm blue Firth of Forth. A handful of fat solan geese wheeled into the brilliant spring sky, chattering and screeching, then took up their sentry posts against the dark hulk of Bass Rock. Alex watched and laughed as one plunged back into the water and came up flapping its huge black-tipped wings, a silver fish in its beak.

Genna pushed open the door to her dressing room, long jet hair hanging loose over her bare shoulders. Her dark eyes glowed as she smiled at her husband, sprawled out on the huge bed. "What are you laughing at, love?"

He pointed to the window. "Our guards are having their breakfast. Come and see."

She came and perched on the bed beside him, giggling at the ungainly birds. "What do you think they'd do if we tried to escape?" she whispered.

He put his arms around her, kissing the nape of her neck, hands reaching around for her breasts. "Peck us to death," he murmured, nibbling her ear. "Well, what news?"

She dangled a pair of snowy linen drawers before him. "See for yourself. That makes it two months now."

He pulled her closer, running his hands through her hair. "Nonetheless," he said gravely, drinking in the beauty of her naked body, his mouth claiming the bud of her nipple. Genna sighed with happiness as he began again the slow, hot caresses she loved so well. His long fingers played down her belly and between her legs, gently insistent. "Monster," she mumbled into his shoulder, as he followed with his tongue.

There was a discreet knock at the chamber door. Genna pushed away his eager hands, laughing, and hastily pulled up the covers. "Oh, it is only you, Althea." She relaxed as she saw the housekeeper's broad red face.

"Only me, is it? That's a fine way to greet your gaoler." She set the heavy tray she carried on the table beside the bed.

There was silence in the room for a moment as Althea stared down at her master and mistress. "Well?" she demanded finally.

"Well what?" Alex's blue eyes were dancing.

"Well, is Genna with child? Can we leave this wretched place?"

"What's so wretched about it, Thea?" he asked innocently. "Your cooking is as splendid as ever. Look here, my love, she's made your favorite biscuits, and brought blackberry jam."

"Oh, good. I am simply famished." Genna sat up, pushing back her hair, and broke open a steaming golden biscuit. "I'm not certain this will be enough for us, though, Althea," she said, slathering the biscuit with preserves. "Perhaps, if it's not too much trouble, you might bring up some eggs? And some butter? And maybe some sausages." She bit into the biscuit eagerly. Alex reached over and wiped a spot of jam from her chin.

Althea glowered at the couple in the bed. "And who is it that you two think you're fooling?" she demanded, chin quivering indignantly. "It's been nigh on three months since either of you budged from that bed! Young Mistress is eating up every lick of food in the castle, and both of you sit there grinning like monkeys. Why, if I didn't know better, I'd swear you didn't want to go home!"

"Oh, Thea," Genna mumbled through a mouthful of biscuit. "Of course we miss Aros. It's just that it's so—so peaceful here."

"Peaceful?" Althea snorted. "You'd not think it so almighty peaceful if 'twas you that had to spend the livelong day explaining to the prison commandant what's become of all his flour and sugar and fruit!"

"Bake him one of your pies, Althea," Alex suggested. "Your pies would placate the devil himself."

"Oh, Thea, that reminds me. Bring up some strawberries too if you can find them. I've had the most outlandish craving for strawberries all this morning." Genna took anther huge bite of biscuit, dark eyes open wide.

"And cream too, didn't you tell me, my love?" Alex prodded.

Genna nodded happily. "Cream, too. Thank you, my love. I nearly forgot."

Althea crossed her arms over her bosom, stamped her foot, and stormed huffily back out the door.

"Pass me a biscuit, would you, little one?" Alex lay back against the pillows as Genna spread the roll with a thick layer of jam and fed it to him in pieces. He licked the sweet preserves from her fingers with the tip of his tongue.

"Delicious," he said with a sigh, pulling her over atop him, caressing her cool white buttocks and back.

"What were you saying before Althea interrupted?" Genna leaned down to kiss him, her hands caught in his long gold hair. His mouth tasted of berries, of honey and sunlight. He kissed her slowly, leisurely, reveling in the warmth of her small lithe body against his, her exquisite dark beauty, the clean fresh scent of her hair. "Something about 'nonetheless,'" she murmured, prompting.

Alex rolled her onto her back, kneeling over her, smiling wickedly. His blue eyes were deep as the ocean, and brimming with love. "Nonetheless," he whispered, reaching for the jam jar and spreading a crimson trail over her pale white breasts. He licked it away bit by bit, until she laughed and pulled his mouth up to hers again. "Nonetheless," he whispered, "it could not hurt to make sure."